The
LOST
GARDEN

BOOKS BY ANGELA PETCH

The Tuscan Secret
A Tuscan Memory
The Tuscan Girl
The Tuscan House
The Postcard from Italy
The Girl Who Escaped
The Sicilian Secret

The
LOST GARDEN

ANGELA PETCH

bookouture

Published by Bookouture in 2025

An imprint of Storyfire Ltd.
Carmelite House
50 Victoria Embankment
London EC4Y 0DZ

www.bookouture.com

The authorised representative in the EEA is Hachette Ireland
8 Castlecourt Centre
Dublin 15 D15 XTP3
Ireland
(email: info@hbgi.ie)

Copyright © Angela Petch, 2025

Angela Petch has asserted her right to be identified as the author of this work.

All rights reserved. No part of this publication may be reproduced, stored in any retrieval system, or transmitted, in any form or by any means, electronic, mechanical, photocopying, recording or otherwise, without the prior written permission of the publishers.

ISBN: 978-1-83618-956-5
eBook ISBN: 978-1-83618-955-8

This book is a work of fiction. Names, characters, businesses, organizations, places and events other than those clearly in the public domain, are either the product of the author's imagination or are used fictitiously. Any resemblance to actual persons, living or dead, events or locales is entirely coincidental.

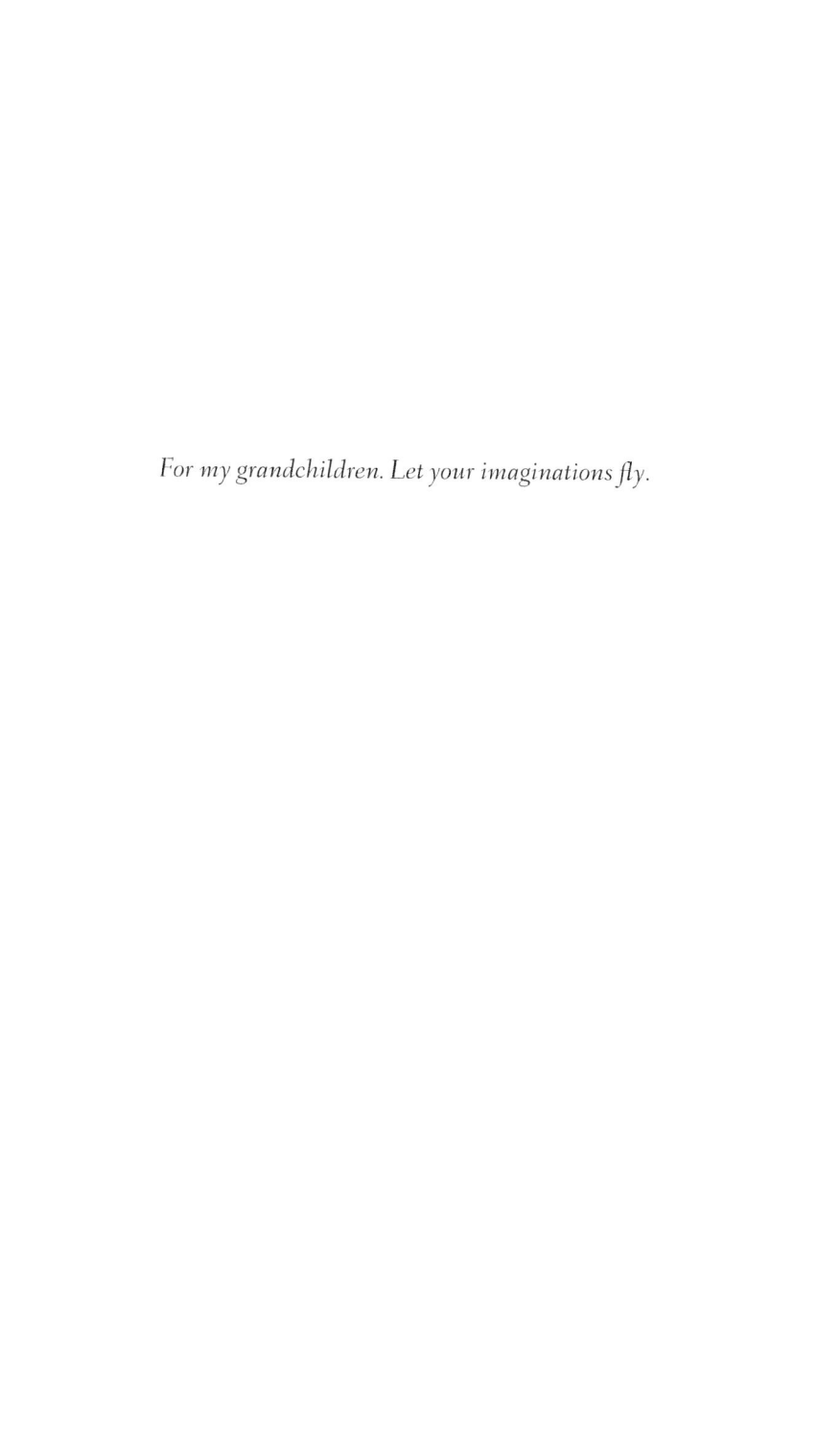

For my grandchildren. Let your imaginations fly.

'*Tutto è fiaba*' 'Everything is a fairytale'

— (AS SEEN IN A STORY EXHIBITION IN THE CASTLE OF SANT'AGATA FELTRIA, EMILIA-ROMAGNA).

'All fairy tales are merely dreams of that world which is everywhere and nowhere.'

— (NOVALIS, 18TH CENTURY)

PROLOGUE

September 1946, Romagna, Italy

In the tower room of the Castle of Montesecco, a young woman watches with guilt as her maid kneels with creaking knees to tend to the hearth. The fabric of the building is deteriorating and she can no longer afford fires in all the fusty rooms. So, she moves between her eyrie on the top floor and the warm kitchen where the old *stufa* is kept alight with wood from the forest.

Here her maid prepares nourishing country meals and when the young woman was desperately ill, she fed her spoon by spoon with *ribollita* soup as if she were a child. The young woman's health has improved since then but her mind is still fragile. Accusations, false rumours, injustice and finger-pointing have dragged her to the blackest places imaginable. But the old lady hauls her back with love.

The time has come to take action.

Outside, summer fades from the neglected grounds, leaves twirl rusty to the floor and birds prepare to migrate to warmer lands. It is chilly within the thick stone walls and the young woman wraps herself tight in an old shawl found in a trunk pushed far back in the eaves of an attic room. The maid's face was ashen when she wore it the first time.

'*Gesù, Maria,*' she'd said, blood draining from her face. 'Your mamma's shawl.' She had come over, fingering the wool, finding moth holes. 'I made this for her years ago.'

Here in the tower room, flames lick the hearth, sending shadows to dance around the wall where photographs, notes, receipts and maps show the results of the young woman's research. She moves to her desk beneath the tall arched window from where she observes the countryside spreading like skirts about the castle. She gazes over the expanse of *cotto* roofs of the small town of Sant'Agnese towards a haphazard pattern of fields and woods. In the far distance hazy purple-grey peaks of the Apennines mark the border between Romagna and Le Marche. Sitting up here, surveying the contours in the landscape, she likens herself to a general plotting a campaign.

She picks up her old-fashioned quill pen and dips the nib into the pewter inkwell. The first attempt is shaky and ink splatters across the vellum notepaper headed with the castle's heraldic emblem: an eagle perched proudly astride its portcullis. The paper ruined, she scrunches it up and throws it to the flames.

From the secret drawer within her writing box, she removes more paper. Taking a deep breath and steadying her hand, she copies the first of five addresses onto envelopes that will each contain an invitation.

You are cordially invited, she starts afresh.

Is 'cordially' the correct word for her message? 'Cordially' derives from the heart but is there warmth for these people who will receive invitations? In truth, it *is* her heart that has begged her again and again to beat with more life than she's felt over the past two years So, the word 'cordially' remains.

You are cordially invited to attend luncheon at 13.00

hours at the Montesecco castle of Sant'Agnese on the feast of the dead, 2nd November 1946, to remember the martyrs of this town.

She signs the signature with a flourish she has practised over and over:

Cristiana della Silva

Nobody will recognise the name because this woman has no past. If anybody attempts to trace her, they will not find her. Cristiana della Silva is the new owner of the Montesecco castle. That is all the knowledge they require.

Gossip spreads as suddenly as autumn mist in these remote mountains of the Marecchia Valley, insinuating itself through spiky branches of mountain firs, along twisting alleyways, through gaps in wooden shutters of simple homes. The people of Sant'Agnese yearn to discover who is this new woman arrived to purchase the castle after the death of conte Ferdinando and the disappearance of his daughter. Various theories are bandied at the washing fountain in the marketplace: she is a rich woman from the north; a widow come to bury her grief in a project to restore the castle; a Carmelite nun who abandoned her convent, disillusioned with restrictive life; a past lover of the conte; or even a long-lost relative from overseas.

All their theories are wrong.

A while later, as the young woman finishes the fifth and final invitation, the gong for supper echoes from below. She dries the address with her blotter and pulls close her shawl for the long descent to the kitchen below the ground floor.

The meal is simple but the maid still insists on waiting on the young woman, laying the table with a clean cloth, silver cutlery neatly arranged, a single rose in a glass vase in the centre. Old standards die hard.

'It is done,' the young woman tells her as the maid ladles soup made from home-grown vegetables.

The maid nods, a faint smile hovering on her lips, the dimmest of twinkles in her rheumy eyes.

'I shall take them to the post office for you tomorrow morning, *cara mia*,' she says.

But the young woman shakes her head. 'No, no. I shall go myself.'

Gone are the days when people hurled insults, pinned dead birds to the castle door and spat behind her as she walked through the town. For that woman no longer exists.

CHAPTER 1

June 1939, Castle of Montesecco

If cats could talk

Contessina Ernestina di Montesecco sighed as the colours ran again, smudging her painting. The patterns on the terracotta roof tiles of the little town of Sant'Agnese below the castle were impossible to capture and she grimaced at her attempt. Something furry brushed her feet released from the uncomfortable leather pumps her father liked her to wear and she recoiled. But it was only the cat she'd seen earlier.

'You most likely belong to somebody,' she said as she bent to tickle the well-fed tummy, his paws clawing the air with satisfaction. 'But you can be mine too. And I shall call you Tigre. You look like a tiger with your handsome stripes.'

Grown bored with her as the girl returned to daub paint on paper, he stalked off tail in the air, jumped onto the wall and disappeared from view.

Alarmed, Ernestina leapt up, fearing he'd plunged to his death and, peering over the edge, saw that he'd landed on a narrow ledge merging into a path that disappeared within a clump of trees. She had never noticed this before and today she wanted to investigate.

At sixteen years old she had never properly explored her town. Her father forbade it, especially now her latest English tutor had been banished from the castle and she had no chaperone. And anyway, she didn't like being stared at in the piazza. She stuck out with her fancy clothes. Not for the first time she wondered if her mother would have been so strict, but she'd never had the chance to know her as her mamma had died at childbirth.

The path at the end of the ledge led in the opposite direction from town. There would be nobody about to bother her and she was tired of walking round and round the castle courtyard.

Later that afternoon, after making sure her father was snoring in his bedroom, she pulled jodhpurs from her wardrobe, a light cotton short-sleeved blouse as well as old plimsolls and hurried through the castle doors, still carrying her paints. Strident cicadas dominated all sounds in the afternoon heat whilst the world rested in siesta. Glancing at her watch, she calculated she had two and a half glorious hours to herself before she had to return to her easel. Allegra, the cook and housemaid, usually started evening meal preparations just gone four.

Checking there truly was nobody else about and after erecting the parasol and leaving her painting box strategically open, she carefully put one leg over the wall, averting her eyes from the sheer drop. Taking one perilous step at a time, she held on to the brickwork and made her way to where Tigre had disappeared within the clump of Mediterranean pines.

She hadn't realised until this moment she'd been holding her breath and she let it out to join the gentle soughing of the breeze that sifted through the branches like the sound of the sea. Save for the continuous raucous sawing of crickets, the afternoon was peaceful. The ground was soft with pine needles. Once or twice her foot slipped and she grabbed the wall of the castle, her heart thumping. A picket fence, the wood rotten in places, had once formed a barrier against the drop but there was little left of it now.

The path, following the line of the castle wall, was overgrown with brambles and when her jodhpur leg caught, she tugged to release the material, causing it to rip. After another four metres or so, the path came to a sudden end as it met the castle ramparts draped with thick blankets of ivy. There was nowhere else to go.

To her left, steep slopes of scrub were impenetrable and to her right, tall ramparts soared far above. She peered up, shielding her eyes to the sunlight ricocheting through the pines and worked out she was standing below the walls of one of the towers, its arched window panes glinting in the afternoon sunshine. Disappointed, she turned to retrace her steps, wondering at the purpose of the path. Maybe it wasn't a path at all but some kind of reinforcing ledge. But, if so, why the fence that had once run alongside? As she turned, a rustling movement from the ivy-covered wall made her start. A snake? Most likely. There were vipers in the countryside and, stupidly, she was wearing thin footwear. Her heart battering her ribs, she peered at the ivy and jumped again as two lizards scampered across the tendrils. One of them fell to the ground, while the other curled itself around a metal ring visible amongst the thick leaves.

Somewhere to tie the reins of a mule or horse. Or... might it be a handle? Was there a door concealed behind the ivy?

Tina gripped the iron ring but there was no give. She tore at the plants, flinching when ants and a large yellow spider crawled up her arm as she pulled on woody tendrils. She really could have done with a knife but that would have meant returning to the castle to fetch one from Allegra's kitchen and precious time was ticking by. Increasingly curious, she pulled with vigour at the greenery, breaking nails as she worked, her fingers bleeding as she strained to free the wood from its prison-frame of plants.

She tried the handle again but without joy. It took all her weight to shove against the surface before it suddenly gave and she fell into the other side, winded and panting. Tina stood up, brushed dirt from her hands down her jodhpurs and gazed around.

This place was like nothing she had ever seen. Her father never came here, she was sure of that; he'd never mentioned it. Had she stumbled upon a secret place, right under his nose?

CHAPTER 2

Fiammetta

The door to the garden is opening... she is here. At last, my child has been drawn to the corner of the grounds where I spent long lonely hours with my secrets...

I am a thousand things and nothing: the sparkle of sunshine on river stones, the feather that flutters free from a dove. I am blossom drifting from wild cherry trees. I am the robin singing in the pines. And I am everywhere in this castle. I linger in oil paintings, in dried-flower posies on dressing tables. I stir up draughts in winter to whistle through window frames. In summer I direct the sun to fade tapestries in the hall. I wait. I watch. I listen. I am the spirit, the liberator. I am the persecuted woman but I have the power to be any woman.

Sometimes conte Ferdinando stops to hold his breath when he thinks he hears me sing or laugh down the echoes of time. But I disappear. I turn into the nightingale that chants its song. Or the cuckoo calling from the woods.

Over the years, tangles of wild rose, thistles, old man's beard and ivy have concealed the old door. I caused the lizards to move within the strangling plants, the sun to glint upon the metal ring, which was all that was needed to bring my child to the magic of my garden. Nestled beneath the soaring rock of the wolves on which the castle perches, where oaks and pines have formed a forest, it is where I escaped when conte Ferdinando grew tiresome.

My child wears flimsy shoes. But I always trod the forest floor barefoot to remind myself of my origins and days when I roamed free. We were very poor. Back then I longed for shoes and thicker clothes like the rich folk from the castle, seated in their comfortable front church pews. But if I'd understood how restricted their lives were, with their stiff etiquette and garments, I would have known we were not poor at all. With a wiser head on my younger shoulders, would I have let myself be wooed by the conte? I think not. If only I had known earlier – before he slipped the ring on my finger. But regret must be banished as I watch over my beloved child in the only ways left to me now.

In the garden I hover near the oldest olive tree. Through the tangle of briar roses and convolvulus I watch my pretty one survey my neglected garden from my stone bench. She looks up to the branches and I imagine she is wondering why the cicadas have ceased. They always do when I am near. The trees interrupt their rustling dances and the plants hush their whispers and the air holds its breath. But Nature need not fear. I do no harm but only come to watch over my child to reassure myself she is well. I shall save her from the future I made for myself. A future that tethered me, stopped me from living when I let myself be seduced by the conte and his castello *above the town.*

I wanted my baby to be named Margherita – after the daisies picked from the fields where poppies thrive amongst the corn. But Ferdinando chose Ernestina instead. A stiff, ugly name and so I took to calling her Tina instead, which greatly annoyed him.

Whenever he was away, I cast off my shoes and trailed through the grass to gather wild flowers to plait into garlands. I collected seeds and dug my fingers into the rich earth of my garden to plant, careless of my dirt-encrusted nails. Allegra, my young maid, scolded me and scattered rose petals in my bath, hung rosemary from the taps to perfume the water and washed my long hair with scented aquilegia petals.

I shall make sure my child ventures again and again to the furthest corners of my garden and she too shall learn to love the pink and white oleanders, scented tea roses from England, white hibiscus and purple lavenders. They are leggy now and choked with docks, dandelions and thorny saplings that will tear at her flesh. But before next time, perhaps I shall magic a pathway between the forget-me-nots for her to tread. For I have missed her and I long for her to find her own way and understand what I endured.

I am happy she has found our garden. And I have seen her spirit is as restless as mine. It is a beginning.

CHAPTER 3

June 1939, Castle of Montesecco

Tina

'If you have a garden and a library, you have everything you need.' Cicero

Tina found herself standing on a path, gravel barely visible beneath waist-high weeds. As she walked forwards goosegrass clung to her. A thorny acacia branch gouged a scratch along her forearm and she yelped in pain, whereupon a pheasant flapped from its hiding place, its coughing, rasping call making her jump.

Her heart beating loud in her chest, she stopped still. At the end of the path, a stone statue of a boy-child perched on a tree trunk. Arms hunched round drawn-up knees he looked life-like, despite brambles entwined around his neck. Someone in the past had created a garden in this place: a long-abandoned garden that once must have been beautiful.

Tina knew little about plants but could tell not everything

was a weed. Along the walls, splashes of yellow and red from rose heads punctuated rampant old man's beard that grew quickly once it took hold. Allegra had taken her along country lanes to pick tips to steam and add to her delicious egg frittata. These *vitalba* tips were the poor man's asparagus and one of Tina's favourite dishes.

She wandered over to the rose bushes, the scent intoxicating even before she reached up to inhale the petals and disturb a fat bumblebee from its foraging. She stepped over broken glass, the fragments crunching underfoot, and behind one of the straggly roses she made out what was a dilapidated greenhouse built against the wall, sun glinting from cracked panes between the leaves. Vines bound its entrance shut and she peered through the grubby windows. Along the width of the back wall a wide bench held upturned terracotta pots with mouse droppings trailing patterns between. Wicker baskets and sacks hung from rusty hooks and she dreaded to think how many mice were using these for nests. A robin flew out, startling her with its noisy chirruping and as she stepped back, she caught her hand on a shard of glass and she staunched the gushing blood with her mouth.

She resolved to return to explore and maybe even tidy up a little at the next opportunity. And she decided not to tell anybody, not even Allegra, about her discovery. It would be her secret. Goodness knew she had little space to call her own, despite living in a rambling castle.

'What on earth have you been up to?' Allegra asked when later in the kitchen Tina reached out for her cup of lemon tea and grabbed a freshly baked *cantucci* biscuit.

'Oh, this,' she answered, nonchalantly, pulling at the sleeves of her blouse to cover the grazes. 'Oh, nothing. Really silly of me. I was painting and... I tripped up a step as I was holding out my brush to gauge perspective of the castle... against the roofs of the town...'

She was pleased with her rambling explanation plucked from the air but Allegra frowned and grabbed hold of Tina's hands, examining her dirty torn fingernails and rolling up her ripped sleeve to find a deep scratch on her forearm. 'Looks more like you fell in a ditch. That needs attending to,' she said, reaching up for a jar on her shelf. 'Calendula oil should do the trick.' She bathed Tina's seeping wound in the sink and gently patted it dry, before applying her home-made lotion.

'Ouch! That stings.'

'I'm sure it does and I'm sure it stung when you fell up your... step,' Allegra retorted.

Tina changed the subject, anxious to be gone from Allegra's scrutiny. 'Shall I take tea to Father? Save your legs?'

'Thank you, *cara mia*.' The housekeeper set to, laying a tray with cup, saucer and a fancy porcelain dish. 'And we'd best give him some biscuits before you demolish the lot.' She gave Tina's hand a playful tap as it reached again for the baking tray.

Tina swept up the tray and hastened from the kitchen, slopping tea onto the tray cloth as she climbed the stairs. Allegra had eyes in the back of her head and Tina suspected her explanations had not been believed. Best not to sit with her for too long in case the truth crept out. She wanted her visit to the garden to remain her own.

'Thank you, Ernestina,' her father said as he hauled himself up to lean against his pillows on the four-poster bed. 'How did you get on with your painting? You must show it to me when I'm dressed.'

'Er! I... actually spent more time thinking about the perspective, to be honest. In the end, I decided it wasn't quite right. So, I didn't finish.'

She left her father to his tea and went to wash and change into a frock. At least Allegra hadn't noticed her torn jodhpurs or asked why she was wearing them when she couldn't exercise her bay. Baffi was lame at the moment. It had been weeks since she'd been able to ride him.

Before dinner, she made her way to the library and spent a happy half hour at her piano mastering the final bars of Liszt's 'Liebesträume', the mood matching her own: dreamy and questioning. Who had created the garden she had found this afternoon? Why had the entrance been locked? She was sure her footsteps were the first in many years to have crossed its tangled paths. Why hadn't her father ever mentioned it? Something told her she shouldn't ask; she was not meant to find it. But she couldn't wait to explore further.

Happy with how she'd played the nocturne, she climbed the library steps to see if there were any gardening books amongst the hundreds of volumes. When the gong sounded, she was immersed in a manual on roses and she slipped it back in its place before making her way to the dining room.

Papà was already seated and she went to his place at the end of the long table, bending to receive a kiss on the top of her head.

He pulled at a leaf from her hair and held it up. 'I expect you to look decent when we dine, Ernestina. You are turning into a ragamuffin and I am certain spending little time at your studies.'

'Sorry, Papà. I... while I was painting... it must have fallen on me.'

A slight raising of his thick eyebrows. 'Really, Ernestina? In early June? I can't imagine even *you* have the power to change the seasons? God knows you are capable of getting up to all kinds of tricks but leaves tend to fall in autumn.'

'It was very windy here today, Papà. Didn't you notice?'

When her father shrugged, Tina thought to herself she was becoming a really good liar, relieved she'd managed to pull wool over not only Allegra's eyes but also her father's.

Tina went to her own place at the other end of the long dining table. How senseless it was they sat metres away from each other, shouting their boring conversations. Suppers in the kitchen, seated at the scrubbed pine table with Allegra whenever her father was away, were much cosier.

There was silence during the soup course but while they waited for Allegra to return with the main dishes, Tina's father dropped his bombshell.

'I have been considering matters and decided the time has come for you to go away to school in Arezzo, Ernestina. You have been without a tutor for too long, so I have secured you a place at the Convent of the Sisters of Mercy starting the first week of September.'

'But, Papà—' Tina started, her heart filling with dismay.

'No buts, my child. You grow wilder by the day. It's time you learned how to conduct yourself as a young lady. I have checked you'll be able to continue with your music and painting lessons. It's high time you mixed with girls of your own class and learned proper etiquette.'

It was on the tip of Tina's tongue to point out that she never mixed with anybody of her age at all, Papà having excluded the possibility of attending school in Sant'Agnese, but he was already in bad humour and her point would fall on deaf ears.

A convent. That meant nuns, and strict rules. In Arezzo would she have even less freedom than she had here in Sant'Agnese?

Tina toyed with the food on her plate, willing herself not to cry. She pushed the uneaten meat and courgettes beneath her cutlery and willed the minutes to pass. The Venetian clock in the alcove beside the large stone-cold hearth ticked away too slowly before her father rose to adjourn to his study for his evening cigar and *digestivo*.

. . .

Tina hurried down the flag-stoned corridor that led to the kitchen where Allegra was scraping food from plates into a waste pail for the chickens.

'Are you not well, Tina, *carissima*?' Allegra asked, looking up from her job. 'You've hardly touched your meal. You're not on a silly diet, are you? Trying to watch your waistline? You're healthy and beautiful as you are.'

Tina's face crumpled at her kindness and she sat at the table, cradling her head in her hands.

'Papà is sending me away. I think he hates me; can't bear to have me under his feet, even though he's hardly ever here. To Arezzo. A convent... Oh, Allegra, what am I to do?' Tina sniffed. 'I can't bear it. How will I live without Baffi and the cat I made friends with today? And you?' she added, getting up to put her arms around the woman who had cared for her since she was tiny: the nearest she had come to being loved by a mother.

'Always so dramatic, Tina.' Allegra picked up a clean towel from a neat pile on the shelves above the sink and handed it to Tina. 'Wash your face, dry your eyes, take deep breaths and calm yourself while I make you my gnocchi. I was going to make a portion to take to Mother. She's not so good today. But I'll make extra for you too – you've hardly eaten a thing. Now tell me everything.'

'Papà is sending me away this September as that English tutor has left.'

Allegra looked up from the trestle table where she always mixed bread and pasta dough. She sliced half a loaf and placed the pieces in a bowl of cold water.

'It's good, isn't it? Without that woman? You told me often enough you didn't like her.'

Tina wiped her face dry. 'I suppose so. But a convent... Allegra, it will be like going to prison.'

Allegra laughed. 'Have you ever been in a prison? Or a

convent school, for that matter? Haven't you thought it might be good to meet other girls like yourself? Make friendships?'

'But I like it here. With you and Baffi.'

'We're not going anywhere. We'll always be here when you return in the holidays. *Su, coraggio,* Tina. It might not turn out so bad. You've a few months yet. And it could be the making of you.'

Tina watched the woman she loved most in the world as she worked her magic to produce the gnocchi dish from an old recipe handed down through Allegra's family. She always felt comforted in her presence, soothed by her advice. Maybe it would not be so bad to escape from the castle after all and discover another world, albeit from a convent school. Sitting in the cosy kitchen, surrounded by copper pots and pans, sauce bubbling on the old-fashioned stove, she began to calm down. She still had the best part of two months before leaving the castle. She intended to make the most of it and spend time in her secret garden.

CHAPTER 4

'Three things remain with us from paradise: stars, flowers and children.' Dante Alighieri

Tina checked nobody was about before climbing over the low wall and stepping carefully along the narrow ledge towards the path to the garden. Tigre emerged from behind a tree, miaowing and purring, and Tina bent to pet him. 'Come and keep me company, *piccolino*,' she whispered.

She carried a small rucksack containing a pair of strong scissors used for cutting up chicken carcasses 'borrowed' from Allegra's kitchen table drawer. Her first task, she'd decided, was to start pruning as many rose bushes as possible before they were completely eaten up by *vitalba* that would strangle them. This time she'd chosen to wear a thick cotton shirt to cover her arms. She wanted no more telltale grazes on her body today.

The garden was as enchanting as the first time she'd discovered it, despite its neglect, and for a few moments she stood, holding in her breath, drinking in the sight of the many plants she needed to rescue. She spied more statues almost concealed by undergrowth: two large stone frogs and the figure of a young woman holding a child, as well as a stone bench and table covered in moss. She would work hard and clear as much as she could. Maybe she would bring picnic lunches in the future to make the most of her remaining weeks before leaving for the dreaded convent school. Tigre prowled about and disappeared from view whilst she worked. As she hacked at thorny brambles round the foot of a deep-red climbing rose, she was showered with scented petals, like a bride with confetti. The walls surrounding the garden were high and thick, one area was in shade where there was less vegetation. A thick carpet of ferns encircled a kind of folly and in the centre, she found what might once have been a fountain in the shape of a dolphin, its open mouth completely dry.

I must stop flitting from one side to another and make a plan, otherwise I'll achieve nothing, she told herself as she sat on the stone bench to assess the huge task facing her. And yet, she wanted to do it all by herself. It would be easy enough to ask Allegra if she knew of a handyman who could help. But she wanted this place to be her own world. There was something magical about this walled garden; she couldn't explain what it was. But she felt in her bones that, somehow, she was destined to find and rescue it before it was too late.

The problem was how to discover more about the garden without giving anything away. Why had it obviously been concealed? Out of bounds? Her father must know but if she asked him, she sensed he would forbid her from working on it. He was so prickly, so hard to engage with. She was closer to Allegra than him and his coldness saddened her.

After three full days of hard work and more scratches which she took pains to cover up by wearing long-sleeved blouses despite the intense heat of summer, Tina had cleared the ground around a dozen old roses. At the foot of each one, she had unearthed small metal discs bearing their names: Le

Vésuve, exceptionally fragrant; Madame Isaac Pereire, a shade of ivory-pink; and the perfumed Duchesse de Brabant. The names were romantic and foreign and she wondered about the women who had inspired the names. In her rucksack she now carried the rose manual found in the library and she consulted it frequently. Nobody would miss it and it had provided invaluable advice on how to care for these beautiful scented blooms. Unable to resist, she'd carried a dozen light-scarlet stems of Mutabilis back to her room and placed them in a jug on her bedside table, the perfume irresistible and better than anything in the bottles her father occasionally brought back from his trade fairs in the big cities where he sourced business interest for his leather factory.

Allegra was no fool and the following evening over a kitchen supper of *tortelli di patate*, pasta shapes filled with potatoes, she confronted her charge.

'Those roses, Ernestina, by your bed… where are they from? An admirer?'

Tina knew when she was cross. Hardly ever did she address her as Ernestina.

'Hah! Admirer? And how do you think I've met a tall, dark, handsome stranger round here? Chance would be a fine thing!' She laughed, the laughter covering concern that Allegra might be about to discover her secret. 'I discovered them on one of my walks. Growing outside an abandoned house – before you accuse me of stealing them from somebody's patch.'

'Where did you walk?'

'Er… towards Rocca Petrella. It was such a wonderful day and I still can't ride Baffi. Although when I can, you won't see me for dust. Maybe we'll run away together,' Tina said, tetchy from Allegra's questions. 'I'm so bored. In fact, I'm almost missing that stupid English governess.' She laughed again – a nervous sort of laugh.

'Next time you go for a long walk, warn me where you're going. You never know who you might meet these days. Those young men from the city, those paramilitary Blackshirts camped outside town by the river, practising their marching and exercises. You want to keep clear of them. I've heard bad things. They're too ready with their fists... and other things besides.'

Teasing her, Tina put her head to one side and asked, 'What other things besides, dearest Allegra? It might make my life more exciting if I were to have some "other things" in my life.'

'*Tssk!* Your father is quite right to be sending you away to school. Other things indeed! You be careful.'

Tina rose to kiss Allegra's soft cheek. 'Thank you for worrying about me, Allegra *carissima*. But I can look after myself.'

However, it was becoming increasingly difficult to hide her grubby fingernails and scratches, particularly the one on her nose, earned when trying to clear round a deep-maroon barberry that had lost its shape and was concealing clumps of gorgeous creamy-white day lilies. All these plants she'd identified from metal name tags uncovered in the soil beneath most of the species.

She hadn't seen Tigre lately but as she was scrubbing away at the moss-covered stone table on the following morning, the cat came to her, mewing insistently before walking away and then returning twice to her side.

'What is it, Tigre?' Tina asked, bending to pat the cat. 'What is it you're trying to tell me? Do you want me to follow you?'

She laid the bristle brush down on the half-clean tabletop and followed the cat to the far end of the garden she hadn't yet tackled. The cat pushed its way through an untidy yew hedge and Tina did the same, realising it had once been a wider opening – another pruning task to add to the list. Tigre stalked ahead along what was another overgrown path, taking a left turn through another narrowed gap, then left, right and left again. They were in a maze, parts of which Tina had to push through to reach the next section. In the centre, Tigre jumped onto a metal bench beneath a broken arbour held together by a sprawling mass of wisteria. The cat mewed plaintively some more, before disappearing beneath the seat. Tina bent to see the cat carefully lie down beside a wriggling heap of kittens that immediately latched on to feed.

'*Dio mio!* You're NOT Tigre after all! How did I not notice? *Congratulazioni*, Tigressa!' Tina whispered, a smile on her face as she rechristened the cat as female. 'Clever you! You've been busy. No wonder I haven't seen you for a while.'

She was careful not to touch any of the kittens but had already decided to bring milk to them.

'No more excuses, my girl,' Allegra pronounced, hands on hips, a pan of sauce bubbling behind her on the stove when Tina entered the kitchen. 'Tell me the truth about why you appear so dirty and have new scratches all over you each day at my table. There'll be no food until you tell me. And I've prepared another of your favourites: partridge stuffed with juniper berries.'

She stood firm, waiting for Tina to confess.

Tina had no more excuses. The garden, with the new discovery of the maze beyond the formal rose garden, had turned into a project vaster than imagined. It was time to come clean and find help. And besides, she yearned to discover who had created it.

'I found a garden,' she told Allegra. 'It's really wonderful. But it's very overgrown and I've been trying to tame it.'

Allegra's hands flew from her hips to her mouth before she slumped into her chair. '*Madre mia!* You've found it. I knew it couldn't remain hidden forever.' When she looked up, Tina saw fear in her eyes. 'Tina – you must never mention this to your father. And it's not safe for you to spend time in that place. You've found your mamma's garden.'

CHAPTER 5

The only secrets are secrets that keep themselves

'What do you mean, my mamma's garden? And why is it locked up? Why has nobody told me about this? I don't understand.'

Tina stood over Allegra, desperate to find out more about her mother, who was hardly ever mentioned. When she'd dared ask questions of her father, he always changed the subject. And now there seemed to be some mystery about her. Tina felt she had a right to know.

Allegra puffed a huge sigh and hauled herself up to the stove to push a pan aside. 'Your father ordered it. He commanded me not to tell you.'

'But why?'

Allegra shook her head.

'Please, Allegra,' Tina said, taking her hands. 'Talk to me. *Why?*'

'He ordered me not to tell you about it and, to be honest, as years passed, I'd pushed it to the back of my mind. It was easier to forget...'

'Forget what?'

Allegra sat down again. 'Your father was furious. He blamed your mother's garden for her death.'

Tina shook her head. What on earth had happened in the garden to cause her death?

'I don't understand. You're not making sense, Allegra.'

There was a pause while Allegra fiddled with the pan on the stove again, her back to the girl, ignoring her.

'Allegra, I beg you. Talk to me...'

The old lady turned, her words hesitant.

'She grew all manner of herbs in there to make medicines, along with beautiful flowers and roses...'

Tina waited as Allegra stopped, a look of anguish on her face.

'And so? Why should that matter?' she asked, prodding the old lady on.

'You see, her own mother was a *medicone*, a healer and herbs-woman who passed on her remedies. People from Sant'Agnese came to your mother when they had maladies and she cured them. Your father became increasingly angry that she spent so much time away from him in that garden. He was so possessive and when he came home from his work trips, he expected her to be with him. I think he always worried he would lose her. But then...' Allegra returned to stir the food, her back to Tina again.

'Then, *what*? Tell me. Oh, this is so frustrating. You're killing me. Why should all this have led to her death, for goodness' sake, Allegra... I hardly know anything about Mamma. Nobody ever talks about her. What did she do that was so wrong?'

'*She* did nothing wrong,' Allegra said, turning, holding a wooden spoon out as she spoke.

She broke off.

'But I've said far too much. Your father, if he could hear me talking like this, he'd dismiss me immediately and... then who would care for you? *Basta*, Tina! Enough! No more questions.'

'But I *need* to learn more about her, Allegra. Surely you can understand that? Your mother still lives with you. You see her every day. I've been denied all that. What was Mamma like? Papà never tells me, although I've asked.'

Allegra gave a deep sigh as if worn down. 'Very well, *carissima*. I'll tell you a little – just a little, mind – while we eat, otherwise this partridge will be as shrivelled as a robin. And today, we'll take wine with our lunch. We need it. Fetch a bottle from the larder, there's a good girl.'

The food served, generous tumblers of wine poured, Allegra talked while they ate, her words flowing more easily as she drank.

'You look very like her with your red hair and fair skin. She was named Fiammetta, little flame, on account of her hair: as red as fire in winter and rich as the brightest sunsets. And she had the spark of fire about her too. When she was in a temper, oh beware her biting words and fists! As for the boys, many a scratch they sported on their cheeks if they dared insult her. *Ahi*, she was a special one, the way she was so determined to help her own people, and sometimes I see a spark of her in you. Something waiting to burst out. And that is why your father keeps you at bay, I think. You remind him too much of Fiammetta: the wild girl he fell in love with and brought to the *castello*. Fiammetta and I were more like sisters than cousins and I loved her so much.'

'How did my father meet her? Was it at a *festa*?'

Allegra paused. 'I've said enough, *carissima*. *Basta, basta!* Enough!'

Tina observed how Allegra kept glancing at the kitchen door as if expecting someone to burst in, but Papà was away.

As frustrating as it was, she decided it was unfair to subject the woman she loved so dearly to further anguish. Allegra wasn't young; she didn't want to make her ill.

'Thank you, Allegra dearest,' Tina said, her appetite gone as she toyed with her food. 'Any scrap you can share with me whenever you're able is precious when I know so little.'

Unable to check her emotions, Tina knelt beside the woman who had given up so much and pulled her close as tears ran down her cheeks and onto Allegra's pinafore lap, while the older woman stroked her hair. 'I so wish she were still alive.'

'More twigs and thorns in these curls,' Allegra, said ignoring Tina's words in her no-nonsense way, wiping her eyes on the corner of her apron and pushing Tina up. 'Fetch me your brush and I'll sort you out.'

Tina loved having her hair brushed and Allegra was gentle, despite the tangles that always knotted her long, thick hair. It relaxed her. When she was little Allegra had always been there for her, stroking her head, singing her lullabies, telling her silly stories to banish nightmares when she woke screaming.

'Allegra, about the garden. I know you've said I shouldn't but now I've found it and as long as we keep it a secret between us, I *really* want to work on it before I leave for school. But I'll need help from someone discreet so Papà doesn't find out. I have pocket money saved to pay someone. Can you think of anybody?'

She didn't confess that working on the garden might make her feel closer to the mother she'd never known.

Allegra bit her lip and stared into the distance while Tina waited for an answer.

'I absolutely shouldn't let you be in there,' she said eventually. 'But... perhaps it doesn't matter when your father is away and soon you'll be off to school anyway and likely forget all about it. And if you are in there, better to have somebody keeping an eye. I shall ask Olivio, my nephew. He's a good boy. Just left the seminary. His mother is disappointed because she thinks he's wasted an opportunity. Olivio needs the extra work. Leave it with me.'

'He *must* understand not to talk about it to *anybody*. If Papà were to find out, that would be the end of the garden, I'm sure.'

'No need to tell *me* that. I'll pretend to my sister I need help in the *castello* with heavy jobs. Which we do, *Madre mia*. There's work enough in this big old place for a small army.'

'*Grazie*, Allegra.' Tina planted a kiss on Allegra's cheek.

'How did you find the way into the garden, *carissima*?'

'I followed the cat and found the path to an old door.'

Allegra's eyes widened. '*Madonna mia!* What are you talking about? Your father had that path knocked away.'

'It *is* very narrow but I'm careful.'

Clasping her hands and shaking them up and down, Allegra wailed. 'I've always said that garden is unsafe. It casts a spell on everyone who enters.' She made a hasty sign of the cross. 'You mustn't go anywhere near that old path. You'll kill yourself, child. That's a steep drop. I thought you'd found the other way in.'

'Which other way?'

Allegra walked towards the larder and flung open the door. 'If you're so determined to be in there, come this way. *Vieni...*'

Tina followed and watched as Allegra stepped over to shelves on the end wall of the larder where jars of preserved fruit and vegetables were stored. She moved aside two large stone jugs on the middle shelf to reveal a knob which she turned. With the utmost care not to dislodge the jars, she opened a concealed narrow door, whereupon a cool rush of air sifted in, rustling her long skirt. '*Ecco!* There you go,' Allegra said, pointing down a dark passageway. 'If you are really bent on going in the garden, you must use this in future. The other way is far too dangerous.'

Allegra reached for a paraffin lamp hanging from a hook on the right-hand side of the passage and, pulling matches from her pinafore pocket, lit the wick. 'Come, *carissima*,' she said. 'Tread carefully. It might be slippery underfoot.'

The two women had to stoop in parts to avoid banging their heads against the roughly hewn stone ceiling. At one stage Allegra yelped as something brushed her face and she swung the lamp up to reveal a mass of cobwebs veiling the passageway like shrouds. Water dripped from the ceiling beyond the spiders' work to show half a dozen maidenhair ferns growing in cracks where thin shafts of sunlight broke through. A little further on, they stepped out to birdsong and daylight.

'Where are we, Allegra?'

'Inside the grotto your mamma designed. The fountain was fed by a pipe from the kitchen but I'm not sure if it works anymore.'

Tina took in the mosaics of colourful seashells and fish plastered into the ceiling and walls of the tiny space. The dolphin statue she'd seen on her first visit was at the end of this folly and she imagined how charming it must have been when it was working.

'The conte took your mamma to Viareggio on honeymoon: the first and last time she ever went to the seaside. She loved it and she wanted her own seaside here in her garden. *Ahi!* It makes me sad to see this again.'

'I shall bring it back to life, Allegra. I promise.'

At this comment, Allegra seemed to withdraw within herself as she gazed about the tangled garden, tears filling her eyes. Maybe she was thinking back to Mamma, Tina thought. Her mood seemed to suddenly change and she grabbed Tina's arm, pulling her back. 'I shouldn't have shown you the passageway and as for your promise to bring the garden back to life... I absolutely can't have you working in here. It's more than my life is worth. Come, child. Best to lock up and forget about your mother's garden.'

Respectful of Allegra's obvious panic, Tina trailed after her and helped push shut the shelving covering the entrance.

There was no way she was going to obey Allegra and now she knew the name of her nephew, she would track this Olivio down herself. And maybe he might know the reason for the garden being locked away. She knew very well from everything Allegra had told her there could never be many secrets in Sant'Agnese. Everybody knew each other's business. But it shouldn't be so difficult to work on the garden with Allegra out of the castle each evening tending her ailing mother. Nothing was going to keep her away from this forgotten garden that had obviously meant so much to her mother. Nothing. The very thought of maintaining the secret of this wonderful place made her tingle with excitement.

CHAPTER 6

Sono il factotum della città (*I'm the city handyman*) 🎵🎵

Every now and again, Tina stole a glance at Olivio while he worked: a strong young man, a head taller than herself with thick wiry curls falling over his forehead as he cut away at the yew bushes along the maze. Occasionally he broke into song, his voice perfectly pitched, but then stopped abruptly as if remembering he was not alone.

He came to the garden via the kitchen most weekday evenings when Allegra had departed and after he had finished work at the leather factory on the edge of town, his hands stained with tannin on arrival. When he left, tannin was replaced by earth-soiled fingernails and rings of sweat on his shirt.

If her father was away, Tina stole to the garden for most of the day to work on her own and after only a couple of weeks of Olivio labouring with her in the evenings, they had cleared paths, pruned all the roses and the garden had begun to take shape. Tina had even tried her hand at neatening a line of topiary bushes into obelisks and mounds. Not all of them had survived and so she'd asked Olivio to dig out the roots while she thought about how to replace them.

He was mostly quiet, uncommunicative, except when he sang refrains from popular operas: '*Che gelida manina*' from Puccini's *La Bohème*, his voice tuneful and assured. One early evening he burst out with the lively tune from Rossini's *The Barber of Seville*, '*Largo al factotum*' and she laughed outright. He stopped immediately and looked towards where she knelt tending to a clump of butterfly plants, embarrassment on his face.

'*Mi scusi*, signorina. I'm sorry.'

'Please don't stop, Olivio. I only laughed because the words are so true. You *are* my garden factotum: completing all the tasks I find hard.'

The smile on his face was almost indiscernible when he replied, '*Grazie*, signorina. My mother says I'll wear out my voice, but... I can't stop singing. I had lessons at the seminary, you see.' He added in an even quieter voice, so she had to strain to hear his words, 'That was the only part I enjoyed.'

Then he clammed up and she rose to sit near the maze on the now clean stone bench.

'I'm a good listener if you want to tell me about it,' she said. 'I have to go away to school soon and, quite frankly, I'm very nervous about it.'

He paused and looked at her for long seconds, as if considering whether or not to share his thoughts.

'I imagine living in a seminary must have been hard?' she prompted.

'Yes and no. At least I had food in my belly and a bed of my own. And an education. I liked studying. Sometimes after lights out, I'd go to the toilet and lock myself in to read.'

She waited for him to continue, sensing he was not the type to easily open up.

'My mother is disappointed in me, signorina, because I left

the seminary. Since my father died, it's been difficult and she would have liked a priest in the family to get her to heaven.' He smiled wryly and lifted the shears to continue his work.

'You see, I was guaranteed a job for life as well as respect for my mother. But I'm not cut out for the priesthood. Never was.'

After the longest exchange of words they'd had in the past weeks, he resumed cutting the yew with even more vigour and she couldn't help thinking as she watched the biceps on his arms straining at the thin shirt material, he would have been wasted anyway as a priest.

On the following evening, when her father requested her to play the piano for a group of men he'd invited to dinner, she leafed through her musical scores until she found the same Rossini largo that Olivio had sung, her fingers flying over the keys as the pace increased, imagining what fun it would be to have Olivio singing at her side. The exciting music matched the sense of danger she was enjoying by keeping the garden secret from her father as well as Allegra. Her life suddenly seemed less bland.

'*Brava, bravissima,*' one of the men cheered as she finished, his clapping loud in the library. He wore dark trousers and a black shirt and his smoothed black hair and good looks reminded her of the main star in a film she'd seen at the local cinema with Allegra. It prompted her to search for the sheet music of one of her favourite songs from the film: '*Parlami d'amore, Mariù*'. 'Speak to me of love, Mariù'. He smiled when she finished and bowed low, reaching out for her hand to plant a kiss on the back.

Tina blushed and made her excuses to leave the men to drink their *digestivi* of brandy and *liquori*. '*Buona notte*, signori. I am tired so I wish you all goodnight.'

. . .

At breakfast next morning, her father asked her if she had liked the young man who had applauded her. 'Bernardo Fara was very taken with you, Ernestina, and asked if you might go out to dinner. But you're too young. I told him to wait until you've completed your studies in Arezzo. Then, you might be ready. He's a fine young man. Climbing the ranks of the party. He'll go far. He's from a good family. Il Duce has his eyes on him. You could do worse.'

Appalled that she had obviously sent out wrong signals, she escaped to the library, staring from the window seat, counting the time until Papà's Maserati disappeared down the hill, the sun glinting from the windscreen as the car curved away along the road. Then she rushed to the kitchen, through the larder room and out into her garden. There was work to be done before Allegra arrived and Olivio came later.

Tina was brewing an idea to replace the small arbour with new wood and rocks in the middle of the maze, in honour of her mother, to create a memory shrine. Instead of the overgrown wisteria, she visualised a white, scented climbing rose she would plant to curl over it. Maybe Alba Maxima. Later she would look up species in the library.

Olivio had barely arrived, looking tired when Tina asked him, 'Can we tidy up the grotto next? I want to see if we can manage to get water flowing again from the dolphin's mouth. And I'm thinking about repairing the arbour in the middle of the maze. I—'

'Signorina, I was going to ask if today I could leave early.'

'Please don't keep calling me signorina. It makes me feel... old and, oh I don't know, it's too formal.'

'Well, you're not old. I know you were sixteen in March because *zia* Allegra has talked about you often enough. I'm almost eighteen and I don't think of myself as old although my parents keep reminding me I'm no longer a child and to hurry up and earn more money to help the family. But, signorina, you are my employer, so I have to be formal with you.'

'*Tssk!* Are we living in the Middle Ages? It's 1939, Olivio. Call me Tina. It's more relaxed.'

'Right... Tina. Well, my friends are nagging me. They say they never see me these days. And... I'd like a break this evening; it's so humid. What about you? Don't you have friends to relax with? We never see you about town.'

She pulled a face. 'I didn't go to school here. How would I meet friends? You're the first young person I've met from Sant'Agnese. You could almost say my best friend is Allegra, but—'

'Come to the river. It's been boiling today in the tannery. Come for a swim and meet people of your age.'

She frowned, feeling suddenly shy, panic filling her. 'I don't know. What would I talk about?'

He laughed. 'You don't have to talk about anything. They will do all the talking and ask you nosy questions.' He paused, taking in her expression before commenting, his tone gentle, 'You're very anxious, aren't you, signo— Tina? It's not an exam. Come on, *dai*! It will do you good. Fetch your bathing costume and slip away for an hour. The garden can wait for today and yes, I *promise* to help with those things another time.'

While he waited, she took the stairs two at a time to search for her bathing suit and then realised it was too small. Since the last time she'd used it a couple of summers ago, her figure had developed and she'd grown upwards and outwards. Tina's excitement at meeting young people from Sant'Agnese was tinged with anxiety as she pulled items from her wardrobe. In the end, she plumped for a pair of shorts and a sleeveless blouse together with a pair of plimsolls, before dashing down the stairs, through the kitchen, and pulling the larder door shut behind her. To her dismay, she heard the crash of splintering glass as it closed. She'd clear the mess up later before the eagle-eyes of Allegra discovered proof of her using the passageway.

As she made her way down the passage, she thought of her mother: would she have been pleased her daughter was making new friends?

CHAPTER 7

'If donkeys could fly'

The air was sultry, still of birdsong as the two youngsters followed a path below the castle ramparts and along a dirt track through tobacco fields towards a line of willows.

'They're already there,' Olivio said when shrieks and whistles drifted from the valley bottom. 'Let's surprise them.' He put his finger to his mouth and she followed as he diverted from the path to creep along the riverbank, parting clumps of pungent yellow broom until they reached a towering willow tree, its branches extending to the middle of the current. Again, he mimed to keep silent and mouthed, 'Wait here!'

Tina watched as he stripped off his shirt and climbed the tree barefoot until he reached a sturdy branch. A couple of metres further on, a group of boys and girls were lounging on the bank. With a warlike cry, Olivio hurled himself down and with an almighty splash landed in the water, showering the two sunbathing girls on the bank.

'*Ma come sei scemo*, Olivio! What an idiot you are,' they shouted. One of them made a great fuss about being wet, towelling herself down and waving her fist. Two boys jumped into the river to join Olivio and the three of them ducked each other while Tina looked on, feeling out of it until Olivio shouted, 'Tina, come and join us.'

She emerged from her hiding place to stand on the bank, only too aware of his staring friends.

'Meet Tina, my new friend from the *castello*,' Olivio said, paddling water as he shouted his introduction.

Tina already felt gawky and out of place in her shorts. It worsened when the group fell silent. She wanted to turn tail and flee back to the safety of the castle as they gawped but she forced herself to remain.

'*Buona sera*,' she said shyly, quickly changing to the less formal, '*Ciao*.'

Olivio climbed from the water, grabbed her hand and pulled her in, whereupon everybody followed.

After a quarter of an hour of ducking, diving and much squealing from the girls, they sat together in the sun and Tina started to field a barrage of questions.

'What's it like in that big *castello*?'

'They say it's haunted. Have you seen ghosts?'

'What do you eat?'

'What do you do all day?'

'We only see you in church,' said a pretty girl wearing a swimsuit revealing a voluptuous figure. 'What *do* you get up to the rest of the time?'

Tina shot a warning look at Olivio, desperate he would understand not to mention the garden.

'Oh, you know. I ride sometimes when my horse isn't lame or I have music lessons and English practice. Of course, I had lessons too in other subjects with tutors. And I love reading,' she replied. 'What about you?'

The girl's eyebrows had shot up, almost disappearing into her fringe. 'Me?' She held up her hand, counting the fingers off as she listed her tasks. 'As soon as I wake, I light the fire to make coffee for my father and bake the *pagnotta* I've left to prove overnight and then I make breakfast for my brothers. After that I feed the chickens and rabbits, clean the pots and pans, sweep the floor and by eight o'clock I'm at my sewing machine, making bags and belts for your father's factory. I hurry through my household tasks in the evening and once in a while, like today, I come to the river with my friends. But as for reading, riding and music... well, I'd have no time. Oh, but I do know how to lead a donkey to the mill with grain to grind.' She laughed.

'Donatella's mother died three years ago,' Olivio explained. 'She has a lot on her plate.'

Tina took in Donatella's adoring gaze as the pretty girl smiled at Olivio.

He pointed to his other friends as he introduced them one by one and Tina tried her best to remember their names.

'Antonio Gerico. He's still at the seminary, worse luck for him.'

A skinny lad, slightly cross-eyed and with thinning hair, nodded at Tina. '*I* like it there. I know Olivio couldn't wait to leave.' He patted his stomach. 'The food is far better than anything at home and I get peace and quiet away from my brothers and sisters.'

'There are eight of them,' Olivio explained. 'His parents have nothing better to do at night.'

There was laughter from the others and Tina envied their free and easy companionship.

'And this is good old Sergio Pancotti. The baker's son, who as you can see, Tina, *loves* his food. Never sit next to him at a *festa*, because he'll devour anything from your hands before you have time to start on it.'

Sergio was indeed robust: his stomach bulged over trousers cut off at the knees and he lunged at Olivio. Tina watched the pair wrestle each other playfully until they rolled too near the edge of the bank and toppled into the river, continuing to fight like two water rats.

The other girl held out her hand and Tina recognised her. She served behind the counter of the chemist store in town. '*Sono* Luisa, my name's Luisa,' she said with a smile. Small and wiry, she wore thick glasses and two long black plaits hung down her skinny back. 'I like reading too,' she added.

Tina smiled, thinking she might have found a kindred spirit.

Olivio finally scrambled up the bank and clapped his hands. 'Right, my friends! Tina needs to perform the initiation ceremony, don't you think?'

'*Si, si, si,*' they chanted and Tina's heart hammered as she wondered what on earth it entailed.

Seeing the look on her face, Olivio said, 'Don't worry. You'll enjoy it. You *can* swim, can't you?'

'Yes, but not well.'

'Well, there are plenty of us here to rescue you if things go wrong.'

'Maybe I should get back,' she stuttered. 'It's dinner time and I think Father might be home tonight and I'm leaving for school soon and there's so much to do.'

'No excuses,' Donatella said, grabbing her by the arm. 'Show her, Sergio. But don't empty the river of all the water when you jump in, you great water buffalo.'

Sergio unwound a rope secured to the thick trunk of the willow and clung to it before pushing himself from the bank and swinging back and forth to eventually let go and drop into the deepest part of the river. His friends cheered as he emerged a couple of seconds later from the water, looking like a sea lion, his hair plastered to his head.

'*Tocca a te*, your turn now,' Donatella shouted, catching the rope as it swung back towards the bank and putting it into Tina's hands. '*Forza*, Tina! Go on!'

It suddenly became the most important thing for Tina to do.

She'd passed music exams, competed at horse shows and owned certificates to prove all these accomplishments, but to swing across the fast-flowing current in order to become part of this friendly group of youngsters counted far more.

Her heart thudding, her head urging her to go ahead although she wasn't confident, she pushed herself from the bank and swung once, twice, three times over the swirling water before dropping much further from the bank than she'd wanted, screaming as she did so. She swallowed water as she went down and when she pushed against the weight of the current to return to the surface, she couldn't.

The belt around her shorts had stuck fast to something and despite kicking and wriggling with all her might, she could not budge. She pushed her arms up to signal her distress but the water was too deep and she didn't break the surface. She was going to drown. Images flashed before her: her horse Baffi cantering over the poppy-studded meadows, his mane streaming behind him, Allegra sitting by the fire in the kitchen wiping her eyes.

The final image was of a beautiful woman with wild auburn hair beckoning to her to follow as she ran with Baffi. Tina's lungs were fit to burst. This was it – and all because she'd wanted to feel part of this group of young people. Well, at least she wouldn't have to go to the stupid school in Arezzo when she died and—

Somebody fiddled with the belt on her shorts, unbuckling it before yanking her by her hair as her body whooshed to the river surface and then her head was above water and she was gulping in delicious fresh air as she spluttered and coughed.

Olivio ordered her to relax, to lie on her back, to stop thrashing about as he held one hand under her chin and paddled on his back, dragging her over to where the others helped pull her out. She lay on her stomach like a landed fish until Luisa rolled her over and told her to sit up, whereupon Tina vomited over Luisa's legs.

'That's good,' Luisa said, patting her back, her voice calm. 'Get all that river water out.' She ordered the boys to disappear and then told Donatella to stop gawping and to help remove Tina's wet clothes.

'She's had a huge shock and we need to get her warm.'

'I'm fine,' Tina croaked. 'No need to make a fuss. I'm so sorry I was sick on you.'

'It will wash off. No worries. In fact, if Donatella keeps an eye on you, I'll jump back in the river now. Then we must quickly get you home.'

Olivio called from within the copse where the lads had retreated. 'Is she decent yet?'

'Two minutes, Olivio.'

When she was dressed in an assortment of mismatched garments, Sergio's spare trousers that Tina held on to lest they slipped from her waist and with her own dry towel wrapped round her top half, they called to Olivio and the others to come out.

'I'm so sorry, Tina, *scusami*,' Olivio said. 'It's all my fault. Such a stupid idea. I thought you'd be a better swimmer.'

Tina was shivering now despite the warmth of the early evening. 'I didn't have to do it. It's as much my own fault.'

'I'll take you back to the castle. Can you walk? Otherwise, I'll fetch my donkey and you can ride him.'

'Please. No fuss. I'm fine.'

She said her goodbyes to the others, her teeth chattering. 'It's been good to meet you all and I'm sorry to break up your evening.'

'Oh, don't you worry,' Donatella said. 'We all have our jobs in the evenings and it was time to leave anyway. Not like you with your cushy life.'

'Hope to see you again, Tina,' Luisa said, frowning at Donatella. 'But maybe not in the river.'

Tina stumbled once or twice on the way back, her plimsolls soggy and slippery. It was difficult to balance as she held on to the trousers and towel but Olivio was immediately there to steady her.

At the castle gates, he apologised again. 'Nothing like that happened before. I'm so sorry. I don't know what I'd have done if you'd drowned.'

'Please, Olivio, don't go on. I didn't drown and it turned out well in the end. Thank you for getting me home. *Grazie.*'

She watched him walk slowly away, turning a couple of times before waving and disappearing through the archway back into town. Papà's car was parked on the forecourt, the engine cooling down, and she pushed open the large front door to the castle. Thank the heavens, she thought, he wasn't in the hall.

From downstairs, Allegra's tuneless singing and the clattering of pots and pans told her she was preparing the evening meal. She slipped off her filthy plimsolls and crossed the hall on tiptoe, the marble tiles cold underfoot.

Upstairs, the bathroom next to her room was free and she locked the door, turned the hot tap to fill the tub and added a spoonful of Allegra's dried rose petal and lavender mix. Sergio's ill-fitting patched trousers she dumped in a soggy pile before sinking into the scented bath, a mixture of excitement and fear after the afternoon's events adding to the crazy thumping of her heart.

Slowly she calmed down in the water as she reflected on what had happened. It had been both thrilling and terrifying. Beneath the fast-flowing waters she'd truly believed she would never see tomorrow. But Olivio had been wonderful and so had his friends. She wasn't sure about Donatella. There'd been a spikiness to her acerbic throwaway line when they'd said their goodbyes: 'I wouldn't try that trick again, Tina. It might not work out twice.' Had she *really* thought that Tina had done it on purpose to attract attention to herself?

It had pulled Tina up short. She'd looked at Donatella, thinking at first she might have been joking, but her turned-down mouth had hinted otherwise. Luisa on the other hand had been kindness itself. Professional in the way she'd tended to her after her near-drowning. Later when they'd said goodbye, she'd squeezed Tina's arm, gently warning her, 'Don't be surprised if you're weepy. It'll be the shock.'

'You should be a doctor,' Tina had told her.

'*Magari!* If donkeys could fly,' she'd replied, pulling a face. 'Talk to my father about that one.'

Tina had felt a wave of sympathy. What was it about strict fathers?

The water growing tepid, her skin wrinkling like a raisin, Tina climbed from the bath and wrapped herself in a clean towel. Of course, she wouldn't be telling Allegra where she'd been or what had happened but Sergio's clothes would need laundering. For the time being she stuffed them behind an ottoman containing clean towels. It shouldn't be too complicated a task to wash them in the morning before Allegra came to work.

As Papà was home she dressed with more care, choosing a green silk frock that fell below her knees and matched her eyes. As she combed her unruly hair back, the reflection in the mirror showed a smiling young woman with sun-kissed cheeks and arms. More freckles graced her nose and she dabbed on face powder to tone down her complexion. Otherwise Papà would doubtless comment, as he often did, that she looked like a peasant woman who worked in the fields. Oh, how she longed to please him and to hear him say, 'Darling, how lucky I am to have a daughter like you. You make me so proud.'

If she were ever to hear such a thing, then Luisa's expression, 'If donkeys could fly', would come true.

She whistled as she stepped from her room – another thing Papà considered common. But, all things considered, she was happy and she wanted her contented mood to last. For one of the first times, she'd met youngsters of her own age and it was all down to Olivio. She'd make the most of the rest of the summer in his company, that was for sure.

On a whim, at the top of the long flight of stairs, she thought what fun it would be to slide down the bannisters. Just as she began to bunch up the skirts of her frock in one hand and swing a leg over the bannisters, she heard the clip-clop of her father's shoes on the hall floor and she stopped, stepping instead demurely down the stairs.

'Good evening, Papà,' she said, slipping her arm through his as they made their way to the dining room.

He patted her hand awkwardly as he led her to her seat opposite his.

'It seems so silly to sit so far away,' she said, moving her setting nearer across the polished mahogany table. 'It's only us after all, Papà.'

She observed the almost imperceptible rise of his eyebrows and stifled a giggle. No doubt he was wondering why his daughter was behaving out of the ordinary. But this afternoon by the river had made her feel different, less shackled. Tonight, she planned to ask him questions about her mother, who was now ever present in her thoughts. Why did he refuse to speak about Mamma?

Tina waited until the second course of roast rabbit and fennel was set on the table and topped up her father's wine glass.

'I was wondering, Papà,' she said, her heart beating faster within her silk bodice. 'Do you have any photographs of Mamma I could take to school?'

He looked at her, his fork midway to his mouth and set it down on the plate.

'There are none. Why this sudden interest? You've never asked before.'

'It's not sudden, Papà. I think of her often but I know very little about her. It seems only natural to me to want to know more about her and—'

He interrupted. 'There is nothing you need to know, Ernestina. Really, you can be so tiresome in your conduct. The sooner you start school and learn how to be more discreet in social situations, the better. September cannot come soon enough as far as I am concerned.'

With that he pushed back his chair and rose. 'You can ask Allegra to bring me a *digestivo* in the study. And you should take yourself off for an early night. You are overwrought and highly strung. Such a difficult child.'

Tina watched him stride across the dining room, a lump in her throat. She sat for a while watching the candle flames flicker until she snuffed them out. The events of the enjoyable afternoon, despite her near-drowning, were now tarnished by her father's attitude. What on earth had her mamma done to cause Papà to clam up whenever she asked questions about her? And how was she ever going to find out? Would the garden reveal anything? She had received little joy from Allegra or Papà. But she was determined to find out.

CHAPTER 8

September 1939 onwards, Arezzo

'Motherhood is to the woman as war is to the man' (As printed on girls' exercise books in the fascist era)

But it was to be a while before Tina could find out more about her mother, whisked away as she was to the completely different world of the convent school in Arezzo. Her life was regimented, leaving little time to dwell on the *castello* and her mother's garden. Two by two, always two by two. Dressed in black pleated skirts and white shirts, seated in twos at hard benches, the students' desks overlooked by framed photographs of a stern Mussolini, the word '*Obbedire*', Obey, written in large italic script beneath his portrait. Two to a dormitory room, walking in pairs from classroom to classroom or when promenading through the town.

Tina had always craved company in her lonely childhood but there were times in this place when she longed for quiet and isolation.

However, to her immense relief, she spotted Luisa on her first day in the convent and rushed over to greet her.

'Nobody told me, Luisa,' she said shyly, whereupon Luisa hugged her. '*Grazie a Dio* you're here.'

'I didn't know myself I was coming until the last minute,' Luisa said. 'My father decreed, as he always does, that I need a better education.' She raised her eyes and pushed her glasses up her nose. 'Nobody told me *you* were a scholar here. *Che fortuna!* How many years have you attended the *convento*?'

'I'm new too, Luisa. My father thinks I need to be tamed.'

'Huh! And *my* father wants me to become a compliant young woman, *una giovane italiana* for Il Duce. This convent, apparently, is the nearest ideal institution.'

'*Che barba!* What a bore. But I can't tell you how much you've immediately lightened up my whole life. My father is difficult too and it's so hard to defy him. I wish it were different.' Tina sighed.

Luisa gave her an understanding look.

One morning during an outdoor art lesson when the girls were set the task of sketching foliage in the convent grounds, Tina spotted a gardener working in a parterre. It made her think of her mamma's garden and she wandered over with the pretence of drawing a tall artichoke plant. She ended up gleaning advice on how and when to prune various shrubs. For the remainder of that day her emotions were all over the place so that Luisa asked if she was suffering from her monthlies.

'No, Luisa. But I suppose this place is taking me time to settle, that's all.'

As sweet as Luisa was, Tina couldn't open up to her. How to explain what was on her mind? Something so new and unfathomable to herself even: the discovery of a forgotten garden that held a mystery about her dead mother?

There was some respite from the cloistered existence during the chaperoned walks through the ancient city of Arezzo, especially the visits to museums such as Vasari's House and the art galleries, when the pair always made sure they were walking partners. She liked less the sight of Blackshirts parading in their severe uniforms across the Piazza Grande. They were menacing with their unsmiling, aggressive expressions, carrying guns, their shiny black boots reminding her of stag beetles.

One evening, they were taken by the nuns to listen to Il Duce broadcast on a large screen in the piazza. He spoke to his *popolo*, urging them, amongst other instructions, to create large families to swell the nation's numbers, to populate the Italian Empire as well as giving birth to soldiers to protect the nation. There was a presentation of a medal to an Aretine father who had produced eighteen children, and afterwards Il Duce chastised bachelors for not playing their part, reminding them he was introducing further taxes for single men. Families, on the other hand, with seven or more children, were eligible for free schoolbooks and medical care.

'What about the poor women?' Luisa whispered, behind her hand to Tina. 'Nobody ever mentions how bad it is for a woman to bear child after child. I despair.' She'd looked around at people in the crowd and muttered, 'Best not to talk about that here. You never know who's listening.'

Tina's mind opened and broadened as they shared such discussions. She was learning more from her intelligent friend than from school textbooks and biased teachers.

The girls were not room-mates but they made sure to spend time with each other whenever they could, sitting together in the refectory or stepping round the cloister gardens when they exercised. There was a gymnasium where they practised 'ladylike respiratory exercises' and callisthenics, as Il Duce did not approve of women practising heavy, aggressive sports. Sport distracted women from childbirth and encouraged female liberation. Skiing, riding and cycling were all disapproved of too as he believed they caused infertility and altered the spinal column. In fact, Papà had broken Tina's heart just before she came away to school by selling Baffi.

'You won't be riding him in future, Ernestina. I've sold him to a farmer.'

Tina had wept many nights afterwards, soaking her pillow with her sadness, not bearing to imagine what work Baffi might be doing: pulling heavy hay carts, nobody brushing his mane or covering him at night.

'I hate my father, and I hate Il Duce,' she'd told Allegra, who'd taken her to her soft bosom, warning her to keep down her voice but letting her cry until she couldn't cry anymore.

During one of the afternoon walks around the city, Luisa hatched a plan to escape for a precious hour. Increasingly, Tina was realising how strong a personality Luisa was, despite her skinny, frail appearance.

They were approaching the top end of Piazza Grande when Luisa swayed and clutched a hand to her forehead.

'*Ahi!* I'm going to pass out,' she wailed, timing the moment perfectly with the start of another newsreel about the war in Libya, showing Italian tanks rumbling through the North African desert, clouds of dust in their wake, soldiers waving happily at the film crew. The nun on duty came over to see what the fuss was and Tina stepped forward.

'Don't worry, *suor* Chiara, I can look after her. I'll take her into the shade during the broadcast. It's no problem. That way we don't cause a disturbance.'

Permission granted, Tina led Luisa up the stairway, her arm round her friend's waist, muttering under her breath to her, 'Act a little feebler; you're taking the steps too fast.'

This comment was met with a giggle and Tina pinched her friend's arm hard, so that Luisa let out a yelp of pain. '*Va bene, va bene. Dio*, you're behaving worse than a Blackshirt thug.'

At the top of the hill, past the library building, they sat on a bench in the shade of tall umbrella pines and gazed over the view of Tuscan hills studded with villas.

'Oh, to be cantering my horse Baffi up there. I miss him so much. I hope he's being well-treated. I wonder if he misses me,' Tina said.

Luisa squeezed her hands. 'I'm sure he's all right, Tina. Don't think about him.'

They sat in friendly silence, grateful for this brief interlude of freedom.

Luisa sighed. 'I cannot abide listening to that monster Mussolini on those reels. But apart from these awful rallies we have to attend and the flag hoisting, prayers and salutes to Il Duce each morning, I enjoy studying,' she said. '*Suor* Chiara has recognised my passion for science and she's hunted me out extra textbooks. I haven't told anybody yet,' she added, clutching hold of Tina's arm, her eyes shining behind her thick lenses. 'But I plan to persuade Papà to let me study pharmacy at university. I'll tell him it will be good for the business if I deepen my knowledge. But' – she lowered her voice, as if there might be eavesdroppers about who would inform her father – 'my real dream is to study medicine.'

'Didn't I once say you'd make a great doctor?'

'But so few women study medicine. It's ridiculous. I mean, I believe many women prefer to be tended by a female physician. And it goes against what that monster dictates: that women should only study living-related subjects so they can stay at home and become housewives and mothers. What is not living-related about medicine? If Il Duce' – again she lowered her voice as she mentioned his name – 'wants *me* to stay by the hearth, bear children and look after a man, then he can think again.'

Tina looked at her wide-eyed, full of admiration for Luisa's fiery spirit as she continued passionately.

'That is *not* what I want for the rest of my life, Tina. This country is going backwards, not forwards as many believe. Do you know, the first female doctor was Italian? Right back in the *eleventh* century. A woman called Trotula from a noble family like yours. She *really* cared about women's health. *She's* my heroine. She, together with Maria Montessori, who has had to flee to India because that odious man closed all her schools and threatened to imprison her. All because she refused to take the fascist loyalty oath. He has a *terrible* attitude to women. And he has mistresses too. The situation in our country makes my blood boil, Tina, it really does.'

She pushed up her glasses, dislodged during her vehement outburst, and turned to Tina. 'Oh, I'm sorry to go on but we have to be ridiculously compliant in that school. You should tell me to be quiet in case I get you into trouble. But what about you? What are your dreams, Tina?'

Such conversations with her friend made Tina think her life was shallow. There was no way on earth she could talk to her father in this way: a staunch party member, the fascist eagle emblem displayed prominently next to the family crest over the main entrance to the *castello*. What had she done so far to be proud of? She didn't even know how to cook. Allegra looked after the domestic side of life. In what way could *she* look after a man? She remembered how Olivio had snorted when she'd handed him back Sergio's trousers and told him she'd washed them and to please return them. He'd held them up to point out muddy stains. 'I can see you've never washed down at the river like my mother, beating clothes against the stones to get them clean.'

What earthly good would she be to a man? She could play the piano but how did that help anybody except herself? Her father wanted her to be ladylike, to wear pretty frocks like a doll. For the first time, Tina considered what she might properly achieve in life. Decisions had always been made for her. She had no doubt Papà would plan to choose a husband for her and expect her to be a good, submissive wife.

'You're so clever, Luisa. You know so much. I'm honestly not sure yet what I want to do,' she said, feeling inadequate and unimportant.

'Perhaps you will become a famous musician and tour concert theatres abroad and give joy to people who come to listen to you.'

Tina's musical prowess had quickly been spotted by the convent choir mistress and she now played the baby grand in the chapel at all services. 'I'm good, Luisa, but not that good,' Tina replied.

'Practice makes perfect.'

But Tina knew she could never be as good as the famous Centa della Morea, whom she listened to with Papà on his wind-up gramophone player.

'If she were still alive, Ernestina *mia*,' he'd said on one of the rare occasions they'd sat in the library listening to music from his long players, 'I'd take you to one of her concerts in Milan.'

Tina had enjoyed these evenings with her father and had worked hard on her piano practice to please him, despite promises he made that never came true.

Yes, meeting Luisa and getting to know her better was the one saving grace about the Convent of the Sisters of Mercy. But their discussions left her feeling there should be more to her life. Her goal to feel closer to the mother she had never known and to discover more about her life by working on a neglected garden seemed somewhat small-minded in comparison.

CHAPTER 9

1940, Sant'Agnese

Il Duce ha parlato: The leader has spoken

Barely three months after her seventeenth birthday, on a boiling hot day in June, days before Tina and Luisa were to finish their education at the Convent of the Sisters of Mercy, Mussolini joined the Axis, combining forces with Adolf Hitler. The newspapers the following day declared, '*Il Duce ha parlato*': the leader has spoken.

Radios blared the news from every window, as the voice that was revered, scorned, hated and feared in turn, announced from the balcony in Piazza Venezia in Rome:

'*Fighters on the ground, at sea, in the air, Blackshirts of the revolution and legions; men and women of Italy of the Empire, the Kingdom of Albania, listen to me... we are descending to the field against those plutocratic democracies and reactionaries of the West who have in every way impeded our way and so often undermined the existence of the Italian people...*' and so on and so forth his voice boomed.

The news was met with mixed feelings. Luisa whispered under her breath that she couldn't understand why they should suddenly become enemies of the *inglesi*. Mussolini was living like a leech in Hitler's back pocket. And she wasn't alone in her thinking.

Tina was summoned back to the castle and all the girls in their final year, no matter their standard, were all hastily passed with full marks.

Allegra hugged Tina fiercely as she stepped through the doors into the cool of the castle hall.

'*Carissima*, how tall you've grown,' she said. 'I'll have to alter your clothes. Welcome home!'

'You don't have to worry about sewing for me anymore, Allegra. The nuns have taught me. Whether it's up to your level is another matter.'

Allegra laughed. 'I'll hand you all my mending, then, *carissima*. We'll catch up later this evening, but your papà wants to see you in the library straightaway.' She pulled her into another hug. 'I'm so glad you're home. You'll be much safer in the countryside. We hear dreadful things about life in the city. And we have plenty to eat here. In fact, many people travel up here from Rimini to buy food from the *contadini* because rationing is starving them. Off you go, *carissima*. My, you look quite the signorina now. Your papà will be pleased.'

Papà was standing by the window talking to a woman, their backs to Tina as he pointed through the windows open to the warm breeze.

Tina coughed and they moved apart.

'Ah, Ernestina,' her father said, coming over to greet her. Whereas before he had always dropped a kiss on top of her head, now he kissed her formally on both cheeks.

'You look well,' he said, appraising her. 'The sisters have done a good job.'

'But it is *so* good to be back, Papà. I've missed Sant'Agnese.'

'Well, for the time being, as long as this war lasts, this is where you shall stay. I had intended to send you to a finishing school in Austria, but events do not permit.'

He turned to the woman and Tina took in her generous hour-glass figure, accentuated by a fashionable nipped-in-at-the-waist skirt and tailored jacket. Red lipstick, slightly smudged in the corners of her mouth, exaggerated full lips and with her brassy blonde hair and deep-blue eyes, she reminded Tina of a tired film star.

'This is Fräulein Eleonore Huber – but we can call her Lorli.'

Tina noticed the look that passed between them and wondered what this stranger was doing in the castle. She didn't have to wait long.

'Instead of sending you to Austria to a finishing school, I have brought Austria here,' her father said, looking down at Fräulein Eleonore, who inclined her head at his words, a smile playing on her lips.

'Lorli speaks very good Italian and she has worked in our office in Vienna for some time, but she was willing to leave her home city and come to work here. She is to be your new companion-cum-governess, Ernestina. You can learn German, which will be most useful now we have joined forces with signor Hitler. It will be of great use when you come to work in the office factory. And she will show you how to touch type and keep the books.'

Tina's heart sank. Yet again, she had not been consulted about what she might like to do with her life. And working with an Austrian to boot. Hadn't they been enemies in the Great War?

'It is a pleasure to meet you, Frä—' she said, stuttering over the word and telling a huge lie for no way did she relish the idea of this woman as a companion. 'But, Papà, I *had* wanted to continue my music studies. I—'

He waved away further discussion. 'I want you safe here while the war against the *inglesi* is waged. You can by all means continue to enjoy music as a pastime, but you can forget about further studies.'

Thinking of how Luisa would react in this situation, Tina plucked up courage. 'Do I have no say in the matter at all, Papà?'

'What do you mean "say in the matter"? While you are under my roof, you do as *I* say, Ernestina. Don't tell me you're turning into one of those militant women? You'll be wanting to wear trousers next and tie a red kerchief round your neck.'

'Papà, excuse me. I... I'm hot and tired after the journey.' As usual it was pointless to argue with him and embarrassing in front of this stranger too. Tina needed time to arrange her thoughts. As soon as possible she would escape to the garden and make a plan.

As Tina changed into a pair of jodhpurs and pulled on an old shirt, she wondered why jodhpurs were considered all right to wear but trousers were frowned upon. It was illogical, like so many things with Papà and these ridiculous rules Il Duce imposed.

Tiptoeing down the stairs in case Papà should catch sight of her and ask why she wasn't resting, she hurried to the kitchen. As ever, Allegra had left it immaculate. Pots drained on the stone counter, the surfaces shone and there was the scent of lemons and Marsiglia soap. For a while she sat at the scrubbed table where Allegra had arranged a jug of marigolds and drank in the quiet and calm of Allegra's workplace. She felt far more at home in this rustic setting than in any of the cluttered rooms in the castle, stuffed as they were with ornate antiques, oil paintings and heavily embroidered wall hangings. Tina picked a peach and a fig from the fruit bowl and bit into the sweet flesh before passing through the larder and opening the secret door to the passageway.

She'd longed for this moment as she lay in her dormitory bed and yet now the time had come she was apprehensive and for a moment almost wanted to turn back. Would sharing time in Arezzo with Luisa and her aspirations have erased the special bond she'd experienced with the garden? Her heart beating faster, she stepped forwards.

She breathed a sigh of relief as a refreshing draught met her in the tunnel She smiled as splashing water alerted her and clapped her hands. Water trickled from the dolphin's mouth into the pool. Olivio had kept his promise to restore it. She knelt to dip her hands in the water, thinking she should try to acquire water lilies and maybe goldfish to complete the project.

Her spirits lifting, Tina walked on beneath the shade cast by orangey-red acers, the cool of her garden embracing her. *Nothing can take away the special feeling I have in here*, she thought. *Nothing.* She dawdled round her little kingdom, as she had started to call it in her mind, examining new growth, deadheading plants that had gone over. The wisteria on the south wall needed cutting back, its pale-purple blossoms withered. The herb garden had recently been hoed, which told her Olivio had been dropping by and work had begun on mending the greenhouse. She picked spent flowers from a straggle of melissa and crushed the aromatic lemony leaves in her fingers. For a few moments she sat on the stone bench drinking in the sights. Allegra didn't want her in this haven and her father refused to open up about her mother but she was overwhelmed with a new sense of purpose. It was her right to know what had gone on in here and, no matter what, she was determined to solve the answers to her questions. She wasn't a child anymore and had the strong sense that to be able to move forward, she needed to do this.

Olivio was curled up in the middle of the maze, shaded by the restored arbour she'd requested. It was perfect and squares of freshly dug and manured earth on each side awaited the planting of white roses she must somehow purchase. How wonderfully kind and thoughtful he was to have remembered her request. She stopped to gaze at him.

He too had grown and stubble darkened his chin and upper lip. His hair was shorter, his wayward curls shorn. One arm was tucked beneath his head; the other arm rested on the side of his thigh, his muscles visible through the thin material of his work trousers. She coughed gently, not wanting to startle him from his deep sleep, but at the same time eager for him to wake up to chat. He moved, turning onto his back, his eyes still shut.

'Olivio,' she whispered. '*Svegliati!* Wake up!'

His eyes flickered open and he jumped up, his expression worried before he relaxed, muttering, 'Oh, it's only you. I didn't realise you were back.'

'You've been working hard, I see,' she replied. 'Sorry to disturb you.'

'Are you being sarcastic? Yes, I *have* been working. All morning in the factory that steams hot as an oven. Am I not permitted to take a short rest, signorina?'

She shook her head, holding up her hands to pacify him. 'I didn't mean it that way at all, Olivio. I'm so grateful to you and I really meant what I said. And...' she added, wondering why her friend was so prickly and had reverted to the formal signorina. When they'd said goodbye at the start of her final term at the convent, he'd called her Tina. '...I am truly grateful for all the work you've done while I've been away.'

'Yes, well,' he said, picking up his cap from the ground and shaking off the dust before pulling it on his head, 'I shan't be able to do any more work in here for a while. I've been conscripted and tomorrow we leave.'

'That's dreadful, Olivio. Do you have to go so soon?'

He raised his eyes, his voice full of scorn. 'Of course I have to go. What choice do I have? If I don't go to fight for Il Duce, then it will be prison for me and shame on my family.'

'Will you... write to me? So I know where you are?'

Once again, his reply was disparaging. 'You have no idea, do you, signorina? Do you think the army will let me write letters to announce to the world where we are and what we are up to? We're likely bound for Africa. And no, I won't be posting you cards from the desert.'

She gasped, understanding now the reason for his sullen mood. How anxious he must be.

'I'm sorry, Olivio. Shall I see if Papà can do something to help? Maybe he could put in a good word and ask if you can be sent elsewhere—'

'Your father isn't interested in me. I'm a mere peasant, a nobody as far as he's concerned: good for working all hours in his factory but for nothing else. I expect he'll be employing my young brother in my place to carry on my work. He's only ten years old but that won't stop your father.'

He strode towards the gate which Tina had originally used to gain access to the garden and Tina watched in dismay.

'I hate to see you leave like this, Olivio.'

'Well, how else would you like me to go? With a song and a dance? *Arrivederci*, signorina. Or at least I hope I shall live to see you again,' he added bitterly, interpreting the word '*arrivederci*', ''til we see each other again', literally.

'*Addio*, Olivio. Go with God,' she whispered after he'd pulled the old door shut behind him. For a moment she stood still, hoping he would return and revert to the friendly Olivio she remembered. The cicadas sang their persistent notes and a robin flew to perch and trill its song on the handle of a spade left in the soil. But Olivio didn't return.

Tina pushed by the fountain spray and stood listening at the secret door to the kitchen, making sure there was no movement on the other side before carefully pushing it ajar. The kitchen was empty, the only sounds the tick of the old clock on the wall and the dripping tap that was past repair.

As she crossed the hall, she could hear her father talking in the parlour, punctuated with laughter from the Austrian woman. She continued to the library and for a while she sat in her favourite spot on the window seat and looked down on the higgledy-piggledy rooftops of Sant'Agnese.

Seeing Olivio upset in the garden had thrown her. She was disappointed with how niggly and aloof he'd been but she'd no doubt he was afraid at what lay in store. Who wouldn't be afraid of being sent to fight in Africa? Especially somebody who hadn't travelled, whose world had always been here in Sant'Agnese, the town Olivio knew blindfolded. She'd wanted to tell him about the Austrian woman Papà expected her to put up with, but there'd been no time and, anyway, in comparison with setting off for battle on another continent, it was a trivial concern.

She decided to venture into town later and see if Luisa was free to listen to her tangle of thoughts. In the meantime, instead of torturing herself with self-doubt, she would start on garden plans. Even though Allegra was dead against her going anywhere near the garden, she could almost hear her muttering: 'Idle hands are the devil's playground.' Well, Allegra was another item to tackle on Tina's list. Allegra had told her how close she'd been to Mamma and Tina was going to persist this time and confront Allegra to fathom the mystery surrounding her life. Luisa was not the only one with determination.

Tina climbed the library steps to reach the top shelf where the gardening books were arranged. She pulled out a thick volume bound in leather with gold writing on the spine she hadn't yet consulted, *The Planter's Almanac*, and carried it down to place on the table in the middle of the room. Her foot slipped on the last rung and the book fell to the carpet, dislodging some loose pages bound with a faded ribbon. Bending to retrieve them, she saw they were handwritten notes and diagrams of plants. Each page was dated. She took the bundle to the window seat and started to read.

The heading, decorated with fancy swirls, read: THE GARDENING JOURNAL OF FIAMMETTA BISICCA, 1921

Her heart skipped a beat. She had in her hands something her own mother had written and she traced a trembling finger over the letters. The paper was old, yellowing. It crackled as she turned the pages. It was the first time she'd seen her mother's handwriting and a single tear trickled down her cheek. Brushing it quickly away before it blotted the fading ink and tucking the notes back within the thick volume, she hurried to the privacy of her bedroom, turning the key in the lock twice before sinking on top of the bedcovers to read the bundle of pages. Maybe now she might uncover the mystery of the forgotten garden.

CHAPTER 10

Castle of Montesecco

Fiammetta's words from the past

Although the notes were headed THE GARDENING JOURNAL OF FIAMMETTA BISICCA, Tina quickly realised she was reading a personal account by her mother: a kind of diary pouring out her feelings. She read the words hungrily. Finally she had an opportunity to draw closer to her mother. But why had she concealed her story this way?

> *On the afternoon before I turned eighteen, Mamma warned me that on the morrow I would be on the way to becoming an old spinster if I continued the way I was going. She urged me to find a husband. But my body was strong, my skin smooth, my eyes bright, unlike hers, and I didn't need a man to tie me down with babies and more toil than I had already. I was named Fiammetta on account of my auburn hair. 'Your curls are like flames that play in the fire,' Mamma told me each time she*

combed my tangles. When she was angry, she tugged too hard, telling me I needed to be tamed, like my untidy mane, that if I wasn't careful nobody would want me and I'd turn into a lonely old maid.

At the time, I could think of nothing better but then something happened to change my mind.

How can I ever forget that August day of 1919? As usual, the sun, so cruel on my fair skin, beat down relentlessly. The only place I found relief was my pool deep in our valley, hidden by beech trees and vast gunnera plants where the sun's rays didn't penetrate. After labouring all day even though it was my birthday, having busily hoed between rows of tobacco, I slipped away, shouting to Mamma that I wouldn't be long and to keep some supper by. She had a fair idea to where I disappeared; she knew that nobody else, save for the occasional hunter of a Sunday, ventured there and she felt it safe. Perhaps because it was my special day she turned a blind eye to my escape.

I remember how I startled a hare as I reached the gap in the trees where I pushed through to the glade and so I stood for a few moments to let her run free. The jill was far from me and I couldn't really tell she was female by looking but I have a sense for such things and I waited some moments to let her run back to her leverets. She had been feeding on a clump of plantain and later I planned to gather their broad leaves to make a balm to soothe insect bites on my body.

Oh, the bliss of shedding my skirt and blouse, flinging the coarse itchy garments to the forest floor, not even taking time to hang them on a bush as I hastened over the flat stones at the edge of the pool and sank into the blessedly chill clear water where tiny trout darted from me. I squealed at the cold and then laughed, startling a pigeon, its wings flapping like Mamma's tablecloth when she shakes away our supper crumbs. On my back, my limbs spreadeagled to keep me afloat, I closed my eyes for a moment and listened to the music of my pool: water gurgling from the lazy summer stream that fed it, the splash of a frog as it plopped into the water, the buzz of a bee gathering pollen from a blackberry flower. I opened my eyes to watch three damselflies chase each other as they skimmed the pool. One landed on my outstretched palm, its delicate black-turquoise wings trembling with a hundred swirling movements. How wonderful it would be to wear gossamer-thin wings instead of thick skirts. I remember thinking at that moment that if this is what paradise was like, then I should change my ways, for Mamma told me frequently I would never get to heaven with my wayward behaviour.

Just at the moment when cool turned to shivery-cold and goosebumps prickled my limbs, there was a loud splashing and, startled, I looked up to see a large dog – I feared it was a wolf. It approached me in the water and I shrieked, 'Aiuto, aiuto,' knowing full well there was nobody around to help. But I knew it was best to make a din if encountering a wolf. Paddling water, I clapped my hands and shouted at the beast to go away and then I heard a man order him back.

'Vieni qua, Nero. Come here!'

His tone was imperious, and the hound – for it was no wolf after all – immediately turned to paddle in his direction and I dropped my legs beneath the water's surface to hide my nakedness, crouching low as my long hair fanned around me.

The man laughed. 'I didn't know sunflowers grew in water. Your hair is like floating petals, signorina.'

'Go away, se ne vada!' I yelled, my teeth chattering from fear and because the water was now icy on my body.

'I shan't go away, signorina. But if you wish, I shall turn my back so you can make yourself decent in my presence.'

'Of course I wish it, damn you, signore. And if you dare turn round, I shall—'

'What will you do, signorina?' He chuckled again.

I was almost pleased he interrupted me, because in truth, what could I do to defend myself? Biting, kicking and scratching would be pointless against him and his hound. Defiant words were feeble weapons and so I rose from the water, cupping my nakedness with my hands, my eyes directed on the man's back all the time as I waded towards my clothes. His horse stamped, stirring the forest leaves, his harness jangling as I suddenly realised who this man was: conte Ferdinando Montesecco, the owner of the castle at Sant'Agnese. Our landowner. Rich and powerful and, according to the villagers, not to be trifled with. I had seen him in his pew at the front of our church on special feast days: tall, sturdy, not unhandsome but his nose a little flat and crooked so that some villagers said he had perfect vision from both eyes for when he hunted wild boar and deer.

Within two months, we were joined as man and wife in the castle chapel of Sant'Agnese. He told me he had fallen under my spell that day when he came across me in my pool.

I had proved to my mother I would not be a lonely spinster. But, my life at the castle was no paradise. My lord controlled me and with each month that passed, my spirit withered a tiny bit more.

The gong for dinner sounded, snapping Tina back to the present. She wanted to read on but Papà was a stickler for starting meals on time and it wouldn't do to upset him on her first day back from Arezzo. She hid the journal in her bottom drawer, pulling garments over the pages, and after dragging a brush through her hair, she hurried downstairs, her head full of her mother. It was going to be difficult not to react to her father now she had read about his controlling nature.

Somehow, she managed her resentment, concentrating on

the food on her plate whilst fielding a couple of questions from her father about school. But it was the Austrian woman who commanded his attention during the meal and as soon as she could, Tina left the dining room to rush to the privacy of her room to read on.

CHAPTER 11

Glimpses of another life

My garden is beginning to take shape as I gather herbs and seeds from the wild. But there is a long way to go. It takes more than a year and couple of months to achieve results even though I have time on my hands.

Yesterday I visited the Cinquetti family. Twelve-year-old Innocenzo was tending the sheep on the slopes of Petrella when he'd been bitten by a viper. There is no money to take him to hospital. His mother is beside herself with worry and the boy has a fever they can't bring down. I took sage powder with me and told his mother to boil water with a good pinch of this and make him drink it three times a day to bring down the inflammation. As well, I gave another infusion of cicoria *leaves to heal his liver. But the most vital of my cures, and one I know will help with the snake bite, is agrimony, from which I made a poultice to tie round the wound on his leg. Thank God he wasn't dozing when it happened, as young shepherds tend to do out in the meadows, day and night. For if he had been bitten in the neck, he would not have survived.*

I returned today and am pleased to report his fever is going down. He is hungry and signora Cinquetti was delighted with the cooked chicken I took. For her, I prepared my lavender tea to calm her nerves, poor woman. She has six other children and is tired, poor soul.

This evening, Ferdinando asked where I had been all day and when I told him, he was angry.

'You will contract diseases if you mix with peasants.'

'Am I not a peasant myself?' I reminded him. 'You knew where I came from when you wed me and I shall not abandon my own people.'

He hates it when I answer back but as time in the castle passes, my courage grows. And if Ferdinando does not want me anymore, I know I can survive on my own. In many ways he is weak because he is hopelessly, madly in love with me. Sometimes I think I should add my luppolo, *hop powder to his wine to deaden his sexual longings. There are a good few wives in the town who are grateful to me for my* luppolo *remedy as it gives them a night's rest from their lustful husbands. Most nights, Ferdinando wants me and he is impatient for a son.*

August 1921

The days are hot and the plants in my garden wither. How I wish it would rain. The water I collect from the gutters is gone from the barrels and I have lost my beautiful jasmine on the south wall.

But, as long as my herbs grow, I shall continue to help my friends. There has been an outbreak of whooping cough in Sant'Agnese. The doctor's fees are high. I cannot pay everyone's bills, for Ferdinando would stop my allowance if he found out. So, I have made several bottles of poppy leaf infusion and distributed them round the houses myself. I have a pony and cart now to transport my baskets. Ferdinando refuses to let me ride a bicycle, saying it is not fitting for a contessa to pedal around the streets. It will impede my fertility. Such nonsense! But, anyhow, I'm fond of Stella, my pony. She has a star between her eyes to match her name. And she understands when I talk to her. To passersby I must sound like a madwoman as I chatter away. The only person I can really talk to and who understands me is my dear cousin, Allegra. That is one kindness Ferdinando allowed me and for which I am thankful. He let me choose my own maidservant. There is such comfort in having someone near and dear who understands me without explanation. True friends are constant, not only when it is convenient. Allegra is happy to listen when I need to pour out my feelings, whether it is convenient or not.

Tina's mother's notes were interspersed with landscape sketches and drawings of plants, carefully painted in watercolours. She ran her finger over the details, recognising the schemes she was attempting to bring back to life herself. She felt such a close bond with her mother as she read on. But, oh, how wonderful it would have been to talk to her instead.

I am throwing myself into adding designs and new plants to my garden. Ferdinando is away for long stretches promoting his leather business. When he returned from Milan last time, he was upset when I told him we had lost our baby. Ferdinando blames it on the work I do in the garden and asked Allegra to stop me going there. But Allegra and I both know that physical labour in moderation never killed anybody. If he would have me lie on my chaise longue in my boudoir all day long, that will surely kill me.

I have created a large wheel from old bricks and tufa stone found about the castle walls. The wheel is divided into segments where I have planted my most important herbs: ruta (*herb of grace*), *rue for making my oils to massage cramps and sore limbs. Calendula that I use for an infinite list of ailments: anti-inflammation, disinfectant, unguent to help heal scars and the petals to soothe menstrual pains. Allegra throws the petals into salad, which Ferdinando refuses to eat. 'I am not a rabbit,' he rages if he finds a single flower petal on his food. He is such an obstinate man.*

I have taken to using milk thistle lately. This needs to be used wisely as it can cause vomiting and poisoning to the stomach but it is also useful in aiding milk production. Malva, *alchemilla, aquilegia, wild ginger and fennel are amongst other herbs I am using.*

Along the central path I have planted cuttings from lime trees that flourish in the park near the piazza. Its leaves are calming and anti-spasmodic. Of all ailments I have come to understand that worry and unhappiness are the cause of many ills. Ferdinando has his townspeople working too hard in the leather factory and when he returns, I shall suggest I run a clinic there and keep an eye on the working conditions. I shall persuade him his people will work better in the long run if he looks after them. But this is not the real motive. I love my people of Sant'Agnese. They need looking after. I am one of them even though I live up in the castle now and no longer in the stone house in Petrella. The priest can tend to spiritual worries but even those are intensified through bad health. I am proud to be able to help.

Tina read the handwritten pages painstakingly, her mother's handwriting small and spidery and in some places smudged. And she pored over more neat diagrams of cross-sections of flowers with labels indicating the properties and uses of each plant. There were plans too showing the design of the grotto and its fountain. She read a footnote that the marble dolphin had been commissioned from a sculptor in Massa-Carrara – a present from Ferdinando for conceiving another baby. At long last she was learning something about her mamma. Why oh why had Allegra thought to keep all this from her? It made little sense. She read on, devouring her mother's words. There was no further mention of this baby she had carried, no name or sex and Tina felt sad for her parents' loss. Allegra would be sure to have information about these miscarriages; she and Fiammetta had been close. Tina couldn't help wondering how different her childhood might have been with siblings to play with and most likely a happier household to live in if her mother had survived and carried her babies to full term. She had obviously been unhappy after the first blinkered flush of romance had wilted. But she had made the most of her life. And Tina admired that. It made her think about her own purposeless life. Upset about losing the mother she had never known, she had a sudden longing to leave the remaining notes for another day and go to the garden to search for the features her mother had detailed.

The light was fading fast as she slipped into the garden and squeezed by the dancing fountain waters. Shadows from the dying sun cast fingers along the ground but there was still enough light to guide her round her mother's secret kingdom. She now understood from her mother's notes the purpose of the heap of old stones and bricks: the remnants of her mother's herb wheel. The plants had long withered and a mesh of old man's beard threatened to completely engulf the stones. But she would resurrect the bed and refer to her mother's notes for replanting. Maybe Luisa would have some medical knowledge about other herbs to add for healing. She longed to deepen her friendship with Luisa, the first friend of her age she had ever had. Very soon she would let her visit her garden. It would be good to have the opinions of somebody her own age.

The tall line of lime trees her mother had planted from saplings to make her calming tisanes, provided shade and a heavenly scent. Tina thought a bench beneath would be a wonderful addition and she could sit here and conjure a better image of her mother now she had discovered her diary. There were still more pages to read and she longed to find out more about her.

With dusk melting into night, it was growing too dark to make out any more features, so she returned to the passageway. But as she drew nearer the pantry door, she stopped. She could hear voices, then smothered laughter followed by a squeal.

'Ferdinando, not here, you naughty boy. Not now. What if your maid were to walk in on us?'

It was Fräulein Huber and Tina stopped still, feeling nauseous. Her father's voice when he replied was distorted and muffled.

'The servant is never here at this time. She lives in her own house down the hill. But don't you find it exciting, little *Liebling*? I've never made love to you in a kitchen. Shift your plump bottom nearer.'

Tina was both fascinated and appalled as she waited. Silence fell, ending with her father shouting, '*Dio mio*,' followed by another of those ridiculous squeals from her new governess. The sound of crockery smashing to the kitchen floor was met with laughter from the ghastly woman.

Tina waited until she was sure the couple had left the kitchen. She was anxious about what the future held with her father obviously under the spell of Fräulein Huber. One thing was sure, however: she would evade her whenever possible. The garden would be her sanctuary but she needed excuses to cover her absences.

Back in her bedroom, she yawned. It had been a long day. She wanted to read more of her mother's journal but her eyes refused to stay open. As she fell asleep, it was as if her mother was sitting by her bedside. She inhaled the perfume of roses and thought she felt someone brush against her hand but it was simply the summer breeze slipping through the open window.

CHAPTER 12

A garden is a solace to the soul

Tina woke early and picked up the journal. It was like reading a romance. But her mother's account was real, not fiction. Tina felt her mother's words deeply, as if they were part of herself. She read on.

August 1922

I have been busy with the garden. There's been little time to write up my notes and I've been sickly. I am with child again. This time I feel nauseous in the mornings and Allegra brings a lemon balm tisane to my bed. She tells me it is normal and a good sign but I feel truly awful until midday when the only food I can keep down is Allegra's chicken broth with her tiny home-made pasta squares.

I told Ferdinando the news last night when he came to my room and he, thankfully, agreed he would leave me alone and not visit me during this pregnancy. He also made me promise not to work in the garden and to tell the truth I have no energy to labour there at the moment. Allegra has asked her neighbour, Benedetto, to do the heavy work and he has told her he is pleased to have extra money for his family. He has a little boy and his wife is expecting another child soon.

October 1922

Ferdinando has gifted me a statue of a child and told me it is a present for my garden. I cannot believe it. Usually, he will have nothing to do with my precious garden but he is so delighted I have not lost this baby.

The vomiting in the morning has ceased. I am still listless but determined to bring the child within me to the world and so I rest for most of the day. Whether it be boy or girl, I shall teach my child to be true, follow their heart and believe in their dreams. It is too easy to be swayed by others. Look at how we Italians are being taken in by this new fascist on the scene: Mussolini. The women swoon over him, call him handsome and admire his virility but I think he is ugly the way he struts around in his shining black boots and tight jodhpurs. He is brainwashing people with the idea that Italy must rule the world and have no more 'bastard relationships', as he puts it, with other nation states.

The newspapers are full of his activities at the moment. His march on Rome was followed with passionate interest, with him decreeing at the start, in Perugia, that everybody should credere, obbedire, combattere, *to believe, obey and fight. It sounds terrifying to me for we do not need another disastrous war. There are photographs splashed across the pages of hundreds of followers jostling to salute him along the route from Perugia to Rome and Ferdinando is sure Mussolini will soon stand for government again.*

I fear for our people. They cannot think for themselves. Anybody who stands up to him flees abroad, fearing for where our nation is bound. If they speak out, they are beaten or disappear. When I mention this to Ferdinando, he is scandalised and angry that I have what he calls wayward thoughts. He says it must be due to my pregnancy. Does he not realise I have a mind of my own? That I can form my own beliefs? He asked the doctor to prescribe me a sedative to calm me but I pretended to sip at it and when the doctor left, I threw the liquid out of the window.

Instead, I asked Allegra to massage me that evening with ruta *oil to relax me and to prepare an infusion from alchemilla leaves to help me sleep.*

November 1922

We are enjoying mild weather. The sun shines kindly in the mornings. Not with the fierce heat of summer but a temperature that offers soothing warmth. I was compelled to sit in the garden for an hour. Benedetto was there, hoeing carefully between my herbs and I told him his name was fitting, for he is indeed a blessèd one: carrying out tasks I cannot manage at the moment and saving my precious garden from turning to wilderness. Now that I no longer have the energy to take my pony with me to town, I pack a basket for Benedetto to deliver on my behalf. And I include money sometimes. I fear Ferdinando is suspicious. He saw me take Benedetto's hand and wish him well as I bid him farewell the other afternoon.

'You are too familiar with the servants, Fiammetta. That is not how a contessina should behave. What is that man to you?'

'You know what he is, Ferdinando,' I replied. I felt a pain in my stomach as we spoke and doubled up and that put an end to his angry words as, full of concern, he helped me up the stairs to my chamber.

Benedetto knows this castle well. His father worked here when he was alive. He knows of secret passageways used in time of siege. One day he pointed out a low entrance at the furthest end of my garden, barely visible, covered as it was by the trailing branches of a fig tree, and he pulled out a large rusty key hidden behind a loose stone in the wall. 'You never know when this might be useful to you, contessina. Remember where it is.'

I thought it a strange message. Did he fear for my safety? Could war return so soon? Would we not be safe up here in our fortress – on the rock of the wolves? As I considered a future danger, I banished those cold thoughts and pictured instead the days after my baby is born. I shall place my child in a basket beneath the shade of the frothy smoke tree and sing lullabies while I work the soil. I cannot wait. I picture little bare feet and fists waving in the fresh air and hear happy baby gurgles mixing with birdsong.

Benedetto has a gentle face. I remember his smile shy from schooldays. His eyes are a deep brown and his right eye is flecked with hazel which is quite endearing.

'I like to work in here,' he told me. 'It's a place of peace. It doesn't feel like work to me either.'

Mornings, he works at the leather factory where the noise of the machines is deafening. I only managed a couple of visits there before I was with child, but I found the place stuffy and unbearable. When I had suggested the windows be opened wider, Ferdinando had retorted it would make the workers gaze outside to daydream and cause mistakes. 'Work will slow down,' he scoffed. If he were to try their work himself, he would experience how hard it is. But I can only drip feed my suggestions so as not to antagonise him and at the moment I am bent on remaining serene and positive for my baby.

Benedetto walks with a limp. He told me it is the result of a war wound from when he was in the trenches in Asiago. 'War benefits nobody,' he said, 'but men do not remember this.'

We left it at that but I agree with him.

He suggests clever ideas for the garden and is building me a greenhouse to overwinter my tender plants and conceal the entrance to the passageway better. Sometimes he brings me seeds and cuttings from the wild that he thinks will thrive in the garden. I have started a corner where orchids and gentians flourish and I particularly love the bee orchid he brought me, tenderly wrapped in his scarf. Delicate and aptly named. Not all my plants are of medicinal benefit but they provide a feast for the senses. How wonderful is nature. How wonderful to be able to nurture these delicate blooms. Benedetto's wife is a fortunate woman. I cannot imagine him being stern with her like Ferdinando is with me. Sitting in the garden observing him working, I always feel a deep sense of calm.

The remaining pages of the journal were blank and, anxious to know more, Tina climbed the library steps to the top shelf and reached around to make sure she hadn't missed any stray pages. Perhaps the rest of the journal held the reason for her father locking the garden from view. But even though she leafed through all the remaining gardening volumes, apart from a couple of bookmarks, she found nothing else.

Dispirited, she prepared herself for the day, pushing away any ideas of what her father and Fräulein might be up to this morning. Her head was full of her mother's words and her work in the garden. *You were a wonderful woman*, Tina thought. *Oh how I wish I had met you, Mamma carina, so I could tell you myself.*

CHAPTER 13

1940

Fiammetta

So, my darling is at last back from that school and is discovering something of the past before it grows too late. Like a rose before its petals wither and fall, it is time to pick her while she blooms.

I am pleased she found my notes. But she needs to uncover the secret concealed within the remaining pages. It will help her towards further independence, as it did me. I hope to guide her to continue the work I started. Now, more than any other time in her life, it is necessary. My countrymen and women are bound to suffer in the coming months, maybe long into the coming years. Life will turn increasingly perilous and I hope my child chooses the right path.

In these difficult times, my baby will have decisions to make. If I were still with her, it would not be as difficult. We'd talk and I'd counsel. Her new friend, Luisa, is a good girl but she is not her mother. But my little Tina is little no more and the time has come to break the shell that for far too long has protected her. My notes help her understand the past but there is work to be done in the present.

If I do not work my magic, Ferdinando will mould her as he tried to mould me.

I see he sent for a woman. Up to his old tricks. He used to pretend he was on business trips when he left the castello *but I always knew he had been with someone: he had the scent of a woman on his clothes and telltale marks on his body from lovemaking. But I never said a word. That way he left me alone for days, which to tell the truth, I minded little. Especially when I was with child. It was consolation he was sated by another. He was always a demanding selfish lover, even when I told him I was tired or unwell.*

To have this Austrian woman in the castle influencing my beautiful girl concerns me, however. I know that what this woman believes is dangerous. I see her snooping about the reception rooms when she believes nobody is nearby. But I am always there.

I have plans and it is time to direct events as far as I am able. A whisper in a dream to stir new ideas and cause second thoughts. The curdling of milk to upset the digestion, a thunderstorm to wreck plans and alter arrangements. Because I must rescue my child. Like the bloom of a flower so easily damaged by a cluster of greedy aphids sucking out its life, I must administer my remedies now.

When darkness falls, I shall visit the Austrian woman. Her nights in this castle will not be peaceful. The shutters at her window will fly open to disturb her, even after the winds have calmed. Her bottles of perfume will fall to the floor and shatter; the strings of her river pearl necklace bought for her by Ferdinando in Paris will snap and the beads will scatter between the floorboards. She and her beliefs are not welcome at Sant'Agnese and if I am clever, her stay will not endure. It won't be easy because Ferdinando lusts for her. She in turn yearns to own the betrothal ring that once was mine and which Ferdinando slipped from my finger even before I grew cold as marble. She schemes to have him place it on her own. I don't care about the ring, or Ferdinando: only my Tina, and what this war will do to her. So I shall conspire to see the woman gone.

CHAPTER 14

June 1940, Castle of Montesecco

Thread by thread, the silkworm spins its fate

While Tina pulled on her clothes, a furious summer storm sprang from nowhere, causing the shutters to slam. Heavy gusts of sultry air swept into the room and tipped a glass bowl of roses on her bedside table to the floor. She rescued her mother's journal from the wet rug and as she picked it up, she noticed brown marks on one of the blank pages.

Taking it to the window, she made out faint lines. Were they letters – a draft of what her mother had been writing? She peered closely at the page concluding the marks were probably not letters at all, but water stains from the bowl of spilled roses. In her desire to know as much about her mother as she could, Tina was seeing things. But would Allegra know more?

Closing the shutters and wandering downstairs she found Allegra kneading dough in the kitchen, grumbling as she pounded the mixture. 'This flour from the *ammasso* store is so awful. What do they add to it?' she moaned as Tina entered.

'Sawdust, apparently,' Tina suggested as she helped shape the greyish mixture into rolls.

Afterwards, they sat at the table sipping chicory coffee and Tina pulled the paper with the brown marks from her pocket.

'I found this in a gardening journal my mother wrote,' she said, handing it to Allegra, who squinted at it. 'Do these squiggles mean anything, do you think?'

She knew she should tread carefully with Allegra, so reluctant to divulge anything about her mother, but it was too late for shilly-shallying. Tina needed to know much more about Mamma; she had so little of her. The time for Allegra keeping information to herself was over.

Allegra frowned as she squinted at the page. 'Where did you find this? Have you been meddling again, Tina?'

Tina picked up one of the dough balls from the table and hurled it across the room. '*Basta*, Allegra! It's *my* turn to say "enough".' Her voice raised and, prodding a finger to her heart with each angry word, she shouted at the old lady. 'I need to know about my mamma. I am part of her, after all.' She pointed her finger at Allegra. '*You* were her best friend, were you not? I feel certain Mamma would have wanted you to talk to me about her. Forget about Papà and his threats of banishing you. *Basta!* Even if he were to send you away, I'd come too. I'd never ever wish to be apart from you, Allegra; you have absolutely nothing to fear about that.' She stood in the middle of the kitchen, quivering, her cheeks flaming red, watching as Allegra's eyes rounded before her face broke into a smile.

'*Mamma mia.* "Nothing to fear", you say. *Ahi*, I have nothing to fear except your temper just like your own mother's.'

She covered the remaining dough with a clean cloth and sat at the kitchen table.

'Well then, my little Fiammetta, pour us both a glass of what's left of that Vin Santo I was going to use for dessert but it's you and I who need sweetening up. Nothing to fear, you say.

Ha, ha, ha. And while you're on your feet, fetch the flat iron and set it to heat on the stove.'

'If you think I'm going to do the ironing as a punishment, think again, Allegra. And there's no need to laugh at me. I'm serious.'

'I know, I know. Patience, child. You never had much of that as a little one and you still haven't learned. Good things come to those who wait. Your mother had the spark of fire about her too. When she was in a temper, oh beware her biting words and fists! Beware anyone near the little fireball.'

'How I love to hear you tell me these things, Allegra.'

When they were settled opposite each other, Tina reached over to pat Allegra's hand. 'I'm sorry for my outburst. But you do understand, don't you? She's even more in my heart now I've found her journal. I know now how she met my father.'

Allegra paused. 'Well, it was very embarrassing for your mamma,' Allegra said as she sipped her sweet wine. 'Naked in a pool where she went to cool down after working in the fields.'

'It's so risqué, like a romantic story. I'd always thought he'd seen her in church or something and talked to her afterwards.'

'He'd have taken note of her, yes. She was so striking. But it was the meeting at the pool that did it.' Allegra poured more fortified wine in their glasses, the look on her face dreamy, lost in her memories. 'She filled me in on every detail, right from how she shouted at him to go away, telling him how she would kick and bite if he took one step nearer. I told you we shared all our secrets. She hadn't realised who he was, you see, and was very rude. Frightened of course – on her own with a man. I mean, we were warned always about falling pregnant if we even so much as looked at a man. And she was alone, as bare as the day she was born, *madre mia!*'

'Oh my goodness. Embarrassing, indeed. I can't imagine what I'd have done in her place. I was going to say "in her shoes", but...' Tina giggled. 'Of course, she wouldn't have worn shoes in the water.'

'And we didn't wear shoes anyway. We mostly went barefoot – even in winter. Sometimes, if we were lucky, we shared our brothers' boots when we worked in the fields and they weren't using them, or wooden clogs bound to our feet with strips of cloth, made by the menfolk in the evenings round the hearth. We were very poor. Do you know, one family in the town was even evicted for cutting down a tree on the conte's land to make new clogs for their children to walk to school? He was harsh I'm sorry to say, but your mamma softened him a little. We are less poor now, but to be honest I often wonder if your mamma was attracted to the idea of comfort, fine clothes and, most of all, the ability to help her family, rather than being in love with your father.'

Tina leant back, thinking over everything she was learning: her mother growing more real to her by the minute. '*Please* tell me more, Allegra.'

Allegra rubbed at a mark on the table with her finger as she spoke. 'She was very clever. She had a thirst for learning. The *professore* at our little school saw that in her. He suggested she should study to become a schoolteacher herself. But there was no money to pay for college. Your mamma loved the library here in the castle. She used to say to be surrounded by books was to be surrounded by treasures. When she wasn't in her garden or helping in the town with the sick, she spent hours curled up in a window seat, her nose in a book. The conte brought her books back from his trips. And perfumes, silk scarves, fine leather gloves but it was the books she liked most. And she'd started to invite children from Sant'Agnese to come to the library to help with their reading. She used to say a life without books was worse than a life without food. But I scoffed at her for that. An empty belly is far worse.'

'So, I've inherited her love of reading. Did she like music too?'

'She sang and danced earlier on but there were no possibilities in our childhoods for learning to play an instrument like you do, *carissima*. Now see if that flat iron is hot enough.'

Tina wanted more. She burned to know more about how her mother died. What did it have to do with the garden? But, with enormous self-control, she held back. Like a bottle of wine uncorked, it did no good to drink it all in one go. She watched as Allegra spat on the iron, her way of testing the heat, and smoothed the iron over the page.

'What on earth are you doing, Allegra?'

'Your mother and I used to send each other secret messages written in lemon juice this way.'

Tina had to stop herself from snatching at the page as she peered over Allegra's shoulder as letters started to show up. 'The ------ holds the -ey,' she read out. 'Or something like that. How frustrating! What holds what? Can you try again, Allegra? Maybe you didn't press hard enough with the iron.'

'It doesn't always work and with time the letters can fade completely. But… let's see.'

This time an additional two faint letters appeared.

'The second word now has a couple more: possibly a ch and a b? And the last word an r or a k? What does it mean, do you think?' Tina asked.

'I have no idea.'

Tina fetched a pencil and traced over the words, fearful they would disappear.

The enigmatic phrase read: **The ch---b holds the ?ey**. Could the final squiggle be 'the key'? It made little sense to Tina and added yet more questions to her puzzle.

'None of this explains why Papà locked the garden, Allegra.'

'*Pah!* That blessèd garden.'

'Yes, that blessèd garden, as you put it. The garden I'm growing to love.'

'I felt in my bones you would.'

'I do.' Tina sat up straight, defiance in her voice as she told Allegra, 'And Olivio and I have been working hard on it. You didn't really believe you could keep me away from it, did you? I feel close to Mamma in there, somehow. I can't explain...'

Allegra shook her head. 'At times you're so like the wild girl your father married and brought to the castle. Yes, she loved the garden. I can understand why you feel her presence in there but in no way must your father find out you've found it.'

She hauled herself up from the table. 'We'll speak again, I promise you. But I have work to do. And it won't do it by itself.'

Tina hugged Allegra and trailed up to her room with the lemon-coded message. Why had her mother written something so cryptic? And why had she felt she had to hide a message? The *castello* held many secrets but at least she no longer had to keep hers from Allegra.

In the afternoon, her head full of her mother's strange phrase, Tina made her way down from the castle to see Luisa, stepping over fallen branches brought down by the sudden early storm and passed through the archway that led to the main street and piazza of Sant'Agnese. Everywhere was a bustle: shops open, voices clamouring, people jostling to reach army vehicles parked at the exit of the piazza, windows of houses wide open, women leaning out calling to loved ones. Usually at this hour of stifling heat, the town's streets and squares were deserted, shutters on the stone dwellings pulled tight against the sun's unforgiving rays while people rested in the siesta hours. But not today.

A little girl pushed past Tina, her bare feet slapping over the cobbles as she called, 'Gianfranco, wait! You forgot this.' She held up a bundle wrapped in a rag and the contents spilled out only to be snatched by a stray dog who ran off. She tried to push through the crowd in pursuit of the animal and then sat on the ground sobbing her heart out.

Tina bent to help the desperate child. 'Mamma will be so angry. It's my brother's lunch.' Tears streaked her grimy face.

'*Non ti preoccupare,*' Tina told her. 'Don't worry! We'll get another *panino* for him.'

'But I don't have any lire, signorina.'

'Come,' Tina said, taking the child by the hand. The *alimentari*, usually closed until late afternoon, was open and they waited in a queue behind women and a couple of young men dressed in black trousers and shirts, their caps adorned with hideous badges of silver skulls displaying daggers clenched between teeth. Tina shivered.

'What's his favourite food?' she asked, bending to talk to the little girl.

'Sausage with Mamma's *strozzapreti*, signorina. But he can't carry pasta with him on the journey.'

She began to cry again and Tina tried to console her. 'We'll buy him two *panini* with *salame*. And some chocolate.'

The child's eyes widened and then she hugged Tina round her legs.

The purchases paid for, Tina watched the child scamper towards one of the trucks in the centre of the piazza. The little girl called out, her voice barely audible above the chatter of the townspeople. 'Gianfranco, *dove sei*? Where are you?'

A gangly youth packed in amongst others waved. '*Sono qui, Leonora. Eccomi!* Here I am.'

The vehicle was crammed with young men and surrounded by clusters of mothers and sweethearts bidding farewell. Some of them were crying whilst others looked on, lost.

She spied Olivio standing near the back of the vehicle, close to his two friends she had met once at the river, Sergio and Antonio. Donatella was in a group of girls waiting nearby and Tina, although she wanted to bid the boys Godspeed and good luck, hung back. Olivio had made it more than plain she was not one of them.

She watched as Donatella handed up an envelope to Olivio and he took it, stuffing it into his jacket pocket before the truck's engine started with a rattle. There were more shouts of '*Addio*' and '*Mi raccomando*': make sure to write soon, eat well, sleep, stay out of danger and other recommendations that Tina couldn't help thinking were more comfort to the bidders. The Blackshirts on the road brandished their rifles, pushed the women back and with a cough of exhaust issuing from the trucks, the men were conveyed away, a cloud of dust stirring as the vehicles disappeared from view.

Then the tears fell and Tina watched as one by one the women left the square, trailing over the cobbles, heads bowed, muttering to each other as they went.

'When shall we see them again?'

'Where are they bound?'

'My son has a weak chest. Who will look after him?'

She heard the older women warn that it was like last time and how cruel there should be another war so soon. '*Il Duce vuole.* Our leader wants it,' one of them muttered. '*Il Duce ha parlato.*' Our leader has spoken.

Luisa's elderly father looked up from the counter as Tina stepped in to the pharmacy and he smiled.

'Ah, *buongiorno*, signorina. Can I help you?'

'I've come to see Luisa.'

He gestured to a door at the far end of the shop. 'My wife is poorly so Luisa is tending to the silkworms. She'll be pleased to see you. *Prego*, signorina.' He gestured her forwards as he moved to open the door. 'Tell her I need her here in fifteen minutes to help me make up the medicines.'

'*Certo.* Of course. *Grazie.*'

Like many other families, Luisa's family reared silkworms to earn extra lire, contributing also to Italy's profitable silk industry. Very little equipment was needed after the first batch of larvae were bought. Delicate handling by the silkworm mothers, a clean, dry environment, boxes with holes to provide air and a plentiful supply of fresh mulberry leaves were all that was subsequently needed.

'It's only me, Luisa,' Tina called as she walked beneath the mulberry tree that filled the courtyard garden and tapped on the door to an outbuilding.

Luisa opened the door wide enough for Tina to slip inside and hugged her friend.

She smelled of nicotine and Tina frowned as she saw a cigarette smouldering in a saucer on the window ledge. 'I didn't know you smoked.'

'I don't as a rule and Papà would skin me if he found out,' she replied, wafting smoke away with her hands. 'But it calms me. This situation, entering the war against the *inglesi*...' She lowered her voice. 'Il Duce is mad. No good will come of this. I despair, Tina.'

'The trucks outside. Olivio and the others. They've gone.'

'I know. I said goodbye to them earlier.' Luisa shook her head. 'That man believes that by joining forces with the other madman, Hitler, he'll bring strength to our country. But it will ruin us. He's already wasted too many lives and money in his crazy quest for expanding his Empire. My cousin was one of those lost in his Abyssinian campaign. And what for? Papà is sick with worry. He's even talking about leaving Sant'Agnese and moving to Switzerland.'

'I couldn't bear it if you left, Luisa. I've only just found you.'

'We have family there, Tina. And he insists it will be better for Mamma's health. There are good sanitoriums there.' She picked up the cigarette and took a deep drag. 'I don't want to leave. But, what can I do?'

'Stay with me. You could live at the castle, study your books and apply to do your medical degree.'

Luisa laughed. 'Life is simple for you, isn't it?' She stubbed out the cigarette and threw it into the ashes of the fireplace. 'I have to get on, Tina. I'll come and see you later if I have time.'

'I'm sorry, Luisa.' Tina turned to leave. 'Before I go, can I leave this puzzle with you? I need your brains. Look at it in a spare moment and see what you come up with.' She scribbled the message with its missing letters on a scrap of paper and left it on the workbench. 'And by the way, your father wants you back in the shop in ten minutes. But, do have a think about what I said. I know your duty is with your family, but we can look after you.'

She thought of Fräulein Huber and Papà and how they might object to Luisa staying but the castle had so much space – and it would be special to have Luisa with her. She could show her the garden.

'Oh, Tina, Tina. You really don't understand, do you?' Luisa washed her hands at the sink and after drying them carefully she lifted the lid of the silkworm cocoon box to check on the larvae.

As she hurried back to the *castello*, Tina wondered about Luisa's remark. What didn't she understand? Her head was already filled with question marks. Life was turning into one huge puzzle.

CHAPTER 15

Pulling the pieces together

As Luisa handled the larvae, gently prising out dead grubs to discard, keeping the healthy ones, she set fluffy white cocoons on twigs standing vertically in another box and couldn't help thinking that Tina was like a silkworm herself, entrapped in her cocoon.

She had a lot to learn, but her suggestion of staying in the castle wasn't so bad. Luisa really did not want to leave Italy with her family. Her dream was to study medicine and if she moved to Switzerland, it would be harder under her parents' noses when they wanted her to stick to pharmacy. It would be difficult to be apart from her family but maybe she could persuade her father that if she stayed behind, she'd keep the *farmacia* going for their return. It would be a shame to let years of hard work go up in smoke. And her identity document, fortunately, had *razza ariana* stamped across it: Aryan race.

She had as much right as everybody else to stay in Italy. It was different for her parents. Nobody could tell simply by looking at her she had Jewish blood. Her parents had never practised their faith or proclaimed their Jewishness in Sant'Agnese. They didn't even possess a menorah, but Papà was concerned about ominous news from Germany and recent racial laws in Italy.

As Luisa worked, adding handfuls of mulberry leaves to the greedy larvae's supply, she calculated it would not be too long before the silk threads could be collected to spin. And just maybe, a plan for herself could be spun at the same time.

On a whim, she fetched sharp scissors and hacked at her plaits, flinging them into the bin. As she raked through her cropped hair with her fingers, she knew her father wouldn't approve, but it was time for Luisa to make a stand and do what she had to do. She tied a scarf around her cropped head. She'd face the music later.

The maintenance of the larvae complete, she glanced at her watch. She had five minutes before Father would come looking for her. Lighting up another cigarette, she looked at Tina's slip of paper, listing letters that might fit in to complete the first word. It was easy. There weren't others she could think of that made sense.

The cherub holds the key. That was it. What it signified was another matter.

She slipped the paper into her blouse pocket and returned to the shop where her father locked up and she told him she was going for a walk. 'I have a headache and need fresh air.'

Her father had his back to her as he sorted the depleted stocks and she was relieved he hadn't noticed her dramatic haircut, despite her earlier courage.

'Make sure to be back before curfew, Luisa. The authorities grow stricter with each day that passes. And your mother has prepared chicken soup tonight.'

Luisa hurried up to the *castello* and knocked at the big door. After a while Allegra answered, wiping her hands on her pinafore.

'*Buona sera*, signora Allegra. May I have a word with Tina, please?'

'She's in the kitchen. Come, follow me, signorina.'

Luisa looked about the cavernous hall as their footsteps echoed from the stone walls. Sombre portraits stared down, as if saying 'What are you doing here?' and she wondered if she would ever be at ease in this place if she took up Tina's offer.

But, down in the homely kitchen, she relaxed. Tina sat at the table topping and tailing green beans. 'Welcome, Luisa. Allegra's got me working. How lovely to see you again so soon.'

Luisa pulled off her scarf and Tina gasped. 'Your hair! What have you done?'

Luisa shrugged. 'I'm sick of my plaits. This will be far easier to look after. Anyway, I haven't long but I think I've solved your puzzle. It wasn't difficult.'

She handed the scrap of paper over and Tina read out: 'The cherub holds the key.' She looked at Luisa. 'But, of course. It wouldn't be anything else.'

'What does it mean?' Luisa asked.

Tina shrugged her shoulders and her expression was sad. 'The only thing I can think of – because I found it in my mother's journal. She wrote these words when she must have been carrying me so maybe *I* am the cherub in her womb. The message is about me: hoping I'd make her life happier. Because I've found out she wasn't happy. She wasn't, was she, Allegra?'

'Not really, *cara*.'

Allegra looked at Tina for a long moment, her eyes pools of sadness, and then she turned abruptly to pull scissors from her drawer. 'Signorina, allow me to straighten the longer bits of your hair. You've missed some at the back.'

'Fine by me, signora.'

Luisa picked up the scrap of paper while Allegra snipped away.

'But why go to such lengths to hide a message like that, Tina?'

'Your guess is as good as mine. There's a lot of mystery surrounding my mother.'

Allegra's job finished, Luisa jumped to her feet. 'I'm sorry, Tina – we'll talk it through another time but I've got to get back for supper.' She hugged her. 'I felt it was important to let you know as soon as possible what I'd come up with.'

Turning to Allegra, she said, 'Thank you for my haircut, signora. I can see myself out. You've enough to do without trailing up and down the stairs.'

After she was gone, Allegra said, 'What a pleasant young woman. She's always so helpful when I go to the *farmacia*. I'm pleased you've found a friend here in Sant'Agnese, *cara*.'

'So am I, Allegra. I've offered her a bed here if she wants, as her parents might be leaving for Switzerland and she really doesn't want to go. Would you mind?'

'Not at all. I'm sure she won't expect to be waited on hand and foot. But, of course, your father has the last word.'

Tina picked up the solved sentence and read it again. 'What did Mamma mean by the cherub holding the key? I wish I knew more about her, Allegra. Do you know, sometimes when I'm working in the garden, I want to turn and talk to her? I feel her close. Ridiculous, I know.'

Allegra reached for Tina's hand. 'Not ridiculous at all. She put heart and soul into that garden. It used to annoy *il conte* so much so she made sure to limit time in there when he was around. But, when he was away, she was there for hours.'

'She was busy in the town too, helping people in need, wasn't she?'

'Yes, *cara*. She belonged to them and they loved her. Everyone will tell you that.'

Allegra sighed. 'Your mamma really never felt she belonged in this big old place. But she'd made her bed and had to lie in it. That is the way it was when we were young. The way your papà met her, it was as if he'd captured her and for a while everything was fine. But he was frightened of losing her. He is a jealous man and I know she regretted marrying her rich, titled conte, and little by little the flame in her dwindled until it was only a fizzle.'

'That's so sad. Why would he be jealous?'

'Your father became increasingly jealous of the gardener who helped her. A lovely townsman called Benedetto. He couldn't believe there was nothing going on between them. Such a foolish man.' She turned to see to the food on the stove. 'Your father blamed her death on those herbs. She'd already lost two babies very early and... your birth was difficult. She refused to have the doctor from Sant'Agnese. She didn't like him and she... wanted you to be born naturally. She said her herbs were all she needed...'

'She mentions Benedetto in her journal: how kind he was. But...' Tina broke off in anguish as she concluded, 'Oh, Allegra, it was my fault then. My birth killed her and that is why Papà spends so little time with me. I've always known he blamed me—'

'My dearest child. I feared you would think that. It was *never* your fault.' The middle-aged woman took Tina's face in her hands, looking her square in the eyes. '*Never* think that, *carissima*. Your mamma was *testarda*, strong-willed. She had so little freedom once she married. Your father wouldn't let her out of the castle without him, so the garden she created became a comfort for her, an escape, and it was really the only time she was happy. She couldn't wait for you to be born; she longed for something more in her life. Oh, it's so complicated, my dear. So very difficult when two people from such very different backgrounds make a life together...'

. . .

That night in bed, filled with melancholy, Tina read the whole journal again, but there was no mention of a cherub anywhere. In the end, she decided her theory was correct. *She* was the cherub – not that Papà considered her that way. Despite what Allegra had said earlier, she, Tina, was the cause of her mamma's death – but at the same time, she was the key to her mother's happiness, or so Fiammetta had believed when she had written the message, presumably when she had been expecting her.

Tina could not rid herself of sadness that her mother had died during her own birth. She'd been deprived of a mother's love, a grounding that others took for granted.

Why oh why, however, had her mother hidden her sentence with lemon juice? She wondered if she would ever discover the reason.

That night she dreamt she was a baby in a basket, curling her fists in the shade beneath the lime trees.

CHAPTER 16

TWO YEARS LATER

October 1942, Sant'Agnese

The golden thread of friendship

It was as if everybody was going through the motions, their hearts not in it. Nobody was brave enough to speak up about the decline of the country over the past couple of years. The piazza was almost empty for the celebrations of the twentieth anniversary of the March on Rome.

As Tina glanced round the sparse crowd, she took in the hollow cheeks of the townspeople, the frayed cuffs and collars of the women's patched dresses, the boys: Mussolini's young fascist youth group the GIL dressed as little soldiers, parading with wooden guns resting on skinny shoulders. Earlier in the parish church, the priest had blessed the fascist flag at Mass and not complained about soldiers wearing hats or carrying daggers in their belts.

Nobody railed openly about the regular bombardments on the cities. Milan had been almost destroyed a few days ago. And despite the Pontine Marshes drained and malaria eradicated by

Mussolini's Law, and education available for more children, it didn't stop people feeling hunger pains in their bellies, or the flour being thinned with sawdust, or posters on the walls warning people not to eat cats. Dio mio, *we're not allowed to eat cats, for who would eat the mice? What has our world come to? Where have all the promises of a better life disappeared to?*

Such thoughts were shared between husbands and wives in bed at night when only walls could hear, or by men gathered with close friends in stables of a cold evening, seeking warmth from the cattle and sharing vinegary wine hidden in bottles beneath the straw. But to utter such things aloud in the piazza? *Per carità!* God forbid. They all knew what would happen if they complained. *The* squadristi *would burst into our houses, force castor oil down our gullets, throw us in prison, while well-dressed wives and children of the* fascisti *continue to wear expensive clothes and eat like royalty. Before this damned war it cost four thousand lire a month to live on, but now we need at least twenty thousand to survive. Where to find that kind of money,* Dio mio. Mah? *The world has gone crazy.* Pazzo!

Even the soldiers looked gaunt and shabby, Tina thought, and, as she often did, she wondered how Olivio and the others were faring. There had been no word from Olivio since he'd left two years earlier but his mother still believed he was alive. Hope was the only promise left to her.

'I think she would have heard if he'd passed away,' Allegra said, 'but the waiting is hard. Still, we must console ourselves with no news being good news.'

The only visits Tina had during this time were from Antonio when he was home from his seminary studies over summer. The first time he'd come up to the *castello*, she'd been more than surprised to see him: he was the member of Olivio's band of friends she knew hardly at all. Quiet, studious and a little too polite, she thought, he came alive when she brought him into the library. He'd gazed in wonder at the shelves of books, his words of admiration pouring out in a sudden cascade and she'd joked to Allegra afterwards she'd almost expected him to genuflect before the dusty volumes.

'You are so fortunate, contessina,' he'd said. 'There is not a single book in my parents' house but... I can't believe how many you possess.' He'd turned full circle, his eyes on stalks as he gazed at the leather-bound tomes, so that for Tina it had been easy to let him borrow a couple. Over the rest of that hot August month, he returned several times, borrowing academic books she was never likely to open.

She quickly picked up he was not keen on chat, apart from when asking after Olivio and Sergio each time he arrived. But she hadn't heard anything and so that line of conversation was closed to them. Allegra felt sorry for him, so skinny and weak-looking, and as she knew his parents were very poor, she always sent him off with a parcel of spare food.

Allegra had grown thin. Now that her own mother had died, she stayed at the castle most nights sleeping on a truckle bed in the kitchen where it was warm and where she could guard her precious provisions in the pantry. Bread rationing was down to one hundred and fifty grams per person per day and there were warnings posted everywhere about buying and selling on the black market. *RISPETTATE IL PANE.* Respect bread, warned the notices, and *LA CARTA È ORO*, paper is gold. But Allegra was a wizard at conjuring meals from nothing.

In the secret garden, rows of cabbages and winter fennel flourished where Tina's flowers had once bloomed and there were still plenty of tomatoes from the bountiful summer crop and Allegra knew how to make the best soups and dishes of *pan cristiano* in the whole region. She collected nettles from the wild and conjured delicious soup from their tender tips.

Fiammetta's journal was always on Tina's mind and she read and re-read her mother's words. They brought her comfort, but in two years of reading and wondering she had still never discovered why her mother had wanted to write messages in secret ink.

Luisa had turned out to be a welcome house guest at the castle, unlike Fräulein Eleonore, about whom Allegra never failed to say daily was the laziest woman she had set eyes on. Luisa did her utmost to help around the castle after her day's work in the *farmacia* and was a cheerful companion for Tina. Sometimes, Tina helped Luisa behind the counter in the chemist's and the pair had become inseparable. In her discussions with Luisa, Tina was learning that life had horizons infinitely vaster than she imagined.

The young women shared a room on the top floor of the castle tower, the view extending far and wide over the countryside. Leaning from the window, Luisa enjoyed a cigarette or two in the evenings, blowing smoke rings in the air from her pungent Nazionali. Tina had tried a puff but the smelly cigarettes made her cough. She couldn't see the point. Luisa was a hoot: a particularly excellent mimic of Fräulein. She strutted around the room, imitating the Austrian woman's guttural accent, a cushion stuffed up her flat chest, lifting her legs high as she marched like a paratrooper across the carpet. 'Vee most have ze sausages *ogni giorno*. Effery day. A *Wurst* a day keeps the *Doktor* away.'

Twice a week, when she was not accompanying Papà on business trips, Fräulein gave Tina German lessons. 'We speak it a little differently to the Germans,' she told Tina. 'But you will manage well enough. You have a good ear. Maybe it is something to do with your love of music, signorina Ernestina.'

Tina thought it an ugly language but accepted the difficult grammar as a challenge and she understood a fair bit, although was less proficient at speaking.

One evening, Papà invited guests including Bernardo Fara, the young owner of a wine estate, for dinner. Afterwards there followed a musical *serata* and Tina performed arias from

Puccini. She had finished playing the 'Anvil Chorus' from Verdi's *Il Trovatore* when, horror of horrors, Fräulein insisted on asking her to play the fascist triumphal hymn, 'Giovinezza'. Her voice was totally off-key and her rendition of the top notes sounded like the screeching of a barn owl. But Papà didn't seem to notice as he smiled benevolently at his mistress.

Tina concentrated on the sheet music, not daring to look over towards Luisa, whose lips were tightly pursed. Afterwards, the pair made their excuses and walked swiftly to the terrace, collapsing into helpless giggles against the marble balustrade.

'Ahem, *scusate*, signorine. May I join you?' Bernardo stepped forwards. 'It was indeed awful,' he said. 'She should be imprisoned for torturing music. I don't know how you endure playing for her, signorina Ernestina.' He bowed low and laughed.

He looked totally different when he relaxed, Tina thought, her mind going back to the evening he had first heard her play and kissed her hand. He had wanted to take her to dinner and she had hated the thought of his attentions at the time. But now, the three of them leant against the marble balustrade and chatted. He lit a cigarette for Luisa, cupping his hands round hers to stop the draught as he talked about concerts he had attended.

'The most magical location has to be Torre del Lago where they perform Puccini's operas. They set up a stage with the lake as the backdrop. It's breathtaking, especially when the moon is high and the stars shine. Ernestina, I think you would love it. Some day you must let me take you there. But, alas, there are no concerts at the moment. So much on hold with this war.'

Tina exchanged a look with Luisa and steered the subject away from invitations. 'The thing I miss most is my beautiful horse, Baffi. I would give anything to ride him again along the mountain trails.'

Bernardo touched her arm. 'I have stables at Podere Fara. You can come and choose a horse to ride whenever you wish.'

'But does Il Duce not forbid us women to ride, signor Fara?' Tina asked. 'Does he not say that riding alters the statistics of the spinal column?'

He shrugged. 'Some rules are made to be broken. I, personally, do not hold with all his beliefs, especially about the sports women should or should not practise. My sisters are excellent riders and competed at high level. And my mother too. It never stopped her from... bearing children.'

Tina's estimation of him had risen a notch at the mention of horses and stables. How blissful it would be to climb upon a horse again.

'But what about other rules our leader lays down?' Luisa asked, grinding her cigarette underfoot.

Bernardo paused before answering. 'Il Duce has grand visions for our country. He is determined to resurrect the Empire and you must agree by raising the school leaving age to fourteen, he is ensuring our nation will be better educated.'

'Yes, but at what cost?' Luisa continued. 'In conducting these wars overseas, he sacrifices the same young people he's educating and starves his people back home. And as for our bellies – yes, we can eat rice, "*il buon riso italiano*", good Italian rice – there is plenty of that – but what about bread? Our staple food? The price of flour has risen exponentially.'

'You are quite the young revolutionary, signorina,' Bernardo said, standing up straight and buttoning his shirt collar. 'You should be careful of what you say.'

'Or what? Am I not allowed to have an opinion? Shall I be dispatched for my opinions, like poor signor Matteotti—'

Tina interrupted before her friend could continue. 'I think we'd best go in now. Bernardo, Luisa likes to stir things up but you mustn't take heed. And, I'd absolutely love to go riding. What about tomorrow?'

Distracted from Luisa's outburst, Bernardo beamed at Tina. '*Perfetto!* I shall pick you up in the afternoon. Shall we say three o'clock in the piazza?' He took Tina's hand and bent low, before taking his leave.

'How could you think of spending an afternoon with that man?' Luisa hissed when Bernardo was out of hearing distance. 'He's an out and out fascist.'

'He's a young man caught up in the system,' Tina answered. 'Keep him off the subject of politics and he's not too bad.'

Luisa shook her head. 'Politics is not something you can simply switch on and off, Tina. For people like him it's a way of life. He didn't *need* to be "caught in the system", as you put it. I, personally, wouldn't want to spend a minute in the company of somebody without principles.'

'You take everything too seriously, Luisa. And, anyway, I want to go horse riding.'

Luisa turned on her heel and marched through the library without bidding the guests goodnight and Tina returned to the piano to play another piece, a version of Vivaldi's 'Storm', her fingers galloping over the keys as she thought how much she was going to enjoy riding on the following afternoon. She couldn't wait for the hours to pass. The last two years had been so dreary. Was she bad to want to switch off? She stumbled over a chord as she remembered how poor Olivio was caught up with the war and there'd been no news of him at all. As she finished the final bars, she knew Luisa was right in a sense: politics couldn't be ignored.

Bernardo left not long afterwards and the party broke up, but not before Fräulein had wailed her way through another German song, totally ruining Brahms's lullaby forevermore for Tina.

When she tiptoed into Luisa's bedroom, her body was turned away to face the wall. Tina wondered if she really was asleep.

CHAPTER 17

The colour of the heart

When Tina woke next morning, Luisa was gone, a note left on her pillow: I shall sleep in my own house tonight. Don't fall off your horse.

Tina felt a twinge of guilt. Luisa's note came over as a reprimand. Maybe she was right about Bernardo. But the thought of being on horseback again was so tempting. What harm could an afternoon ride possibly do?

Her breeches were loose at the waist and she tightened her belt, rubbed mould from her riding boots and as she did so, she hummed. Tina was as excited as a child as she sat on the stone steps to the door of the castle waiting for her lift. She heard the rumble of Bernardo's sports car approach in the valley and hurried down to the piazza. By the time she arrived, he'd parked outside the bar and a crowd of little boys had gathered round his shining machine.

'*Via! Andate via,*' he shouted at them to scram as they crept nearer to bend over the bodywork of the Bugatti, commenting on the dials, chrome headlights and leather-covered steering wheel. He flapped his gloves at them like a fly swat. '*Via!* Any damage to the paintwork and there'll be trouble.'

As Tina drew nearer, he opened the passenger door and ushered her in, muttering about leaving speedily to get away from the urchins.

One of the boys was Olivio's young brother, Paolino: a sweet child who suffered from a weak chest. Tina had made him up bottles of cough linctus, copying a recipe she'd found in her mother's notes, and had sent it via Olivio originally, but she had taken to dropping in at his home with more since he'd left. Sometimes Allegra visited with her and they took a plate of *cantucci* biscuits or a pan of vegetable broth. Tina smiled at the boy, not liking Bernardo's testiness.

'They're no harm, Bernardo. Just doing what little boys do.'

'Yes, well,' Bernardo said, accelerating and scattering the children as he sped off. 'You can never be sure. Little thieves, some of them.'

He reached for a headscarf from a pocket beneath the dashboard 'Wear this, otherwise your hair will be a mess,' he advised. She wondered how many other women had worn it. It was impossible to hold a conversation over the roar of the powerful engine and she settled back to enjoy the ride. He was a careful driver, slowing down at the many potholes along the way and fifteen minutes later, further into the valley, he took a right turn and steered the car up a dusty white road lined with cypress trees planted at the edges of vast olive groves.

'Welcome to Podere Fara, the family estate,' he said, removing his driving goggles. He pulled up at the edge of a meadow where half a dozen horses were grazing head to tail amongst a clump of trees, their tails flicking away each other's pesky flies. 'Aren't they magnificent?' he said.

She climbed from the car and leant on the fence, wishing she had thought to bring a carrot to entice them over.

Bernardo came to stand beside her. 'Well? Do you not recognise him?'

It couldn't be. It just couldn't. What was he doing here? Hadn't Papà said he'd sold Baffi to a farmer? Tina shaded her eyes to gaze across the meadow, focussing her attention on a bay horse at the far end.

She called and immediately Baffi looked up from his grazing and moved towards her, sedately at first but breaking into a canter as he whinnied and recognised her. And then he was nuzzling her and Tina was crying as she turned to Bernardo to say, 'Tell me I'm not dreaming.'

He laughed. 'You're *not* dreaming.'

She scaled the fence and pulled herself up onto Baffi's back. He wasn't saddled, but it didn't matter. She squeezed her heels against his sides and clung to his mane, bending to whisper in his twitching ears to tell him how much she'd missed him, loving the feeling of once again being high up on his sturdy back as he walked a few steady paces parallel with the fence, almost knowing he had to be extra careful of his special rider perched bareback.

Bernardo laughed again. 'Let's get him properly tacked up and then I'll ride with you on my horse, Principe. There's a route through the forest you'll enjoy.'

A sturdy black Maremmano cross had approached as they talked. Bernardo pulled a lump of sugar from his pocket and Baffi moved closer to investigate, nuzzling at Bernardo and blowing air through his nostrils.

'*Sì, sì*, there is one for you too,' Bernardo said, holding flat his hand.

The rest of the afternoon became a wonderful blur of cantering and galloping, stopping only to pause and admire the extent of Bernardo's family estate along the forest route. Tina was in heaven. To be with Baffi again was the best gift she'd received in a long time and when Bernardo invited her to dine with him, she accepted straightaway.

'My family is away but our housekeeper will rustle up something for us.'

'How did Baffi end up here, Bernardo?'

'I had a word with your father. He asked if I knew any farmers who could do with your horse and I persuaded him to sell him to me. He agreed, on the understanding I didn't tell you. I think he thought it best that way. And I didn't tell you, did I? I kept my word.'

'You did indeed. But... oh, I've missed him so much. Now that I've found him again, would you mind if I rode him occasionally?'

An incline of his head and a benevolent nod prefaced his answer. 'I was rather hoping you'd ask, signorina Ernestina.'

'Please call me Tina. Papà won't accept the abbreviation but Ernestina is so... stuffy, don't you think?'

'Tina it is, then. Now, let's eat. Pierina is an excellent cook.'

As the sun trailed fiery streaks along the horizon, they dined at a table on the terrace that looked out on the estate's vineyards.

'We used to export our wines to America,' Bernardo told Tina as he held up a glass of white Grechetto, 'but now we're exporting to Germany. So far, business is going well.'

With the spell of the afternoon – being reacquainted with Baffi and now seated at a table laid with a white damask cloth, being served steak and feeling slightly tipsy from the delicious wine – Tina had almost forgotten there was a war on and Bernardo's comments pulled her up. Here she was, being wined and dined in style whilst Olivio was missing and the people of Sant'Agnese were suffering privations across the board. She didn't want Luisa's admonitions to intrude on this short, glorious interlude but it was impossible to push them away.

'Papà tells me you're a rising star,' she said, placing a slice of beef as soft as butter in her mouth.

'I have ambitions, yes,' he said.

'What exactly do you do, Bernardo?'

'I'm in Rome most of the time, working in the Quirinale for our Duce.'

'Aren't we *all* working for him in one way or another?' Tina said, wishing Luisa could hear her provocative remark.

He raised his eyebrows, giving her a long look before replying. 'In what sense?'

Suddenly not hungry, feeling bad she was dining on meat that had been unavailable to most of the population of Sant'Agnese for months and months, she placed her fork on her plate.

'I mean...' She paused to find the right words. 'The way people have to sacrifice so much with each instruction from Rome. It's unfair. Women have given up their gold wedding rings to be melted down to provide funds for weapons. Nobody has tasted *caffè-caffè* in ages and they make do with ground acorns or chicory roots. *Everything* is risen in price and rationed, while officials and their wives can afford to wear satin and silks and soft leather shoes.'

'Yes, I admit there are advantages to being in the party,' he said, lighting up a fat cigar and tipping his head to exhale towards the stars. 'But *you* should know that. Your father, after all, is no communist.'

'But the difference is, *I* can see how the other half live. Or don't,' she added. 'Their lives are hard. They're good people and I think Il Duce has forgotten about them in his quest for making Italy great.'

'I had no idea such thoughts were in your head, Tina. You should be careful how you express yourself. Once words exit the mouth, it's hard to retract them.'

'I'm sure I'm not the only one with such thoughts, Bernardo.' She drained the rest of her delicious wine, not caring about her loose words. 'What do *you* really think about it?'

He ran his finger and thumb up and down the stem of his empty glass as he gave a reply that sounded considered to Tina.

'I obey. Sometimes it's easier to do so and not give away one's inner feelings, my dear.' He quoted a line from Dante's *La Vita Nuova*: '"*Lo viso mostra lo color del core.*" The face shows the colour of the heart. Tread carefully, Tina.'

'I think it's the poor who suffer most in war. The ordinary person,' Tina replied, 'and if I show the colour of my heart with that assumption, then so be it.' She repeated something she'd overheard in the piazza, the mutterings of an old man. '"*Quando i ricchi vanno in guerra, sono i poveri che muoiono.*" When the rich go to war, it's the poor who die.' Bernardo was not the only one who could spout quotations.

She shivered in the chill of the October evening and Bernardo removed his jacket to drape round her shoulders. He called for Pierina to bring coffee. 'Let's not spat,' he said. 'Come and watch the full moon rise. I have to return to Rome tomorrow and I don't want to go with a quarrel ringing in my ears.' He moved Tina's chair away as she rose and offered his arm. She didn't take it, pretending instead to hunt for a handkerchief in her pocket.

'I'm not quarrelling, simply telling you how it is.'

'*Va bene*. That's fine. And after you've drunk your *caffè-caffè*, as you so charmingly call it, I shall drive you home. It's late.'

The coffee was excellent, although she didn't admit it, and Bernardo was the perfect gentleman on the drive back to the castle. He didn't kiss her hand as he had done on other occasions, although Tina was sure he wanted to. No further mention of horses was made and neither did she push with more requests to come and ride Baffi. Now that she knew where her beloved horse was, maybe she could borrow Luisa's bicycle and steal a ride from time to time. Or walk. It was not so terribly far.

She waited for a couple of minutes after Bernardo had dropped her at the castle. Bernardo's car purred away before accelerating down the hill, the glare from his headlights stroking the edges of the road as he wound his way back to Podere Fara.

The castle was in darkness and she lit a candle to light her way up the staircase. Luisa's bed was empty again and Tina was disappointed. How satisfying it would have been to share the evening's events with her friend and tell her how she'd stood up in her own small way to Bernardo. She'd hoped it would have been enough to dispel doubts Luisa held about her. But her friend had obviously taken umbrage and was staying away from the castle. First thing tomorrow she would find Luisa and patch things up.

Tina wasn't sleepy at all. Her garden called to her and, grabbing her mother's shawl, she slipped down the stairs to the kitchen where the clock ticked away the minutes of the night, before making her way through the pantry to the secret passageway. Allegra wasn't sleeping in the kitchen having decided she needed to catch up at home. As Tina came from the passageway, the moon, silver and sombre, shed a spectral light over the pathways and between the branches of the lime trees.

As she explored the moonlit garden, her head was full of plans for a new bed. She would plant all in white: with long fronds of gaura with their white flower tips that resembled dancing butterflies, a white scented rose with pink-tinged petals, white cosmos and bidens that would self-seed and fill in gaps and last long through the summer until first frosts.

She was compiling the list in her head when the sound of an animal in pain stopped her. A low moan came from over by the far wall near the greenhouse and she tiptoed towards the sound. She couldn't bear to hear such agony. Maybe a cat had been savaged by a fox or a boar. Could it be Tigressa or one of her kittens?

The sounds grew more insistent as she approached. There'd been plenty of boar about this summer. Allegra had told her the men in Sant'Agnese poached them from her father's land. There were sausages and hind legs hanging from hooks in the outhouses of some homes and who could blame them? Meat was expensive and scarce; delicious cured boar meat provided for winter. If somehow a boar had made it into the garden, she must be wary though. If cornered, they were capable of killing or gravely injuring.

But as she grew nearer the greenhouse, the sound was less animal to her ears. She pushed open the door and stopped, her heart pounding as she made out the shape of a person curled on the floor.

'*Chi sei? Cosa fai qui?*' she asked. She really should turn tail and flee. What could she do, defenceless, if the person attacked her? Picking up a spade leaning against the bench, she repeated the question. 'Who are you? What are you doing in here?'

By the light of the moon, she made out his features: pale, wan, sickly – barely recognisable. Falling to her knees, she cried out, 'Olivio! What have they done to you?'

His eyes flickered before he slumped back and she brushed a straggle of curls from his clammy forehead. Olivio was burning up and he needed help.

CHAPTER 18

Fiammetta

Voices from the past

Oh my little Tina, what are you doing? Leave Bernardo alone. You will singe your wings, my beautiful girl.

Don't you realise he is bewitching you, that he doesn't care about your horse? He wants you... he only bought Baffi so he could ensnare you. Yes, dramatic words but I know what men are like.

Your father did the same. Me, a simple country girl, he wooed with fine silk dresses and rich promises. He promised me the world. He said we would visit famous cities, dine on fine food and wine for the rest of my life. We met once or twice secretly by my pool. I was as chaste as a novice nun when I was with him, would not even let him kiss me on the cheek or hold my hand. I think I drove him to a frenzy, waiting.

'Only if we are man and wife can you make love to me,' I told him, threatening to stop our visits if he dared touch me. For that is what we had been taught, we girls, from very young. 'You

will fall with child,' the older women used to say. '*Don't let a man near you.*' That word '*fall*' was laden with shame. My mamma had told me more than once how she had met Papà. '*He used to come and watch me when I fetched water from the well. And one day, he winked at me. And that was that. We were as good as married and I made him come to our home and ask permission of my father for my hand. Be careful, Fiammetta. A man only has to look at you a moment longer and you know what he wants. They cannot control themselves.*'

I knew no better, you see. And so I believed what she said. I was a good girl.

But when I was back in our stone family house, seated at table with my parents, sharing bean soup and dry bread, always serving Papà and my brothers first, my mother and I eating what was left over, chewing on crusts, I imagined swallowing the tenderest meats that Ferdinando talked about.

'*You will not have to lift a finger if you live with me,*' he told me often enough. '*You will have servants to do everything. My library is full of books for you to read. You won't have to fetch water from the well or wash in a tin bath by the hearth. You will have a bathroom to yourself and soft cotton towels to dry your body.*'

His words wore me down; he tempted me with dreams of luxuries. Eventually he captured me and we married quite soon after our first meeting. And my parents, oh, how proud they were; how Mamma boasted down at the river as she pummelled away at her laundry; how she told the women her Fiammetta never had to do such menial work and what a lady I had become. I believe the women grew sick and tired of her and one by one her friends abandoned her, choosing different times to go to the river so as not to hear her boasting.

And over the years Ferdinando's actions wore me down too. What else was there for me to do in the daytime save prepare myself for when he returned home and wanted me in bed? At times I felt like a cut of meat served for him on a platter, his mouth devouring me, nibbling here, nibbling there, turning me over, issuing commands to do this or that for him.

I was a doll. Dressed for undressing, hair combed up in perfect curls, my hands as smooth as a newborn baby's skin now that I had no washing to do down at the river or digging in our meadow. And he berated me when I showed no pleasure in our marriage bed. I felt nothing except pain most of the time when he thrust himself into me and I feared I would split in two. And afterwards, I lay awake, my ears full of his snoring, wondering if this was all there was to life. I lost two babies very early on before you and that increased his anger.

'If you enjoyed me more, then your babies would grow properly,' he berated. 'It's like making love to a wooden skittle.'

I tried. Oh, how I tried. I pretended, moaning like he moaned, but still I felt no pleasure and as my unhappiness grew, I lost weight and he in turn grew angrier until eventually he stopped coming to my room each night.

I helped my townspeople as much as I could and learned of the discontent in the factory. Kind Benedetto helped me and showed me the way to come and go in secret. I believe Ferdinando was suspicious of the time I spent with Benedetto so I had to time my visits to town carefully.

It was you growing inside me that saved me. And my garden. I planted seeds and nurtured them. And when the plants flourished, I had such joy. 'When you are born,' I would whisper to you, cradling my belly, 'I will nurture you too and show you how to grow.' Some plants withered and I identified myself with them. Some I fussed over and watered too much and they were not strong. The plants that self-seeded were the best of all. I learned so many lessons. The garden and all that it led to showed me how I should be myself, find a place where I too could grow and find a reason for living.

This, my darling girl, is what you must do too.

Think what you are doing. Think for yourself. Listen to others, yes, of course. But choose for yourself how to act and then you will grow strong like the plants that resist weather, sun and the meddling of others.

Look to the garden for my herbs to heal your friend. He is very sick. Make him strong again, Tina.

And look to the garden to solve the meaning of the message from the cherub. It holds the key, my darling girl.

CHAPTER 19

Tina

True colours

Pulling one sack from a hook to form a pillow and another to place over and beneath Olivio's body, Tina hurried to the kitchen to fetch medicinal herbs. She had to bring down his fever, rehydrate him, get food in his stomach. She threw a couple of sticks on the glowing embers in the stove to heat a pot of water and lifted down a jar of dried *Filipendula ulmaria*, meadowsweet. From the meat safe she took the remainder of the chicken broth and *cappelletti* pasta Allegra had prepared for dinner. Olivio looked half-starved. She would do what she could for him tonight and then involve Luisa tomorrow. Tina guessed he would need more medical attention than her herbs.

A noise from upstairs caused her to blow out the candle and stand motionless while the water simmered on the stove. Then, the flush of a toilet, footsteps on the landing and a door closing told her she was safe to continue.

Olivio had thrown off the sacking and was muttering as he thrashed around. She knelt again by his side, touching his shoulder to wake him gently. 'Olivio, *sono io*. It's me, Olivio.' He jerked to a sitting position and his hands went to her neck, gripping so hard she resorted to slapping his face.

Her strangled words, 'I'm Tina. You're safe, Olivio. You *must* calm down so I can help you,' eventually got through and he shuddered before flopping back.

'You need to eat and drink. You're safe,' she repeated.

He allowed her to feed him small amounts of broth, but she insisted he drink all the herbal potion. She made a mental note to find something more comfortable to bring from the *castello* to arrange into bedding: blankets, pillows. The floor was hard and cold.

He muttered a weak '*grazie*' before settling and she sat with him until she was sure he slept. It was a fitful sleep but he seemed calmer. There would be time enough to talk when he was stronger and find out why he was here but for now he needed her to care for him and remain strong. Covering him again and pulling the greenhouse door to, she left as daylight seeped through the trees. She had to tidy the kitchen. Allegra would be in her kitchen very soon to prepare breakfast and Tina had left pots and pans on the surfaces.

It would not do to reveal there was a visitor in the garden. Even if it was Olivio. The fewer people who knew the better.

Her mind wired, the events of the night repeating themselves in her brain, Tina lay awake and kept glancing at her wristwatch until the hands pointed to six o'clock. Luisa would surely be up by now. Tina stole from the castle and ran through the alleyways until she reached the shop and went to the back of the *farmacia*.

The door was ajar. Luisa, still in her nightgown, was turning her coffee grinder.

'Luisa, Luisa, you have to help. Come quick.'

'*Buongiorno*, Tina. What on earth has happened? *Calmati!* Calm down! Is it your father? Allegra? Can you not fetch the doctor?'

Tina grabbed Luisa's arm and lowered her voice. 'It's Olivio. He's turned up out of the blue. Hiding in my garden. He's feverish. Looks awful. I need your help, Luisa.'

'I'll go and dress. You deal with the coffee. I'll grab some medicines. Fever, you say? Anything else?'

'I don't think he's wounded. There's no blood. But... oh, Luisa, he's in a bad way.'

'You need to stay calm and we need to walk back to the castle as if nothing has happened. I swear there are eyes and ears behind every shutter in this town. *Calmati!* Take deep breaths.'

Within ten minutes, the two young women were walking up the hill, arm in arm. Luisa with a wicker basket on her free arm, a large lettuce resting on top of a cloth covering medicine packets she had pulled from the *farmacia* shelves. She chatted to Tina as if they had no cares. Every now and again she burst out laughing, muttering to Tina to do the same, although it was the last thing in the world Tina felt like doing.

As Tina pushed through the great doors of the castle, she heard sounds of her father stirring upstairs and water gurgling in the pipes but, fortunately, the kitchen was empty, Allegra still not at work.

Leading her to the greenhouse, Tina watched as Luisa pulled a stethoscope from her basket to listen to Olivio's heart where he lay on his makeshift mattress of sacking.

'Lie still, Olivio. You're in safe hands,' she said, her voice calm, authoritative. 'We'll sort you out, but lie still.'

She next measured his temperature and shook her head gently. '*Caspita!* What have you been up to, *amico mio?*'

'I gave him an infusion of *Filipendula* to calm his fever,' Tina explained.

'You did well,' Luisa answered, pulling a phial of tablets from the basket and asking Tina to fetch fresh water. 'These *aspirine* contain much the same thing so stop your infusions from now on. He needs to take two of these every three hours and plenty of fluids. Boiled water will do. Can you manage to sneak away regularly to do this? The next twenty-four hours are crucial if we want this temperature down. When will it be safe for me to come again, do you think?'

'Whenever Allegra is sleeping in her own house. Hopefully tonight. She says she sleeps better in her own bed. But sooner or later, I'll have to tell her what's going on. Olivio's her nephew, after all. In the meantime, I'll root out blankets and pillows to make Olivio more comfortable. It's freezing in here.'

Luisa nodded. 'Good idea! I can bring a couple from my place too. Now, help me remove his filthy clothes.'

Tina, embarrassed at first, joined in with raising Olivio carefully to a sitting position so they could remove his rag of a shirt. When it came to his trousers, she hesitated and Luisa said quietly, 'He's our patient, Tina. Forget he is Olivio while we do this.'

Tina found it hard to see Olivio naked and she averted her gaze from his manhood. He was vulnerable, helpless and she was glad he was, for this moment at least, not fully aware of what was going on.

On removing his boots, Luisa gasped. The big toes on each foot were blackish-purple, one of the toes on his left foot oozing pus. '*Porca miseria*,' she hissed. 'Damnation! Frostbite… that toe needs lancing. We may have to get the doctor involved in this or he could lose his foot. And worse… Poor Olivio. I'll come back later to check on him, there's danger gangrene might have set in. Ideally, we need sterile conditions to work in and he'll need fresh clothes. I'll look in Papà's wardrobe to see what he's left behind. They're about the same height.'

'Come to supper tonight, Luisa. It's easier. I'll tell Allegra you've decided to return to sleep here, that your house is too lonely without your family. As you say, we need to try to act normal.'

'*Assolutamente.*'

'*Grazie*, Luisa. For everything. You're amazing. And I'm sorry about our tiff. I'll tell you about my visit with Bernardo some time.'

Luisa sighed. 'We have more important matters to worry about, *amica mia*.' She gave Tina a sweet smile and the two women embraced.

As they prepared for bed that night, pulling nightdresses over day clothes so they could sneak out later to the garden, Tina told Luisa about Bernardo, explaining how she'd probed him for his beliefs and stood up to him. But she was also honest about how much she had loved riding Baffi and how she hoped to sneak away to ride him again.

'I'm glad you said that to him. I know it's not easy, standing up for what is right, Tina. I suppose I'm lucky because I was brought up by parents who openly discussed such matters. You... you've not been so fortunate. But there comes a time...' Luisa paused, obviously searching for tactful words. 'I mean, we're not children anymore, are we, you and I? We've been given minds of our own to decide between right and wrong. I hate the way our country is going with this crazy man at the helm. You only have to look around to see fear in people's eyes: the... the way people are pitted against each other, fearful of acting according to their true principles. People spying on each other, people following the *partito* simply because of the favours on offer...'

Tina was quiet. She knew her friend was right.

'Anyway, we'll concentrate on Olivio for now. By helping him, you're on your way to showing your true colours, you know. If he has run away from the army, the authorities will be looking for him and we'll be punished too if we're caught helping. So, we go carefully. But we both know there is no question we're doing the right thing.'

By the pearly light of the moon, Luisa worked on Olivio. As well as woollen blankets and a couple of cushions they had fetched warm water and cloths and first they washed him down thoroughly, Tina by now come to terms with seeing him undressed. In her head she was a nurse following instructions from a doctor. The patient wasn't Olivio. Or so she told herself as she willed him to pull through and make a good recovery. Tina had sneaked a bottle of brandy from the drinks cabinet in the library and they made him swallow a couple of glasses, Luisa warning Tina to lie across his body if he should later thrash about when she lanced his toe.

'It will hurt,' she warned and she was right. Olivio swore as Luisa cut into the flesh, releasing bacteria and a stream of pus which she wiped away with a clean cloth. He gripped Tina's outstretched hand so hard she thought he would crush her bones.

'Soon be over, *amico mio*,' she said soothingly. 'It's for the best.'

Luisa bound the toe with sterilised bandages. 'You have to keep this clean, Olivio. No digging for you in the garden today.'

'As if,' he murmured. 'How can I thank you both?'

'By getting better,' Tina said, helping thread his arms into Luisa's father's shirt, the sleeves too short. She rolled them up and with fresh underwear and trousers, too wide for Olivio's skinny frame, he began to look more human.

'*Grazie*,' he said, grasping her hand and squeezing it gently this time.

Tina's stomach did a little flip and she swiped away a tear. 'We'll get you well again,' she said, trying to make her voice ring with confidence she didn't feel.

CHAPTER 20

November 1942

Night movements

For a while, Olivio continued to look ghastly, his temperature high and Luisa worried he might need the hospital down in Rimini.

'How on earth will we get him to the city?' Tina asked.

'Good question, but once he's there, he'll be in good hands. Papà had a friend, a *guardia medica*, I think we can trust. But it's a long way and at the moment getting him there would do more harm than good. I think we have to continue to keep him clean and watered and... pray,' she added.

Ten days later, and Luisa pronounced he was at last turning a corner.

'You might always walk with a limp and it will be a while before you can put proper weight on that foot. Then, you'll need to wear comfortable shoes. It's a good thing it's not too cold yet and you don't have to wear boots. Fresh air will do no harm. But... you *must* keep the wound very clean.'

'Yes, ma'am,' he said, saluting Luisa as she rose to leave.

'I'm not joking, Olivio.'

'I know and I'm grateful. Truly I am.'

When Luisa had gone, Tina fetched food from the kitchen. When she returned, Olivio was sitting outside the greenhouse, leaning against the brickwork.

'What are you doing? Are you mad? *Pazzo?* I hope you didn't put weight on that foot,' Tina said.

'I dragged my body along. I needed a change of air from the greenhouse.'

'You have to be careful. Didn't you hear what Luisa said?'

He made a disparaging noise, huffing air through his mouth. 'It's bad enough having Luisa nagging me, but two bossy females telling me what to do is too much. If you can find me a couple of sturdy sticks, I can use them as crutches. I can't fester here for the rest of my life. I have things I must do.'

Tina placed the pot of food at his side. 'For a while longer, you must be patient. Otherwise, all our hard work will be pointless.'

He had the grace to look apologetic and she watched him tuck in, pleased his appetite had improved.

'I've not tasted anything so good in all my life,' Olivio said as he mopped up the last of Allegra's broad bean soup with a heel of bread. 'I've been living on what I could grub from fields and hedgerows for God knows how long.'

She waited to hear more about his ordeal but he didn't elaborate and she had the sensitivity to let him be. If he wanted to tell her, he would. If he didn't, then she would respect his silence.

. . .

One week later, Tina supported Olivio's weight as he hopped to the glade beneath the linden trees to sit on the stone bench. They sat together and she watched as he nibbled on fresh bread and cheese, only eating half before he carefully wrapped the remainder and put it in his pocket. 'I'll eat it this evening. I've grown used to keeping something spare for later. No need for you to keep stealing away to come and see me, Tina. Won't your father become suspicious you're never about?'

'He's away at the moment. As usual. It's to Allegra and that Austrian woman I have to keep making excuses. I tell her I'm going for a walk and she thinks I'm very fit.'

He smiled. 'It's only the rich and the *fascisti* who are fat these days with their privileges. Mind you, I could kill for a decent smoke right now.'

'I'll see what I can do.'

'I became a dab hand at rooting around for fag ends in the gutters,' he said. 'When you're desperate, there's a lot you can't be too fussy about.'

Breaking the silence that hung in the air after that statement, she asked tentatively, 'What actually happened to you, Olivio, all this time? You haven't said. We all believed you were sent to Africa.'

'I almost wish I had been,' he said, pointing to his bandaged foot. 'No frostbite to be had in Africa.'

She waited, aware it wasn't simply the body that needed healing after trauma. His words were faltering at first but as he continued, she sensed his need to share what had happened.

'We were sent to hell, basically. Only two weeks after we left here in October '40, Sergio and I ended up in Albania for the invasion of Greece. Il Duce had planned a glorious entry into Athens. Another crazy scheme. But we never made it, although he'd assured us it would all be over by early November. *Huh!*'

He was quiet and she took in the tremor of his hands as he continued.

'We were holed up forever in the Greek mountains and, *Dio mio*, was it freezing! Minus twenty, Tina. It gets cold here, you and I know that. But this was a different cold and we were badly equipped. We had no warm clothes. And the Greek soldiers... well there were fewer of them but they were better supplied and no way were they going to let us take over their land. Il Duce withdrew but then in the spring, once the rain stopped, the bloody fool urged us to make another attempt. He even turned up to give us a pep talk in person. All bluster.' Olivio spat in the flowerbed. '*Pazzo!* Crazy fool. The *inglesi* in the meantime sank our ships in Taranto and we were dispirited.'

'So, what happened?'

'I'd had enough, that's what happened. I love my country but why die for a pointless cause? I want to fight for a better cause: the liberation of my country from the tyranny we're enduring.' He paused, his mind somewhere else. 'It's taken me all this time to get back here. There were times when I thought I wouldn't make it...'

'You've had to travel a long way. How did you do it?'

'I'm not sure myself now. Some of it is best forgotten. I smuggled myself onto a fishing boat, walked by night, hid by day, jumped on trains... you name it. It's taken me longer than I wanted, but... I'm grateful to be here at all.'

There was silence when he'd finished. What a lot he'd been through. She couldn't imagine it but the state he was in clearly indicated great suffering. Her heart went out to him and she reached out to hold his hand. It was still trembling.

'Shall I see if I can find that cigarette? Papà has a box in his study. And I'll find some cognac.'

'Would you mind, Tina? Smoking calms me.' He smiled and she wanted to scoop him up and care for him forever.

Allegra was busy chopping vegetables in the kitchen when Tina emerged from the pantry.

'I'm missing a couple of candles, Tina. And did Fräulein finish off that soup? I thought there'd be enough left for your suppers. What shall I prepare instead? I'll not be here tonight, so I'd planned to leave it for you to heat up.'

'Oh, that's strange. It definitely wasn't me. But that woman *does* have a huge appetite. It was most likely her,' Tina lied, feeling relief at how much easier it would be to steal away to visit Olivio this evening with Allegra out of the castle kitchen.

'Could you do us stuffed zucchini flowers? You know I love them and there are still a few growing in the greenhouse. Once the frosts arrive, that will be it.'

'*Va bene*. Stuffed zucchini flowers it is, then. *Perfetto*.'

'I need to fetch a gardening book from the library. One of the roses has black spot; not sure how to treat it. Won't be long, Allegra, then I'll pick the flowers.'

The box of cigarettes was on a side table next to Papà's armchair and she grabbed a handful, stuffing them into her blouse pocket after climbing the ladder to grab the first gardening manual to hand. The cognac was almost finished, but the dregs would give Olivio some cheer.

'Take this basket,' Allegra said, handing her one from a shelf next to her copper pans as Tina rushed past her through the kitchen. 'Bring the flowers back as soon as you've picked them. Otherwise, they'll shrivel and not taste good.'

'You're a wonder,' Olivio said as Tina handed him the cigarettes and little wax *cerini* matches.

While he smoked his first cigarette, she cut off the remaining courgette flowers, selecting only those that grew on the edges of long stems and hurried back to the kitchen. She met Allegra halfway along the passage and Tina's heart hammered in her ribcage. What if Allegra had come through to the garden and discovered Olivio?

'Allegra! Goodness, you startled me. Are these good enough? It's the last of them.'

'I'm sure they are. I was coming to see what else there is in the vegetable beds. There's hardly anything in the *alimentari* and what there is costs *un occhio della testa*, an arm and a leg. I don't know how people are managing. We must share what we can.'

Thinking on her feet, desperate for Allegra not to come further, Tina said, 'I'll pick you a basketful and then we can visit those in need. There are more broad beans, the last of the tomatoes and some spinach beet. And there's that sack of potatoes. Don't you worry, I'll do it. See you later; I must finish one or two things today before Papà returns.'

'Maybe I'll pop into the garden before I leave and take a look. It must be looking lovely now with all the time you spend on it.'

'I'll most likely be finished by then, Allegra *cara*. I'll say goodbye now.' She embraced the woman, not liking the subterfuge, but it was in Olivio's best interests.

Olivio read her face when she returned.

'What's up?' he asked.

She sank onto the bench where he was smoking another cigarette.

'I bumped into Allegra in the passageway and had to stop her from coming into the garden. Luisa thinks it best not to tell anybody you're here. But, what about your family? Isn't it cruel not to tell them?'

'In my darkest moments it was the thought of seeing my mother and brother again that kept me going. So, of course I want to see them. But I also don't want to put them in danger. I don't want to cause you any trouble either but... I didn't know where else to turn.'

'I'm so glad you came to me. And, you know I'll always help you.'

Any reply from Olivio was never to be heard. They were interrupted.

'I knew it. Ernestina di Montesecco. I *knew* there was something going on.' Allegra's strident tone startled them as she stepped from the shadows. 'You never were good at telling fibs and I've wondered why things have been missing from my kitchen.'

She rushed over to Olivio and crushed him in a warm embrace, her voice choked with sobs as she cried, '*Madre mia e Dio buono*. You are alive, *piccolino*. I've been saying the rosary every night for your safety. And here you are, my prayers answered. But you look terrible and… what have you done to your foot?'

Tina hissed at her to keep down her voice. 'Allegra, you don't know how loud you are. If anybody discovers Olivio is here, it will be curtains.'

'But, *madre mia*, he can't possibly stay here. In a garden. In the cold and dirt with winter sneaking up. He must come to my place. My house is outside the walls, away from neighbours. He'll be safer there. The shutters to my bedrooms are always closed and he can stay quiet. Nobody comes to visit.' She clasped her hands together in delight at her plans. 'Clean sheets, my special chicken broth. Fresh water from my well. I can look after him and… oh, but what about your mother, Olivio? She needs to know. I shall tell her this evening.'

Olivio grabbed her hand. '*Zia*, Aunt, slow down! We don't want the news spreading all over Sant'Agnese. You know what it's like. I'll be arrested and you too, most likely. There'll be trouble. *Of course* I want to see them again. But in good time. Tell me they're well.'

'They will be much better for knowing you're back in Sant'Agnese.'

Tina agreed with Olivio. 'Let's wait until Olivio is better. It will be a shock for his mamma to see him like this, Allegra. For the time being, we keep this to ourselves and when the right moment arrives, there will be the most amazing reunion? But...' Tina paused. 'Allegra, I'm not happy about Olivio staying at your place. If you're caught harbouring him, you'll be punished. Imprisoned, even. We keep him here, make the greenhouse more comfortable.'

Olivio was not so sure. 'Here I'm like a rat in a trap. There are no easy ways in or out of this garden and the way you keep coming and going, Tina, through the kitchen... if Allegra was suspicious, others will be too. But I do agree I can't possibly tell Mamma yet, hard as it is.'

'You'll be safe here, Olivio. If needs be, I can find you one of Papà's guns. I know where he keeps the key to his cupboard. And you're not going anywhere for the time being. Don't you worry about me coming and going to the garden; I do it all the time. No, we carry on with our daily routines, Allegra,' Tina advised. 'Perhaps together we can find a truckle bed for Olivio from the attic and extra blankets. Pick the vegetables you need while you're here, but the garden has to be out of bounds to you from now on. What if Huber comes to find you in the kitchen for one of her snacks and you're not there?'

'Very well, *cara*, but I'm going to make sure he eats well: my thick vegetable and chicken soups and fresh pasta.'

At dinner, Tina toyed with her food, her stomach churning with plans for hiding Olivio. Fräulein Lorli sat opposite at the dining table, tucking into her starter of fried zucchini flowers. When she saw Tina's full plate, she asked if she could have them if they were going to be wasted. The same happened with the veal and mushroom main course. It made Tina furious to think of all the people needing food in the village.

'I hope you are not sickening for something, Ernestina. You look pale. Perhaps you should go to bed early tonight. Your father returns tomorrow and I'm sure he won't want to pick up any of your germs. And neither do I. No need for our lesson this evening.'

Tina needed no further excuse to escape to her room. She bolted the door and dressed herself in the darkest clothes she could find in her wardrobe, pulling her nightdress on top. As Tina lay waiting on top of the covers, the windows open to the night, she went over the list of tasks already completed. She'd found a truckle bed in the far end of the attic and a spare torch and candles. Over the next days, Olivio could do his best to make the greenhouse weather-tight, now he was capable of simple jobs. Yes, she had made the right decision. She'd been worried about Allegra. If Olivio were found in her house, Tina didn't want to think about the consequences and despite her protesting her house was not in the centre of town, you never knew who might be in the shadows of the alleyways. Lovers looking for a quiet rendezvous away from the ears and eyes of watchful parents or the *postino* delivering mail, the *guardia vigile* doing his rounds after dark. In truth, nowhere was really safe these days but the garden was the best place.

Olivio had a point, however. Danger could pounce at any time. And if he ever had to flee the garden through the passageway into the kitchen, he might come face to face with Huber, or even her father.

What would her father say or do should they be discovered? A conte, at the heart of the *fascisti*, harbouring a fugitive from the war? Luisa was right. At a certain point, Tina had to choose what side she was on.

CHAPTER 21

Volontà è vita – Good will is essential in life

Papà had taken Fräulein Lorli to inspect a possible new outlet in Bolzano, near the Austrian border, so fortune smiled on the three young people. Tina had the castle to herself for a few precious days and she and Luisa took it in turns to slip away each night to check on Olivio.

They'd adapted a wooden framework over his leg from an old bedwarmer known as a *prete*, a priest, to keep the covers from weighing on his sore foot. But during the day if it was warm enough, he had taken to sitting in the garden and had taken over the task of mending the greenhouse. Allegra had remembered an old brazier in one of the outhouses and on cooler evenings, it was now cosy enough in his hideaway.

'You look much better,' Tina told him. 'At last you have colour in your cheeks.' She pulled a couple of books from her basket: *Addio alle Armi* by Ernest Hemingway and *Via col Vento* by Margaret Mitchell. 'I found these in the library. Thought they would help pass the time. I loved both.'

'*Grazie*, Tina,' he said. 'I'm going stir-crazy in here. Can't wait to be on the move again.'

Tina frowned. 'But where will you go?'

'I can't stay here like this forever. There's work to be done.'

'Work?'

He tapped his nose.

'Why can't you tell me?'

'Talk to Luisa.'

'Luisa isn't here. I want to talk to you.'

He laughed. 'Are you sulking, Tina?'

'Why should I be sulking?'

She was peeved. After everything she was doing, the risks she, Allegra and Luisa were taking, it wasn't fair Olivio couldn't open up to her as if he didn't trust her. She left him after half an hour. He said he was sleepy, needed to rest and she knew he wasn't going to enlighten her.

Late the following afternoon, although it wasn't her shift, Tina was bored and decided she would join Luisa in the garden with Olivio. Papà had returned with Fräulein Lorli to the castle the previous night and almost immediately left for another work trip, but Tina was taking advantage of Fräulein Lorli having her usual long siesta to join her friends. What Papà saw in the Fräulein, she had no idea. But going on the noises coming from his bedroom, the groans and moans, she guessed.

Emerging from behind the fountain, Tina caught the tail end of a conversation between her friends.

'We have to be so careful, Luisa,' Olivio was saying.

She stopped to listen. What was going on? Was everybody at it like Papà and the Austrian woman? Her heart sank but as there were no moans and groans, she called out softly, 'It's only me, you two.'

Luisa was leaning over Olivio, snipping away bindings on his foot.

'Good!' she said. 'It's healed nicely. You can leave the bandage off now and let the air do the rest. But...' She wagged her finger at him. '*Non esagerare.* Don't go overdoing it.'

He nodded.

'What do you have to be so careful about?' Tina asked. 'I know we have to be vigilant about Olivio being here, but is there something else I should know?'

The look that passed between them didn't escape her and she felt a pang of jealousy. Annoyed, she asked, 'Tell me what's going on? Am I not involved up to my ears in all this? I have a right to know what you're discussing.'

Another look, a fleet second of conspiratorial silence that spoke more than any excuse.

'Well?' she demanded, hands on hips. 'Am I *not* to be trusted?'

It was Olivio who spoke first.

'Luisa's heard word that Sergio is badly injured. He's been sent back from the front and he's in hospital. We're trying to work out how we can help. He'll want out of the army more than ever now.'

Tina sank down next to them. '*You* can't get him out of anywhere, Olivio. Not in your condition.'

'I know that. I'm not intending to leave for a while. More's the pity. But—'

'Olivio and I were trying to come up with a plan, any plan,' Luisa took up. 'Working out details. And, of course, we have to be careful.'

'How badly injured is he? And where is he?' Tina asked, relieved there was nothing else going on.

'Sartina. In the next valley. And the poor blighter's lost half his leg.'

'*Caspita!* Goodness! Poor chap,' Tina breathed. 'So, he won't be able to walk across Monte Aquilone pass. What have you come up with so far?'

'Cart and horse. Hide him under merchandise, firewood maybe. Something like that. We haven't got far with anything significant,' Luisa said.

'But as sure as Il Duce is destined for hell,' Olivio said, 'Sergio will not be wanting to return to arms. We know he doesn't support the *fascisti* – we need him with us here to help in the fight. We've also heard Antonio is back at the seminary. Convinced of his vocation, the friars are protecting him.'

'Couldn't Sergio pretend he has a vocation too?' Tina suggested. 'And hide in the same place?'

Olivio spluttered. 'Sergio is more atheist than atheism itself. There's no way he'd settle in a seminary and there'd be no peace for the poor friars either. He'd start a riot.'

'Why didn't you want me to know about this?' Tina asked. 'To be honest, I'm offended. I thought you trusted me.'

Luisa leant nearer and took her hand. 'We didn't want to involve you any further in this mess, Tina, *cara*. You've already done so much. And your father... let's say his politics are very different from ours and it must be hard for you. We don't want to put you in more difficulty, Tina. We were trying to think of where we could hide Sergio.'

'I'm not my father. Being his daughter doesn't mean I follow his beliefs, Luisa. You must know that by now. How often did we talk about all this at that dreadful convent?'

'All the same—' Olivio started to speak but Tina stopped him.

'All the same, *nothing*,' she snapped. 'I know you think I'm spoilt and rich, Olivio. Yes, I've had a different upbringing and I haven't had to work hard like you. But, don't think I particularly enjoy my life. More and more I realise my father has controlled me, isolated me from the world. Meeting you both has been a revelation. I *want* to help.'

She looked at Luisa, who was looking at Olivio. Their silence was deafening and disappointing.

'And if it's a horse and cart you need,' Tina continued, 'then the horse is absolutely no problem. I know where Baffi is and I can easily fetch him. There's an old cart at Allegra's. She hasn't used it for years. Let me check it over. *I* can go and fetch Sergio.'

'And trot away with him in broad daylight,' Olivio said, sarcasm filling his words.

'There you go again, Olivio. You have no faith in me. Well, here's what we shall do.'

Tina paced the small space in the greenhouse. 'I shall disguise myself. In fact,' she said, pointing to Luisa, 'you can accompany me in disguise. It will take two of us to get him into the cart anyway if he's so badly injured. We'll dress as nursing sisters. Turn up with paperwork – I can easily sort that. Papà has any number of stamps in his office and I can type something that looks official – and explain we've been requisitioned to transport him to the hospital we run for *invalidi* because there's a shortage of beds at Sartina Hospital... something like that. Where there's a will, there's a way,' Tina finished up, staring intently at her two friends for a response. 'Well? What do you think?'

'It *might* work,' Luisa said after a short pause. 'After all, what alternative do we have, Olivio? Sergio's not going to be able to get himself away from Sartina.'

'But then what? Where do we take the poor blighter?' Olivio asked.

'Back here of course,' Tina pronounced. 'Hide him in my garden with you, in this greenhouse. It's cosy enough now. And Luisa can help nurse him, like she did you.'

'Right under the nose of your fascist father,' Olivio said, doubt still colouring his tone.

'Yes, exactly. Right under his nose. Who would ever imagine there were deserters hiding in a castle that prominently displays the fascist emblem on its main door? Leave it with me and I'll start the arrangements. Luisa, you concentrate on the medication Sergio will need. It shouldn't take too long to sort the rest. A week, I reckon.'

CHAPTER 22

Fiammetta

Be careful, my lovely. Lay your plans well. Consider the loopholes and dangers. I will do my part as far as I can. But that Austrian woman, she is absolutely not to be trusted. She is wily, like the wolves that lurk in the rocks waiting for their moment to pounce. Did you not know the castle is built on the sasso del lupo? *The wolf's rock?*

When you wake in the morning, you will find my book of remedies beside your bed, open at the section on sleeping draughts. Take heed!

As I foresee, the weakness in your plan is depending on Bernardo to release your horse. You will need to play on him, use your charms. He is a stupid man. Tonight, I shall fill your dreams with schemes and scenes but for now, the first half of the night, sleep sweetly, my lovely. In the following days you need to be strong and alert.

The time has come to reveal to you your next trump card. It will make all the difference to your future activities. So, don't forget about my message: the cherub holds the key.

CHAPTER 23

The best-laid plans

On the following morning, Tina woke, groggy from an interrupted sleep. She'd had crazy dreams about her garden where she'd wandered in a dramatic rainstorm, her nightdress clinging to her body as lightning forked the sky above the castle turrets. When she'd tried to shelter in the passageway to the kitchen, she couldn't find it. The dolphin fountain was gone and she'd raced here and there searching for it, her hair catching in thorny rose branches, her bare feet slipping on paths. She'd fallen over a statue and grazed her knees and arms but when she cried out in anguish, her mouth wouldn't open.

The dream was very real and when she examined her arms in bed, she found grazes and bruises she couldn't remember from the day before. Worries besieged her: what about Papà and Fräulein? If they were around, how was she going to manage this crazy plan of rescuing Sergio under their noses? How would she bring him into the castle and manoeuvre him down the steps to the kitchen and through the passageway? Maybe the grazes had been caused by her tossing and turning in bed:

she'd knocked herself against the metal bed end or the sharp corner of her bedside table. Yes, that was it.

She was a nervous wreck. There were too many loose ends: fetching Baffi without being seen, when to check Allegra's cart was fit for purpose, how to bring Sergio unnoticed up to the castle? How long did she need to be away on this venture? She'd announced at dinner the night before she was helping Luisa at the *farmacia* for a few days and Papà hadn't objected, wrapped up as he was with the Austrian woman. But if she and Luisa took longer returning from Sartina with their cargo or were held up in any way, how would she account for that? What if the weather turned for the worse as in her nightmare and they were stranded on the mountain?

Sitting up, leaning against the pillows, her head a whirl of concerns, a sudden gust of wind caused the curtains to billow at her window and the pages of her open *Planter's Almanac* to flap in the current. As she leant to close the book, she caught sight of the heading at the top of the page:

Tonics for deep sleeps and calming the nerves

Yes! That was it! Apart from needing a dose herself, she would ask Allegra to add a strong sleeping tonic to Papà and Fräulein's meals and afternoon tisanes on the day she was to leave with the cart. That way, they might retire to bed early, before she and Luisa returned with Sergio.

Allegra was only too pleased to be included in the latest plans. There was no hesitation in her reply when Tina spoke to her after breakfast.

'*Certo!* I shall do it for your poor mamma, *cara* Tina. And I believe it's what she would have done herself. She never forgot where she came from, who her own people were. Not for her the hoi polloi and *borghesi* who clustered round your papà for favours.' She tutted as she spoke and pummelled harder at the dough she was mixing. 'And the cart is sturdy. There's room for Baffi too in the storeroom where Father stabled our mule. But we must be careful.'

By now, Allegra was one of them. She joked that for all her life she had been well behaved, *per bene*, but now she had joined a group of *banditi* and she was enjoying being a renegade. It was never too late, she told Tina, as she sat in the kitchen putting finishing touches to two tunics cut from a length of homespun dark-brown woollen material pushed to the back of the laundry cupboard. 'Your mother brought this as part of her dowry for blankets but it was too rustic for the castle. She'd be pleased, bless her, that we're using it to help her people.'

Allegra adjusted the glasses on the end of her nose and finished sewing the hems, breaking the thread with her teeth. 'Just as well you and Luisa are slender. There was barely enough material. Now, let's have a glass of grappa to celebrate finishing these ugly things before you try yours on.'

She fetched a clean white towel from her cupboard and tied the corners at the back of Tina's head to fashion a wimple for the headdress. 'All you need now are rosary beads to tie on a cord round your waist and to tuck that flame-red hair of yours well away and practise a pious look. *Ah sì! E i sandali...* I'll fetch you a pair of sandals from home. Those boots of yours are too fancy.'

Tina cast her eyes down, joining her hands in prayer and Allegra laughed. '*Perfetto!* You'd win the prize at next year's Carnevale. *Madre mia!*'

'If only it were simply Carnevale, Allegra. I hope we manage to pull it off.'

Allegra wiped the smile from her face and busied herself rooting in her cupboard for another towel for Luisa.

'I'll be in the stable cleaning Baffi's reins. Come and warn me if Papà returns,' Tina told her.

Tina lingered for a while, leaning against the wooden partition where the tack still hung. Baffi's strong scent was long since gone, the straw swept away to reveal a cobbled floor. How often had she crept in here to seek comfort from her horse whenever she felt lonely or exasperated with the latest stupid nanny employed to keep watch on her. No words were needed with him and he seemed to understand her moods. She'd often fallen asleep, her back against his, and been woken by the gardener. 'Best pull the straw from your hair, signorina, lest your papà notices.'

Damn Papà and damn Il Duce for their stupid, stupid ideas. Did her father really believe getting rid of Baffi was for her own good? If only she could smuggle him back to the stable and keep him secret, how wonderful it would be. But, of course, it was impossible: Papà now parked his precious Maserati alongside and there was nowhere else to hide her horse. She couldn't exactly walk him through Allegra's kitchen and pantry to conceal him in the garden and the perilous path was absolutely out of the question.

The bridles and harnesses were stiff with age but she found the lanolin she'd used on Baffi's tack and she was pleased with her morning's work. A couple more days and she'd steal away to fetch him. It was a good distance, but if she strode out, it would likely take her a little under two hours. She'd have to ride him bareback, the saddle would be impossible to carry all that way, but even if she had to walk him along the rockier terrain, the night hours would be plenty long enough to bring him back to Sant'Agnese. Allegra's outbuilding would serve as his stable for the short time needed. Tina's heart pounded at the thought of everything that could go wrong. Once the plans were actually set in motion, maybe she would rest easier, rather than going over and over details in her head.

In the evening, she dressed in a long raincoat, the weather having turned for the worst, and took a pan of broth to Olivio.

The garden beds were a quagmire and her shoes were soon sodden. The wind had snapped several branches and upended pots. As she stepped over the storm debris, she nearly fell over the statue of the boy, blown down from his usual tree trunk perch and leaving the wood exposed. She tutted and went to pick him up, not wanting him to get further damaged – it had been a gift from her father to her mother when she was pregnant, she remembered reading. But he was far too heavy, the side of the statue embedded in the mud. She leaned on the tree trunk to catch her breath – and saw a rusty key, right in the middle, almost pressed into the wood. As if it had been underneath the statue. A key to where?

And then it came to her: the message her mother had written in lemon juice. 'The cherub holds the key.' She'd almost forgotten about it. Could this be what her mother was referring to? She spoke the strange phrase slowly in her head: *the cherub holds the key*. But of course! The stone boy child resembled a cherub, now she looked closely. She bent to pick up the key, heavy and rusty, and placed it in her basket.

'You're soaked,' Olivio said. 'You shouldn't have bothered coming out in this.'

'Shall I take this soup away, then?'

He looked sheepish. 'It smells so good. That would be a waste. Come and sit near the brazier. You look like a drowned rat.'

'Always so charming, Olivio.' Tina handed the pan and spoon to Olivio and watched as he devoured Allegra's hearty broth. How much better and stronger he looked.

She picked the key from her basket and held it up. 'I found this near an upturned statue and it fits with something my mother wrote in a secret message.'

Olivio looked up with a grin. 'Have you been drinking Allegra's grappa again? What nonsense are you spouting?'

Even as Tina explained, the whole account sounded bizarre

to her own ears. 'So, I've learned through her journal, together with what Allegra has told me, how unhappy my mother was and how she hid stuff from my father. I have to admit I'd forgotten about her cryptic message but now I've found this key, it's got me wondering again. Where does it fit?'

He took it from her. 'Looks like an old key to a door.'

'I have this feeling it belongs in the garden,' Tina said. 'Otherwise, why was it hidden here?'

'Leave it with me if you like. I'll see if I can find what it opens. And, *yes*, Tina, before you say it, I *won't* overdo things but it will give me something to do.'

There was a lull in the rain. It was late and a little while later, Tina reluctantly bid goodnight to Olivio. She'd enjoyed his company, despite his teasing.

Three nights later, soon after midnight, Tina crept from the castle to fetch Baffi. Allegra was waiting outside the door to her house and hugged her tight. She pushed a string of rosary beads into Tina's hand. 'Put these in your pocket, *carissima*. I'll be waiting here all night for you to return. Tap and I'll open the gate to the yard. May *Santa Maria* and all the saints watch over you tonight.'

The moon was full but Tina wasn't afraid of the shadows cast in its other-worldly light. As she stepped quietly past the houses, the world was her own. But from one of them a faint glimmer of candlelight seeped through shutters and a baby cried. A woman sang a lullaby. It was a warning to Tina she wasn't the only person awake. She took heed and more care as she continued. Would the sound of Baffi's hooves on the cobbled road wake the citizens of Sant'Agnese on her return? Or would they simply think it was somebody bound for work? Doubts besieged her from all sides and she wondered if the whole plan was too crazy. But then she thought of Sergio and

Olivio, two fine friends in need of her help, and she pressed on.

Once she was out of town, she breathed easier. A fox ran across her path, owls hooted, the moon shone grey-blue on fields of unpicked grain and before long she was at the gate to the field where Baffi and the other horses grazed securely. She whistled low to him in the way she always had. A whinny, a thudding of hooves and he was there, nuzzling her. She pulled a carrot from her jacket pocket and whispered they were going on a huge adventure and he had to behave because it was vitally important. '*Stai buono, Baffi, stai buono.*'

It had been too long since she'd ridden any distance bareback and her thighs ached by the time it came to slip from his sturdy back. At the top of a steep rise, she tied the length of rope she'd carried over her shoulder to walk him down the shortcut: a rutted mountain path leading to Sant'Agnese. The castle on the opposite crest was outlined against the stars in the blue-black sky and shapes of houses beneath the moon were a Christmas cut-out. She stood for a moment while Baffi drank from a stream that tripped its way down the slope. Tina wanted time to stop and wondered how come she'd never thought to steal away before with beautiful Baffi for a secret night ride. The air was frosty, still. She felt free.

But she knew the next hours of her life were likely to be the trickiest, most dangerous moments ever. The plan simply had to work. So much depended on it. She felt alive, invigorated. Terrified, yes. But now she had purpose. At long last she was really doing something worthwhile.

CHAPTER 24

Nothing ventured, nothing gained

On Tina's return, Allegra made a great fuss of girl and horse and Tina urged her to quieten down. Together they tied squares of sacking round Baffi's hooves to deaden the sounds while he was distracted with his nosebag of hay.

'We will have to hope he doesn't try to whinny to you, Tina, whilst he's with me. Thankfully I have no neighbours.'

'We shall have to hope *many* things, dear Allegra. There is much to go wrong.' She embraced the housekeeper and patted Baffi before slipping away.

A great wave of fatigue washed over Tina. She wanted nothing more than to sink into bed and sleep the sleep of the dead. And indeed, she needed all the rest possible before the most dangerous part of the plan that would take place in less than twenty-four hours.

She dragged herself up the hill where the inhabitants of Sant'Agnese still slumbered. The castle doors she'd left ajar were shut tight and she swore under her breath. They must have closed in the night breeze. Allegra kept a key to the kitchen entrance beneath a bucket of mint, so she made her way round the walls and let herself in, stopping when she heard a noise in the room above. Somebody was awake. *Dio Cristo!* Papà? Maybe up early because of some unforeseen business trip? She pressed herself against the wall next to the dresser. If he came down the stairs, which was highly unlikely, she would have to hide in the pantry. Then she heard a sneeze. Definitely not Papà's. It could only be Fräulein's. What on earth was she doing up at this hour? Had the sleeping draught not worked, *porca miseria?*

Tina crept up the staircase and moved across the hall to peer into the living room. By the light that blinked silver through the French windows to the terrace, she watched the Austrian woman opening drawers in Mamma's lacquer-work sideboard. She pulled out a box of coffee spoons Papà had brought back from Paris one year. Fräulein Huber held one up in the beam of a pocket torch before placing the box on a side table. *Che diavolo sta facendo? What the hell is she doing?* Tina wondered. *Stealing? Or assessing what might be hers one day if she manages to ensnare Papà? Porca miseria! I hate the meddling woman.*

But now was not the time to confront Fräulein Huber. Tina was dressed for outdoors and no way did she want to arouse suspicion in the awful woman's mind for why she too was up and about at this time. She vowed to keep a careful watch on her in future. Tina tiptoed past the lounge door and hurried up the carpeted staircase to her bedroom, closing the door gently behind her. She leant against it for a few seconds, her heart pounding. So far, so good. She fell into bed and within seconds was fast asleep.

There were nervous giggles as Tina and Luisa dressed in their disguises.

'We haven't chosen names for ourselves,' Tina said. 'But I shall be *suor* Maria Immacolata of the Immaculate Misconception.'

'*Idiota!*' Luisa smirked as Tina adjusted the band with the red cross around her upper arm Allegra had stitched to show they were nursing nuns. 'I shall be plain *suor* Rita who the women revere during the month of May when they bring roses to church. Now, let's go!'

Luisa packed her bag of medication into the back of the cart, every sound seemingly magnified to the two young women in the quiet, chilly first hours after midnight and it didn't take long to harness Baffi to the cart, Allegra fussing about them as they worked. Within ten minutes they were moving away.

Tina was stealing into the night yet again but this time she didn't feel free. Apprehension verging on abject terror gripped her, for their passage was far noisier than when she'd passed the houses on foot. The sacking bound round Baffi's hooves helped to somewhat soften his paces but to Tina, the clip-clops and the rolling of the cartwheels bounced alarmingly loud in the narrow alleys. What if at any minute a door opened and somebody challenged them? What if they were recognised, despite their disguises?

Too many ifs assailed her brain and her heart pounded furiously in her ribcage. She was sure Luisa must be experiencing the same fears but her friend seemed calm. Before long they were out of Sant'Agnese and Tina brought Baffi to a halt before jumping down to remove the sacking from his hooves, rewarding him with another carrot from Allegra's store. '*Bravo*, Baffi,' she whispered. 'Now the real adventure begins. *Coraggio! Su! Andiamo!* Let's go!' She realised she was talking to herself, urging *herself* on, rather than her faithful horse.

Tina filled Luisa in about Huber's night prowling but their minds were intent on their mission. 'Let's concentrate on tonight,' Tina said. 'But I've never trusted that woman and I trust her even less now.'

'Forget about her, Tina. In the scheme of things, Sergio is more important.'

'Absolutely. He's worth far more than Huber. She's hand-in-hand with the *milizia*, I'm certain of it. I see the way she kowtows to those men when she has her soirées, huddling with the officers and discussing who knows what. I really can't bring myself to like her and I hate the way Papà is so enamoured.'

The two young women remained quiet for most of the journey over the mountain pass. There was no need to go over their plans again, no need to waste energy when they would need all of it later. Nobody would know them in Sartina so that was one less complication but they would have to act better than the best actresses of the Italian cinema.

The first performance came sooner than they had bargained. At the gates to Sartina, a sleepy nightwatchman dressed in a grubby black *squadrista* uniform roused himself from his chair by the brazier and squinted at them in the half-light. 'You're up early, Sisters,' he said, as he held out his hand for their documents.

Without hesitation, Luisa responded. 'We have come on a matter of medical urgency and you should know we nuns do not carry about our own documents. They are back at the convent with Mother Superior.'

It was an oversight. They had not thought to supply themselves with papers and could hardly have passed over their own. Luisa's invention filled Tina with admiration for her friend, totally in command with her improvised excuse.

Miraculously, the man waved them through the archway, informing them of a quicker route to the hospital, and Tina urged Baffi on with a click of her tongue and a slight tap of the reins. With a barely perceptible glance at each other, the two nursing sisters made their way into the town. They passed the town bakery, delicious aromas wafting from an open door, and Tina's stomach rumbled. But she knew her nerves would not let her swallow a single mouthful.

As they entered the doors to the small hospital, it was still early: fifteen minutes before five o'clock. Already there was a bustle about the place. There were patients everywhere: on the floor, on camp beds, slumped in chairs. It was obvious the hospital was overstretched. An orderly carrying a pile of fresh linen hurried past; a tired-looking doctor, stethoscope slung round his neck, dashed towards a flight of stairs. They asked a woman sweeping the floor where the main office was and took the same wide stone staircase to the first floor.

'We are here to collect Pancotti Sergio,' Tina announced to a man at the desk, her voice calm but firm. She pulled out the forms she had painstakingly typed, the round stamp at the top deliberately blurred so as not to show her father's emblem.

'We were told he would be ready to transport to Maria Magdalena Hospital,' Tina continued.

'Where is he?' Luisa asked, tapping her foot impatiently and looking at the clock on the wall.

The young man at the desk needed sleep. His hair was tousled, his shirt creased. He peered at the forms through bleary red-rimmed eyes. 'I knew nothing about this,' he said eventually, a frown puckering his forehead.

Tina huffed a sigh of disapproval. 'It has all been agreed, signore. By *telefono*. Yesterday. With our *madre superiora*. We have come a long way. We were informed you are short of beds with the influx of wounded from the front. It is all arranged but time is of the essence with this particular patient.'

'We have an excellent consultant who works at Maria Magdalena,' Luisa said. 'He specialises in problems with these amputees.'

'We shall need help to carry him down those stairs,' Tina said, looking up at the clock above the harassed man.

'I... er... haven't been told anything about this,' the man stuttered, rubbing the stubble on his chin.

'It may have been before you came on duty,' Tina said. 'Perhaps somebody forgot to inform you.'

'Please hurry up,' Luisa said, sounding less demure than she should. 'The man is gravely ill. We can save him, give him hope for the future. Surely you would not want to be responsible for causing the demise of a compatriot, signore, because of missing paperwork?'

He placed the forms on his desk and turned to consult a list on the wall, running his hand down the names. 'Second floor. I'll find two porters. *Un attimo.* One moment. Wait here, *suore.*'

'Do you think he believes us?' Tina hissed when the harassed clerk disappeared. 'Has he cottoned on?'

'We have to hope not. *Coraggio, suor* Maria.'

With the faintest of grins, Tina swept up the forged forms and stuffed them down the front of her habit. 'We don't want to leave incriminating evidence behind,' she said.

Agreeing it was best not to be confined in the office in case they had to flee, they stepped into the corridor, the minutes passing far too slowly as they nodded demurely at staff hurrying by. Eventually, a stretcher bearing a patient came into view. The porters handled Sergio carefully down the stairs and helped the two nursing sisters arrange him as comfortably as possible in the restricted space at the back of the cart. Sergio was almost unrecognisable, his face a ghostly blue and even if he had opened his eyes, Tina thought it highly unlikely he would recognise them.

'It's a pity you can't take more than this one,' the older porter said. 'I've never seen the likes of it. We're inundated and can barely cope.'

'Perhaps we shall be sent back for more patients,' Luisa replied. 'But we only have room for one today, signore.'

'We were told we'd be supplied with a stretcher for the journey, signore,' Tina said, holding out her hands, and the older porter rolled it up and stored it in the back of the cart next to Sergio. 'We shall return it when we come for the next patient,' she added.

The porters out of sight, Luisa administered a strong sedative and painkiller to poor Sergio and within a couple of minutes, the two young women were on their way back to Sant'Agnese.

'Brilliant move about the stretcher, Tina. *Brava!*'

'Well, we'd forgotten about carrying him into the garden. Thank goodness they didn't question it,' Tina replied.

As the cart made its way back to Sant'Agnese, Tina thought if she'd truly been a nun, she'd have spent the whole return journey mumbling interminable novenas to Our Lady on Allegra's rosary. As it was, she spent the whole time anxiously glancing behind, hoping Sergio was still alive.

CHAPTER 25

The cherub holds the key

The town of Sant'Agnese was busy as the cart and its load made its way to Allegra's house. She was ready and the high gates to her backyard were open. Between them, the women helped Sergio into the house where Allegra had made up a bed in the corner of her kitchen. Later that night Tina and Luisa would return to take him up to Tina's garden.

Sergio's eyes flickered open as his nurses made him comfortable and on seeing their faces, he muttered, 'Am I in *paradiso*?' before slipping back into unconsciousness.

'Keep a careful eye on him, Allegra,' Luisa said. 'Come and fetch me if you're at all worried. He's very poorly. A light broth if he can manage and *plenty* of water.' She signalled a goodbye with one hand and slipped away. 'I must get to the *farmacia* to open up. I'll try not to fall asleep at the counter.'

'I'll sit by him for a while,' Allegra said to Tina. 'Go and rest. He's in good hands now. What a team.'

As she walked up to the castle, Tina felt she had passed

some kind of crucial test. She belonged. Despite feeling bone tired, she felt more alive, more needed than ever.

In days to come, Luisa and Tina would shake their heads and marvel on how on earth they had managed to pull off stealing Sergio from the hospital and squirreling him into the garden. It had been an outrageous plan. Maybe so outlandish that nobody would have dreamt it possible and that was why it had worked. All the various aspects had pulled together. Allegra had added more sleeping infusion to the soup and Huber and the conte were dead to the world when Tina and Luisa used the stretcher to carry Sergio up to the castle, through the pantry passage and into the garden.

The two young women hoped there was no way of tracing them back to Sant'Agnese. Nobody in town had queried the comings and goings of Allegra's cart. In times of war, routine thrown into the air, nothing was normal. The two nursing nuns were never seen again but Luisa was kept busy with her two patients in the greenhouse.

Tina had wept when she'd returned Baffi to his field. 'I don't know when I'll see you again, *amico mio*,' she'd whispered, his ears twitching as she leant into him. 'I'll try and come soon.' She pulled off his bridle and hid it in a thick bush at the edge of the paddock, wondering if she would ever manage another ride.

Every time Tina visited the garden, heart in her mouth, she wondered in what state she would find Sergio and Olivio. Over the following weeks they slowly regained strength. Allegra washed their clothes and managed to feed their ever-growing appetites. Olivio fashioned a pair of crutches for his friend and each time Tina visited, bringing books and news from the outside world, Sergio looked better. And Olivio was no longer hobbling about on his damaged foot. She loved the evenings when all four of them huddled together in the greenhouse playing cards or chatting quietly about anything and everything. During this precious time of convalescence, Tina's heart was lighter despite the risks. She could hardly wait for the daylight hours to pass to slip to the garden.

It was Olivio she thought about during the day. The way his handsome face lit up when engrossed in discussion, his eyes no longer sunken and feverish. She admired his spirit and ready wit. Olivio was adamant his beloved country needed change. Tina sensed the growing discontent in the community and more and more people were disenchanted with their leader, who had sided with another fanatical leader.

'Mussolini is a madman,' Luisa agreed. 'What he proclaims and what he does are two different things.'

'Power has gone to his head,' Sergio added. 'One thing for the people: the downtrodden us, and another for him and his cronies. We are worse off each day that passes.'

'And the way he flaunts his mistresses,' Luisa said. 'Poor wife! It makes me sick. If I were *donna* Rachele, I'd cut off his genitals.'

'Ouch!' Olivio winced and clutched his groin.

They smothered their laughter. For although the garden was concealed behind thick walls, sound easily travelled in the still of the evenings. The owner of the *alimentari* shop in the piazza had been arrested only last week for selling black-market flour. Somebody had informed on him and he was in prison, his wife left to fend for the shop and six children. Not everybody was against Il Duce and the once-neighbourly atmosphere of Sant'Agnese was tainted.

On the following evening, they all had news.

'One of Antonio's sisters passed away this week,' Luisa told them, 'and he returned from the monastery to help with her funeral. Afterwards, he came to the *farmacia*, to see if I had antibiotics for his family. He didn't seem to believe I had none left. And... he wanted to know if I'd seen anything of Olivio and

Sergio recently.' The friends looked at each other. 'When I told him I had no idea where you were, I'm not sure he believed me. I made up an excuse about having to work on my silkworms but he still hung about.' She shivered. 'He wanted to know why I hadn't left with my parents for Switzerland and asked if I felt safe in Sant'Agnese.' Luisa shrugged. 'I mean, who's safe anywhere these days? I'm not sure why he asked me.'

'Perhaps he was practising how to deal with the public,' Olivio suggested. 'It was one of the things we had to do at the seminary: how to talk to your congregation, blah, blah, blah. He found that difficult. He was never the most sociable student.' Olivio shrugged.

'I found him rather awkward too,' Tina said. 'He's visited the *castello* a few times. But I've never had a real problem with him, to be honest; he's always been friendly, despite his strange ways, once he got over his shyness or whatever it is. We chatted a fair bit but he was really only after my books,' she said, laughing. 'Do you know, now I come to think of it, I've never seen him smile, except when he was looking through those library shelves. He borrowed a couple of books on the last occasion – stuffy academic works on *The Divine Comedy* I'll never read and he asked about you both,' she said, looking at Olivio and Sergio. 'Naturally I told him nothing and acted vague. You're the only people, apart from darling Allegra, who must know about this garden.'

'We won't tell anyone,' Sergio said. 'How could we?'

'Well, you won't be staying here forever, I imagine,' Luisa commented.

'Definitely not,' Olivio said, shaking his head vigorously. 'But don't worry, Tina, we'll keep shtum about this place. Won't we, Sergio?'

'*Certo*. Of course. And are you going to tell Tina what we've discovered?'

Olivio picked up the old key from behind a pile of pots.

'Last night, Sergio and I were trying to work out where a draught was coming from which was blowing the flames in the brazier. I thought I'd made this place weatherproof but I'd missed something. Look!'

He shuffled down beneath the workbench and the girls bent to watch as he pushed aside three heavy crates.

'Tah dah! Look what we found!'

Olivio fitted the key into a crude lock set in a low door built into the rockface that formed the back wall of the greenhouse.

'Wow!' Tina exclaimed. 'Why've I never noticed that before?'

'You wouldn't have unless you moved those crates,' Sergio said.

'I actually explored it last night,' Olivio said. 'It's the way in to another passageway. These old fortresses are riddled with escape tunnels used during times of siege. This particular one leads to town and emerges near the church crypt. The exit is concealed by a column holding a station of the cross, covered in thick creepers – really hard to detect.'

'Oh my!' Tina said. 'I wonder if my mother used it to come and go. She wrote how she helped the townspeople but had to do so without Papà knowing.' She thought of the words in the diary, written in invisible lemon juice. *The cherub holds the key.* This key was the key to the door: an escape route.

And Olivio's words confirmed what she'd concluded herself.

'Don't you see? It's perfect if we have to get away too. I've always felt trapped in here,' he said. 'It's not been used for a long time. There are fallen rocks I had to climb over and at one stage it's very low.'

'Tomorrow, I'll explore it with you, Olivio. What a find,' Tina said.

But on the next day, Olivio didn't show Tina the tunnelway. As she stepped into the garden carrying a basket of provisions, she saw the greenhouse was empty, the embers in the brazier glowing faintly in the dark.

Tina flicked on her torch and looked round. Sergio and Olivio were gone. The hidden door beneath the workbench was slightly ajar, the key still in the lock. She pushed it to without locking it, rearranged one of the crates to conceal it and replaced the key in its hiding place beside the pots. The entrance had to be kept accessible for their return.

The sacks they'd used for makeshift coverings had been neatly folded and on top she found a scrap of paper.

Her heart plummeting, she read the message:

Don't worry about us. *Grazie di cuore*. Thanks from the heart.

They really were gone. She crumpled up the note and threw it in the ashes, watching as it slowly caught light. Her heart hollow, she sat for a while, deeply upset they hadn't informed her they were leaving. She knew they weren't coming back. Had they known when they'd told her about the doorway or had they come up with their decision during the night? Either way, she worried for their safety. Sergio still had a long recovery ahead of him. How would he manage?

She trailed to the library and played the first few bars of Beethoven's 'Les Adieux', until she grew too melancholy and stopped abruptly, mid-sonata. Were they going to be safe? When would she see Olivio again? And where had they gone?

CHAPTER 26

December 1942

Libiamo – Let's drink!

On the following day, the *farmacia* was closed, a note on the door stating, Back Soon. *Mannaggia! Damn it!* Tina wanted to tell Luisa about Olivio and Sergio leaving. Perhaps the trio had left her out again and Luisa already knew. What did she have to do to prove her loyalty to her friends?

Downcast, Tina trailed back to the castle. Bernardo's Bugatti was parked next to Papà's car, along with two more smart vehicles. The last thing she felt like was entertaining Papà's friends from the *partito*.

Fräulein Huber waylaid her as she climbed the stairs. 'We are to have a pre-Christmas gathering, Ernestina. And you must play the piano for our guests and accompany my singing. Get changed. I have been looking for you everywhere. Where is the cook? She must be here to help.'

Tina glared at the woman. Who was she to issue orders? 'Allegra is at home, resting.'

'That woman is never here and when she is, she does little work. She is a typical lazy Italian peasant.'

Tina bristled. 'Perhaps *you* could cook tonight, Fräulein, and make schnitzel with dumplings and that sickly pudding you so love.'

'Me? I am no cook. Signora Allegra must come here straightaway. *Sofort.*'

'She's no longer young, Fräulein. It's unfair to spring such a do on her so last minute. Our guests will have to be content with bread, cheese and prosciutto.' She added pointedly, '*If* we have any left. And Papà's wine from his cellar. I shall go and talk to him now.'

'You do not issue orders to me, signorina Ernestina.'

'Perhaps you are forgetting that *you* are in my father's employ and I am his daughter.' Tina fumed as she walked away. She may want to distance herself from her father's politics but that didn't mean Huber got to tell her what to do.

Tina watched Huber deep in conversation with a high-ranking *milizia* officer who leant in close as he examined a folder in her hands. Was she flirting with him? She moved nearer to see if she could eavesdrop but her father walked over and suggested she entertain the party with some music.

Bernardo insisted on turning the pages of the aria from Puccini's *Tosca*. The sadness matched her mood and when she came to the end and rested her hands on her lap, he leant towards her and suggested she play something lighter, sorting through the sheet music until he came to the drinking song '*Libiamo ne' lieti calici*' from *La Traviata*.

'This piece fits better with your father's excellent supply of Sangiovese. I haven't enjoyed a party so much in ages: simple bread and cheese. *Very* rustic. A charming kind of indoor country picnic. It's impossible to find decent cheese in Rome these days.'

Fräulein Huber interrupted further conversation as she handed Tina her own score.

'It's time to play for me, Ernestina. But first I must warm up. Play some arpeggios.'

Huber inhaled deeply, her bosom swelling and nearly escaping from her dirndl blouse, before squeaking out a few *La, la, la, la*s in no way in tune with what Tina played.

'I think the signorina is tired, Fräulein,' Bernardo said, taking Tina by the elbow and steering her from the piano. 'Maybe later? After more refreshments?'

'*Grazie*, Bernardo,' Tina whispered, genuinely grateful to escape as he led her to the French windows, closed to the December chill. 'Thank you for rescuing me.'

'I believe you're not the only one I rescued,' he said.

She smiled. 'I find her... challenging.'

'And she has the most appalling voice I've ever had the misfortune to endure. Here, I think you need this more than I,' Bernardo said, handing her his glass of wine.

Tina sipped from the glass and gazed from the balcony at the view of the snow-freckled mountains on the horizon. Where were Olivio and Sergio? Were they safe? Although they were both much better, Sergio had still found it difficult to move about on one leg, even though he had practised hour after hour in the garden with crutches. She couldn't imagine how he'd managed down the narrow tunnel Olivio had described. And out there, on uneven icy paths, how would he cope? Olivio was improved too, but too much walking would surely undo the benefits of his convalescence. *Dio buono*, where in God's name were the fools?

'You're thinking about your horse, aren't you?' Bernardo said, interrupting her concerns. 'He is fine, signorina Tina, I promise you. Very soon I shall fetch the horses to overwinter in our stables. Don't worry, I'm sure he's more than fine since you came to ride him... again.'

Tina gasped. 'How... how did you know?'

And how much else does he know? she wondered.

'I found his bridle under the hedge. And he hadn't been rubbed down. There were sweat marks on his body from what must have been a vigorous ride. It could only have been you. I'm correct, aren't I?'

Her heart skipped beats and somersaulted. Any moment now he would tell her he knew about Sergio's rescue. She cursed inwardly at how stupid she'd been. Why hadn't she taken more care in concealing his bridle?

'If you want to ride him, you only have to ask, Tina,' Bernardo said, touching her arm. 'I am not an ogre. There's no need for you to be secretive. In fact, while I'm here this week helping your father arrange meetings for when we go to Rome, we must enjoy a splendid winter ride together. How about tomorrow before I turn too busy?'

Of course she agreed. How could she not? She had to keep on the right side of Bernardo. If she refused, it would appear strange. She must do everything not to arouse suspicion. What were these meetings in Rome about? Maybe she could find out when they rode together. It might be useful information to pass on if the boys returned.

'That would be wonderful, Bernardo. I'm free in the afternoon after my lesson with Fräulein Huber. Thank you so, so much. You don't know how much I miss Baffi.'

'I think I do. Now, shall I help you slip away from that awful woman's clutches? I'm sure you see quite enough of her. And I too am tired of her caterwauling.'

He kissed her hand as he left her at the foot of the stairs and she hurried to her room to change back into the dark clothes she used for her escapes from the castle. She had to update Luisa about Olivio and Sergio's departures. She winced at the squawking voice of Huber accompanying herself on the piano in the library, the occasional wrong chord adding to the racket.

The lights were out in the flat above the *farmacia* and although she tapped twice at the door, it remained closed. She made her way along the side alley to the back of the building where Luisa slept. It took a third handful of pebbles to waken her friend. The window opened abruptly and Luisa leant out.

'Who is it? The shop is closed. If you need a doctor, then go to the *ambulatorio*. I—'

'*Sono io.* It's me. Tina. Let me in.'

Tina hurried to the door of the shop and Luisa let her in, moaning at how tired and cold she was and why couldn't it wait until the morning.

'They've gone, Luisa. Sergio and Olivio. I couldn't come earlier. As it is, I've had to pretend I'm asleep in my bedroom.'

Luisa pulled on Tina's sleeve. 'Come in, come in. We can't talk out here.'

Nursing camomile tea, the two friends discussed the latest turn of events.

'I'm not surprised they've gone,' Luisa said. 'Apart from worrying about the danger to you harbouring them, they were restless. Olivio doesn't like to be far from action.'

'What do you mean? He surely won't want to return to fight.'

'Not with the army, he doesn't.' Luisa lowered her voice. 'But I've heard them talk about joining with other rebels. With the *partigiani*.'

'I suspected as much but I couldn't be sure. They still don't trust me enough to open up, do they? Even after everything I've done to help. I could help even more if you'd all just let me.'

Luisa paused. 'You have to admit living in the castle, your

father a bigwig in the *partito*... it's difficult at times to know how much to involve you.'

'*You* trust me, don't you, Luisa? Tell me the truth.' Tina grabbed Luisa's wrist, causing her to spill some of her drink.

'Of course I do. You must know that. But—'

'But what, Luisa? But what?'

'It's dangerous for you. I don't have anybody to see me come and go. If your father were to discover you had connections with the resistance, the consequences would be too awful to contemplate.'

'None of you have ever talked openly to me about what you're up to, but I'm not stupid. Just think how useful I could be to the cause. I've said this before but nobody listens. The fact my father is a high ranking *fascista* is an absolute advantage. And I could do so much more. Who would suspect *me*, the daughter of conte Ferdinando di Montesecco, of being *antifascista*? I can get away with many things.' She sighed. 'So many things.' She counted off on her fingers. 'Special passes. Listening in on meetings. Keeping abreast of events and plans. Don't you see? Why, tomorrow I'm riding again with Bernardo and he's mentioned some big meeting in Rome that's coming up. I could try to find out more, but—' She rose from the table, the chair behind her clattering to the floor. 'Oh for goodness' sake, I *want* to help. But I know when I'm not wanted.'

'*Shh!* You're wasting your dramatics on me. Keep your voice down, Tina. Look... If Olivio gets in touch with me somehow... and that is a huge "if" because I don't have the faintest idea where he's buggered off to, I shall tell him all this. Because... I agree with everything you say. And in the meantime, spy on your father and Bernardo as well and we'll see what the two of us can manage together, eh?'

Tina nodded, grateful Luisa at least understood. She was learning to fight her corner. For too long she'd been the obedient daughter, compliant despite the rebellious streak she knew she had within her. Now was the time to change all that, before it was too late.

Before leaving for her bed, Tina chatted about Bernardo and their appointment the following afternoon.

'Phew! I bet you nearly wet your drawers when he talked about you riding Baffi.'

'Absolutely. I thought the game was up.'

'But I can understand why you need to keep in with him. And' – Luisa clinked her glass against Tina's – 'Bernardo can be your first victim. Practise on him and learn as much as you can about this big Roman meeting he mentioned.'

'What exactly do you mean by "practise on him"? Don't like the sound of that,' Tina said, pulling a face. 'I don't fancy him at all.'

'Sometimes spies have to do what they have to do, *amica mia*,' Luisa said, a wicked twinkle in her eye.

'You've been reading too many *gialli*. Too many thrillers.' Tina finished her tea. 'By the way, you haven't come across an easy method in any of your books for getting rid of unwanted Austrian tutors, have you?'

The two women spent the next ten minutes suggesting ridiculous ways of bumping off enemies, including mincing them into pasta sauce and feeding them poisonous mushrooms. But when it was time to leave, Tina had been filled with a greater sense of purpose. She had much to discover about the visits of these *fascisti* who visited the *castello* more frequently as the hateful war progressed. Maybe Bernardo might give something away tomorrow if she played her cards right. Her father and Bernardo trusted her – they saw her as a good girl, she knew. But her father's beliefs were not her own and she was tired of living a lie.

As she returned up the hill to the *castello*, she thought of what she had learned from her mother's journal: how, despite her unhappiness, Mamma had found ways to help the downtrodden citizens of Sant'Agnese and do her own thing for her people. Her mamma was truly an inspiration. Tina felt as if she had been meant to find her words and work on them. She walked with increasing confidence up the slope as she understood how in a sense she was taking up her mother's mantle.

CHAPTER 27

Spinning the web

When she pushed open the door to her room, the outline of a figure sitting by her bed made Tina jump and snap on the light.

It was Huber. She sprang to her feet. 'Where have you been, Ernestina? Your father entrusted me with your care and this is not the first time you have been out at night.'

'I... I needed fresh air after the party. The wine was strong and I'm not used to drinking.'

'*Humph!*' Fräulein Huber crossed her arms beneath her large bosom. 'I do not believe you. It is too cold to walk outside at this hour. Although I believe you are rather fond of night excursions.'

Tina's heart stopped. Did the loathsome woman know about the garden?

'Believe what you want, Fräulein.'

'I am not stupid. You left with signor Bernardo. A handsome chap. You have been with him ever since, *nicht wahr*? Without a chaperone. As a single woman, this is not correct.'

'I am not the only person who... misbehaves... Fräulein. And I'm not the only person who roams the castle at night.'

Tina had hit a nerve. The woman's expression changed from defiance to perplexity.

'So, I think we are equal in our list of misdemeanours, are we not?' Tina stated.

'Your father and I, we are betrothed. You on the other hand are only nineteen.'

'I wasn't talking about your sharing his bed, Fräulein. I refer to your examining of our family heirlooms at night when you believe we are asleep. And... by the way, should I therefore openly offer my father congratulations on your betrothal? There has been no announcement and you wear no ring, *liebe* Fräulein.'

The woman drew herself up to her full one hundred and fifty centimetres but Tina was well aware of the fear in her eyes.

'Shall we call it quits, Fräulein? I keep quiet and you do likewise? And, as far as Bernardo is concerned, I said goodbye to him soon after you asked me to play your awful music. Good night, I'm very tired.'

Fleeting seconds passed while the two women stared each other out, but it was Tina who won when Huber turned with a flounce, one of her curlers dropping to the carpet as she spun to leave. As she closed the bedroom door, she muttered words that Tina had not been taught in any of her lessons.

I shall have to be extra vigilant from now on, she thought as she perched on the edge of her bed.

Bernardo and Tina cantered higher and higher over the fields, skirting the bad lands – the arid slopes where nothing grew – until they reached a beech forest ringing the summit of Monte Piccione. Bernardo led the way to a viewpoint where they dismounted to let the horses graze as reward for their work.

Bernardo leant back on a large rock whilst Tina gazed on the view, an unexpected gift on a mild December afternoon. In the distance, the castle dominated its little town. Whenever winter mists spun their way in and out of the folds of the mountains, the castle floated as if without foundations atop white breakers, rising above the hidden world below. But it was clear today. She could make out Papà's Maserati parked in the stable block, sun glinting from the windscreen. Up here was an excellent vantage point for anybody wanting to spy on the town, a spectacular landmark in all seasons. With strong binoculars, it would be easy to keep an eye on comings and goings and she noted this for the future. Her garden, however, was completely hidden, a thick canopy of pines obscuring any view of that section of the castle walls.

'I come up here often,' Bernardo said, his voice lazy. 'To survey my estate and keep an eye on things.'

'What do you have to keep an eye on?'

'Wild boar digging up our crops. People. Poachers. Peasants helping themselves to grapes and olives at harvest time.'

'They are hungry, Bernardo. Would you begrudge them the odd pheasant and handful of grapes?'

'I am referring to thefts of mule-loads of grapes, two crammed-full baskets per beast. The last culprit is on her way to prison right now.'

She sighed. Tina could not think the way her father and Bernardo did about the citizens of Sant'Agnese, as if they were a race apart. They were an Allegra or an Olivio, a Sergio, a Luisa. From families who were hungry with menfolk away fighting, in exile or in prison. Widows trying to scrape anything together to feed their children, whilst Il Duce continued to exact more and more hardship on ordinary Italians in his quest for an Imperial dream and money for armaments.

'You should have pity, Bernardo, and help our people when you have so much.'

He sat up. 'I'm helping them by working towards a better Italy, Tina. Towards the promises our leader is directing us to. Unfortunately, there is no gain without pain.'

'How much pain are you and I feeling from these promises, as you call them? We have plenty of food, clothes, a warm place to live. Think about it, Bernardo.'

'It's as well there's nobody listening, save me, Tina,' Bernardo said.

His hand was warm against her back where she sat facing the view and she stiffened, before rising.

'Shall we go back now? I have a lesson with the Austrian singer,' she said.

'I thought we could stay longer. Get to know each other better. You're an intriguing young woman, Tina. Different from any other young woman I know.'

What to do? No way did she want a dalliance with Bernardo. But she and Luisa had agreed he was a good start towards gleaning potentially useful information. Reluctantly, she sat down.

'And you are different too, Bernardo. Tell me more about how you'll fill the next days.'

'Meeting upon meeting. But I'm sure I should be able to fit in another ride, weather permitting. And if not, perhaps dinner. I know an excellent trattoria in the next village down towards Rimini.'

'I'd like that, Bernardo. Is there a meeting tomorrow? What *do* you talk about at these party meetings that go on for hours and hours? It must be so boring,' she said, artfully, stifling a pretend yawn. 'By the way, I'm free in the morning.'

'Unfortunately, I am not. Your father has invited important guests from Rome and I have to keep minutes. The day after, perhaps?'

'In the afternoon,' she said. She made it sound as if her diary was full, when in fact it was not but she didn't want to sound too keen. Which she definitely wasn't.

Important guests, he'd said. Guests who would talk about important things, she hoped.

The next day, Tina joined Allegra in the kitchen.

'Tell me what to do and I'll help,' Tina said brightly, thinking this would be an excellent chance to listen in on the officers invited for lunch. She was sure Papà would not be inviting her to sit at table with them.

Allegra looked dubious, despite her grumbles about the expectation to provide lunch to a large delegation of visitors, her age and the work involved.

'But you don't know how to cook,' she said suspiciously.

'I can follow instructions, and you need the help. *Su!* Let's get going. *Andiamo!*'

For the next twenty minutes Tina sliced fennel, opened preserved jars of tomatoes for *bruschette*, arranged *salame* and prosciutto on a huge platter, washed winter salad, beat up eggs and sugar for Allegra's famous creamy dessert, ground coffee grains ready for afterwards and helped lift roasted rabbit and pork that Allegra had been basting in the wood oven into which Tina fed more logs.

It was a lot of work and Allegra was getting older, Tina thought sadly. Maybe Luisa would know of a girl in town to help out. It would mean Tina couldn't slip in and out of her garden so easily but if the help was only in the mornings, that would still leave afternoons.

'I'll help serve,' Tina said. 'You keep control in the kitchen and hand me everything in the right order.'

'But—' Allegra protested.

'I'm enjoying myself. And Papà will be so preoccupied with his *ufficiali* he'll barely notice.'

The conte did notice, however, as Tina swept into the dining room wearing a clean apron, her sleeves rolled up. He frowned as she bore platters of cold cuts and *bruschette* to the table but she simply smiled, bending down as she served him, whispering she would explain later. He didn't introduce her as his daughter but Bernardo winked at her from the other side of the table.

When she emerged again from the kitchen with the first course of thick pasta ribbons of homemade pappardelle with wild hare sauce, a large man, his grey-green uniform jacket undone revealing a black shirt straining to hold in a well-fed stomach, was talking, holding everyone's attention. Although he was obviously in mid discussion, she picked up there was about to be a drive to hunt down deserters.

'It does no good for morale with these cowards out there whilst other brave young men are sent to battle. We have calculated that many hundreds have run away, shirking their duties. So, we are directing our attention to this matter and moving a platoon from Parma to intensify searches in the area.' The officer looked up as Tina leant forward to serve the pasta, indicating she should add more to his plate. She wished she could accidentally serve it into his fat lap, but resisted. The less attention she drew to herself, the better.

'I am ashamed to admit I know of several deserters from Sant'Agnese,' the conte said. 'You'd do well to chase *them* down first. I'll furnish you with names after we've dined.'

Tina halted in her serving and the man sitting next to her father held up his plate as if to ask, 'Where's mine?' Her hands shook as she served him pasta and a few strands spilled onto the white tablecloth.

'*Mi scusate*, signore,' she said before moving on to her father.

'Where is Allegra?' he muttered while the discussion about absconders continued around the table.

'I told you, I'll explain later.'

That was all the information Tina picked up for, as the wine flowed, the raunchy anecdotes began. She could have sworn when she handed dessert to the portly militia man, he touched her bottom, but it was a furtive movement and, anyway, what could she say? She got her revenge later by pretending to trip as she poured coffee and the hot liquid splashed down his shirt.

'*Mi scusate tantissimo.* So sorry,' she said, hoping her tone didn't sound too gleeful as he mopped at his front with a napkin.

'You can leave us now,' her father said, his face etched with fury.

She caught Bernardo's look and the slight shrug of his shoulders.

But she had learned important information and wherever Olivio and Sergio were hiding up, they needed to be warned.

CHAPTER 28

Fiammetta

Brava! Bravissima, *my daughter. You are beginning to emerge from that chrysalis and show the courage that lies deep within. Oh, how I wanted to laugh out loud when you spilled coffee down that oaf's fat stomach. I remember Martelli well. He was already odious with those wandering hands. Back then, he was leaner with oilier hair. And when I told Ferdinando, he laughed, telling me it could not be true. That monster was not interested in women and I was obviously imagining it, he said.*

Ferdinando often brushed aside my complaints. 'You do not understand the ways of society,' he would say. 'You still have much to learn. There is nothing wrong with a little flirtation now and then. It keeps a marriage alive.'

But that was not the way of my parents. They were happy, despite little overt demonstration in front of their children. A hand on the shoulder as my mother leant to serve my father his soup, a wild canina rosa picked from the meadows by Papà when he returned from bringing in our cow from the slopes of Monte Benedetto, a rabbit snared for Sunday lunch, wrapped in wild rosemary and sage leaves. Tiny gestures that spoke of their affection.

I wanted nothing of flirtations from men who were not my husband. One night after a dinner with his friends where the wine flowed more than usual, he pulled me onto his knee and kissed me long and deep in front of them and when one of them suggested he should stop it or share me, he laughed and said, 'Why not, amici?' Whereupon, he pulled the sleeve of my low-cut silk dress down too low on my shoulder and revealed my breast. I slapped him hard on the cheek and he laughed. 'My woman has spirit, you know. I fell in love with her wild ways. No harm in sharing her.'

I tore myself from his lap and ran from those hateful beasts, knocking into Allegra as I rushed across the hall. She asked what was wrong but I, too choked and ashamed to reply, sped up the staircase and locked myself in my bedroom. I was so shocked I was unable to shed the tears that filled me. How could my husband behave in such a way? The man who, before the priest and the whole of Sant'Agnese, had stood at the altar promising to God he would respect and love me for the rest of my days. That evening, he had shown his true colours. I tried to calm myself and find reasons for his behaviour: he was drunk, it was the wine. Hadn't Mamma talked by the fireside about the blacksmith's behaviour: how sometimes, after an evening in the osteria, Diulio's anger would get the better of him and that was why Costanza, his wife, was often covered in bruises? She'd tell the women she'd slipped or not been concentrating when milking their cow and so the cow had kicked her. But we all knew it was no cow that had caused the blue and purple patterns on Costanza's pretty face. Easy for us to mutter she should leave him, to say he was a beast who couldn't contain his fists. But easier said than done for her to up and leave. Where could she go? Her family were from the south and from all accounts had been only too pleased to be rid of her: she was one less mouth to feed.

And now, here was I, confronted by a man who had disrespected me. And I knew that no excuse should justify his lewd behaviour that evening. It was wrong. Furthermore, it would be too shameful to return to my family and ask to be taken back. What could I tell them? They wouldn't believe conte Ferdinando di Montesecco behaved in such a way. I was on my own.

In the morning, when Allegra came to help me dress, even though she wanted to know what had upset me last evening, I was still too ashamed to tell her. I had chosen this life, this castle in the air, and I had to make the most of it.

For a while, Ferdinando was good to me. He returned from a business trip to Florence and showered me with gifts: a pair of fine red gloves, the leather as soft as a baby's skin, scented soap made from gardenia blossom, dainty shoes with little heels and a volume of Dante's love poems bound in leather. And so I let him back to my bed. He was gentle with me and that was how we made our first baby, which I lost before eight weeks.

Tina, Tina, think wisely before you accept lavish gifts and words from men. It is not expensive presents that bring love and happiness. I think you are at last beginning to understand more about life and I shall be with you in spirit to guide you while I can. I do believe you have stepped out along the right path now. May it continue, my darling girl. I am glad you have found the cherub's key. The tunnel will be of use to you now, as it was to me.

I watch you asleep on your bed tonight, your hair the colour of fiery autumn leaves spread across your pillow. I shall stay by your side, banishing worries from your beautiful head. Oh, how I wish I could reach out and take you in my arms. Instead, I hold you in my heart, my darling, as you continue on your journey. May it be smooth – although I fear danger is ahead for you all.

CHAPTER 29

Tina

Paving the way

In the early hours, Tina woke from a deep, calming sleep, a lingering scent of roses in the air. The vase on her dressing table was empty and she wondered about the fragrance. Maybe Allegra was using a different polish on the furniture. In her dreams she'd felt warm and protected and she hadn't wanted to stir from bed. But she was wide awake now and she flung back the covers. The light in her room was a dirty-grey and through the flimsy hand-crocheted lace curtains, she saw snow had fallen in the night.

Rubbing sleep from her eyes, she padded over to gaze at the view, loving the pristine white blanketing of the roofs of Sant'Agnese. She knew it wouldn't last long. When the extreme cold weather came, icicles hung for days from gutters and snow clogged alleyways until an army of men and boys dug pathways through. But this was a mere dusting, a softening of the landscape, always beautiful at first but quickly turning to grubby slush. She splashed water on her face from the jug on her washstand and then remembered her task for today.

Somehow, Olivio and Sergio needed to be warned about the pending hunt for absconders. Where were they? If they were up in the mountains somewhere, was their shelter weatherproof? How would they be coping? Neither young man was fit. The castle was quiet. Her watch told her it was only five thirty, too early for Allegra to be in the kitchen, but she craved coffee. Papà had found real coffee grains on his last trip and her mouth watered at the thought of a strong morning brew. She would take some beans from the packet and put them in a twist of paper to bring to Luisa. Proper *caffè-caffè*.

She pulled on her clothes and dragged a brush through her tangles before slipping from her room. The door to Fräulein's room was ajar, her bed empty. No doubt she was keeping Papà warm. Oh, how she wished she could banish the woman from the castle, make him see she was only after his wealth. On a whim, she tiptoed over the floorboards and carefully pulled open the top drawer of the dressing table. Her fingers met with the woman's flimsy underwear before she felt something hard beneath. Nestled in the cup of a corset was one of the Fabergé eggs Papà had purchased in Paris, one of a dozen displayed in a glass cabinet in the sitting room. *Thief!* Tina thought. *And sure as hell there'll be other stuff hidden in her room.* Tina left the precious ornament where it was. No need for Huber to know she had been rifling in her room. Instead, she would add it to the list of items compiled so far in her head: silver spoons, the egg… there were bound to be more. Papà should know about this before too long and then the woman would be gone.

Tina had woken with a plan. It involved taking a travel permit from her father's desk, fetching Baffi once again, *oh the bliss*, and a little help from Luisa.

Twenty minutes later, she let herself into Luisa's kitchen, after removing her wet boots, and set to grinding the *caffè-caffè* beans. She placed the coffee pot on the stove top after adding a handful of kindling to strike a flame. Before too long, the delectable aroma of proper coffee filled the kitchen as rich brown liquid bubbled up in the percolator.

'*Dio mio*, you gave me the fright of my life, *porca boia*,' Luisa cursed, as after placing the little coffee cup on her bedside table, Tina gently shook her friend awake.

'Don't ever do that again! I could have stuck this in you,' Luisa said, pulling a carving knife from beneath her pillow.

'What? Never bring you proper coffee in bed?' Tina laughed. 'Put that thing away, for God's sake. Who were you expecting?'

'Best to be safe than sorry. Many people know I live alone. To what do I owe this early visit, Tina?'

'Drink first and then I'll tell you.'

Luisa groaned with pleasure at the coffee and asked if there was more but it was time to talk. Tina told her everything she'd heard at dinner the previous evening and Luisa listened, her hand to her mouth, a look of horror on her face.

'I've racked my brains to think where they might be. It can't be far,' Tina said. 'Not with Sergio's injury. And I don't imagine Olivio would have let him fend for himself. No, they're together somewhere in the area and so I'm fetching Baffi again to ride up to the seminary to see if Antonio has discovered where they might be. Can you give me some medicines to take as a reason for my trip if I'm stopped? I should be back by afternoon. If I'm not, then come and find me.'

Luisa shook her head, hunching her knees up under the covers, concentration furrowing her brow. 'I'll come too.'

'No need, Luisa. I'll be quicker on Baffi. Far easier than hitching up the cart and all that palaver. And no way am I dressing up again as a nun.'

She accompanied Luisa downstairs to the shop, where Luisa selected a couple of items. 'These are antiquated tablets for typhus. Lay on the life-threatening, contagious aspect if you're queried but nobody other than a medical practitioner will have heard of this medicine. It's out of date. Do be careful, Tina. I shan't relax until I know you're safely back.'

They celebrated with the rest of the coffee. Lukewarm but still heavenly.

'I've got to dash. Let's hope I can find them, Luisa. Cross everything for me.'

Tina hugged her friend and set off in the direction of Bernardo's estate, halfway to the seminary, her father's words about deserters ringing in her head. *'You'd do well to chase them down first.'*

CHAPTER 30

A litany of lies

She was weary. Oh, so weary. The bareback ride was harder this time and took far longer, the tracks slippery and perilous where snow still lingered in sections that never saw the sun. And twice on the way to the Seminary of San Francesco in Verna, she'd been stopped by guards who took ages over her documents, looking backwards and forwards to peer in her face, examining the boxes of medicine stowed in her knapsack so that she'd turned snappy and warned them not to damage the contents.

'I need to get this medication to the seminary as quickly as possible. There's been an outbreak of typhus and it's spreading everywhere down the valley. Please hurry and be careful how you handle those packets.'

She was waved on but not long afterwards she took a wrong turning, ending up in a farmyard where an old man shouted and brandished a hunter's gun, ordering her to vacate his premises.

'I'm sick and tired of strangers from the city begging for food and stealing my poultry.'

'I'm lost, signore,' Tina had said. 'If you could tell me the right way to the monastery, I'd be very grateful.'

'Be off with you. No need for tricks. I know your kind.' He fired a shot in the air and Baffi whinnied with terror.

Tina had trouble stopping him rearing up. '*Woah*, Baffi! Good boy,' she said, steering him away from the unpleasant man, talking to her horse calmly although she felt anything but calm.

She took the other fork and eventually bells chiming the midday Angelus call to prayer, told her she was nearing her destination. The monastery was cut into the side of the mountain, almost camouflaged by sharp pinnacles and folds in the rocks. Dating back centuries, it was a feat of construction that seemed to defy possibility: more a fortress than a place of worship. A bastion against the wider world. Easier to tame souls within those walls when there were no outside distractions, Tina thought.

She slid from Baffi when she reached the vast oak doors of the monastery and turned him loose. He had worked hard. '*Bravo!* Baffi. *Grazie, amico*. Thanks for your efforts. You've done well again.' Baffi tossed his head and snorted as if to say, 'I know.'

Tina pulled on a chain at the side of the doors and waited as chimes echoed within. A friar welcomed her with hands clasped and, after asking about her business, she was shown into a side room and told to wait for the abbot.

'*Fra*' Alvise is busy at the moment,' the friar who had opened the huge door to the seminary told her, indicating a tray containing a bowl of fruits on a side table: juicy red plums and sweet apples. 'You say you have come all the way from Sant'Agnese, so please refresh yourself. Antonio is it, whom you want to see? Antonio Gerico? A studious young man. Are you related?'

'Distantly,' Tina lied, hoping she would not be struck down

there and then in this place of God. 'Most of us are related in Sant'Agnese. He's my father's cousin's nephew. So complicated.'

The friar lingered, obviously enjoying their chat. Tina thought maybe he missed the company of women.

'It is often the case in these small towns,' he said. 'Nobody moves about, do they? And so cousins marry cousins and what have you. There was nobody suitable for me in my village.'

He stopped his chat immediately as the door opened and a tall thin man dressed in the grey-brown habit of the order of St Francis stepped into the room, bringing with him an aura of spirituality. He immediately folded his hands within his sleeves and nodded to the voluble friar. 'You may leave us now, *fra* Piero.'

Fra Piero scuttled out, shutting the door quietly behind him and Tina wondered about the man's vocation. Maybe his family had pushed him towards a life in the Church because they didn't know what else to do with him. It happened sometimes in the poorest of families.

'I hear you wish to speak to young Gerico. I have to ask why of course, signorina.'

'I have news for him, *frate*,' Tina said. 'From his mother. His father is unwell. And, apparently Antonio is prone to neglecting his medication. I've brought some. He needs to take it regularly.'

'I see. I had no knowledge of any maladies.'

'He tries to deny his affliction. His parents cannot write and there is no access to the telephone in Sant'Agnese,' Tina continued. 'So, I told his mother I would bring his tablets.'

The abbot looked at Tina as if weighing up the information, his hands still folded across his thin frame and within his long sleeves.

'Very well. Our community will pray for his father and you may have a few minutes with Gerico.'

He left Tina alone again and from deep within the building, a bell chimed six times.

She heard footsteps approach and then the door burst open.

'Tina?' Antonio said, a look of concern on his face. 'What are you doing here? And what is wrong with Father?' His glasses were askew on his nose and he pushed them back in the gesture Tina remembered from their meetings in the castle library.

'Sit down,' Tina said, patting the chair beside her. 'There's nothing wrong with your father and I only have a few minutes, so, keep your voice down and listen carefully.'

'What is going on?'

'I'm looking for Sergio and Olivio. Do you know where they are?'

The brief pause before Antonio answered, the fiddling of his fingers in the folds of his habit, the biting of the lip, gave him away. He was thinking of something to say.

'Didn't I myself ask the same question of your friend Luisa not so long ago? I have no idea where they are.'

'Think carefully, Antonio. It's a life-or-death situation. If they're here, I need to let them know the *milizia* in Sant'Agnese are looking for absconders. Have they been here?'

Antonio nodded. 'Yes, but Olivio and Sergio are no longer here. The friars are helping others who have absconded, so I shall warn them too about this search.'

'Where are they now?'

'I have no idea.'

'*Think*, Antonio. It's important.'

He shrugged. 'They didn't tell me.'

'If you do hear, please tell them not to come near the castle. They're in great danger. And, take these. I told your superior you needed this medicine.'

She thrust the package in his hands. 'Tell him you have a rare blood disorder or something.'

Antonio's eyes widened. 'I can't tell him lies.'

'You'd best dispose of it then. Luisa told me it's out of date but I had to tell the guards at the road stops I was bringing medication here. It'll look strange if I return with it.'

'What a litany of lies you've told,' Antonio said.

'I'm sure God will forgive me,' Tina retorted.

On the return journey, which took more than four hours over ground which was turning to ice in the falling temperatures, Tina fought to keep her eyes from shutting as light drained from the heavens. Energy-sapping adrenaline to get her through the terrifying journey had done its work, plus the rhythm of riding upon Baffi's back was like being in a cradle.

There was no moon and the torch she'd tied to her wrist cast ghostly shadows back and forth in front of Baffi. Sleet wettened dusk, turning the tracks into muddy quagmires, slowing down progress further and Tina had to concentrate with all her might to keep Baffi steady. The stormy conditions had at least saved her from further stops at road checks, the guards huddled deep in their shelters, not even bothering to wave her on. Tina led Baffi into Bernardo's field. This time she had brought an old towel with her and she made sure to rub him down and then slip the rope halter from his nose. Once again it was hard to say goodbye and she inhaled the smell of him as she rubbed his nose. '*Grazie*, my faithful friend,' she whispered. 'We did it together.'

It was approaching three thirty a.m. as Tina wearily stepped through the town. All she wanted was to curl up in her bed and sleep for evermore. The trip had been only partially successful: she knew Sergio and Olivio had been in the monastery for a while and were in the mountains somewhere, most likely still alive, but would Antonio see them to pass on her message?

Yawning, she pushed open the back door to the kitchen and almost sleepwalked to the bottom of the staircase. A shadow emerged from the hall and her father planted himself, legs akimbo, hands crossed in front of his chest to confront her.

'Where have you been all night, Ernestina?'

CHAPTER 31

Beginnings

She jumped, her heart sinking to her muddy boots. 'I... er... I couldn't sleep, Papà. Last night, I ate too much of Allegra's gnocchi. I—'

'Stop your lies,' he said, slapping her hard across the face so that her head snapped back. The sound echoed throughout the hall and she cried out.

'Lies! Allegra was not here and neither were you when we returned from Rome.'

'But... I thought you were away until tomorrow evening.'

'It would appear you did, you little tart. But our trip was cut short. The railway lines were bombed, so our journey was impossible. Where have you been?'

'Baffi,' she stuttered. 'I... miss him so much, Papà. Bernardo... he let me ride him and then the storm and we went too far... I sheltered in a barn and... I must have fallen asleep in the hay.'

'So, you have spent the night with Bernardo.' Another slap on the other cheek caused Tina to sink to the floor.

'You are not only a liar. You are a slut.'

'No, no... you've got it all wrong. I was on my own. Bernardo was not with me. It's not like that. I meant I was with Baffi...'

Her father turned as Fräulein Huber appeared at the top of the staircase, calling down to them, tying the cord of her dressing gown round her thick waist.

'What is going on? I woke to hear shouting. Do we have burglars, Ferdi?'

'Return to bed, Lorli. I am busy with Ernestina.'

'Has she been out again all night? It's not the first time. She is a wayward girl.' Huber descended the stairs and stared at Tina slumped on the floor, a look of satisfaction behind her sneer.

Tina's dislike of the woman turned to hatred. And the way the pair called each other by ridiculous names, the accusation made by her father that she was a slut when Huber was warming his bed night after night, made her see red at the injustice. She had planned to retrieve more evidence before accusing Huber, but she was too angry to wait longer.

'Your Lorli, as you call her, Papà, is a calculating thief.'

A sharp intake of breath from the Austrian woman and a wide-eyed look of horror encouraged Tina.

'I found silver concealed in her room. *Our* silver, Papà. And one of Mamma's Fabergé eggs. Fräulein Huber is not the woman you think.'

'Get up!' her father shouted. 'You two women behave like a couple of alley cats.' He took them by their arms and marched them to the library, snapping on the electric light and ordering them to sit down, while he stood like a prosecutor, his angry stare flicking from one woman to the other.

'If your daughter is accusing me of these things, then let her prove it,' Huber said quietly, her gaze fixed on Tina.

'That's easy. I'll show you now, Papà.' Tina ran from the library up the stairs, followed by her father and Huber.

She pushed open the door to the Austrian woman's bedroom and pulled open the top drawer of the dressing table to rummage beneath the underwear, her fingers searching for the case of silver spoons and Fabergé egg. They were not there and she tugged the drawer fully out to tip the contents on the floor. Nothing, save for flimsy undergarments and handkerchiefs.

'She's moved them.' Tina wrenched open the wardrobe and started to pull out dresses, rifling frantically through the garments until her father pulled her back.

'Stop this behaviour immediately, Ernestina.'

'But I found spoons and the egg in this room. I promise you.' She pushed past her father and raced back down the stairs to the sitting room, followed by her father and Huber. 'Come and see for yourself, Papà. There were twelve, weren't there? Twelve precious Fabergé eggs you brought back for Mamma from Paris. Look for yourself!' She ran over to the glass cabinet and pointed, turning to her father and Huber. 'One, two...' She stopped counting at eleven, staring in dismay at the glass shelf where all twelve eggs were displayed. 'But...' She turned towards Huber, advancing slowly, wanting to throttle the woman standing there looking so smug and satisfied. 'You've returned them, you—'

'Ernestina! Enough! Go to your room and stay there until I see fit. Your conduct does you no favours.' Ferdinando's words were spoken with chilling finality.

'But I found them in her room. I...'

'Your daughter is highly strung, Ferdi. I have found her difficult in our lessons. Unpredictable. I think she needs a psychiatrist's visit or at the very least a sedative from your doctor.'

'*I* shall be the one to decide how to go forward on this matter, Fräulein. In the meantime, Ernestina, go to your room. Now!'

Tina trailed up the stairs, pleased at least that her father was not influenced totally by the odious woman. Once in her room she pulled a valise from the top of her wardrobe and began to stuff in clothing: a change of underwear, trousers, a thick skiing jumper, toothbrush, soap from her washstand and at the last minute, her mother's journal. There was no way she was going to remain imprisoned in this castle like some character from a Grimms' fairy tale.

A tap on the door. When she opened it, the conte stood alone. 'May I come in, Ernestina?'

'It seems you can do what you want,' Tina replied, touching her cheeks where her father's fingermarks had left painful weals. 'If you prefer to believe that woman over your daughter—'

'Talk like that will get us nowhere, my child.'

'That's half the trouble, isn't it? I'm nineteen years old, no longer a child, but you want to keep me as one. My life has absolutely no purpose.' She continued to ram items into her valise: the novel from her bedside table, a hairbrush, comb.

'So, you want to run away. Where will you go?' Ferdinando pulled a chair from her dressing table to sit down.

She was infuriated at how calm he was, leaning back in the chair, his legs crossed, seemingly not distressed at all about their row.

'I cannot stay here with that woman insinuating herself into your life. Can't you see, Papà, how totally scheming she is? She's waiting to become the contessa di Montesecco.'

He laughed. 'You never had tantrums when you were little but you're certainly making up for it now. Are you really so unhappy? And how do you suppose to support yourself if you leave? You've never had a job in your life.'

She was amazed. It was as if her father wanted to understand her – just moments after striking her in the face. She wasn't used to seeing this side of him. What was going on? She persisted along the same tack. Now or never.

'I cannot *stand* Fräulein Huber.'

'Are you jealous?'

Now it was her turn to laugh. 'Papà, there is *nothing* to be jealous about. To be honest, I have never felt part of your life. You're not interested in me. But... *she's* not to be trusted. Can't you see?'

A small part of her hoped that her father's involvement with the *fascisti* was because he hadn't taken time to consider his actions. Was he so bound up with the success of his factory that he was oblivious of the wider world? He didn't see his workers as family people but cogs in his business machine. Huber offered him comfort. She was from a world he understood and he was too lazy to go against it. She wanted her father to be a good man but she knew in her heart he wasn't and his world wasn't the kind of world she wanted. But what if, away from Fräulein Huber, she could talk to him and make him see sense?

'I'm no good at this... at this kind of talk. I... your mother... she was a very free spirit. I've always been afraid you would turn out like her.'

'Like what, Papà? Like a woman with a mind of her own? What's wrong with that? You've kept me so penned up I've never been able to form my own opinions until recently, experience *anything* beyond the walls of this place. It's become a prison for me. Sending me away to a convent wasn't freedom either.'

'The war... I don't want you out there. It's not safe.'

'Oh, Papà, you've always been like this with me, long before the war began.'

'Fräulein Huber has been a comfort to me these past years. I'm sorry you don't get on. Will you at least try?'

'I *have* tried. And she doesn't like me either.'

She stared at him, anger consuming her. But he looked

somehow different as he sat there – almost helpless. And this was the first time they'd ever had a discussion like this. *Don't ruin it now, Tina*, she told herself. *Calm down. Stay reasonable. Losing your temper won't get you anywhere. He looks lost.*

And maybe – if he listened to her about Huber – he would listen to her about other things. More important things, about those in the village, the resources he gave them. And, even better, things going on in the political world.

If she truly couldn't change his mind, then the fact he trusted her would be enough. She had promised Luisa she would prove herself and a closeness to her father was an advantage for the *antifascisti*. This felt like a moment to get close to him, in a way they never had before. Treachery for a good cause. If he sent her away again, that would be impossible.

'Papà,' she continued, slowing her voice down, trying to affect a mix of meek daughter and independent young woman. 'You told me Huber helped with your office work, translating, interpreting and suchlike. I speak some English and enough German to get by. Why don't I take her place?' She paused before adding in an embarrassed rush of words. 'And I can't believe she's the only woman who can offer what you call comfort. You could do far better. Or are you in love with her?'

His reply gave her hope as he shook his head.

'Let me think over what you have said, Ernestina. But for the rest of the week, you are not to venture from the castle.' And... he sighed before continuing, 'I'm sorry I struck you. I know I've not been a good father.'

She wondered afterwards how he would have reacted if she'd embraced him when he'd said that. But the action was alien to her and she couldn't, her anger still simmering. 'I forgive you, Papà. I've maybe not been the easiest of daughters.'

. . .

Over the next days, however, she made sure to keep herself visible. She sat in the library seemingly reading but spending much of the time peering out at the countryside, wondering what was going on in the real world where Olivio and Sergio were hiding.

Happily, Luisa came to visit, anxious to discover why her friend had not put in an appearance recently. The two young women were able to catch up about Tina's ride to the monastery to see Antonio once they were in Tina's bedroom where they talked in hushed voices.

'The bitch must have guessed I would tell on her sooner rather than later and she replaced everything. I can't stand the idea of her staying with Papà. She obviously has a hold over him.'

'Sexual,' Luisa said. 'Men's needs and all that. She knows what he likes.'

'*Yeuch!* Stop it! I don't need that vision in my head.'

Luisa laughed. 'One day it will happen to you.'

'Have you ever liked somebody that way, Lu?'

'No. Not yet. But when it happens, I want to be swept off my feet and for it to be wonderful. Papà did try to palm me off with one of his friend's sons but there was no spark there. I think there has to be a spark, something difficult to describe – something that creeps up unawares.'

For a moment the pair were quiet, each thinking their separate thoughts.

'I'm terrified Papà will stop me from coming to you, Lu. I've offered to work for him in return for that woman to be sent packing and that will give me more freedom – and I'll find more things out, too.'

Tina and Ferdinando reached a compromise when she was summoned to the library. Her father was uneasy with her as he ran through his proposal, his hands behind his back, addressing her as if she were a member of a committee.

'You need not study with Fräulein Huber any longer but she will stay on to help me out with my Austrian and German contacts. Try to be civil to each other.'

She in turn decided to put her side plainly and to stand her ground.

'*Grazie*, Papà. But I also need to work. I can't rattle around the castle doing nothing. Let me help in the business. And' – she crossed her fingers behind her back – 'I want Baffi back here at the castle. I miss him so. That way, I won't have to sneak along the country tracks to ride him. Bernardo's estate isn't so near. It's ridiculous you won't let me ride him. If harm has been done to my body, as Il Duce says, then it will have been done years ago. I—'

He put up a hand to interrupt her. '*Va bene*. Fine. This I shall permit. And you can help me part time at the factory. In the office. You did well in the past.'

The hug she gave him was awkward, his body rigid as she put her arms about him, but it was a start. Maybe her father was human after all.

CHAPTER 32

Fiammetta

Look at you, my darling, rushing about your tasks in the garden. Did you notice the way the roses have arranged themselves against the wall? I spent an hour while you were riding across the mountains, persuading them to curl this way and that and they listened to me. That Félicité-Perpétue will tangle itself everywhere unless you have control over its waywardness. Oh, how I love that rose, despite the thorns. Perpetual happiness was what I was expecting when your papà took me as his bride. Sadly, it was not to be.

I wandered into his dream two nights ago. He tossed and turned as I painted pictures in his head of what that Lorli woman is really like. Ha ha! I had her dressed up as a serving wench in the ristorante *down in Rimini where he likes to eat fish. On her plump bosoms that threatened to spill from her blouse, I conjured blackheads and deep-grained dirt. She flirted with everybody, especially the rich, and in this dream, he saw her for what she is. But a dream is only a dream. A dream can only do so much and when he woke, he'd forgotten it already.*

Brava, figlia mia, for your courage. Now you shall have Baffi with you again and that is a big success. But be careful. Do not trespass too far into your new freedom. For what Ferdinando gives with one hand, he takes with the other. Too often it happened to me.

Watch over Allegra for me, tesoro. She is tired. I know she only stays on at the castle to care for you because she made me a promise as I lay dying. But, see! You are a woman now and you can do so much more. Slowly you are understanding more about this life. You told your papà so and to him it seemed a surprise that you are no longer a little girl. Sometimes with men, a woman has to show the way.

Do what you can in the factory. Discontent is rumbling amidst the hungry workers. And I shall be near you, doing what I can. Tread carefully, Tina mia. And be very wary.

CHAPTER 33

1943

Tina

Spirits of the dead

Over the following months, Tina survived believing no news is good news. After her mission to tell Antonio they needed to flee, she and Luisa still had no idea of the whereabouts of Olivio and Sergio and in one sense, ignorance was bliss. It was better to believe they were alive than hear the worst.

News of Mussolini's increasing political disasters, the defeat at El Alamein despite the legendary brave Italian paratroopers, brought more doom and gloom to the country. Back in autumn, several cities had been bombed by the allies, Torino coming off worst. And then came the allies forcing the Axis from North Africa. At home, food and fuel dwindled and pitted citizen against citizen. In the little town of Sant'Agnese there were divisions within families, with one brother doggedly hanging on to Il Duce's promises and the other favouring growing communist and dissident movements. Tina witnessed this in the factory herself and had to advise her father.

'You cannot continue to have young Bonaventi on the same cutting bench as his brother, Papà. There will be tragedy with those sharp scissors before too long.'

She worked in the office three days a week and she picked up undercurrents, listening to complaints about conditions, persuading her father to increase rations. 'If they eat better, they work better.' This was one way to apprise her father, but the main motive was because she could not bear to see her townspeople suffer.

'I'm sure, Papà, you can acquire extra provisions from the community store for your workers. Can't you see how tired and thin they are? You do want them to continue working for you, don't you?'

There were no longer many young men on the shop floor, having been either conscripted or fled to the hills to avoid conscription. Mothers, young girls and grandparents had replaced them in order to continue to bring in lire to pay for food. And if that meant on the flourishing black market, then so be it, despite ever-increasing prices and warnings of severe punishment.

Life dragged on and up at the castle, Huber and Tina largely ignored each other. Tina was invited to accompany her father and Huber on occasional business trips, her father tasking her with choosing designs for their leatherwork. She sensed Huber bristling with resentment when the conte went for her choice of a larger style valise over a sophisticated portmanteau favoured by the Austrian.

'But, Papà, in these times of relocation and displacement, when so many are leaving the cities to live in hotels in the mountains, customers will need something larger to carry as many of their possessions as possible, rather than a bit of frippery.'

His nod of approval made up for Huber's poisonous looks.

To Tina's relief, her father had booked a single room for Huber on the ground floor of the hotel overlooking Lake Bracciano outside Rome, whilst her own room was adjacent to her father's on the top floor where they shared a balcony. On the final evening of the business trip, he called for her to join him in a glass of Frascati before dinner. It was the closest she had felt to him and she plucked up courage to ask him about her mother.

He turned to her, his look wistful. 'You look a lot like her, Ernestina. Beautiful. The same colouring.'

But the fleeting moment of closeness disappeared in the air with his cigar smoke as he dismissed further conversation, glancing at his fob watch and saying, 'Fetch a shawl and we'll dine. It's late.'

After this trip Huber stopped her policy of avoiding Tina and instead seemed to be everywhere in the castle, sticking to Tina like a bloodsucker, waiting perhaps for her to make a wrong move. Tina took courage in both hands late one evening and, armed with a torch, she made her way to the garden in the darkness. She never felt scared in her kingdom, as she called it, but as she passed through the low door in the greenhouse and into the rough passageway down to town that Olivio had uncovered, it was as if the weight of history was pressing on her. Leaving the castle this way was better than the chance of Huber discovering what she was up to.

The tunnel had been hacked roughly from the hillside and in parts was narrow. She banned all thoughts of ancient warfare and why it had been built: surely not for a young woman to carry baskets of food to the needy in town. The wind funnelled through fissures, the sound like wailing, and she had to steel herself to continue. It was a perfect nesting place for bats. She wasn't scared of these living creatures: they weren't harmful.

No, it was the spirits of the dead she was aware of: soldiers escaping from bloodshed, the wounded who hadn't made it, their restless souls permeating the damp rocks.

When she pushed through the undergrowth at the end of the tunnel and emerged in the church precinct, she had to sit for a while, breathe deeply to gather herself, before slipping round town to leave her goods on doorsteps. It was worth it in the end to know she was making a difference and helping her people.

On the following morning, Huber followed Tina to the kitchen and sat herself at the table, observing how Tina helped Allegra with breadmaking. Tina almost expected her to question what she had been doing in the night, despite knowing Huber couldn't possibly have seen her.

'You should not be doing such work, Ernestina,' Huber rebuked.

'I enjoy it, Fräulein. It isn't like work.'

After Huber had left the kitchen Allegra paused in her kneading, dismay in her eyes.

'That woman will have your father sending me packing soon,' Allegra said. 'I'm too slow.'

'I won't let you go, Allegra, *carissima*.' Tina hugged her, leaving floury fingerprints on the back of the older woman's dress. Her shoulder blades were sharper now and, as with most of the population, her weight had dropped away.

Tina did as much as she could to help Allegra lighten her load but she had also grown to genuinely love working in the kitchen. She enjoyed working with pasta dough, pummelling out her frustrations which were usually over Huber. She hung the yellow bands over backs of chairs to dry and then folded them over and over to cut ribbons of tagliatelle. She stuffed fresh lengths of pasta to make little hat-shaped *cappelletti*. In fact, this was the only treat with which they'd marked last Christmas. There had seemed little point in celebrating.

Papà had forbidden her to ever serve at table again on evenings when he invited important guests from the *partito* and instead she was frequently a guest. She was careful to store up information about the diners, working out their roles and whereabouts. Bernardo sometimes attended, but he was cooler, remarking once to her that now she had her horse back, he was no longer needed. She had smiled at him, without comment. For what could she say?

It proved impossible for Tina with Huber trailing her to easily escape to her garden and with the greenhouse tunnel to town being out of question during daylight, she resorted sometimes to entering via the perilous path over the wall, waiting for when Huber was out with her father. Yet another section had disappeared over the winter months when snow had lingered on the ground for longer than usual and she had to tread carefully. To be sure nobody would see her, she took to rising early to spend a couple of hours before breakfast tending to her garden, where she felt a deep sense of peace. Her troubles and anxieties melted away as she worked.

In a corner beyond the maze, by the greenhouse, she had set up a beehive with Allegra's instruction. Tina marvelled at the hardworking bees, watching them buzz to and fro, intrigued by the drones as they performed their dances, pointing their bodies in the direction of the best source of pollen for the worker bees. More of her beds were planted for bees now. She'd added buddleia, lavender, sage and field scabious grown from seeds gleaned from the wild. A robin had built her nest in the arbour dedicated to her mother's memory and as Tina worked, she kept her company as she trilled her busy songs.

Conditions continued to worsen as war raged on. Living from day to day became harder and harder and Tina did her best to help as many of the workers as possible, using the tunnel from the greenhouse to make her way into town. With Huber sitting at her bedroom window that overlooked the main access to the castle, it was a better way for Tina to make her escape.

What did Huber know? Did she suspect Tina was making her way out each night – or was she simply suspicious of everything Tina did? Despite these thoughts, Tina continued. She wasn't willing to sacrifice her work for fear of that woman – despite the dangers if she was caught.

CHAPTER 34

Rumblings

As if war was not grim enough, Italy was beset with large-scale strikes that started in factories in the north and percolated throughout the country. There were rumblings in the leather factory and Tina racked her brains to find a solution to keep work going.

'Thank heavens for you,' Tina told Luisa as they chatted about the situation in the empty *farmacia*. 'You and Allegra are the only people keeping me sane.'

'Likewise, *cara*. Everything is so grim but these strikes are a sign people are distancing themselves from the dictatorship. They're fed up with war and our leader's folly.'

Through her work in her *farmacia*, Luisa knew of those in greatest need and was happy to help distribute food deliveries when she could.

'I still think my idea of using the factory for growing food is possible,' Tina said. They had been chatting through Tina's scheme to use it as a large greenhouse now that leather work had slowed right down.

'What's the point? Most townspeople have access to their own vegetable plots,' Luisa said as she sorted through a box of medicines. 'Can you get them to grow *aspirina* instead? My supplies are becoming nigh impossible to get hold of.'

'Be serious, Lu.'

'I'm deadly serious – as ever. I can't remember the time I laughed about *anything*. Italy is on her knees and soon I will have absolutely no pharmaceuticals in my *farmacia*. Hardly anybody comes to me anymore either. They don't have money. The *medicone* in Sant'Agnese, meanwhile, is doing a roaring trade with her witchcraft potions. She's paid in kind: a handful of potatoes, a piece of material, whatever's spare.'

'I think my idea of a food cooperative *will* work. We can grow crops in the workrooms by the high windows through the winter,' Tina said. 'Like in an enormous glasshouse.'

'Have you thought through where you'll find seeds and plants to start off this enterprise? And how to heat this amazing glasshouse?'

'There are stoves in the factory. And surely the inhabitants of Sant'Agnese will have spare seeds.'

'And how will you pay them?'

'From sales, of course. It'll be a cooperative and we'll transport what we grow to the city. I'm going to persuade Papà after you've made me a coffee.'

'If it's *caffè-caffè* you're after, I've none left. Chicory do you?'

Tina wrinkled her nose. 'I'll let you know how I get on with Papà.' She hugged Lu, who wished her good luck with her crazy scheme and shook her head as her friend left.

Her father guffawed at her proposal. 'I'm not having my workforce turn into manufacturers of turnips and potatoes. No! While you've been dreaming up ridiculous ideas, I've been successful in acquiring orders for uniforms to send to Rome. We have the wherewithal already: workers who know how to cut patterns, sewing machines to put garments together. It won't take long to amend their skills. Forget about vegetables, Ernestina.' He laughed again and looked at her with pity. 'Montesecco vegetables indeed.'

On the following morning, the conte made his announcement to the handful of workers in the factory yard.

'I cannot increase wages at this time, but on offer is plenty of overtime at the normal rate. We are commissioned by *milizia* HQ to deliver a large supply of uniforms. I shall need cutters, seamstresses, tailors. Mark this form with a cross or sign with your name if you know how. My daughter will help you.'

More than half the workforce started to queue but a small group of men turned to leave. When Tina caught up with them at the gates to ask them to be patient, explaining she had another idea up her sleeve, their spokesman wasn't interested and told her they flatly refused to sew uniforms for Mussolini. They strode away before Tina could say more. As they disappeared into town, she couldn't help admiring their defiance but wondered how they would manage to feed their families. It would likely be down to their women, as usual.

And she was correct. The rest of the morning was a strain with Tina sorting lists and listening to women share their difficulties. Two were widows, one pregnant and concerned the conte would not keep her on in her condition.

'I don't have family left to help me. My mother-in-law died and my father-in-law is simple in the head. Mine is the only wage, signorina.'

Tina tried to allay the woman's fears, telling her she would do her best to get help when the time came for her confinement.

Another woman begged her to find a job for her daughter. 'She's never worked here but she's a good child and I'm sure she could turn her hand to something. She helps me clean and cook at home.'

'What's her name, signora?' she asked.

'Nella. She's a good girl, she is.'

'Tell her to come and see me this afternoon at the *castello* and knock on the kitchen door at the back.'

The girl was only eleven but Tina had her in mind as a help for Allegra.

The list of those in need was long by the time midday arrived. Tina was exhausted and dispirited as she accompanied her father back to the castle.

Young Nella was quick to learn and Allegra was grudgingly pleased to have help for a couple of hours each morning. Tina found clothing to replace the girl's darned skirt and blouse as well as a pair of leather shoes that had always been too tight. She caught Nella staring at the red shoes on her feet more than once, pointing her toes like a dancer and smiling.

'I've never had a pair of me own, signorina,' she said. 'I've always had me brother's cast-off boots or wooden *zoccoli*. It's like I'm not wearing anything on me feet, they're so comfortable.'

Such a little thing to give so much pleasure. Tina resolved to sort through her wardrobe and take items now and again to the factory.

'Don't just be dishing them out for no reason,' Allegra told her. 'People are desperate, yes, but they're proud.'

Allegra was so wise. From then on, Tina gave items out as a reward for something like neat work on the seams of a black shirt or progress made by a younger worker cutting out trousers from the roll of grey material and made sure to select those who seemed to most need it.

. . .

It was late in July when Mussolini resigned. Marshal Badoglio took over as head of government. The allies invaded Sicily and next came news in September that Badoglio had agreed an armistice with the allies. The headlines were spread over front pages of all newspapers. For a short spell, there was jubilation in the streets of Sant'Agnese as people gathered in the piazza.

'The war has ended.'

'*Evviva gli alleati!* Long live the allies. They'll be here soon.'

'Our men will return home and life will be normal again after three long years of war.'

In the *osteria* in the corner of the piazza, bottles hidden in all parts of the drinking house were retrieved and Sant'Agnese came alive. Tina hunted out a bottle of sparkling wine from Papà's cellar and shared it with Allegra in the kitchen.

'I can't wait to see Olivio and Sergio turn up again. It's been too long since we've seen them,' she said, pouring Allegra a second glass.

'And the shops to be full again. I'm scraping the flour barrel and what they give me is rubbish anyway. Not even fit for the pigs.' She hiccoughed and they both laughed. How long had it been since they'd last laughed?

But the mood did not last long. In the north, Il Duce was helped to settle into the Republic of lakeside Salò by *tedeschi* and fascist cronies and started to issue his orders from there. Nothing much had changed; in fact, the war had worsened now the Germans were in opposition.

By September 12th news spread that the Germans had entered Florence in force without resistance. The Italian army had ordered its soldiers to resist the *tedeschi* but there were insufficient guns and ammunition and many surrendered. Soldiers who had been too slow to escape from their barracks were arrested and marched to trains that took them to Germany. Badoglio and his politicians retreated to Sicily where the allies were now in control and the people of Italy felt abandoned and confused. The *tedeschi* were now the enemy and people feared how they would be treated.

Rome fell to the *tedeschi* and Radio Roma stopped broadcasting completely for several days, starting up again with the fascist anthem, 'Giovinezza', issuing order after order from German command, including curfew from half past nine at night until dawn, no photography, no withholding goods from Germans, no pigeons, no cloaks for men, no radios. The list was endless. Italy was in turmoil. An atmosphere of mistrust ruled in what was now full-scale civil war.

To Tina's horror, a flag with a swastika had been hoisted above the main castle doorway, next to the fascist eagle that Papà refused to take down. Tina was ashamed. She had to stop herself from tearing them down with her bare hands but her task was to spy on Papà's cronies and discover as much as she could about events. How could she maintain her cover if she openly protested? She observed the comings and goings of his visitors but was not invited to take dinner with the men who sat behind closed doors until late in the night. She tried to engage Bernardo in conversation to glean what had been discussed as he emerged from her father's study soon before midnight, but he looked right past her where she waited in the hall and made his way with the other officials to their expensive cars parked on the forecourt.

'Good meeting?' she asked her father, pouring him a glass of grappa where he sat looking morose in his armchair in the library.

He looked up. 'Nothing to bother your head about, Ernestina. But we shall be providing lodgings for a German officer from tomorrow. Allegra and that new girl must make ready our best guest room. Fräulein Lorli will be invaluable with the language.'

He registered the shock on her face. 'Everything will be fine. Life will soon return to normal. Now, go to bed. It's late.'

Normal? Nothing is normal, Tina thought as she trailed up the stairs. *Nothing.* Tedeschi *in our home.* Her heart sank. The guest room was on the same floor as her bedroom and she shuddered as she thought of how near she would be sleeping to a man who was now an enemy of Italy. She would bolt her door every night.

Sleep refused to come as she tossed and turned. Eventually she pulled on her trusted dark clothes and moved to the staircase. The castle was quiet. This might be the last time to safely slip out at night. Her garden called.

A harvest moon hung like a dirty puckered orange in the sky as she emerged from the tunnel behind the pantry door. The wind was still and everything was outlined in a silvery-golden sheen. She sat for a while as motionless as the trees and plants, drinking in the strange beauty of the night. Anybody glimpsing her might have mistaken her for a garden statue. She knew from her mother's notes how she too had often slipped away from her bed to seek solace in this place. Tonight, she felt a strong link with the woman she'd have loved to have known.

A sound jolted her from her thoughts: stones clinking against metal. A sound she knew well. Someone was digging. She rose slowly from her bench and tiptoed nearer. Who was in here? How did they get in? What were they doing at this time of night?

Two figures dressed in long robes were bent over a hole in the fallow section of her vegetable plot. The long habits on the eerie figures were those of friars. Or were they ghosts? But they were puffing from exertion and one of the figures uttered a filthy oath. No, they were definitely real.

The hood fell back from one of them as he stood up to stretch, revealing the shorn head of a young man.

'Olivio?' Tina hissed. '*Che diavolo fai qui?* What the devil are you doing here?'

He started and then grinned. 'We have to stop meeting like this, Tina.'

CHAPTER 35

In the dead of night

'What are you doing up at this time of night?' Olivio asked. 'Shouldn't you be tucked up in your comfortable bed?'

Annoyed at his tone, she retorted, 'What are *you* doing in the middle of the night in *my* garden in fancy dress? And who is here with you? I thought we'd agreed not to tell anybody about the garden.'

'Nice welcome.'

'Well, what do you expect? Coffee and cake?'

He laughed. 'Wine and cheese would be better.'

The other person limped nearer and held out a grubby hand to her. It was Sergio.

She should have been pleased to see them, given them an ecstatic welcome, but they'd frightened her out of her wits and she was annoyed. She ignored Sergio's outstretched hand.

'What the hell are you doing?'

Olivio and Sergio dug their spades into the pile of earth they'd been working on and moved to the bench.

'Tell me what you're doing,' she repeated.

Olivio looked at her for long seconds.

'You still don't trust me, do you, Olivio?'

'I want to.'

'*But*... I am the daughter of conte Ferdinando Montesecco, the most influential member of the fascist party in Sant'Agnese and you believe I'm too much of a risk. You're still not convinced I hate the *nazifascisti*, are you?'

'You're still living in the castle. You can understand how it looks.'

With a long, frustrated sigh, she shook her head. '*O Dio santo*, Olivio. I went up the mountains to the friars and left a message with Antonio warning you the *fascisti* are hunting for absconders and in particular men from Sant'Agnese. You! Did you not get the message?'

At the blank look on their faces, she swore. '*Porco cane!* I despair. Antonio failed to get the message to you. But anyway, I'm sick of you going on at me for being a contessina, as if I don't understand what's going on out there. We've talked about this before. It's getting boring. What it *looks* like, as you put it, is surely an advantage. An excellent cover. Listen, both of you, tomorrow a German officer is arriving to stay here. I *hate* the thought of living under the same roof. But don't you see? I can be so useful. I know some German now. I can find out more stuff for the cause. But trust has to work both ways. If you don't trust me, how am I to trust you?'

There was silence after her outburst, broken eventually by Sergio muttering to Olivio, 'She's right, Olivio.'

'I think you do have *some* trust in me, Olivio,' Tina continued. 'Otherwise you wouldn't be here, doing whatever it is you're doing. I certainly don't believe you're planting potatoes in my vegetable plot.'

'You have to understand that one misjudged decision or comment can lead to catastrophe,' Olivio said.

'It seems to me you've already come to a decision.' She stood up, annoyance mixed with anger and disappointment at his attitude. 'If you're going to continue to talk in riddles, then you'd better leave now. But rest assured, *I* shall not be telling anybody that Olivio Buratta and Sergio Pancotti, absconders from the army, wanted by the fascist *milizia*, were here at two o'clock this morning. Leave the gate closed on your way out. I don't want more strays wandering in and out, playing havoc with my garden.'

Tina moved to leave and Olivio tugged on her arm.

'*Va bene*, Tina. *Scusami.* I'm sorry. You're right. Of course we trust you. But it's been difficult recently. You've no idea. One of our men was tortured by the *milizia*... someone we thought would never reveal anything, but he did... None of us know really if we're brave enough to resist what those bastards can do. I won't tell you what his body looked like when we found him.'

He looked away as Sergio continued. 'We had to pretend to his mother the bastards had already buried the poor sod, his body was in such a state. We dug his grave on the mountainside. One day we'll give him a decent send-off.'

'Oh, that's terrible. Did I know him?'

Olivio shook his head. 'We're with new people. There are Slavs with us, escaped from the camp at Anghiari, a couple of *inglesi* and a South African from another camp as well as ex-soldiers who refuse to take up arms again. We're gaining numbers all the time.'

'Where are you staying now? Did you return to the monastery?'

'We've not been there for ages,' Sergio said, 'but we requisitioned these habits before leaving. They've been a useful disguise because we're too well known in Sant'Agnese. Hence sneaking here by night. We used the greenhouse passageway.'

'I hoped you might return one day. That's why I left it unlocked.'

'Yes, we were grateful,' Olivio said.

'And are you going to tell me why you're here? Why you're digging?'

Olivio hesitated before answering and that hesitation didn't offend Tina now. She understood he was about to entrust her with something important.

'Weapons, Tina,' Olivio said. 'There's a group of us up in the mountains all bent on fighting the enemy and we have to constantly move about. We can't lumber extra arms around with us. We have to travel light, staying in this farmhouse or that. In caves, sometimes. It's freezing and uncomfortable. Sometimes we sleep in the woods but we need somewhere permanent and secure to store guns and ammunition for future attacks. Whenever you hear about bridges being blown up or railway lines damaged, it's invariably us. We have to rid our country of these occupiers.'

Sergio took up the discussion. 'It's not easy, Tina. Hard to trust because there are still many who hanker after Il Duce and are working with the *tedeschi*. Those *nazifascisti* burn houses down when they think the poor owners are hiding *banditi*, as they call us. This place here... nobody would think of it. Ever.'

'You could have asked me without having to go through this charade. What if I'd decided to dig over that plot and discovered the guns myself?'

'I know,' Olivio said. 'I guess the way we live now, it's best not to reveal anything to anybody. None of us use our real names in this work. Less to reveal about our comrades if we're caught.'

'So what names do you go by now? Are you allowed to tell me?'

Olivio grinned. 'I confess I borrowed mine.'
'What?'
'Baffi,' he said in a half-whisper.

'*O Gesù*, Olivio.' And then she giggled. 'You don't look like my horse, but you certainly need a shave.'

He scratched at the whiskers on his cheeks and chin. 'It's easier this way. Adds to my disguise.'

'And I am Focaccia,' Sergio said. 'They know I love to eat bread. I dream about it at night.'

Tina smiled in the darkness. Sergio was no longer the tubby young man she'd known before the war. 'Anyway, my friends, we need to sort a plan for when it's safe or not for you to come here. And how I can get information to you. What do you suggest? You know I have the real Baffi back in the stables? I ride him regularly, so that gives me an excuse to be out and about. Is there somewhere safe to leave messages?'

'What about the river?' Olivio suggested. 'The willow we used to swing from. There's a hole high in the trunk where an owl nests.'

'The tree I nearly drowned from,' she said, a smile playing on her lips. 'A lifetime away. We were so naïve back then. That was my first taste of freedom.'

His hand covered hers as he said, 'You were courageous that day. You still are, Tina. And one day we'll be free again when we rid our country of these *bastardi*. Life will improve. It has to.'

His voice was steely and Tina thought how much he'd changed from the mischievous boy she'd met four years earlier. She'd have liked to talk more, have Olivio's hand cover hers for longer, but this was not the right time to linger.

'Right!' she said, moving to the greenhouse where she kept her tools. 'Let's get going. Three of us digging will make lighter work. Will one of these crates be large enough to hold them?'

'*Perfetto*,' Olivio said.

They dug a deep hole and within the half hour, raked soil back over the box.

'Job done,' Tina said as she straightened her aching back.

'Time for my bed now but I'll come with you to the tunnel and close the door behind you.'

She was agreeably surprised when Olivio pulled her into a hasty hug, his goodbye greeting warmer than their earlier frosty conversation. He was followed by Sergio and her heart warmed. They were both alive. And they had accepted her help.

'*Alla prossima*,' Olivio said. 'Until next time.'

She turned away from them and as she did, she caught a movement over by the gate she'd first used. It was open and she saw a figure move away.

'*Porca Madonna!* There's someone there.'

Olivio rushed to chase the figure, who was now almost at the end of the narrow path where it met with the wall.

The figure turned and hissed at Tina, the voice unmistakable. 'Wait until I tell your father what you've been up to. I saw everything you did with these young men.' Fräulein Huber took a step back and then a shriek split the night as she missed her footing on the narrow ledge and slithered from the edge.

'*Hilfe! Hilfe mir!*' she called. 'Help me!'

The rolling of loose stones, snapping of branches and muffled shrieks were followed by an ominous silence.

The three friends peered over the edge into the darkness, the only sounds now the whispering of pine branches moving in a capricious wind sprung from nowhere.

'*O santo Dio*,' Sergio cried. 'We have to help her.'

'The only safe way down is along the track leading out of town,' Olivio said. 'Wait here with Tina.'

Sergio stood while Tina sat hunched beneath the trees clasping her knees to her chest. Everything was in tatters before it had even started. Huber had witnessed them together. She would tell her father and then Olivio and Sergio would be hunted down. Even if she hadn't overheard their conversation, there would be ructions: what had she been doing out at night, alone with two men? And in the garden that Papà had locked and never spoken about.

She didn't care what happened to herself but she cared deeply about Olivio's and Sergio's safety. Papà would punish her, lock her up, there was no doubt about that. But her friends – oh God, they'd be arrested, tortured like the comrade they'd spoken about. She hid her face in her knees, her body trembling as she tried to still her anguish. She must have made too much noise when she'd crept downstairs and woken the woman. Now, Huber knew about the garden. About the guns.

Moments later, Olivio appeared from over the low wall above the path. He bent over, gasping for air, breathless after his exertions.

'She's dead,' he said and Tina gasped. 'Her neck is broken. I... I covered her in leaves and left her there for the time being.'

'I know it's an awful thing to say, but I'm glad she's dead,' Tina said. 'I really disliked her but... what are we going to do?'

'Sergio and I will move her later, Tina. She's concealed by the foliage, but if her body is found where it is, there'll be questions to answer.'

'Suicide?' she asked.

'Nobody would think of jumping from there. Too many trees to break a fall.'

'Maybe she could simply disappear back to Austria? Leave in the night?' Tina suggested.

'Yes,' Olivio said. 'That's good.'

The world was waking as they discussed the plan in hushed whispers, the sky turning a muddy grey as a new day dawned. One or two birds chirped within the canopy of trees, oblivious to the drama.

'We'll move her tonight,' Olivio continued. 'In the meantime, you have to cook up a convincing story, Tina.'

'I'll write a note, copy her handwriting. It's plastered all over the work she set me. I'll think of something, Olivio.'

She began trembling again, the cold air and the horror of what had happened hitting her. The weapons were secured and life would be easier now Huber would not be around to snoop. But the sight of her plunging to her death had been horrific. Like something from an opera, she thought, with the *primadonna* disappearing over the parapet like in *Tosca*. She knew she would suffer nightmares from the memory. She couldn't stop shivering.

Olivio once again pulled her to him. He was warm from his run to the base of the path and he rubbed his hands up and down her back. 'You're frozen, Tina. Go inside now. Try not to dwell on what happened. It's for the best. Nobody pushed the woman. It wasn't your fault.'

She thought she felt the slightest of kisses on top of her head, but then he and Sergio pulled the cowls over to conceal their faces and were gone. She wondered when she'd see them again and tried not to picture Fräulein Huber lifeless at the foot of the cliff, buried under leaves.

With each second the sky lightened and she hastened back along the narrow path to the garden, pulling the ivy-clad door to and was soon in the kitchen where she threw kindling into the stove to warm herself. She only stayed a few minutes. Allegra would be in to prepare breakfast soon and she tore herself from the warmth, her legs like lead as she took the stairs. As she passed the open door of Huber's room, she steeled herself to enter. First, she checked the bed really was empty and that everything that had happened this night had not been a terrible nightmare. It was ridiculous, she knew, but she hadn't seen Huber's body for herself. What if she had simply been knocked out and come to after Olivio had run back up the hill? But no, he'd told her Huber's neck was broken.

Chastising herself to get a grip, she straightened the covers on the bed after removing the flimsy nightdress from under the pillow. Fetching a suitcase from the top of the wardrobe, she stuffed in various items of clothing. *Think, Tina*, she told herself. *Stay calm!* What would Huber take with her? In a hurry to accomplish what she had to do before her father stirred, she flew back down the stairs and removed six of the Fabergé eggs as well as the box of silver spoons from their places in the cabinet and returned to Huber's room. Hairbrush, underwear, perfume, jewellery, a fancy hat with ostrich feathers and a fox stole were all squashed into the bulging case. Satisfied she'd grabbed sufficient items, Tina sat on the case to close it and hauled it to her own room. For the time being she pushed it to the back of her own wardrobe. When Papà was away, she'd dispose of everything.

She returned to her own room and then cursed. *The letter. Mannaggia. I have to write the letter.*

In Huber's room again, avoiding the sight of the slippers poking from beneath the bed, she took a sheet of writing paper and pen and ink from the desk by the window. An official-looking envelope bearing the town hall stamp and addressed in handwriting to Huber caught Tina's eye and she pulled out the contents. Scanning the lines, to her horror she read a list that had been taken from the census, showing names of a dozen or so citizens of Sant'Agnese. Included in the list was Luisa Levi and her family.

Dio mio! Luisa was Jewish. Of course! That was obviously why her parents and siblings had left for Switzerland. How stupid she'd been not to realise. And Luisa had kept that to herself all this time – of course she had.

But what had Huber intended to do with this list? Jews in Italy had been stigmatised by Il Duce with his racial laws, but now the *tedeschi* were occupying Italy, life for them was perilous. They were being hunted and deported. Why did Huber have this list in her desk? How had she obtained it? Who else knew about it? Tina knew she had to warn Luisa fast.

But for now, she had another task to complete: fabricating a letter from Huber. She stepped back into the corridor. A cough and her father's door opened. She shrank back, hoping her father was not making his way to Huber for an amorous morning meeting. Instead, he entered the bathroom and, heart pounding as she heard the toilet flushing, she rushed to her own room. She leant against her bedroom door until she felt calmer.

Before Papà came down for breakfast, she had about thirty minutes to compose the most convincing letter of her life.

CHAPTER 36

Hurdles

Flicking through her German grammar exercise book, Tina opened a page with several corrections and practised copying Huber's spindly handwriting on a blank sheet of paper a couple of times. Her fingers trembled as she started to form the letters and she rose to pour herself a glass of water from her washstand. Grappa would have been more effective but she downed the water and afterwards breathed in and out deeply before she felt calmer.

Ferdinando, she wrote, after debating whether or not to preface it with *caro*, but 'dear Ferdinando' sounded too affectionate for a woman who was about to leave. She wrote in Italian. The woman had been very strict about Tina's errors in her written German and so she delighted in sprinkling plenty of mistakes throughout the letter.

Il Castello Montesecco, Sant'Agnese.

October 5th, 1943

Ferdinando,

When you read this, I shall be gone.
    It is time for me to take my leave from Italy, where hostilities increase each day. I have arranged to travel to Sant'Arcangelo from where I shall catch a train.
    Your daughter has made my stay most unwelcome. I can no longer endure this unpleasant atmosphere. Ernestina has been successful in driving a wedge between us, Ferdinando. A wedge I do not feel can be bridged.
    I am returning to the bosom of my family in Vienna. Italy no longer holds a place in my heart.
    Do not try to contact me for I shall not return. Anything I have left behind you may dispose of how you think best.

Eleonore Huber

Tina read through her effort, wrinkling up her nose as she folded the letter into an envelope and wrote her father's name on the front with a swirling flourish. It wasn't perfect but with the time she'd had, it would have to do.

Tina pulled off her grubby dark clothes and picked a clean skirt and blouse from her wardrobe. The long mirror reflected a wan figure, dark circles under eyes in a pale face, hair a mess of curls. Although she yearned to curl up in her bed and sleep, she dragged a brush through the tangles before hurrying down to coffee and bread. On her way to breakfast, she shoved the envelope into a pile of mail on the hall table awaiting her father's attention.

Her father nodded to her over the top of his newspaper, *La Stampa*. 'More and more strikes in the north,' he tutted. 'These devils will stop at nothing to ruin our nation.'

The bread stuck in her throat and she could hardly swallow but she washed it down with two cups of strong coffee. Proper coffee that Luisa loved. Poor Luisa. She was in great danger if Huber had passed on the names on the list to the *fascisti*. Where could she hide? The greenhouse. Yes, that was it.

'Fräulein Huber is late this morning,' the conte said, interrupting Tina's worries as he reached for another roll and spread it with Allegra's home-made plum jam. 'I need her to interpret for the German officer who arrives today. Is his bedroom prepared?'

'I did ask Allegra and Nella, Papà. What time is he arriving?'

'Earlier than planned. He was due this afternoon but I received a message to say he's arriving late this morning.'

'I'll go and check with Allegra now.'

Nella had her arms in the sink beneath the window, washing plates, and she turned to smile shyly at Tina.

'*Buongiorno*, Nella. *Tutto bene?* Everything good?'

'*Sì*, signorina. And Mamma asked me to thank you for the fruit.'

'*Prego*. You're welcome. Where is Allegra?'

'In the pantry, sorting what we are short of, signorina.'

Allegra was on a stool, reaching up to the top shelf where the sugar and flour were kept in wooden tubs. 'This will all be gone soon. How am I supposed to feed an extra mouth on nothing?' she grumbled. She stepped down as Tina offered her hand, and took a hard look at Tina.

'*Madonna buona*, child.' Allegra tutted. 'You look as if you've had a *notte bianca*, a sleepless night. What is the matter? You look like a ghost.'

'It's the time of the month, Allegra.'

'Really? I thought you'd finished your bleeding only last week. Are you ill? Maybe you need more iron. Spinach,' she said, 'and apricots if only we could get hold of them. Liver. Pig's liver is the best.'

Before she could go through her list of iron-rich foods, Tina interrupted. 'Is the spare room ready for the *tedesco*? He's arriving earlier than we thought.'

'*Gesù e tutti i santi*, we still have to make the bed. Nella!' she shouted through to the kitchen. 'Take those ironed sheets and pillowcases and I'll come and help you finish the room. Quick now!'

The girl scurried from the kitchen with her load and Allegra turned to Tina. 'Now tell me what is *really* the matter. What is up?'

'Nothing. I... had a bad night. Stomach pains with my monthlies,' Tina said.

'You should arrange to see the doctor. You shouldn't be bleeding so soon after your last period.'

'Oh, I expect it's the stress of everything. The thought of a *tedesco* living here with us. I can't bear the idea. It's playing havoc with my system.'

'The very idea of having to cook for a German when all I hear is the way they are treating our people upsets my system too. In the grocer's the other day they were talking about the Montinis down in the valley. The *tedeschi* entered their farmhouse and took everything: their two cows, all their eggs and poultry. They even ordered Elvira to pluck the hens and to roast them. Just imagine! And while they were waiting, they stole linen from the chest at the foot of her bed. I mean, what good is linen to a soldier?'

'It's called the spoils of war,' Tina said.

'Well, I'm going to hide anything precious we have. I'll give them spoils of war, *Madonna buona*. I've a good mind to spoil his dinners too.' She lowered her voice. 'Perhaps you can help me conceal things in your garden. We could put bottled food and our best linen in a barrel and bury it in one of your flower beds.'

'Not sure about that, Allegra. They might spoil with the damp. What about under the floorboards in one of the attic rooms?'

There was no way she wanted Allegra poking about and discovering the guns.

Before Allegra could suggest anything else, there was a loud bellow from the conte upstairs.

'Ernestina, *vieni qua!* Come here!'

'Got to go. We'll talk later, Allegra.'

Tina rushed up the servants' stairs from the kitchen and into the library where her father stood by his desk, Fräulein's letter in his hand.

'She has gone, Ernestina. Did you know anything about this?' He held up the letter and shook it at her.

'Who has gone, Papà?'

'Eleonore. Lorli. She is returning to Austria.'

'Does she say why, Papà?'

Tina didn't know for how much longer she could continue to ask inane questions about answers she already knew.

'She says it is your fault, Ernestina. That you have made life intolerable for her. What have you done?'

Tina pretended to be shocked, widening her eyes as if in disbelief, shrugging her shoulders.

'It is all because of the accusations you made,' he said, his face purple with rage. Tina couldn't help thinking if he had a heart attack, then that would be two deaths at the castle within twenty-four hours.

'You are impossible, Ernestina.' He sat down heavily, his fingers drumming on the polished desk. 'How am I going to communicate with our German guest?'

'There's always me, Papà. I can hold a basic conversation now. Fräulein Huber was a good teacher.'

The most boring teacher I have ever had, and an unpleasant bitch to boot, Tina thought. *As well as being a thief and a fascist.*

His eyes were piercing as he looked at her. 'How long will it take you to mess that up, Ernestina?'

'Papà, I agree that Fräulein and I didn't always see eye to eye but at least give me a chance.'

'I don't think I have any choice.' He flung the letter on the desk. 'You may leave now. But you really are the most difficult daughter.'

She left before he changed his mind and returned to the kitchen where Allegra was lurking by the door.

'Well, I heard all that,' she said. 'And quite frankly, *grazie a Dio* for this wonderful news.' She made the sign of the cross and looked heavenwards. 'It means one less greedy mouth to feed and a great deal of grumbling gone too. Good riddance to the woman. You should look happy, Tina, not like death warmed up. If I didn't have so much to do and if I had a bottle of Vin Santo, we could celebrate. But even that is finished.'

Tina couldn't quite bring herself to celebrate with Allegra.

Oberstfrontführer Tobler, a lieutenant in the Todt division, responsible for military engineering, was tall and lean, his blond hair slicked back close to his bony skull. Allegra had remarked in the kitchen after seeing him for the first time that in her opinion he wouldn't last long – that he looked as if he needed three large meals a day. But there was no way on God's earth she was going out of her way to fatten him up.

In fact, the officer ate like a horse. He knew very little Italian but had a phrase book of colloquialisms he would pull from his breast pocket frequently in an effort to be more communicative with Tina.

'*Ho fame da lupo,*' he said in his terrible guttural accent each time they waited for dinner, chortling at the expression.

'We also say "hungry as a wolf" in German. I like this similarity.' He beamed at Tina and for a fleeting moment, she thought he actually resembled a wolf with his sharp teeth.

And when he had slept well, he would consult his book and rub his hands together as coffee was brought in by Allegra. '*Ho dormito come un ghiro*. But we do not sleep like dormice in our country. We sleep like a rock. I find it fascinating how our two cultures use animals in our sayings, do you not, Fräulein Ernestina?'

Tina couldn't care less but she smiled as sweetly as she could and continued to interpret as best she could.

'Your German is quite good, but by no means perfect, Fräulein,' he told her more than once during his first two weeks. 'But you will do for the moment, until I find better.'

Tina took to studying her German textbook in free moments, worried she would no longer be needed and always mindful of how she might be useful to Olivio and his *partigiani* with information. She hadn't heard from him yet, despite riding out to the riverbank twice to check in the tree.

Tobler enjoyed listening to Tina playing on her piano and it became a regular after-dinner event. He sat in an armchair, his long legs crossed like a stick insect, smoking a cigar and waving his hand about like a conductor.

'Play me more Beethoven, Fräulein. If I close my eyes when I listen, I can almost imagine I am back in München.'

At dinner earlier, she had made polite conversation, asking him if he had family.

'I am not married, if that is what you mean? But I have sisters. Three. The youngest is about your age. She has the same colour hair as you. Most unusual for an Italian woman, I think. I am guessing you are about twenty or so. Am I correct?'

She regretted hearing this information. She didn't want to

imagine him as a brother or a son. It was best to consider him as an enemy. Going forward, she kept talk to the impersonal, talking about weather or the history of the castle and Sant'Agnese.

He tried to converse with her father, but the attempts, each sentence having to be translated, were more stilted than with Tina.

'You have some exquisite furniture and paintings in your castle, conte Ferdinando.'

'Yes, the castle itself dates a long way back, to the eleventh century, but the castle as it is now was fortified in 1474. My grandfather was a collector of art. In the chapel, we have a small crucifix reputed to be from the school of Cimabue.'

Tina selectively omitted details about any artwork in her translation, advising her father afterwards he should be mindful. If he wasn't careful, anything of value might be requisitioned by the *tedeschi*. They should be prudent and hide the most precious items, otherwise they would be lost forever.

Later that same night, she stole downstairs and removed the painting of her mother, the only image she had of her, and replaced it with an ugly oil painting of an older ancestor.

When at the start of the third week of his stay the lieutenant asked her father to rustle up men for work on a massive project he was ordered to oversee, she concentrated on everything he said.

'We shall build defences across the mountains and valleys from Pisa to Pesaro and the work must start immediately. You must help me find these men, conte.'

The German's tone and attitude had changed. It was as if his first two weeks in the castle had been a brief holiday, but now he reverted to work mode. He was curter in his comments, driven to duty.

'It will not be easy, signor *tenente*,' the conte replied. 'The only young men left in Sant'Agnese are not fit for hard labour.'

'Then you must find me older men. The work must be completed quickly.'

There was a finality to his statement. Tina watched as he carved his meat into small pieces of identical size. She counted how many times his mouth moved before he swallowed each morsel, precisely, deliberately, his eyes directed on his plate like a bird of prey waiting to seize on small animals. She shivered. Her father had a hard task ahead. She wondered what would happen if he didn't fulfil the officer's order. There was no piano playing required that evening and she concluded it might become harder to acquire useful information in the future unless he requested her help in translation.

She rose long before breakfast the following morning and saddled up Baffi. In the pocket of her riding jacket she had a pass that Tobler had written for her on an earlier occasion after she had played his favourite piece of music by Wagner: 'The Ride of the Valkyries'.

'I have no chocolates for you. Or perfume. The luxuries my sisters appreciate,' he had said, handing her the pass. 'But, take this, Fräulein. A thank you for your exquisite piano playing. Keep it, for you will need it when you shall play for my men in the theatre in the square. Such an enchanting building.'

No polite request to play. An order. Tina wondered what would happen if she refused. But the pass was gold dust, so she kept quiet. The pass was in her pocket, but down her boots she had stuffed a note about the Todt construction work.

She showed the pass to the guards at the exit of Sant'Agnese and, once out of town, she urged Baffi into a gallop across the fields towards the river where she dismounted and let him rest. Checking she was alone, she reached up to the hole in the tree and was again disappointed to find nothing. She removed the note from her boot and pushed it in the hole, weighing it down with a river stone.

Within a couple of minutes, she was on her way back to

Sant'Agnese. An army truck bearing the German cross on its side overtook her, veering too close to Baffi, and she swore at the driver. Soldiers seated in the back wolf-whistled as she shook her fist at the speeding vehicle.

'*Bestie*,' she muttered as she patted Baffi. 'The sooner we rid Italia of them, the better.'

As she approached town, she heard the beating of hooves behind her and slowed Baffi to a trot. Turning in the saddle, she saw Bernardo.

He came aside her. 'You're up early. Next time maybe we can ride together.'

Had he seen her at the river? Had he seen her leave the note in the tree? Willing herself to sound calm, she said, 'Oh, I couldn't sleep and I prefer to ride in the cooler hours.'

He nodded. 'Me too. Nevertheless, Ernestina, it's not wise for you to be out on your own. The soldiers... they're far from home. They miss female company and...'

She noted the reversion to using Ernestina, rather than Tina.

'That's kind of you, Bernardo. But I can look after myself.'

'Most probably. However, you are far less likely to be accosted if you ride with a man.'

'If I ride out again, then I'll let you know. But I don't ride often.'

While they had been talking, the two horses flicked flies away from their shining flanks, nuzzling each other. Tina couldn't help thinking how much easier it was for animals to find peace with each other.

'Very well,' he said, 'I shall no doubt be seeing you when your father calls me to the next meeting.' He touched his riding hat in a salute and continued in the direction of his estate.

As Tina entered the town, she told herself she must be even more careful from now on when riding to the river. Fräulein Huber might be out of the way, but there were still hurdles.

CHAPTER 37

1943-1944

Subterfuge

Over the following months, life changed so drastically for Tina she hardly recognised herself. In the castle she came over as dutiful daughter, helping her father at meetings with the *tedesco*, having persuaded him that if she was to understand everything in order to interpret correctly, she needed to be present when he ate with his colleagues. She passed round cigars, poured wine, played whatever they wanted on the piano, always commencing with the anthem 'Giovinezza' until eventually it was normal for her to be there. She tried to remain low profile and soak up every potential useful detail.

Back in her room, she wrote notes in small handwriting on onion skins gleaned from the kitchen or in tiny, handmade notebooks she could hide about her body. She wore two pairs of socks and hid notes within the layers. If, God forbid, she was ever stopped and searched and asked to remove her clothes, she would peel off the socks in one go.

She rode with Bernardo, as promised, but only occasionally. She knew he liked her and he often dropped hints about spending more time together but she found excuses: 'I'm tired today.' 'My father needs me in the factory.' 'Baffi is lame.' Eventually he seemed to get the message and stopped asking.

The winter of 1943 was bitterly cold, the ground stone-hard but still she rode her horse regularly to the riverbank.

On a winter-white December morning, days before the end of the year, she arrived at the willow. Somebody was there. A man was slumped at the base, partly hidden by trailing branches, a green cape covering his whole body. She remained on Baffi's back, unsure if the figure was alive. But then she saw his breath hang in the air. He lifted his head and stood. She didn't know this haggard man with the long beard and she clenched her legs against Baffi's flanks to urge him to move but then the man smiled and she recognised him.

'Olivio,' she gasped.

'I thought it was time we saw each other face to face. God, your handwriting is terrible, especially when you write on those bloody onion skins.'

She slithered from her saddle and they fell into a hug. It was so good to see him after so long.

'You're very skinny,' she said, pulling away reluctantly.

'Our staple food is polenta. The cook in the camp knows a hundred-and-one ways to prepare the stuff but supplies are running out.'

'I can leave you provisions. You only need to ask.'

He looked at her. 'You still have food?'

'Papà manages to acquire—' she started.

'I couldn't eat that. It would stick in my craw.'

'You can't fight on an empty stomach, Olivio. Don't be proud. I'll see what I can do.'

'You can't trust a fat person these days. A hungry appetite is the best seasoning for me.' He turned away and picked up a flat stone to skim across the river surface before asking, 'Any new information?'

She pulled clips from her hair arranged in an untidy bun and her rich auburn curls cascaded to beneath her shoulders. She heard his intake of breath as she produced the folded paper concealed that morning with a clip and felt suddenly shy as she handed it over.

'I copied this from papers on Tobler's desk.'

He perused the sketch, biting his lip and squinting as he examined the diagram and notes.

'What does this say?' he asked, pointing to a line of German.

She drew closer to interpret the words and smelled hunger on his breath. She wished she'd thought to bring food with her but she was never hungry on these rides, her heart in her mouth for fear of being apprehended at any time. But next time, she would leave something in the hollow, despite his earlier protest.

'I had to look that up in the dictionary. *Geschützstand* means gun emplacements for anti-aircraft. And *Hubrettungsgewehre* there,' she said, pointing to equidistantly spaced crosses, 'are aerial guns.'

He gave a low whistle. '*Bastardi*... It's on a spot on the Tre Querce ridge close to where we're camped.' He looked at Tina. 'This is really useful. Any more where this came from?'

'The lieutenant is usually careful and files away his papers. But he was called out suddenly last night, so I took advantage. Trouble is, there's a new recruit turned up recently and he speaks some Italian, so I'm not needed as often, but I'll still snoop.'

'We're going to need those guns I hid now. But it sounds as if the castle is crawling with the *bastardi*. How safe is it?'

She thought for a few moments. 'They're not always there but if you want me to let you know if the coast is clear, then it'll be a question of you or one of your group loitering around town.

You can see my window from the piazza and the opposite ridge. If I hang out a white sheet, then it's safe. What do you think?'

'That could work. I have a contact in town. He knows how to get word to us.'

'I wish you'd let me know where you are, Olivio. It would be far simpler.'

'I told you no. You're already doing your bit. And... it's too risky for you to know. Believe me.'

'I'm playing at one of those concerts in two days' time. That might be a night to retrieve the guns, when lots of the *tedeschi* are there.'

The lieutenant had tasked Tina once a month with playing the piano in the Maraini Theatre in the piazza, along with a group of German musicians. The little theatre was a gem of a building, reputed to be the smallest in Emilia-Romagna, the walls of the stalls and balconies hand-painted with trompe l'oeil and rural scenes. It was a popular evening's entertainment for the *tedeschi* and always packed with officers.

'Are these concerts always on the first weekend of the month?'

'No. It varies but I can send dates.'

He smiled. 'We can use those dates to provide our own entertainment.'

'What do you mean?'

He tapped the side of his nose and she pulled a face, moving quickly to untether Baffi. But Olivio caught hold of her arm, waylaying her.

'Don't take offence, Tina. I told you it's for your own good.'

'Don't treat me like a child.'

She couldn't fathom the look he gave her but he held on to her arm a moment longer and murmured, 'I think of you as anything but a child, Tina.'

As if it were an annoying insect, she batted his hand away and put her foot in the stirrup to climb onto Baffi's back. 'I'll let you know the dates by leaving a message here. And tell your man, whoever he is, to keep a careful check on my window.'

She urged Baffi round with her leg. 'Stay safe, Olivio.'

And with that she was off, pushing forward her steadfast friend to gallop back across the meadows.

CHAPTER 38

Olivio

The desire to win

Two afternoons later, it was Olivio himself who observed the white sheet draped from Tina's window, flapping gently in the cold breeze as he entered the church of San Francesco overlooking the piazza. She'd left a message in the hole in the willow confirming there was to be a big concert this evening and he'd spent an uncomfortable time kneeling in his disguise as a friar waiting for the right moment to move, his habit now the worse for wear as he used it as a blanket and ground sheet when sleeping rough.

His head was empty of prayers and full of plans to retrieve the guns. Tina had warned him to use the greenhouse tunnel instead of the path as another chunk had disappeared in the same direction as the Austrian woman's fall. In dark moments, Olivio recalled coming across her still warm but lifeless body, her eyes open to the stars. He had closed them and partially buried her under leaves. The most difficult part had been disposing of the body a few hours later. Rigor mortis had set in by the time he and Sergio had returned to dig a hole nearby and they'd had to break her arms to get both limbs to fit. There had been little time to dig deeper. She hadn't been the first body they had dealt with in this infernal war and there had been many more casualties since, on both sides. Doubtless the castle held plenty of secrets from the past and Huber was another one. He hadn't told Tina but the first time he'd used the tunnel from the greenhouse, he'd stepped over human bones and pushed them through a large split in the rock.

The church cleaner tapped him on the shoulder to tell him she was closing the doors and he waited by the church steps until darkness fell. In the piazza, din from the *osteria* increased as soldiers in khaki-grey uniforms congregated, their strident voices carrying across the old town, the words unintelligible to Olivio's ears, the sound of their language grating on his nerves.

It was wrong. All wrong. One day soon, Italian would ring out again across the piazza. Children would scamper about playing freely in the portico, men and women would dance on the cobbled street, the trattoria would open its doors again, food would be plentiful and life would return to normal. Except, he knew life could never again be normal. There had been too much suffering. Husbands, lovers and sons had been sent abroad to never return, their bodies buried far away from the little cemetery outside Sant'Agnese where loved ones placed flowers and came to grieve. Votive candles were not allowed to flicker beside their tombs in case bombers used them as a landmark. His hands clenched in anger as he thought of the many stories of suffering recounted by fellow fighters at night by the campfire as they drank rough wine. His men and increasingly more civilians were bent on revenge, bent on revolt.

He forced himself to calm down but dismay consumed him at what played out before him as he shrank against the old door of the church, his habit the same faded rusty-red of the ancient chestnut wood. From the theatre violins tuning up and a pianist playing a series of chords warned concertgoers to stream to their seats. Amongst the crowd, he spotted Donatella teetering across the piazza, arm in arm with a German. She held back her head and her laughter bounced from the walls and he wanted to shake the stupid girl. *Puttana troia!* What was his old school friend doing? But he knew: giving herself in exchange for food in the belly and clothes on her back. She wore red shoes with high heels and as she stepped towards the theatre with the blond soldier she swayed, one heel catching between the cobbles. Olivio watched him pull her tight, kiss her deeply and she laughed again. Disappointed as he was, he had to accept what was going on. She was behaving as she was to fill her belly. *Povera* Italia, poor Italy that her women were reduced to this.

There were dozens of armed *tedeschi* milling about. He moved slowly across the piazza, his head bent in reverence as he made his way towards the back of the crypt and the entrance to the tunnel.

In the garden, weeds had grown over the spot where he dug for the guns and the soil was compacted. It took longer than he'd reckoned. His head was full of Tina while he worked: more beautiful than ever, she was not coquettish like Donatella and unaware of her stunning looks. It wasn't easy to go against one's upbringing. His father had always been a staunch anti-fascist as was his mother and Olivio had never questioned their beliefs. To him it was second nature, the normal philosophy everybody should live by. He hated Il Duce's grip on his people, the anti-Semitic stance, the treatment of women merely as producers of future warriors for the Empire. The man was a hypocrite too, the way he'd travelled first class in a train whilst his followers had walked for days on the march to Rome. Olivio wasn't religious but didn't even Christ want everybody to love their neighbours? There was little love in evidence anywhere at the moment.

It was strange to be working without Tina in this beautiful oasis they had tended back to life. He remembered fondly how they'd discussed music, always keeping their voices down, and to what lengths she'd gone to look after him when he'd turned up a wreck that first time. But she was out of his league. He was a working-class boy from peasant stock. She was an aristocrat with the type of education he'd never had.

Up in the camp at night as he lay on the hard ground, he'd nevertheless comfort himself with thoughts of her, imagining a life together if he survived this bloody war. One day. But he knew they were ridiculous dreams. She was a contessina, unattainable. She'd end up marrying someone from her own social stratum. Maybe she'd call on him from time to time to carry out odd jobs in her precious garden. That would be the sum of it. He'd say no, of course. What was the point of torturing himself in her presence?

The guns retrieved, he helped himself to a couple of cabbages and fennel bulbs to vary his men's diet, knowing Tina wouldn't mind, and placing his haul in a sack he made sure to arrange the vegetables at the top. His load was heavy and he stooped under the weight, which he supposed might lend more age to his appearance, but he wasn't making the whole trip up the mountain by himself. Jancko, Sergio and the *inglese* from his band would be waiting half a kilometre up the path to the hideout. They'd share the load. The tunnel had proved too difficult for Sergio to navigate with his stump.

All in all, it had been a good night. Except for seeing Donatella consorting with the enemy. It saddened him that many countrywomen had to resort to this to survive. But even this served to spur him on in his desire to free his beloved country. Il Duce's word '*VINCERE*', exhorting the nation to obey, fight the allies and win, had once been all over the newspapers and was still legible on faded posters. But now that very word had morphed into a cry for action for his own band of *parti-*

giani. The *nazifascisti* would *not* win this battle. The CLN, the action group for liberation would. He was absolutely convinced of this despite the hardships involved. It *had* to be so.

Once outside the town, he increased his pace and straightened his back. The load was heavy but not his resolve.

By April 1944, Olivio, now officially a commander of a splinter of the Garibaldi brigade, had moved yet again with his men. The farmhouse where they had sheltered before had been too close to the ridge where the *tedeschi*'s slave workers were constructing trenches and dugouts to use as stores.

Now, the *partigiani* shelter was more basic: a cave well-camouflaged in the craggy mountainside. It was damp and dark; spring water trickled down the sides of the walls where strangely shaped stalactites had formed. The only warm spot was by a fire at the back of the cave which the *partigiani* could only light at night for fear of smoke spiralling into the crisp winter air and revealing their hideout.

Twenty-two of them huddled together for warmth, bundled in strange assortments of civilian clothes, uniforms, old blankets, sacking and rags to stave off the cold. One of the Slav fighters, Jancko – a huge man with hair tied back untidily in a ponytail that hung below his shoulders – had tied a wolf pelt around his bulky frame. He presented a frightening, Stone-Age-like figure, fierce in his hatred of the *nazifascisti* and intensely loyal to the resistance cause. In a former life he had worked as a carpenter and thanks to his skills Sergio now wore a comfortable wooden false leg made from oak and had long ago discarded crutches.

There was also a British pilot in the group who had bailed out after his plane was hit. The pilot had been desperate to join up again with the allies, convinced they would soon reach this part of Italy. There was a radio in the camp and much to the group's elation the band managed to pick up Radio Londra and were abreast of the latest progress of the allies' move up the mainland.

There was a spot within the woods on the edge of the escarpment above the cave where Olivio could sit and train his binoculars on his town. He could make out Tina's bedroom window in the tower. Using information she'd gleaned, his group had started with small but nevertheless successful interventions: incapacitating vehicles by pouring sugar into their petrol tanks, stealing provisions from German stores, although the Italians in the group admitted to preferring polenta to the tinned sausages they sourced. German coffee was less strong but infinitely better than ersatz coffee made from ground acorns.

Their acts of sabotage had becoming increasingly annoying to the Todt engineers working on construction of the defensive Gothic Line. They had cut telephone wires, dynamited a railway bridge across the Marecchia river and they were about to embark on another scheme to thwart progress.

It had been easy for Olivio and other *banditi* to enrol as workers as construction sped up on the Gothic Line as the allies progressed northwards. Olivio and Jancko were on reconnaissance to understand what exactly was happening at the Todt camp, assessing the number of guards, the gunpower and machinery they could put out of action. While they were up there, Olivio added salt to the concrete mix to hamper its setting. Before sunrise, Jancko forced a hole in the walls of the wood hut where he and Olivio were confined next to ten other labourers, all lying on the floor without covers. None of them raised the alarm but wished the *partigiani* well as they slipped outside.

The pair crawled through the damp undergrowth towards the sentry guarding the compound gate.

'I want to cut the bastard's throat,' Jancko muttered, pulling out his knife as they lay in the leaves, waiting for their moment to escape.

Olivio had heard often enough how Jancko had been treated in the prison camp in Renicci and he understood his thirst for revenge but he shook his head.

'We go through those gates when he does his next round of the perimeter. No killing, my friend. Otherwise there'll be repercussions. They'll shoot ten workers. Do you want that? Restrict yourself to slashing tyres on that truck.' Olivio pointed to a vehicle parked near the gates.

In the eyes of the *tedeschi*, one of their dead men equalled ten of the enemy. There were posters everywhere directed at *ITALIANI*, warning of this.

As Olivio and Jancko sprinted towards the gates, they were confronted by another soldier they hadn't reckoned on who stepped from the guard hut, his semi-automatic directed at them. Olivio was aware of a shape flying past him as Jancko, howling like a wild animal, leapt for the *tedesco*, kicking the gun from his grasp before grappling him to the ground and slashing his throat. Blood spurted over Jancko's face as the man gurgled his last breath. The two men ran for their lives, slithering and tumbling down the loose stones of the mountainside as shouts and shots and a wailing siren rang out. They came to a stream and Olivio pulled Jancko down.

'Submerge yourself. They'll have the dogs on us next. We lose our scent in the water.'

The water was cold enough to freeze their balls off and, wet through, they continued on their desperate escape, fleeing through the pine forest down to the valley. Metres below them an elderly man was up early scything weeds in his meadow. He shaded his eyes with his hand and beckoned to the pair, pointing to a pile of muck as they ran into the open.

'*Venite, venite,*' he called, his voice full of urgency. They watched as he scraped away manure to reveal an old door flat on the ground. 'Hide down here,' he said, lifting the door. 'Quick!' he urged, signalling to them to be quiet, his grimy finger against his mouth barely visible beneath long, grey whiskers.

Olivio and Jancko climbed down a ladder into a hole and the old man replaced the door behind them and in the pitch black they heard the scrape of a spade on wood as he shovelled back the manure cover. Olivio's lighter worked after a couple of attempts and the men stared about them. A pile of grubby blankets lay in one corner and a candle stub in a rusty enamelled holder. This hole had been used before.

'We are trapped now like rats, damn it,' Jancko hissed.

'I know the old man. We can trust him.'

Jancko had been itching for a kill and the guard had presented himself like a human sacrifice. Jancko had saved their lives but Olivio was going to give him a rollicking when they were out of this mess. He was hot-tempered, bent on revenge and at this rate would cause more trouble. For the time being it was best to keep his trap shut and sit it out. They were both shivering, so they stripped off their wet clothes and sat wrapped in a blanket, waiting. Olivio was not so sure they were going to get away with it this time.

CHAPTER 39

Tina

A tangled web we spin

In the concert interval, on the same balmy April night, Bernardo offered to fetch Tina a drink. Last month one of the young German violinists in the quartet had cornered her. Anxious to avoid his amorous advances, she accepted Bernardo's offer. At least she knew how to handle him.

'*Come stai*, Tina? One of these days we must ride out again now your horse is better. I sometimes see you gallop along the meadows.'

She swallowed. How much had he observed of these rides? 'I love to be free,' she said. 'Shall we go outside? It's stuffy in here.'

He took her arm and they sat on the wall that edged the portico outside the theatre. The voices all around were predominantly German and echoed from the arched roof. She wanted to shout to them to go back to their own country, to leave this place in peace. She clung to the memory of a wedding group before the war congregated in this very portico. Everyone was in Sunday best; the children chased each other, holding on to a long white ribbon. She pictured their smiles, the laughter, the dashing groom and beautiful bride in white, her hair threaded with a band of fresh white roses as they held hands and ducked rice thrown by friends and family.

As if echoing her thoughts, Bernardo leant close. 'Italy is not ours anymore, is it?'

She turned to him, surprised. 'I thought you approved of our conquerors?'

The look he gave her was hard to fathom, his eyebrows slightly raised. 'We are not yet conquered and' – he lowered his voice – 'let's say, my thoughts might be not what they were.'

Before the strange conversation could continue, they were interrupted by Donatella calling Tina. She stumbled over to them and put her arms round Tina.

'Such a long time since I've seen you, Tina *cara*. How clever you are. This is the first time I've been to one of these concerts.' She hiccoughed and swayed as she turned to the tall, very young German hovering behind her. 'Meet my new friend, Wolfgang.' She laughed as she mispronounced the name. 'Such a difficult name.' Cupping his pink face she said in slow Italian, 'Why can't you be called Francesco or Gianni or something easier?' Then, pushing her way to sit between Bernardo and Tina she asked, 'Have you heard from Olivio? I know you and he are good friends now. A postcard or anything? Do you know where he is? He's disappeared from the face of the earth. And who is this handsome man?'

Donatella leant into Bernardo. 'At least you're Italian. Where have all our Italian men gone?'

The German soldier stepped forward and, clipping his heels, he bowed as he said, '*Gute Nacht, Fräulein.*'

'No, no, wait for me, Wolfgang,' Donatella cried. As she rose, she rubbed her fingers together and whispered to Tina,

'This one has plenty of dosh. He's a conte, like your papà.' Stepping towards the soldier, now pinker in the face, she tripped and Bernardo moved to catch her before she fell.

'I think it's time to take you home, signorina,' he said. 'We'll speak another time, Tina. But we must have that ride soon.'

In the second half, Tina stumbled over a couple of chords, her mind dwelling on Donatella's indiscreet questions and Bernardo's strange comment. Was he really disillusioned? Or was he trying to trick her into his confidence? Her instincts told her to not trust him. Wasn't that what Olivio always advised? She was grateful when the last bars were over. Thankfully, there were no cries of '*Bis*' at the end, the audience seemingly eager to be on their way without an encore.

Despite the late hour, she wanted to talk to Lu. It had been a while. She had an updated pass in her purse in case she was stopped.

Luisa had taken to locking her back door now after Tina's warnings about her name on Huber's list. She had disturbed an intruder one night: a drunken soldier climbing the stairs to her living quarters. With the shortages, there were plenty of light-fingered and desperately hungry people about looking for anything they could eat or sell. Tina threw stones at her friend's window instead of calling up.

Luisa opened the window and a triangle of light illuminated the cobbled walkway.

'It's only me. Can I come in for a while?'

The window was shut quickly. There were punishments for showing light at night. There were punishments for everything now, Tina thought ruefully. Soon they'd have to ask permission to breathe.

The back door opened a crack and Tina slipped inside.

'What's up?' Luisa asked, pulling her shawl around her long nightdress. 'Come into the kitchen and I'll boil us water for a drink.'

Tina chatted about Olivio, expressing her concern for him. 'He's living in a cave at the moment. I worry for his safety.'

Luisa shook her head. 'He's certainly brave.'

'He was dressed as a friar again. I hardly recognised him. Oh yes, and I saw Donatella tonight. She was drunk and flirting with a *tedesco*. I've never really liked her but now I like her even less.'

'There are other women in town who go with the *tedeschi*. People won't forget when this is all over.'

'Sometimes I think the war will never be over, Lu.'

Luisa's reply was snappy. 'Well, you should stop that thinking. Otherwise, what Olivio and the others are doing, what we are all doing in our own ways, will count for nothing.'

Tina sipped at her brew made from wild fennel seeds. 'I know you're right but being up in the castle, listening to my father and his men – all of them influential in the region, listening and watching that odious German officer who thinks the castle belongs to him, it's overwhelming. Confusing at times… and, oh, I forgot to tell you…' She placed her cup on the table. 'I had the strangest conversation with Bernardo tonight before we were interrupted by Donatella. She was really tipsy and actually asked after Olivio – said he and I were good friends. Bernardo was all ears and he seemed to be saying he's disenchanted with how things are. Should I believe him, do you think?'

'Hm! If he mentions it again, there's no harm in listening. But don't give anything away about what you're up to, obviously. He could be spying but he's most likely hedging his bets. With the *alleati* making their way north, he'll want to make sure he's on the right side of the fence.'

Tina nodded. 'He's suggested we go riding again. And he said he sees me when I'm in the meadows on Baffi. I'm wondering what else he's seen.'

'That's worrying, Tina. But it will look strange if you refuse to ride out with him. I'd say go, but be prudent. If he really is thinking of changing sides, he could be useful, but we need to make absolutely sure where his loyalties lie.'

To her surprise, Bernardo called at the castle early the following morning, suggesting they ride before it rained.

'The sky was red at break of dawn,' he told her.

'I was dead to the world. Tired after the concert.' For a fleeting moment, she wondered why he had been awake so early. Had it anything to do with Donatella, whom he'd rescued the previous evening?

Bernardo helped her tack up Baffi and they took a back path towards his estate. 'There are no checkpoints along this track,' he said, turning to talk to her. 'Not yet, anyhow.'

He urged his stallion into a canter. For a while, Tina had to admit she enjoyed riding with somebody who obviously loved his horse. Baffi enjoyed it too; Tina could feel it in the way he pressed forward, his ears pricked, his head high. It must be lonely for him all alone in the stables. Once upon a time there had been half a dozen in the livery. Papà no longer rode. But she'd caught him caressing Baffi once before climbing into his car.

It was mid-morning when they entered the stable yard behind Podere Fara. For almost an hour her head had been free of worries and there was a smile on her face as she dismounted and patted Baffi. She loosened off his girth, put a head collar over his bridle and Bernardo handed over a hay net for Baffi to munch on.

A German jeep was parked by the stables.

'Do you have an officer staying in your place too, Bernardo?'

He nodded. 'Yes. He's with the Abwehr, military intelligence. Strange chap. He doesn't like to mix much. We tolerate him. Not that we have much choice.'

Bernardo's housekeeper served a platter of bread and prosciutto on the terrace, with two glasses of Chianti.

'*Cin cin*, Tina,' Bernardo said, lifting his glass. 'I have really enjoyed this morning. We must do it again.'

Hungry after the early start and invigorating ride, Tina's mouth was full of ham and white bread. She thought guiltily of Olivio and his hungry men and she resolved to pack provisions for them and ride to the willow as soon as possible to leave them in the hole.

When the housekeeper disappeared into the villa, Bernardo set down his glass on the wrought-iron table.

'Tina, I suggest tomorrow you stay in the castle. There is likely to be increased activity in this area and you won't be safe riding.'

'What do you mean?'

His fingers playing with the stem of his glass, he lowered his voice. 'There will be extra *tedeschi* and *milizia* all over the place. They'll be raking the whole area for *partigiani* and there'll be reprisals for one of their men killed yesterday up on the construction site in the mountains.'

She willed herself to stay calm, her voice steady, but her heart was beating erratically. Why was he telling her this? Whose side was he really on? Was it a trick?

'I hadn't planned on going anywhere, Bernardo, but I shall certainly warn my housekeeper to stay at the *castello* tonight and not return to her house.'

Did he know she was involved with the *partigiani*? How did he suspect? Was it because of Donatella's comments? She absolutely had to warn Olivio and the others to be careful and wondered how best to do this. Olivio didn't go to the tree daily to pick up her messages, so that was pointless. Would the white sheet on her window ledge simply serve to lure him to danger? Her mind working overtime, she was aware Bernardo was talking but she wasn't registering what he was saying.

He leant forward to touch her hand. 'You seem distracted, Tina. Please don't worry about tomorrow. It shouldn't affect you up in the *castello*. I'm sorry if I've alarmed you.'

She shook her head. 'With this war, Bernardo, we're all in a state of perpetual alarm, are we not? But, thank you for your concern.'

Tina waited for a while, continuing to engage in vacuous conversation and then she yawned. 'I'm sorry, Bernardo. I have a headache, I must be sickening for something. The girl who helps us in the kitchen was sneezing all day yesterday. If you don't mind, I'd like to go home.'

'Of course. I'll ride back with you.'

'I'll be fine. There's no need for you to go to Sant'Agnese and back again.'

'I insist. There are too many strangers about. If you're with me, they'll leave you alone.'

The ride back was interminable for Tina and to avoid conversation, she urged Baffi into a gallop the whole way, Bernardo straining to keep up with her.

She ignored his comment about her headache not stopping her from riding like the wind, thanked him and after tethering Baffi to a ring beside the kitchen door, she rushed in to speak to Allegra.

CHAPTER 40

The web closes

Allegra was beating eggs into a mound of flour on the table for pasta and she looked up as Tina stormed into the kitchen.

'*Gesù Maria*, what on earth is the matter?'

Tina paced the room. 'Allegra, you *have* to help me. You're Olivio's aunt. You must have *some* idea where he and Sergio are in the mountains. I can't believe you know nothing. I have to get an *urgent* message to warn them today. It's a matter of life and death. There's to be a raid. They're being hunted in reprisal for the death of a German soldier.'

Allegra abandoned her pasta preparations. 'Wearing out my kitchen floor is not going to help. Come, sit. I'll make you something to eat. I know what you're like when you're hungry. Ever since you were little, you—'

'I am *not* hungry, Allegra. I'm *seriously* worried and we have to hurry. Please try and think where exactly they might be. I absolutely have to get word to them.'

A sound of a plate smashing in the pantry alerted Tina and she strode over and wrenched open the door.

'Nella. Come out from there. Why are you hiding? Were you eavesdropping?'

'No, contessina. Signora Allegra asked me to tidy the shelves, I—'

'Leave her be, Tina. She's a good girl.'

'Were you listening to what I was saying just now?' Tina shook Nella hard and she yelped in pain.

'*Ahi*, contessina, that hurts.'

Allegra came between the pair.

'Shame on you, Tina.'

'If she blabs, then there'll be even more trouble,' Tina said, lifting her hand to threaten the terrified girl.

'Papà knows,' Nella said, her voice barely audible.

'Papà knows what?' Tina asked, still holding the girl in case she fled.

'Let her go,' Allegra intervened. 'I *told* you: she's a good girl.' She lowered her voice. 'Sergio is her brother, Tina. *Calmati!*'

'*What?*' Tina blurted.

'Papà warned us to keep it to ourselves, but I heard you, contessina. If Sergio is in danger, we must tell him.' Nella sank down in tears next to Allegra and the older woman pulled her close.

'Why did nobody tell me this before? That she's Sergio's sister? *Why* the secrecy? I don't understand.' Tina stamped her foot in frustration. Would she ever truly be accepted by anybody in this town? 'You too, Allegra. Why? Why didn't you say?'

'You should know by now we're all related in this town,' Allegra told Tina. 'Olivio is my nephew. You knew that. Sergio's father is my brother. His name is Claudio. *Of course* we know what's going on, where our loved ones are, but we don't talk about it.' Allegra passed a hand across her neck in a cut-throat gesture. 'But now the time has come. Nella, take the contessina to your father but hurry straight back. I need you in the kitchen.'

Nella grabbed her shawl from the peg on the back of the kitchen door and hurried along the alleyway, turning to make sure Tina was keeping up. Her father's bakery was located at the edge of town by the Roman gate and one of the German sentries waved at Nella as she approached.

'*Buona sera*, Nella,' he said, greeting the young girl, his accent clumsy.

'*Buona sera*, Norbert.'

She skirted the back of the building where the aroma of baking bread wafted from an open door.

'He has a sister my age and he's friendly,' Nella explained. 'Papà gives him little cakes. He says it's best to keep on his side.'

Still smarting, Tina couldn't help wondering if this same attitude extended to her too. Best to keep on the contessina's side. You never knew. Oh, where was the sincerity in anything? She knew she shouldn't be taking all this so personally; the most important thing at the moment was to make sure Olivio and the others were aware of the imminent danger. Her feelings shouldn't count, but sometimes she felt like a parasitic cuckoo without a place of her own. Would she ever belong? Would she ever be accepted for who she was? Herself?

A stooped man of middle age, his face and arms coated in ghostly white flour, turned as they entered.

'Why aren't you at work, Nella? Are you sick?' Then, seeing Tina, he inclined his head. '*Buona sera*, contessina. Can I help?'

Tina closed the bakery door. 'Yes, signor Claudio. Nella tells me you know how to reach Sergio and Olivio. They're in great danger. I need to warn them of a *rastrellamento* tomorrow. They're combing the whole area and rounding up absconders and dissidents. Their blood is up at the death of one of their sentries up in the construction camp.'

Claudio turned on his daughter. 'You little vixen. *Puttana troia*. You opened your mouth. I—' He came towards his daughter, his fist raised, and Tina stood in front of the girl.

'Don't be angry with her. It's my fault, signor Claudio. I forced it from her but for good reason and we have no time to waste. Can you take me to Olivio and your son?'

'I cannot drop everything and leave right now, contessina. The guards at the gate, they know my routine. And... how do I even know I can trust you? Your father, *il conte*, he—'

'I do not see eye to eye with my father, despite what people continue to think. Baffi and Focaccia are my friends. I'm on their side and have helped them—'

The baker held up his hands at that. 'Ah! You know their battle names. You must not go round dropping them in your talk. But it's proof enough to me you know what's going on. I'll meet you at the castle entrance tonight at midnight. Come dressed for a climb up the mountains.'

He took a couple of loaves from a pile on the side and thrust them into Tina's hand. 'Take these. Otherwise, the guards will wonder why you're here. *A dopo*. Until later.'

At twenty minutes before midnight, Tina, in dark clothes and walking boots, trod silently to her father's study. He was slumped in his armchair, snoring, a glass held against his stomach, an empty bottle of whisky on its side on the carpet where it had spilled its last dregs. Tina coughed but he didn't stir. She'd noticed his increased drinking since Huber was gone: how he downed entire bottles of his favourite Sangiovese each evening at dinner whilst Lieutenant Tobler looked on in disapproval.

She reached for the key taped beneath the desk drawer and tiptoed to the gun case. Papà's hunting gun would be her weapon. She'd fired it since a young girl on his boar shoots. Still his snores rang out without interruption and she hurried from the study into the night. The sky was star-spangled and there was no sign of Claudio until a shadow moved away from the trunk of a plane tree and stepped forward. His face was blackened and he pulled a rag from his pocket and gestured her to approach. 'Your face shines like the moon. Here!' he said, roughly daubing charcoal dust on her face and hands. 'And careful with that gun. No need to fire it and wake the countryside. Don't talk. Tread lightly. Stop when I stop and move fast,' Claudio instructed.

Tina followed Sergio's father along a back alley she had never used, overgrown with brambles and fallen debris. At the end, he vaulted over a stone wall into the forest. Once or twice Tina's feet slipped on pine needles as they climbed steadily for the next half hour. Claudio stopped stock-still and crouched low at the sound of twigs snapping nearby and she followed suit. A magnificent stag, his horns glinting in the moonlight, bounded further into the trees and they continued on their way.

At one stage they came to a track. When headlights from an approaching truck swept the pine branches lining the road, she followed Claudio's action and dropped face first, her body at one with the leafy forest floor. The truck passed and when it was safe, they dashed across. Within the hour they came to a dead end where a sheer rock face barred further progress. Claudio cupped his hands round his mouth and imitated the sound of an owl, repeating the cry three times. To Tina's astonishment, half a minute later a man shimmied down a creeper and jumped to the forest floor beside them.

Tina held up her gun and Claudio knocked the barrel down. '*Puttana Eva*,' he hissed. 'Bloody hell. No need for that. You're amongst friends. Now tell him what you know.'

'I need to speak to Baffi himself,' Tina said.

A chuckle, followed by the man pulling the scarf from his

face. 'You're looking at him, Tina. What the hell are you doing up here?'

She wanted to hug him in relief. Instead, she kept her emotions in check. 'I need to warn you of a *rastrellamento*. They've planned a raid to search for you.'

'Come,' Olivio ordered. He led the pair to a curtain of creepers and pulled it aside to reveal roughly hewn steps in the rock face. 'Can you manage?' he asked Tina.

It was steep but she was fit and she followed Olivio up the rock edge, Claudio bringing up the rear. Faint light glimmered from within an opening in the cliffside and they were ushered inside. A dozen or more shapes were huddled near the fire and one stood as they approached.

'Papà!'

Claudio pulled his son to his feet and embraced him. Sergio's eyes were wide in astonishment when he recognised her. 'Tina, why are you here?'

Tina filled them in on what Bernardo had told her. 'I don't know what time exactly they're carrying out the raid. He told me it was today and warned me to stay in the castle.'

'Which order I see you obeyed,' Olivio said with a grin. '*Porca boia*, bloody hellfire. There's no telling when they will strike. Could be early morning when they think they can catch us asleep. We can't stay here like sitting ducks. We'll have to disperse. Sergio, wake the others, tell them we're abandoning camp and to carry arms and only the absolute necessary. We leave in fifteen minutes. Put out that fire.'

Turning to Tina, he said, 'I applaud your coming all this way to warn us, but you're a bloody nuisance. We can't nursemaid you if anything happens.'

She pulled her gun round from where it was slung on her back. 'I can look after myself.'

'Have you ever killed a man? Shooting game is very different.'

'If I have to, I shall kill.'

The two stood for a few moments, staring at each other before Claudio broke the silence.

'I'll look after her. I brought her up here and I'll bring her down.'

Further discussion was impossible as the forest was suddenly lit by a searchlight scanning the area below the cave. Tina instinctively covered her eyes, blinded, her heart pounding in terror. It was too late. She had come too late.

An order followed from the mouth of an Italian speaker. 'Come out with hands raised. You are surrounded.'

Olivio held his hand to his mouth and whispered, 'They can't see us up here. It's a bluff.' He pointed behind him and indicated they should crouch and follow him. 'When we reach the peak, we disperse.'

The light continued to strobe the forest, beams playing through the trees and up to the stars but the way to the cave was hidden and the canopy thick. It was hard to step lightly in the undergrowth and each time a twig snapped underfoot, Tina's heart stopped. After the lights came explosions from hand grenades lobbed into the undergrowth below them and then there was a shout.

'Over here, *tenente* Fara. They're up here.'

Her mouth round in horror, Tina understood that one of the aggressors was Bernardo. Had he tailed her? Had he given her the information on purpose so he could follow her? Was it her fault the *partigiani* camp had been discovered? But there was no time for questions. The steps to the cave had been discovered and shots were fired at the first men arriving on the clifftop. She heard Olivio urge everyone: 'Run! Run for your lives. Every man for himself.'

Tina's hand was grasped and she was dragged along through the trees, the sound of gunfire reminding her of fireworks at a *festa*, except this was no celebration and she wanted it to stop. Cries from injured men behind her pierced the air and then the rat-a-tat-tat spewing of a machine gun's bullets hit Claudio and, with a cry of pain and his hand still in hers, he dragged her down into a ditch between a line of holm oaks.

Something grazed her face and pain like she'd never felt exploded in her eyes, her nose, her cheeks as blood filled her mouth so that she was drowning. She felt a huge weight collapse on top of her, the weight of death, and as she fell towards it, a vision of a woman in a long cloak, her red hair loose around her face like flames from the hottest fire filled her head before everything turned black.

CHAPTER 41

Olivio

To the depths

Olivio slithered down the mountainside, always turning to check on Sergio, who, though nimbler with his false leg, was nevertheless still hampered. The friends had the advantage of knowing the rocky terrain like the back of their hands. Much of their childhood had been spent in the forest foraging for mushrooms, hunting for deer, hare and wild boar and now they were making for a smaller cave where they had sheltered from rainstorms in the past, known to themselves as their secret *tana dei lupi*, wolves' den. It was large enough for two adults at the most and they knew wolves sometimes sheltered in there. It was better hidden than the large cave where the *partigiani* had been camping and could only be reached through a narrow cleft between two huge limestone boulders.

As they crouched sharing sips of water from a flask, Olivio prayed Tina, Claudio and the others were safe. In the distance, shouts and an occasional volley of gunshots cracked the night air and each time they flinched. Who was firing and who was in receipt of these bullets was impossible to tell.

'How long are we going to stay holed up here?' Sergio whispered.

'Until darkness falls. We'll take it in turns to get shut-eye. You first, my friend.'

While Sergio slept, Olivio tortured himself with what might have befallen his men. But most of all he worried about Tina. If anything happened to her, he would never forgive himself. Somehow, she must have worked out the identity of his messenger and tracked down Claudio to find them. She was brave, foolhardy maybe. But he himself had told her more than once not to trust easily and she'd obviously wanted to pass on her information face to face instead of leaving it to someone else.

He let Sergio sleep on. With his disability, he expended twice as much energy and as the first dirty light of day stole into the hollow, Olivio studied his friend's face: white with fatigue, etched with pain. He was a good man, never complaining, always the first to volunteer, angry with Olivio if he made allowances, insisting he be treated as an equal. He'd been through a lot. Olivio couldn't imagine having a better man by his side.

After spending another uncomfortable night amongst the bones and droppings the wolves had left on the floor of their lair, their rifles at the ready, Olivio and Sergio emerged cautiously before daylight illuminated the forest. They stood tall to stretch their cramped limbs, listening for sounds of soldiers. Gunfire had ceased hours ago, replaced by birdsong, a nightingale having continued its song of beauty at intervals during the night and

Olivio envied its peaceful existence. They split up, making their way in parallel but metres apart, and crept through the trees, turning this way and that to ensure they were alone.

Olivio heard Sergio's warning whistle, his imitation of a siskin's call, and hid behind a tree, peering through the foliage to check the reason. On a rock ten metres in front of Sergio two *tedeschi* sat, smoke from their cigarettes spiralling in the air. They had their backs to the two *partigiani* and as far as Olivio could see, were alone.

Pulling out his knife, he gestured to Sergio, who armed himself similarly and when Olivio held up his hand and silently counted down his fingers, the two men lunged forwards, gripping each soldier by the throat and slicing through the skin in a single motion. It was over before it had begun, without a single shot fired.

And then, they saw what the soldiers had been guarding: a dozen or so bodies scattered around this place, their last moments frozen in time.

Jancko, so powerful in life, was now nothing more than a lifeless puppet, flies feeding on stumps where legs had been. Olivio moved to close his comrade's eyes that stared blankly to the green canopy. There were six more of his men amongst three *tedeschi* and a couple of *milizie*, the axe insignia on their caps ugly symbols befitting death.

He heard Sergio cry out, '*Noooooo*, Papà,' his hands stretched before him as he stopped over another body. Olivio watched in pity and anger as Sergio fell to his knees over his dead father. He made the sign of the cross and moved over to pat his friend's shoulder. There were no words as they gazed, horrified, at the older man's body. At first, Olivio thought the red he could see on the forest floor was the rust of dried blood from Claudio but awful realisation dawned and, his turn to cry out in horror, he dropped to his knees.

Tina's hair, her beautiful rich-auburn hair. It was snagged beneath Claudio's body, her features undistinguishable in a mess of blood that had once been her face. He felt for her hand – cold as ice – and in that moment, his fury knew no bounds.

At the sounds of men marching up the forest track, the two young men tore themselves away from the carnage.

'When it's safe we'll return to bury our dead. I promise this, Sergio. But for now, we return to Sant'Agnese. The bastards will never expect us to go back to town.'

Nothing was expected or normal any longer. The pair followed animal paths down to Sant'Agnese, their hearts heavy. Somebody had betrayed them. Or Tina and Claudio had been careless and allowed themselves to be followed as they'd made their way up to the camp. Consumed with guilt, he vowed to avenge her death and the death of all his men. Revenge was all he had left.

Back at the *castello*, Allegra was beside herself. Tina's bed had not been slept in. She had searched the garden. Maybe the crazy girl had decided to sleep under the stars in her happy place. But, no, the garden was empty save for Tigressa curled up on a pile of sacking in the greenhouse and a robin chirping madly from its nest in the arbour.

'Where is she, Tigressa?' she asked, bending stiffly to stroke the cat, who stretched, arched her back and then settled down again.

She hurried to the bakery to talk to Nella but she wasn't around, so next stop was the *farmacia* where she found Luisa tending her silkworms in the back room.

'She might be out riding with Bernardo,' Luisa suggested. 'She's been seeing him recently.'

Allegra shook her head. 'She went off with Nella's father to warn Olivio but she's not returned. Her horse has been in his stable all this time. Something's wrong, Luisa. I'm really worried.'

Luisa frowned. 'Maybe she's fallen and hurt herself. I'll go and look in the forest. You stay up at the castle, Allegra, and wait. I'll be quicker by myself.'

As Allegra trudged up the hill, she had to stand back as a fleet of cars swept up the road towards the castle, swastika pennants streaming on the bonnets. Something was afoot. She quickened her pace.

The cars were parked on the castle forecourt and the huge front doors wide open. Allegra slipped inside. Two German officers, accompanied by Lieutenant Tobler, stood in the hall as well as half a dozen *milizia*, their red and gold badges prominent on their uniforms. She noticed Bernardo amongst their number.

'We need to talk, conte,' Allegra heard Tobler say. His voice was steely and the conte was quick to reply.

'Of course. Come to my study.'

In the confusion, Allegra was overlooked as she hovered by the open study door.

'A number of our men were killed in a skirmish last night when they came across a band of *banditi*,' she heard the major say. 'Unless the perpetrators come forward within the next hour, there will be severe consequences. You are to make an announcement outside the *comune* immediately to explain the situation to your townspeople.'

'One hour is very short notice, Lieutenant Tobler.'

'One hour is all the notice you have, conte.'

'I think we should search these premises too, Lieutenant,' Bernardo said, stepping forward.

Ferdinando was indignant. 'I shall not permit this. I am a loyal member of the *partito fascista.*'

'We have to ensure nobody has slipped in to hide here. I suggest, conte, that you hurry along to warn your townspeople,' Bernardo replied.

'*Our* townspeople,' Ferdinando corrected, his face thunderous.

Allegra frowned and hurried down to her kitchen to make sure she had properly closed the shelving-entrance in the pantry. This had something to do with Tina going missing. *Ahimè*. Where was she? The world was going crazy. Her poor old heart strained with anxiety.

When a couple of young *milizia* soldiers clattered down the kitchen stairs, she stood, barring the way, her arms crossed in front of her bosom. 'If you make a mess in here, *ragazzi*, there will be trouble. I know your mother, Gino, and I'll have something to say to her too when I see her in the piazza.'

'Don't worry, signora,' the brawnier one called Gino said, stepping past her and picking up a *cantuccino* almond biscuit cooling on the rack. He popped it whole into his mouth. 'I'm sure there's nothing in here, but our orders are to check.'

Allegra stuffed half a dozen biscuits in a paper bag and poured them cups of lukewarm coffee from the pot on the *stufa*, willing her hands to stop shaking. 'Have some *caffè-caffè* and then be off with you.'

They beamed at the treat and left after opening the door to the pantry, glancing cursorily at the lines of mostly empty jars of flour.

'Nothing in here,' Gino said. '*Grazie*, signora, and I'll pass on your best wishes to Mamma.'

After they'd gone, their hobnailed boots noisy up the steps, Allegra sank into a chair, her hands shaking so much she had to clasp them together. For a moment, she'd feared her distraction techniques would imply there was something to hide but her baking was famous in town and her *cantuccini* had done the trick. Where on earth was Tina? What had happened to her? She hurried down to her house where she joined her hands in prayer to ask the blessed Vergine Maria and all the saints in heaven to protect her special charge. Maybe Luisa would soon be back with good news. She must not let her imagination work overtime. All would be well. Please, God, all would be well.

The shooting in town started within two hours.

The first shots were fired by Tobler up in the castle where he strode into the library and aimed his gun at the conte's head. Before he climbed into the jeep, his eyes steely cold, he dispatched Baffi too.

By the end of the killing spree, thirty-six innocent civilians of Sant'Agnese were added to the tally of six dead *partigiani* and the four German soldiers and Italian militia up in the mountain forest. Neighbours two doors down from the *farmacia* recounted how Luisa had been dragged from her shop, beaten and kicked where she lay bruised and bloody in the road, German soldiers shouting at her: '*Tu dire dove banditi? Dove partigiani? Sporca ebressa. Juden.*' Their Italian was incorrect but the message was only too clear as they cursed her for being a dirty Jew, blood pouring from her mouth as they beat her over and over trying to extract a confession, urging her to tell them where the *partigiani* were hiding. Nobody came to her aid, fearful for their own lives as they cowered beneath their beds, children pulled close to parents as they waited for the nightmare to end.

Neither were infants or the elderly spared or two invalids in the doctor's infirmary. They were pulled from their sick beds and shot. A woman's body lay on top of her baby by the front door where a ribbon announcing his birth still hung crisp and blue. When his tormented mother cried for mercy as she cradled her infant, she was dispatched with a single bullet to her temple.

Little Nella in the bakery was shot where she worked, her blood coating loaves she was setting to prove. Paolino was shot as he ran across the piazza to warn her to hide. The butchers went from house to house with death in mind to avenge their fallen comrades and there was nothing anybody could do to stop the massacre.

Afterwards, even the birds fell silent and the stench of cordite hung over the town. The bodies were collected by the *nazifascisti* and taken to the bridge where they were laid out one by one as a terrible warning to the rest of the inhabitants of Sant'Agnese.

But Luisa's body was hung from a lamp post and the letter J daubed in yellow paint on her blood-soaked clothes. Her feet were bare and her life-blood trickled down her toes to splash on the wall of the bridge as her body swayed in the wind that funnelled along the river.

The dead lay in the open for three days, despite the priest entreating Lieutenant Tobler to let them be buried. On the fourth day, the remaining citizens of Sant'Agnese, word having passed between them, exited their houses en masse. *Padre* Tommaso knocked on each door, as he progressed through the silent town, holding the crucifix from the church aloft as the mourners processed to the *questura*, the local police station, where *milizia* and *tedeschi* had set up headquarters.

'You will have to shoot all of us,' *padre* Tommaso declared, his voice unwavering as his words rang out over the piazza, 'but I insist we bury our dead. What you have done is against the conventions of war and when this war is over, you will all be held to account. And God spare your souls.'

Despite the machine guns aimed at them, the people of Sant'Agnese stood firm, their eyes fixed on the crucifix depicting the agony of Christ held up by the little priest whose voice echoed across the piazza as he recited Pater Noster over and over. After one hour, Lieutenant Tobler relented.

'You have until midnight to do what you have to do.'

The door slammed behind him as he returned inside the town hall and preparations for burial commenced immediately. Allegra cornered the elderly priest and explained how the daughter of conte Ferdinando was missing; she believed she was up in the mountains and he promised her he would find help.

The two young men *padre* Tommaso sent to Allegra were militia, sickened by what they had witnessed in the last hours. They had presented themselves to the priest in his presbytery with a crying baby swaddled in a shawl and confessed how, in shame, they had pulled the child from beneath his dead mother's body and retreated from the murderous fray. He handed the infant to his housekeeper and sent these young men to Allegra. She insisted on accompanying them up the mountain track and they were patient, putting their arms around her to guide her on, each perhaps reminded of their own grandmothers, their guilt spurring them to drag any remaining morsel of goodness from their damaged souls.

When they found Tina in the dirt beneath Claudio's body, Allegra collapsed to her knees, pulling out her rosary to pray over her darling charge, smoothing back the blood-encrusted hair from Tina's mangled face. She cried silently, kissing Tina's forehead over and over, the only part of her face not caked in dried blood.

For a moment she was confused when she felt the slightest of breaths. It was the mountain breeze playing with her, she told herself, but she pressed her ear to Tina's chest and yes, there was the faintest of movements. She felt for a pulse on the girl's neck and, oh *Vergine Maria e tutti i santi*, it was a miracle.

Her eyes glistening, she called to the two young men standing respectfully at a distance. 'Help me. *Aiutatemi!* She is alive. We must get her back to my house. Be careful. Be quick. She's alive.'

And in all the town's confusion of mourners scurrying here and there, the church filling with hastily made coffins nailed together from any wood the townspeople could spare – floorboards, tabletops, wood put by in stables and stores – and amidst the mourning and lamenting, the tolling of bells in the church tower of San Francesco, nobody noticed Allegra and two young men in civilian clothes, their *milizia* uniforms discarded, slip into Allegra's house below the castle with their burden. After they had carried Tina to the bedroom and stayed to help heat water and take buckets upstairs for the old lady, Allegra extracted a final duty of them.

'You are to tell nobody how you helped me this day. And, for your own good, I suggest you get yourselves far from Sant'Agnese. Once this town has buried its dead, there will be lynchings. You will not be safe anywhere in the vicinity.'

When they were gone, Allegra locked her door and started her nursing of Tina, first gently dropping water and soft bread into her mouth. It had been four days since Tina would have had nourishment – a miracle she had survived.

Allegra bathed her ruined face with warm water, gently removing dirt and hardened blood to reveal a gaping wound across her ravaged face. It stretched from cheek to cheek, across her smashed nose and near her mouth where a bullet had torn through her flesh, mercifully missing her eyes.

Tina winced and muttered as Allegra worked and the old lady spoke in soothing tones as if to a fretful child while inside, she seethed with rage. She used lotions of wormwood and nettles to disinfect, as well as honey from her own bees and bound the wound with clean cloths. But she knew it needed stitching. Dirt from the forest floor had seeped in and she feared infection. Ordinarily she would have fetched Luisa but Luisa was gone and she wept as she thought of the way that lovely young woman had been treated. Man's cruelty over these past days had sunk far beyond the imaginable. The little town of Sant'Agnese would never be the same again.

After spooning more water and some light chicken broth through Tina's parched lips, she whispered to the girl to sleep. She would be back soon.

The doctor was not at his infirmary and a woman mopping up the mess in the tiny ward told her she should go to the presbytery where *dottor* Brilli was tending to many more wounded.

'He reckoned it's safer there, with *padre* Tommaso to protect them all. But, if you ask me, nobody will ever be safe in this cursed town.'

Allegra waited for more than an hour for the exhausted doctor to finish his rounds. Despite his fatigue, he fetched what he needed and, carrying his leather medical bag, followed Allegra to her house on the edge of town.

He shook his head as he removed Tina's bindings. 'She should really be in hospital and have a surgeon see to this. But I shall do the best I can. I have no anaesthetic left. Do you have *grappa*, signora?'

Allegra shook her head but fetched the remains of her strong walnut *liquore* and together they held Tina and encouraged her to drink two glasses, the girl spluttering and complaining as they poured the drink into her sore mouth.

'It's for your own good, contessina,' *dottor* Brilli said. '*Bevi, bevi*. Drink it up. Hold the candle high, signora.'

The gash was wide and crooked and the stitching painful. Allegra held fast to Tina's hand, the candlestick in her other, the doctor tutting as he worked, muttering under his breath that not even wild animals would behave like these beasts had done.

After three quarters of an hour, it was finished. 'You must keep this scrupulously clean, signora. And come to me immediately if you fear infection.'

He would not accept payment, shaking his head as he left. 'When all this is over, we shall do our reckonings.'

Allegra fetched a pile of blankets and slept on the floor beside Tina day and night until the worst was over. On the seventh day, Allegra was happy that no infection had set in. She arranged the pillows so Tina could sit up and she managed a whole bowl of broth. Afterwards, Tina asked her what had happened, her words distorted with the pain of moving the damaged muscles on her face.

When she heard about the killings, about Luisa, Claudio, Nella, young Paolino and the many other people she had known in Sant'Agnese, she whispered, 'Tell me I am having a nightmare, Allegra. Tell me.'

'Yes, you are having a nightmare. But the nightmare is real.'

'And Olivio? Sergio?'

'Who knows, *carissima*. Who knows?'

Tina turned quiet, her face to the wall and as there were no words Allegra could find, no words of comfort that could possibly change anything or lessen the horror, she left Tina for a while.

'I have to go up to the *castello*. Your father will be needing to eat and I shall fetch provisions and clothes to bring back here for you. I shan't be long. Rest now, my child.'

The front door to the castle was shut and Allegra made her way to the back to let herself in her kitchen. Flies buzzed on a chicken carcass she had set aside to make broth days ago and she tutted at the waste, throwing it in the bin. Half a stale loaf and the remains of a hunk of pecorino cheese sat on the table together with an empty wine bottle. Her master must have grabbed supper for himself. He would be very hungry by now. She climbed the stairs to his study. Doubtless he would be furious at her absence but she could take that. She would listen to his chastisements and let them go over her head. Little mattered to her except restoring Tina to health.

There were more flies buzzing at the library window. She tutted again. He must have eaten up here and left food lying about. She moved to open the windows and then she saw him: his head slumped forward where he was collapsed in his armchair, legs splayed, one arm hanging over the armrest and... the blood.

Allegra stopped, her hands to her mouth as she gazed in horror at her dead master.

CHAPTER 42

Tina

Tina lingered for weeks in her bed. She had been too ill to attend her own father's funeral but even if she had, what did she feel for the man who had kept back her freedom for so many years, who had sided with Mussolini, who had worked with the Germans – the people who murdered her friends, half the village? She couldn't spill tears for him. The tears would be for what he had denied her. As time passed, all she wanted was to anaesthetise herself with sleep. Allegra tried to coax her into conversation but she had nothing to talk about. And it was hard to talk anyway, her face tight and her mouth not functioning properly, the few words she managed barely intelligible so that Allegra had to lean close to listen to understand.

'It's like when you were a toddler,' the old lady said, trying to be jolly, trying to cajole a response.

'*Stanca*. Tired,' Tina said and turned to the wall, her back to Allegra, who sighed and left the room to prepare whatever dish she thought Tina might fancy: her favourite nettle dumplings or delicate home-made *cappelletti* pasta swimming in rich chicken broth. Tina knew she was behaving badly but why should she bother to behave well? What was the point? Each night she prayed that morning would not arrive, that sleep would take her somewhere better, but each morning she was woken by Allegra bustling into her room, opening the shutters to let daylight stream through.

'A fine summer's day, Tina *mia*, the sun is shining. It's high time you left your bed. I need to change your sheets and you need a bath, young lady. You're beginning to smell like *fossa* cheese maturing in the cellars of Sant'Agnese.'

Finally, Tina let herself be washed. Allegra knelt by the bathtub to gently rub her hair with rosemary and rose-petal scented soap. Allegra kept up her patter, refusing to give up where others would have long since. Tina knew it was pointless to stop her but she had devised a way of switching off, Allegra's words blending into a fuzzy background. If it made the old lady happy to fuss about her, then so be it.

Months later, Allegra swept into Tina's bedroom and flung open the shutters. 'It's a beautiful sunny morning, Tina, and your scar is healing well. Maybe we should step downtown and take a stroll. Or if not that, I'll make us a flask of coffee to carry to your garden. The weeds will be up to our knees by now, strangling your beautiful roses.'

'Garden,' Tina said and Allegra halted, her eyes wide.

'*Brava, bravissima, Tina mia. Bella tu sei qual sole.* You're as beautiful as the sun and you've made my day.'

Tina's legs were wobbly and her head spun as she took her first shaky steps. Allegra found her a walking stick.

'I'm like an old lady,' Tina said, steadying herself on the handrail of Allegra's narrow stairs.

'Well, that makes two of us. *Su! Coraggio.* Slowly! One step at a time. *Pian piano.*'

There was nobody about as usual at their end of town and they would not have recognised Tina anyway, wrapped as she was in one of Allegra's old cloaks like a *vecchietta*, an old woman, her hood pulled forwards to cover her poor face. They stopped for a moment to lean against the low wall along the drive and Tina lifted her face to the sun, breathing in the fresh air as the joyful song of the robin, perched high in the branches of the umbrella pines, filled the air.

'*Brava!* Let the rays heal your scar,' Allegra said, leaning in to arrange the folds of the hood so that more of Tina's scar was exposed.

As they continued along the drive, a flash of orange fur emerged from behind the low wall and Tina laughed as another three orangey bundles appeared behind her.

'*Tigressa, che brava!* Clever girl! More babies.' Tina chuckled as she bent to fondle the kittens before they scampered ahead of the two women, Tigressa keeping a watchful, motherly distance.

Baffi's stall was empty and Tina averted her eyes. Allegra had told Tina of his death, explaining she had no idea how it had happened. Tina wondered if her father had dispatched the horse before he'd turned his gun on himself. Had his death even been suicide? Perhaps somebody else had done the deed: Lieutenant Tobler or one of his men? Who knew?

The two women made their way into the garden via the pantry entrance, the kitchen cold and dusty, the shelf unit stiff and swollen as they worked it open after the long winter.

Tina stopped in her tracks at the sound that met her in the garden. It was as if the birds had conspired to compose a welcome, for a choir of blackbirds, robins, chiff-chaffs and sparrows were chirruping an almighty chorus in the branches, diverting her view from the tangled mess below. She took a deep breath and turned to thank Allegra.

'It was a good idea to come, Allegra *cara. Grazie.*'

Allegra beamed a smile. 'I'll make us a *caffè-caffè*,' she said, turning to leave Tina alone. 'I remember where I hid the last packet. We'll celebrate.'

While she waited, Tina sat on the stone seat and gazed around. The garden had been abandoned for months but maybe she could manage a little tidying each day to bring it back to a semblance of what it once had been. She would start by pruning her roses. There'd been nights lately when she'd woken to their powerful scent and yet, there'd been no vase of roses in the room in Allegra's house. The perfume had dragged her temporarily from a bleak place that swamped her brain, fleeting images of the flowered garden replacing horrific images of the night on the mountain when she was close to death.

Olivio had helped her so much in this place. She rose, her legs still wobbly and, using Allegra's stick, she wandered slowly to the greenhouse. Only a couple of sacks remained from the pile and she remembered how she had used them to cover Olivio when she'd found him half starved, full of fever and later, how she'd helped him and Sergio wrap and bury the guns in a box for his *partigiani*. Where was Olivio now? Allegra had told her he hadn't been among the dead. Neither was Sergio. Where were they? Would they return to Sant'Agnese once this war was over? Were they even alive? Was it too much to hope they had survived?

She took the secateurs from a hook on the wall and once outside, she started to prune her favourite red and yellow China roses. Some of the petals fell into the fountain pool and as she bent to clear them, she caught sight of the reflection of an old woman in the water. She was ugly, her face grossly distorted, and Tina shrank back in horror.

The woman had hair the colour of burnt sienna and Tina drew near the water again, running her own fingers down her hair and watching the same action in mirror image. Tina touched her face where her skin was puckered and the woman in the water did the same. The realisation of being this old woman was a shock. Allegra's room had no dressing table, no hand mirror and Allegra had cared totally for her over the months, helping her with her toilet, washing her, brushing her hair. Once again, Tina touched her scar, her finger tracing the deep furrow across her face that had pulled her features into somebody else's. For an instant, she tried to convince herself it was simply the action of the water crimping the surface as it fell from the dolphin's mouth into the fountain basin. But she knew it wasn't so. She remained there staring at her image and that was how Allegra found her when she set down her tray.

'*Ma cosa fai?* What are you doing?'

'I hadn't realised,' Tina answered. 'I hadn't realised my face was so bad. *Dottor* Brilli saved my life but' – she ran her fingers across the puckered scar – 'he couldn't save my face.'

Allegra pulled her gently away from the pool and led her to the seat. 'But you are still *you*, my darling Tina. *Carissima,*' she said, taking Tina's hands in her own and tenderly kissing the tips of her fingers one by one.

'I am ugly.'

'You are *you.*'

Tina shook her head and after some moments she said, 'Thank you, Allegra. Thank you for not telling me time will heal.' She ran her fingers again over the scar. 'I don't want to be told lies.'

'Your hair is so beautiful, *carissima*. Maybe if you grow a *frangetta*, and arrange your beautiful hair round your face.' Allegra fussed with Tina's curls and Tina stopped her, holding the old lady's hand.

'It's all right, Allegra. No need to say anything. I can cover myself with a scarf; there are cosmetics. But... I need time to get used to it. Let's drink your delicious *caffè-caffè* and talk of something else. Where shall I start on my garden?'

She poured the coffee for Allegra, whose cheeks glistened with tears.

'Don't cry, Allegra. I have my legs and arms, my feet and hands, my head to think with. I'm alive and I don't know how to thank you for everything you've done to help me.' She put down her cup and pulled Allegra to her and they stayed for a while in each other's arms.

They sat quietly. The birds had quietened too and Tigressa lay by Tina's feet, her kittens suckling. In the midst of turmoil, it was a moment of peace.

Over the rest of the summer and into winter, the two women survived as best they could in Allegra's little house, taking life day by day, keeping to themselves. Lieutenant Tobler and his men had left Sant'Agnese at the end of September 1944 before news of the liberation of nearby Sarsina was announced.

The *alleati* had arrived in their jeeps and tanks and women welcomed them by throwing flowers and blowing kisses. The garish red and black swastika flags were ripped down all over the town, fascist emblems removed and defaced from doors of supporters. But it felt impossible to Tina to join the celebrations, with the loss of so many weighing her thoughts.

The *alleati* remained throughout winter and a British army captain took over the room that Tobler had occupied in the castle, on the understanding his own orderly should rustle up meals for him and do his laundry. Allegra had enough on her hands.

Captain Jimmy Metcalfe was a jovial, rotund man in his early forties and had a smattering of Italian. Before the war he had holidayed in Tuscany and told them he had a fondness for their beautiful country. When Tina and Allegra had shown him round the castle, between them they had made themselves understood.

'The war will be over soon and I mean to visit Siena and Florence. I love all the Madonnas,' he told Tina. 'Let's hope Jerry hasn't stolen them all. There'll be a fair bit to sort out at war's end. Our task will not be easy.'

'I'd like to believe you about the war ending,' Tina said. 'But I don't seem to be able to share your optimism, Captain.'

He paused. 'You've had it rough, signorina.'

Involuntarily, she touched the scar on her face. 'Others have fared worse,' she said, turning away from him.

Tina ventured to her precious garden once or twice but she preferred to stay with Allegra. The *castello* was now rightfully hers with the passing of her father but it was a place of bitter memories and no longer felt like home, especially with Captain Metcalfe and his orderly making use of it.

On a fresh spring day in late April when Allegra popped to the *alimentari* to see if there was flour, she heard rumours in the piazza that war might soon be over. But the two women had heard talk like this before and they gave it little credence. However, at breakfast the following morning, an unaccustomed noise broke the silence.

'*Dio!* The bells,' Allegra said, spilling her coffee made from ground chicory roots, the *caffè caffè* long since finished. 'They have only tolled in all these years when padre Tommaso rang them for the mass funeral. Could it really be true this war is over? *Madonna buona* and all the *santi.*' She made the sign of the cross and started to pace the kitchen.

'Let's go into town and find out,' Tina suggested.

They walked slowly, supporting each other and as they approached the archway into the piazza, the noise of people shouting and cheering was deafening.

More British tanks and jeeps had rolled into the piazza and there was a party atmosphere in the little town.

'*È finita. La guerra è finita.* They've signed a treaty at Caserta. *Evviva!* Hurrah! The war is truly over.'

People were hugging, dancing, children thrown into the air as bells continued to ring out as if for a thousand weddings. The owner of the *osteria* dragged a large *damigiana* of wine into the piazza. '*Offro io.* Wine's on me today,' he shouted as he siphoned it into outstretched metal cups and billycans held out by smiling soldiers and townspeople.

The place pulsated with happiness and relief but there were women crying too and some of the youngest of children, bewildered by this unaccustomed merry-making, hid under tables or behind skirts.

Allegra was greeted by some women who glanced away when they saw Tina.

Tina pulled her shawl across her face. She would have to grow used to this reaction to her wounds.

CHAPTER 43

Turncoats

Several days later, Tina told Allegra it was time she returned to the *castello* to stand on her own two feet.

'I can't stay with you forever, Allegra. I must look after myself and you deserve a well-earned rest.'

'But how will you cope?'

'What do you mean how will I cope? It's only my face that's changed. Of course I shall cope. And I shall come and visit you in a few days' time. Don't fret so.'

She refused to let Allegra accompany her. 'I shall begin as I mean to continue.'

Allegra started her off with a few last-minute offerings stuffed into a basket: 'Some *tortelli* with my spinach and potato filling, preserved zucchini, a bag of potatoes and half a fresh loaf.'

Tina hugged the old lady and made her way up the hill, turning to wave goodbye at the end of the alleyway. It was like departing on a long journey and she sensed Allegra would watch until she could no longer see her.

The castle was empty, chilly and damp despite the sunshine outside and her footsteps echoed in the silence. After depositing Allegra's gifts on the larder shelves, she rolled up her sleeves to tidy the kitchen. She was pleased Allegra was not there to witness the grease-spattered stove, burnt pans, cracked dishes and muddy footprints left by their billeted English guests on Allegra's usually spotless kitchen floor. Her English governess had taught her a saying about the Englishman's home being his castle. Well, the *inglesi* had certainly done what they wanted in Castello Montesecco and not cleared up behind them when they'd left for their next posting. If she was to eat, then she must clean up and light the cooking stove.

It took more than four attempts to light the damn thing. Eventually, Tina had to remove all the wood she'd optimistically piled in and start again, running to her garden to find kindling scattered beneath the trees. By the time a decent blaze was going, it was almost midday. She was exhausted and hadn't started to tick off jobs she'd mentally compiled: cleaning away cobwebs, making up her bed with fresh sheets, listing the food she needed to buy in. The supply of wood in the log basket was low and that would need to be replenished. And she hadn't started to think about preparing a hot meal. Exhausted and daunted, she now understood how much Allegra had done to keep this place running. Oh, how she had taken her for granted.

The next day, with the larder empty, Tina decided to go into Sant'Agnese to shop. Her clothes no longer fitted after her months of recuperation and when she looked at herself in the mirror, she hardly recognised the girl she'd been. It was not only the distorted features of her face, it was her stick arms and bony shoulders apparent beneath her clothes. Her hair was the same: her crowning glory, Allegra had always described it, so she chose not to cover herself with a shawl for her outing and let her hair hang loose around her face as Allegra had suggested. She would hold her head high and confront the world as she was. 'Take me or leave me,' she muttered as she strode down the hill.

The sun was shining, the sky a cerulean blue, and everything was fine until Tina arrived in the piazza. A group of women were washing clothes at the fountain, their laughter and chatter drifting across the square as they pounded their laundry, occasionally breaking into song. As she stepped towards them and uttered a cheery, '*Buongiorno*, signore,' they fell silent and stared at her before muttering to each other. She caught snatches of what they said: 'It *was* her, wasn't it? How does she have the cheek to make an appearance? What a nerve.' One of them spat on the floor and, one by one, the women picked up their bundles of washing and walked away.

Tina wondered what they were talking about. If it was the scar on her face, then they were being excessively rude and unkind. She made her way to *l'ammasso*, the community store, to buy her groceries. A queue of customers chatted while they waited to be served. The man in front turned to greet her and his expression changed. He prodded the woman next to him. '*È lei.* It's her.'

Silence fell as they were served and once again she asked herself what was up. What had she done? Was it something to do with her father, perhaps? She wanted to tell them she was no *fascista*, had never been despite her father's politics, but it would sound disrespectful after his death. She held her tongue and waited her turn. But no matter what she requested, the shopkeeper muttered it was *finito*. He had no coffee, no sugar, the bread was reserved. He was sorry but he couldn't serve her. She'd seen with her own eyes the goods the customers were able to buy. He wasn't telling the truth.

She left with an empty basket and walked over to the little bar in the corner where she met with the same treatment. There was no coffee today. Tina knew it was rare for women to frequent bars on their own. Maybe that was why the greeting in here was so hostile. This surely couldn't be the real reason. Why was she being treated like this?

She walked slowly across the piazza, feeling everyone's eyes upon her. A woman leaning from a window slammed her shutters to and then she found herself surrounded by a mob of children. They encircled her, pulling faces, sticking out their tongues, calling her a witch, telling her to go away and never come back and the treatment by such innocent youngsters was more upsetting than the adults who had shunned her.

Allegra's little house was on her route back to the castle and she knocked on her door.

'How wonderful, Tina. I didn't expect a visit so soon. Come in, come in. There's coffee and *ciambella* I made this morning. Your favourite sponge cake.'

The warmth in the little kitchen, tomato sauce bubbling in a pot on Allegra's stove, the cheery greeting was enough to set Tina off. She collapsed into a chair, her empty basket on the floor beside her, head in her hands.

'*Ma, che cosa ti è successo?*' Allegra asked. 'What has happened to you? Oh, but you're not ready to look after yourself yet. It's too much. I feared this might happen.'

Tina shook her head. 'Yes, I'm useless domestically, Allegra. You'll have to show me how to do so many things. I can learn, but—' She wiped a tear from her face with her sleeve and Allegra fetched a clean tea cloth.

'What has happened? Does your face hurt? We can go to the doctor—'

'It's not that.' She sipped the coffee Allegra set down before her. 'In town. The people. They... hate me for some reason. I was treated badly by everyone. What have I done?'

Allegra sat down opposite. 'Maybe it was because of your appearance. People can be ignorant.'

'It was more than that. As if they blame me for something.

What do you know, Allegra? Maybe it's because of Papà. He was never popular.'

'I do know there have been witch hunts to hunt out any remaining *nazifascisti*. There was a lynching in the next village. The war has churned everybody up. But, leave it with me. I'll see what I can find out.'

'I feel weak crying like this. But it was such a shock.'

'You've been ill for a long time. You have to take it steady.'

Tina sat for a few moments to compose herself, thinking how lucky she was to have Allegra care for her. She was quite alone in the world but as her breathing slowed, she was filled with determination to move forwards. Allegra in her usual practical way was right. She needed a little more time.

'Allegra, would you consider coming to me for a couple of hours each day until I learn how to do all the jobs you've always done for me? I need to learn for myself.'

Allegra beamed. '*Ma certo, carissima*. Of course I can.'

Part of Tina felt ashamed that she needed to rely on Allegra. But they could help each other: they had both been through so much and only had each other left. Whatever the people of Sant'Agnese had against her, she would get to the bottom of. She was not giving up yet even though she feared there might be worse to come.

CHAPTER 44

Fiammetta

A sense of purpose is a sense of self

My child, you are a bird with wounded wings and for a while you must stay near your nest to heal and grow strong. I yearn to take your pain, to carry you under my wings but I cannot, my darling girl. It is not time. Be brave. Listen to Allegra. Learn. Grow. Do not give up.

There were times as a young bride when I wanted to end it all and throw myself from the castle battlements. Since childhood I had sleepwalked. I needed to be outside, uncaged. My mother was always gentle, sensing where to find me, coaxing me lovingly back to my bed. She knew not to wake me but she always told me afterwards what had happened. Your father was less understanding. He accused me of inventing stories, shouted at me and said I was feigning sleepwalking, doing it on purpose to escape from his bed.

One night, I woke from my trance to find myself standing on the castle wall along the drive. Snow lay thick on the ground and *in my white nightdress I was an angel, the crisp wind billowing the material about me like wings. I was about to let go and soar above the countryside to be reunited with my family in Petrella, when something tugged at the material, pulling me from the castle wall and I fell backwards onto something soft. It was Nero, your father's dog, and he was whining softly and licking me, tugging at my nightdress to pull me with him inside the castle. He saved me that night. That hound loved me more than he loved his master. It was by my side he always curled, resting his head on my feet when we sat in the parlour after dinner, Your father used to reprimand me. 'You're spoiling him, Fiammetta. He will be no good for hunting if you turn him soft.' Then, he would snap his fingers and remove the dog and lock him in his kennel in the castle yard for the night. Whenever your father was away, I would fetch poor Nero and allow him to lie curled up on my bed. I was his friend and he was my friend and guardian.*

The world seems bleak right now, my tesoro, *my darling My people shunned you in the piazza and wounded you with harsh comments but they do not know what really happened on that dreadful day in the mountains. It was not your fault that they lost their loved ones in the cruel massacre. Search for the truth,* tesoro, *my darling. And search for small signs to bring you back to a better state of mind: the beauty of a leaf gilded with frost, a ray of sun dancing through the trees after grey days, snowdrops, daffodils and tulips thrusting through the hard ground to meet the sun's early warmth, delicate creamy yellows of first primroses. Stay close to Allegra and her kind soul that instinctively prompts her to heal your heart with kindness. The world seems bleak but you will find the truth if you persist. Do not give up, my darling child. You are a bird with wounded wings but one day you will mend and soar again. Attend to your garden, let your favourite place restore your soul. Make new plans. It will pass.*

CHAPTER 45

Tina

The quest begins

'They *what?*' Tina stood, legs apart, floury hands in the air, covered with the sticky dough she had been kneading for the weekly bread supply. 'They think it was all my fault? Where did they get that crazy idea from?' She undid her pinafore and flung it towards the back of the kitchen chair. 'Right! I am going down right now to the piazza and I'm going to give them what for.'

'That will do no good, my girl,' Allegra said, retrieving the pinafore from where it had slid to the floor. 'They are convinced it was you who informed on the *partigiani* and caused the deaths. And it's going to take more than you shouting in the piazza to convince them otherwise.'

'I cannot believe it. Don't they know what I did to help Olivio and the *partigiani*? Allegra, I need to find him. He will explain everything. Can you find out where he is?'

The old lady shook her head. 'Not everybody was in favour

of the *partigiani*. Some of them say they were hooligans. And nobody has seen Olivio. There is talk he went down to Rimini before war's end to fight with another brigade and he hasn't returned. He might not even be alive.' She made the sign of the cross across her chest.

'Sergio, then. What about him?'

'Apparently, he requested to go to America but is down in Rimini somewhere. I can try to talk to his mother but she's not in a fit state of mind since losing both husband and daughter.'

'Then, I'll go and ask around town myself. Surely somebody must know.'

'Tina, nobody will talk to you. Let me do the finding out while I can. Because after some of the comments this morning about helping you up here at the *castello*, I'm not so sure I'll be popular in Sant'Agnese for much longer either.'

'So, do they think I'm responsible for the death of darling Luisa too?' Tina sat at the table, picking dough from her fingers. 'What can I do, Allegra?'

'Somehow prove you are innocent. But not by shouting in the piazza. You're a clever young woman. Use that brain of yours to come up with something. Now, let's finish setting this dough to rise. Show me how well I've taught you. But don't forget the bread will pick up on your mood. That's the way with cooking.'

Tina poured out her anger into the kneading and folding of the dough and Allegra was right when the finished loaf turned out flat and hard.

'Put it down to poor flour,' Tina said later at midday as they chewed on her attempts. 'You keep saying it's mixed with sawdust.' She wasn't hungry anyway, her head full of the injustice of the accusations Allegra had picked up in town.

'And they tell me in the shops we're going to have to put up with meagre supplies for a long while yet. *Maremma mia*, the war is supposed to be over.'

Tina helped clear the dishes away. 'This war will not come to an end for me until I've convinced the people of Sant'Agnese of my innocence. *I* know I'm no traitor but someone is and I mean to find out who. I owe it to the people to find the one who's guilty.'

The thick ropes of fog winding round the *castello* blocked the view of the town and added to Tina's sense of isolation. She spent a couple of hours at her piano. It served to calm her as she played her favourite Chopin nocturnes. But when she started the aria from Puccini's *La Bohème*, she stopped midway. The tune brought back bitter-sweet memories of Olivio singing for the first time in the garden and she closed the lid and trailed up to her room.

At her desk beneath the window in the tower, she pulled a blank piece of paper from her drawer and started a list. She would begin with the people she knew to see if she could winkle out any extra information about the raid. Hopefully, they might provide leads about their fellow fighters who might be guilty of treachery.

1. Track down Olivio and Sergio to question them. Why did they disappear?
2. Talk to Sergio's mother. Sergio might have let something slip.
3. Visit Rimini where Olivio might still be and where Sergio is possibly working.
4. Talk to Donatella: she was friendly with plenty of people during the occupation.

Every item would be hard to tackle. Where could she start in Rimini? It was a big city, a port where people came and went all the time. Hunting for Olivio and Sergio would be like searching for sardines in the ocean and she knew nobody down there. Sergio's mother was distraught, poor woman. She'd have to rely on Allegra to talk to her for his address and if that failed maybe a neighbour might know something. Where was Donatella? Was she still in Sant'Agnese? What did she know? It left a nasty taste in her mouth as she remembered Donatella mixing with German soldiers. But if it was the only way, then so be it. She had to talk to her.

Frustrated she could not simply walk into town to speak to people herself, she threw down her pen, suddenly overwhelmed. Yet again she was reliant on poor Allegra to bail her out. She owed her so much.

Right, Ernestina Montesecco. Get off your backside and in the meantime do something to help Allegra. Tina now knew where the cleaning paraphernalia of mops, rags, carpet beaters and dusters were kept, and she spent the remainder of the afternoon hunting spiders and cobwebs. It was satisfying seeing results and she rewarded herself by popping for half an hour to her garden.

The rain had ceased. Glistening droplets were suspended from plants like miniature chandelier pendants and fingers of shadows lengthened as she wandered through the maze, noting how the thick yew bushes encroached on the paths. Best to hack at that before the maze became impenetrable. As she approached the centre where she had once found Olivio sleeping, the fading light played tricks on her eyes and in the gloom she thought she caught the billowing of a cloak and heard its silken swish as a figure trailed round a corner of the maze.

'Who's there?' she called as she pursued the intruder but there was no answer save for the slightest gust of breeze whispering through the garden and the song of a robin perched on her mother's arbour. Light was fading rapidly. *You're seeing things*, she told herself. The garden had turned sinister to her, echoing her despondent mood.

She took to her bed early that night, her sleep fitful and shallow, with waves of strange dreams that ebbed and flowed on the shallow surface of slumber. She was a bird: a carrier pigeon taking messages along rivers towards cities. The journey was long and strenuous and she took shelter in the rolled-up sail of a pirate ship for part of the voyage, afraid she would be discovered and made into a pie. The pirates' moll resembled Donatella with her low-cut blouse and painted face, large, smudged beauty spots daubed on each cheek. The captain was Sergio, his artificial leg made from shining mahogany and the parrot on his shoulder had Olivio's face. A woman with flowing red hair occasionally flew the length of the ship but where her face should have been, there were no features.

Tina woke in a sweat, her limbs tangled in bed sheets. She lay for a while as early dawn filtered through the shutter slats. What had brought on the strange nightmare? She hadn't eaten a heavy meal last night. The curious dream melted away with birdsong. Maybe it was because her mind was full of her quest for justice. The townspeople's treatment of herself had been difficult and she'd been overwhelmed by everything but what was more important now was to reveal the truth. The bereaved of Sant'Agnese needed closure. Too many people had lost loved ones.

She was not giving up before she'd begun. Oh no. As she lay in bed in the first moments, she thought of her list of things to tick off and then she realised there was somebody from the group she'd omitted: Antonio. No doubt he was still at the monastery. Maybe by now he had taken holy orders.

She knew the way there. Papà's car was still parked in one of the stables. There was no Baffi to ride along the country roads, but she would drive as far as the track permitted and walk the rest of the way.

Books! She'd take him a couple; she remembered how much he'd appreciated her loans and their friendly discussions about their shared love of reading – even if they liked completely different genres. She ran to the library and pulled two leather-bound volumes of Boccaccio's early works – she'd never read those and never would. With a pinch of good fortune, Antonio might know Olivio's whereabouts. Maybe he had returned to shelter at the monastery. Her spirits lifting, she fetched the keys to the Maserati. She hadn't driven for a while but after a couple of tries, the motor spluttered and turned. She was on her way.

CHAPTER 46

Searching for the truth

Tina was shocked at the devastation as she drove along. Several houses along the road were little more than piles of rubble; others were patched with strips of sacking, planks of wood, piles of stones. Children in raggedy clothes sat on steps leading nowhere, their feet bare, waving with grubby hands as she drove past.

She slowed down over a military bridge, the metal frame different from characteristic stone, her wheels bumping over wooden planking. Men fished from the banks and they stared at the car as she passed. Parts of the road bore huge craters and she was forced to drive around holes carefully, sometimes diverting into fields, praying she would not get bogged down or sustain a puncture. She had no idea how to change a wheel.

Eventually, the road stopped where it dwindled to a narrow stony track and she parked the car beneath an oak, hoping the Maserati would still be there on her return. Allegra had told her people scavenged anything these days: leather from crashed fighter planes' seats to make shoes, a cockpit for a chicken house, helmets for water containers. Corpses were looted for warm winter coats that were restyled. Army boots were a great prize for *contadini*, farmers who normally worked barefoot or in uncomfortable wooden clogs. She tried not to imagine Papà's car reduced to a metal skeleton on her return. *Expect the unexpected*, she warned herself. But in the meantime, she was going to do everything she could to pursue her quest.

Walking through the pine forest made a pleasant change from driving, the murmuring wind sifting through the branches a comforting sound. She walked steadily uphill, sun glinting through pines that offered some shade. She was surprised how well she was doing, despite months of inactivity. There was nobody along the way to stare at her mutilated face and she felt her cheek muscles relax. In a clearing where wild garlic spread a misty, strongly scented white carpet, she sat to eat her picnic. Allegra made a delicious pesto from the green garlic leaves and Tina made a mental note to harvest some later. A boulder with a view over the valley provided a perfect resting spot and she munched on her rather hard bread whilst early bees hummed as they lifted pollen from a scattering of pink and yellow flowers.

Her watch told her she'd been going for two hours, so she pressed on, calculating that by the time she'd spoken to Antonio, she would need to leave almost immediately to catch the remaining daylight.

On the ridge she came across an army post where trenches had been abandoned. Spent shells lay scattered here and there along with a couple of *tedeschi* helmets upturned on the forest floor, one of them pierced with a bullet hole. Piles of sacks were lined along the top of the trenches and she shivered as she imagined fear, death and destruction shattering such a wild, beautiful location. No matter what side they fought for, the men involved were sons, brothers, lovers, husbands. What a waste. What an escalation of hatred resulted from war. She wondered how long, if ever, it would take to forgive and forget. Maybe never. She was only one of many looking for answers or revenge. She pressed on.

The monk who responded to her ringing of the monastery bell looked momentarily shocked when he saw Tina. She pulled her neckerchief higher up her face, her hands clenching as she remembered lovely Luisa; how courageous she had been at her side on their mission to fetch Sergio: enterprising, cool and calm as she took over situations. She hadn't deserved to die the way she had and this strengthened Tina's motive for hunting down the traitor.

The abbot showed no recognition of her from her first visit. In this sense, Tina thought, her scars were a positive. When she asked about Antonio, he nodded.

'You are fortunate, signorina. Tomorrow he is bound for Rome. Wait here. I'm sure he can spare you some time.'

Antonio didn't seem to recognise her either, until Tina spoke. 'Forgive me, Antonio. I have no news of your family but I hoped you might have news for me.'

He frowned, a look of shock on his lean features. 'Can it be you? Tina?'

'I was injured. When I was with Olivio and Sergio,' she said, touching her face.

'I'm sorry for your—'

'My face is the least of my concerns, Antonio. I need to know if Olivio has been in contact with you.' She paused while searching for the right words. 'I'm sure you heard about the awful event of April 1944: the massacre of many of our townspeople, reprisal for the skirmish in Olivio's camp? Somebody informed on Olivio and his men. I need to talk to him, pick his brains. It's simply not right that somebody got away with this.'

Antonio crossed his arms, his hands snaking into the wide sleeves of his habit the way the abbot's had done. She wondered if this was something taught to novices, something they did when reflecting or in repose.

'Yes. He stayed here again for a while that April. As did Sergio. The abbot sheltered them but they left after ten days. We tried to persuade them to stay longer because Olivio was in a bad way. Suffering some kind of nervous breakdown, I believe. Olivio, as we know, is particularly stubborn and he refused help. But I have no idea where they are now.'

Tina sighed. 'The consolation for me is he was alive when you saw him.'

'He was very much alive. He had evil bursts of temper. I think the abbot was not disappointed when they left. But... don't say I said this.'

'Of course not, Antonio. The abbot tells me you're leaving tomorrow for Rome.'

Antonio smiled. 'I am most fortunate. I'm taking up a position in the legal department in the Vaticano.' He stood and Tina took that to be a sign their interview was over.

'Impressive, Antonio.' She pulled the books from her basket. 'I hope you'll have room for these. Thank you for your time. Please, please send me word if you hear anything from Olivio. You know where I am.'

'Thank you.' His smile was fleeting as he handled the old texts. 'I'm sure I can squeeze these in. How thoughtful you are.' He frowned as he told her, 'But it's highly unlikely he'll be in touch with me. I won't be here but, good luck, Tina.'

It had not been an entirely frustrating visit, Tina thought, as she strode from the monastery. The sun as it fell lower occasionally blinded her with flashes of light through the trees and the breeze blew cooler. Sometimes snow fell up high, even in May. She fastened the buttons on her jacket and hurried down the path, stepping over tree roots snaking up through the soil, her feet scrunching on old pine cones. A pheasant called from within the forest and, thinking she could hear someone calling her name, she turned and stopped, her heart hammering. But there was nobody there. She had mistaken the fallen branch of an old pine, its drooping needles draped with browned ferns, for a figure with long rust-streaked hair. Tina quickened her pace. She didn't fancy straying from the path to pick wild garlic. *Please, please let the car be in one piece*, she prayed.

At first, she thought the creature, front paws crossed where it rested by her car, was a wolf and she stopped dead. The animal rose and stretched when it saw her, mouth open in a wide yawn, showing long yellowing canines. She knew not to run but to fix her stare at its eyes. She must not demonstrate fear but her crazily beating heart proved otherwise.

Somebody whistled and the dog, for it was an Alsatian not a wolf, bounded over to the edge of a clump of trees from where a man watched over a scraggy flock of sheep.

'Rex was guarding your car for you, signorina,' he said, rising as he spoke. 'As was I.'

'Why, thank you so much.'

'Can't leave anything unguarded nowadays.'

The falling sun reflected gold and red in his round-lensed glasses. He made an unlikely shepherd, she thought. His accent was not local, but his Italian, educated. Strange for a shepherd, she thought. They usually left school very young, once they learned how to sign their name.

'What do I owe you?' she asked. 'I have to admit I've been concerned.'

'You don't owe me anything. I recognised the car and wondered what was going on. I know the owner is dead. *Il conte* Montesecco, am I correct?'

Momentarily thrown, Tina asked, 'Who *are* you?'

He paused. 'I know who *you* are too, signorina. Unless you

have stolen this vehicle, I am speaking with the contessina Ernestina Montesecco. I am correct, am I not?'

'How do you know these things?'

'Shall we sit?' He gestured to a couple of sawn tree trunks beneath the oak tree. A sack hung from one of the lower branches and he reached up to pull out a bottle of wine. 'This is all I have to offer but it is drinkable.'

She shook her head and he returned it to his improvised larder.

'I know who you are because I was with Baffi and his band of fighters from the Garibaldi brigade. You will know him as Olivio, contessina. With his guidance, we staked out the town of Sant'Agnese, knew the exact comings and goings of your father and his *nazifascisti*.' He spat on the ground and then apologised. 'Forgive me.' He shrugged and pulled a face. 'It was not good. Any of it. Your Mussolini considered we Slavs inferior and barbarian.' He gave a wry laugh.

'I can assure you, signore, that Mussolini was never mine, as you put it. The people of Sant'Agnese, unfortunately, some of them believe otherwise,' she said.

'It will take time to sort out the grubby mess of war.'

'Tell me who you are, apart from being an ex-*partigiano*,' she said.

'I was a good friend of another Slav called Jancko. A wonderful man, God bless his soul. You won't have noticed me that day you came to the camp with Claudio – the day everything unravelled. My name is Bogdan and Jancko and I were together in the prison camp Renicci where many Slavs were confined. We fought side by side once we escaped.'

'The world is small. To come across somebody who was with Olivio here in the forest. Who would have imagined?'

'The world is not so very large, contessina. Many of us are scattered about the mountains, with nowhere left to go in our own countries: our families gone. You only have to deviate slightly from the main paths to come across us: the dispersed.'

'Have you no wish at all to return to your own country?'

'To Yugoslavia? It is not easy and, anyway, I have stayed because of the oldest story in the world. A story that cares nothing about frontiers.'

At her look of puzzlement, he chuckled. 'I see it has not yet come your way, contessina. I fell in love. With a beautiful Italian. Caterina and our baby son are the reasons I am still here. Back home I was a professor of language at Belgrade University but here I am learning to be a shepherd. And it is not such a bad life. There are no papers to mark, no lectures to deliver and my office is in the open.' He gestured to the meadow and nearby woods beneath the towering summit where the outline of the monastery was silhouetted against the darkening sky. 'Now, my responsibilities are to my new family. For I have been gifted a second chance at life.'

'Have you seen Olivio? I need to talk to him.'

'I haven't. I have heard tell he was in a bad way after that night.' He tapped his head. 'He disappeared deep within himself. I'm sorry. He's a good man.'

Disappointed at coming to another dead end, she sighed. 'Please, if you come across any information at all about him, can you let me know, Bogdan? You, of course, know where I am.'

'I shall.' He held out his hand and she took his firm handshake as he bowed formally, demonstrating old-fashioned manners. 'I wish you good fortune.'

'Thank you for looking after the car.'

He nodded and by the time she'd started the motor, he and his dog had disappeared with the sheep, the music of bells round their necks the only reminder of their presence.

As she drove back to the castle, Bogdan's words about the mountains concealing the dispersed echoed in her thoughts. Was Olivio living nearby? Would he be able to provide useful information about that awful day on the mountain? Did he have any suspicions about a traitor? But what if he was sick of mind and couldn't remember anything? As she drove through the streets of Sant'Agnese, she fully expected the car to be pelted with stones or worse but it was that time of evening when families were at their supper tables and even the benches outside the *osteria* were empty of customers.

Needing company, Tina felt like confining Tigressa and her kittens to the kitchen that evening, but the cats were nowhere to be seen. The stove had gone out again as she'd been away for most of the day, so she pulled on her jacket and made her way down to Allegra's little house.

There was no answer at her first knock and she peered through the kitchen window but Allegra wasn't in there. Allegra had spoken of the new coldness dealt to her in Sant'Agnese and she was obviously not expecting visitors. From the upstairs window, Tina spied a faint gleam of light. She must be in bed already. Eight thirty seemed early but she wouldn't disturb her, so she made her way back to the *castello* through the shadows. A fox ran across her path startling her and she hoped the hens were locked up. In these hard times, everything edible was gold dust.

An early night and a book for companionship beckoned. As she brushed out her thick hair before the mirror, she glimpsed a face behind her own, merging into her reflection: a face without a scar. She blinked twice. Her scar pulled on her eyes and she was tired or her eyesight was beginning to fail because when she looked again, her vision had improved and she saw her true disfigured likeness. She didn't last long with her book before the lines began to blur and she settled down to sleep.

Her dreams were strange again: of shepherds and wolves, of herself as an old woman, her thick auburn hair longer and silvered rusty at the front. She woke abruptly, crying out as she relived her nightmare on the mountain when she'd been surrounded by death, trying to push off the heavy weight of Claudio pinning her to the forest floor, the ricochet of bullets and grenades filling the forest. Opening her eyes, she was confronted by Tigressa, her face so close that whiskers tickled her nose and she laughed out loud. The weight on her body had simply been her cat pawing her chest and purring like a motorcar.

'*Va bene*, signora Tigressa. I get the message. You want me to feed you. Were there no mice abroad last night?'

Allegra was already in the kitchen, scraping cold ashes from the stove.

'You really need to keep this *bestia* going, Tina,' she said. 'It's a pain to have to relight it every morning.'

'*Scusami*, Allegra. You were in bed early when I came to visit. Were you unwell?'

The old lady paused in her work. 'I was tired. Next time you should warn me and I'll stay up.'

Tina took over from Allegra, laying twigs as she'd been shown, adding increasingly larger sticks and then logs as the flames caught and Allegra smiled.

'Soon you'll not need me anymore.'

Tina hugged her close, noticing how thin she was. She worked too hard. 'I shall *always* need you. You're like a mother.'

'*Ahi!* Don't go soppy on me. Show me how you make a cup of coffee and let's hope the shops will stock the real stuff again soon.'

They sat together to breakfast, finishing off Tina's hard bread with a thin smear of plum jam.

'I have found out where Sergio is,' Allegra announced, when the last dregs of chicory coffee were finished. 'I spoke to his mother yesterday. She's considering joining him as she has nothing to live for here, *poverina*. Poor thing. But I doubt it for she worries about her husband and daughter alone in the cemetery with nobody to bring flowers to their graves, but I have promised to do that—'

'Where is he?'

'In Rimini, as I thought.'

'Why did he end up there?'

'It seems one of the *partigiani* offered him a job as tourists will return again to bathe in the sea. His father owns a trattoria. You know that Sergio cooked for the men on the mountain? This fellow, he liked what he prepared.'

'Do you know where in Rimini, Allegra?'

Allegra shook her head. 'But I can find out. Sergio has written to try to get his mamma to come and be with him. He says there's a house with the job.'

'Can't I come and talk to her myself?'

'No, no,' Allegra said. 'She's another who blames the killings on you. As it is, she only tolerates me because we're related. But... I have to tread carefully.'

'Can you see if she'll show you the letter? Can you copy the address, Allegra?'

'Let me see. She keeps the letter on display on her sideboard. I can try.'

This was a small step forward. Sergio might be the key to not only finding Olivio, but also remembering details of that fateful day. She thought of the seeds in her garden flourishing into large plants. From small things, big things grow.

CHAPTER 47

Late 1945, Rimini

Out of the ashes

Rubble, stones, fallen monuments, remains of people's homes piled up waiting to be rebuilt. Lives waiting to be rebuilt. Pinched faces, guarded faces, skinny urchins playing barefoot in ruins. Unhealthier than the children of Sant'Agnese, where at least food had never been totally scarce: the countryside providing wild mushrooms, edible weeds, snails, rabbits, pheasants, the space for chickens to scratch.

But there was resilience here in Rimini. As she drew nearer the area of San Giuliano and the restaurant where she hoped to find Sergio, she passed stalls with fish heaped in crates and baskets. The Adriatic had witnessed the devastating presence of torpedo boats and landing craft but the waters continued to provide their bounty. She was offered varieties of fish and molluscs she had never seen before: creatures with long tentacles, brightly coloured scales and bony waving feelers.

'Buy from me, signorina,' a vendor shouted, 'the best *garagoli* in Rimini.'

She gazed on strangely twisted shellfish as his neighbour countered with, 'Don't believe a word he says. Mimi's the biggest liar on the coast. Try my excellent *uomini nudi*. You won't find better, signorina.' He winked at her.

Tina smiled as she looked at the so-called naked men: the tiniest of tiny fish in his basket. She declined the good-tempered banter with laughter.

She asked for Da Maria, the name of the fish trattoria that Allegra had copied from Sergio's mother's postcard, and a fisherman mending nets pointed towards the river that flowed wide to the sea. The Marecchia river started in the mountains above Sant'Agnese and gathered in force as it made its way to the plains, the waters muddier here than the sparkling tributaries in the woods.

Sergio wore a scarf round his neck against the December chill. Tina had recognised his gait from afar as he swept the pavement. She stepped nearer and studied the menu displayed outside the door.

'We're not open yet, signorina...' Sergio said, followed by, '*Gesù Maria*, Tina. It's you, isn't it? I'd recognise that hair anywhere.' But as she turned to face him, he didn't seem so sure. '*Mi scusi*, signorina...'

He looked away as most people did, no doubt troubled by the scars that distorted her features.

'You're not mistaken, Sergio. It *is* me.'

'I'm sorry,' he said, leaning his broom against the door to the eating place and coming to take her hands. 'I heard you were alive, but I hadn't realised...' He broke off, embarrassed.

'You hadn't realised I was so ugly,' she completed his sentence.

'No, no. Not that.' He rubbed his hand through his hair. 'I mean, I heard you'd been injured... but not like that.'

'I'm fine, Sergio... I'm fine.' She watched his shoulders relax. 'Can we talk? Are you very busy?'

He apologised. 'I can't stop now. Come back after my shift ends at two thirty. Or better still, stay to eat. We're the best fish trattoria in Rimini. I can find you a table at the back. Out of the way,' Sergio added.

This was the way it would be from now on. Out of view to not offend. She smiled bravely and thanked him. 'I've not a huge appetite, Sergio, but a bowl of spaghetti would be wonderful. *Grazie.*'

The trattoria was clean and furnished simply with plain wooden tables, decor kept to a minimum: a couple of photos of be-whiskered ancestors hung on the walls and portraits of women cleaning sardines, their skirts long, headscarves covering their hair. She enjoyed watching Sergio weave in and out of the customers' tables. Despite his disability, he managed really well, balancing a tray in one hand, a ready smile on his face, obviously enjoying himself.

He has his war injuries but it doesn't seem to faze him, Tina thought. *With his long trousers, you wouldn't know he only has one leg. Yes, he has a slight limp but he copes. And so must I*, she told herself, sinking into the moment but waiting for the right time to discuss in private what exactly happened in the days leading to the massacre in their hometown.

The food was delicious and Sergio explained each homely dish: she started with onions and sardines wrapped in a typical flatbread called *piadina*, followed by a soup made from local squid and monkfish with squares of home-made pasta. Sergio then brought her home-made spaghetti in a rich cockle and tomato sauce. He told her the cockles were known as *'le poveracce'* as they were freely available to pick from the shore by the poor. She declined the next platter of fried shellfish, pulling at the waistband of her skirt with laughter. But she did manage room for a slice of chocolate cake *della nonna*. At the end of the feast, she sat back in surrender and ordered coffee, delighted when proper espresso arrived, made from real coffee beans.

Whilst waiting for Sergio to finish, she wandered outside. On the shore, women and children were bent over rocks with pails, gleaning *le poveracce* she had eaten. They were like the poor back home who gathered edible plants for free, she thought. *We're not so very different after all. People find a way to survive.* And so must she.

It was cold, but not the biting cold of the mountains and she entertained herself by the harbour wall watching stray cats feast on fish heads and entrails discarded by fishermen. Would Tigressa enjoy fish? she wondered. The diet of a seaside cat was obviously very different from a country cat used to hunting mice and birds. Gulls soared and wheeled, keeping up their shrieking calls and she realised it was fun to be away from Sant'Agnese where it was impossible to linger in the piazza without receiving abuse.

'Penny for them.' Sergio's voice broke her out of her musings as he arrived and sat next to her on the wall.

'It's peaceful here, despite the bustle,' she said.

He gave her a bemused look. 'Come again?'

'Back in Sant'Agnese I can't go anywhere without receiving hostile remarks. I'm deeply resented in my own hometown.'

'I heard about that too. I'm sorry.'

'Sergio, can you tell me what happened up there on the mountain? It's all such a blur in my head.' She paused. 'Do *you* believe I informed on your *partigiani*?'

She didn't enjoy his pause before he replied. 'I personally do not, Tina. I know the extent you went to help us. But even my own mother has suspicions and it's hard to persuade her otherwise. You can't blame her, really. She lost her husband and a daughter after you accompanied him up the mountain. She needs to cling on to some kind of explanation to make sense of it.'

'The *tedeschi* were guilty, of course, Sergio,' Tina said, 'but they had to know where you were and whoever betrayed you up on that mountain is the chief culprit. We have to find whoever it was. Was there anybody at all in your group who it could have been?'

Sergio frowned. 'Of course I didn't know everybody in the group and men were constantly joining and leaving, but, no... nobody springs to mind, Tina. What you are saying is deeply troubling but I can't think of anybody.'

She sighed. Her hunch about the traitor being somebody in the band of *partigiani* might not be correct. What next?

'I must find Olivio. He may have some idea. He knew everybody.'

He looked uncomfortable. 'Olivio is...' He tailed off.

'Olivio is what, Sergio? Spit it out.'

'I'm not sure where he's disappeared to and... he wants no one to find him.'

'Do you have *any* idea at all where he might be? Please, Sergio. Think!'

He shrugged. 'He's gone to ground. If I could help you, I would. But I honestly have no idea.'

Tina sighed. 'Well, at least *you* have faith in me. You do, don't you?'

He touched her hand. 'Yes, Tina. I do. But it won't be easy for you. Many people are suspicious of the rich girl from the castle.'

It meant a lot, this first step, to hear Sergio's words. Olivio had great respect for him. Her instinct told her Sergio was no traitor. But she also knew it was important not to let sentiment soften her judgement. She had to keep an open mind in her quest and ask herself all the important questions: why? Where? When? To finally reach the answer to: who?

'Thank you, Sergio. Now, I have to track down Donatella. And please keep your eyes and ears open for Olivio.'

She held out her hand and Sergio took it and then pulled her into a brotherly embrace.

'Donatella is living in Arezzo. Good luck, Tina. When I come to visit my mother, I'll look you up.'

Tina turned to walk back to the railway station, crossing Tiberius's unscathed bridge spanning the Marecchia river. She passed beneath the Roman arch of Augustus which showed only a couple of bullet pockmarks. They were two monuments that had been protected from destruction: a promise adhered to by warring armies. A sign of hope that a glimmer of respect had existed in those awful years. Tina took it as a positive sign as she passed through other ruins waiting to be repaired. That, topped with Sergio's faith in her, was a positive beginning. But the hunt for the traitor was not much further forward. She had work to do.

CHAPTER 48

March 1946

'The hottest places in Hell are reserved for those who, in times of great crisis, maintain their neutrality.' (*Dante, Inferno*)

Tina stood to ease her aching back and examined the wall where she had pinned a chart. She'd written names in bold with lines that led to comment boxes. Sergio's details, where he was working in Rimini and the date she'd talked to him was the extent of information so far. Olivio, Donatella, Antonio and Huber had very little in their boxes. She'd scrawled in the date of Huber's demise and as she'd done so, she'd shivered. Huber had died before the raid but who was to say she hadn't already passed on details of the Jewish inhabitants in Sant'Agnese? How else would the *nazifascisti* have known about Luisa? Why, even she hadn't realised Luisa was Jewish. Tina had checked the file she'd found in Huber's room and it was still in the desk drawer, so she'd hidden it as evidence. But evidence of what? What if the wretched woman hadn't even had time to pass the names on? There'd have been plenty of occasions to do this at her musical soirées. How to find out? She stepped over and drew a huge question mark next to Huber's name.

She sighed. The whole damn thing was a huge question mark. And to make matters worse, thick snow had blanketed the countryside for two long months, making it impossible to move. It was so frustrating. Next on her list was Arezzo and a visit to Donatella but that had to wait until the weather broke. She'd tried to take her mind off her quest and over the following long weeks, busied herself helping Allegra, who insisted on putting in an appearance most days to clean the castle.

The door to the tower room was pushed open.

'You've been closeted up here for too long,' Allegra said. She placed an armful of clean sheets on Tina's bed and straightened up. 'Those stairs,' she said. 'They'll be the death of me. We need a lift.'

'Huh! And how shall we pay for this lift, Allegra *cara*? Anyway, you only have to sound the gong downstairs and I can fetch and carry for you.'

Allegra approached the scribbles on the wall, as she called them. 'How's it going?'

'It's not. And the weather doesn't help. Oh, Allegra, the more I think of it, the more I'm convinced somebody followed me up the mountain with Claudio that night. I feel so guilty. It was likely all my fault. And as time goes by whoever betrayed us has most probably escaped to the furthest corner of the world and had time to embellish their story.'

'Or *their* stories,' Allegra said as she stared at the chart. '*Madonna buona!* Stop torturing yourself. It could have been pure chance that Olivio and the others were discovered. You don't know if you were followed.'

'And I don't know if I wasn't. Oh, my head is spinning...'

'Have you considered it's not a single person involved?' Allegra interrupted her and stepped in closer to scrutinise Tina's chart. 'And why haven't you included signor Bernardo in your hunt? I thought you'd told me he'd warned you to stay put in the castle because a raid was going to take place?'

'*Che stupida!* How very stupid of me,' Tina said, hitting her own forehead and grabbing her thick pencil to scrawl Bernardo's name between the others. '*Grazie*, Allegra.'

She and Allegra had spent hours talking through the need to clear Tina's name and the questions over who may have betrayed the whereabouts of the *partigiani* on the mountain. Allegra herself had recently been isolated in town and was eager to clear her reputation too. Sergio's mother and friends no longer invited her to join in their evening *veglie*, when they gathered to share stories and wisdom while mending or knitting. They disapproved of Allegra having anything to do with Tina.

'This weather will break soon,' Allegra said. Tina didn't contradict her for she knew country folk could tell these things: from the way the wind blew, the first swallow returning, a snowdrop pushing up through the ice.

'Then, I shall try to visit Bernardo first. He's nearer than Donatella. Leave the sheets; I'll make up the bed.'

'Four hands are better than two, *cara* Tina. And anyway, you never tuck the corners in firmly.'

Allegra began to strip the bed and Tina helped, her mind dwelling on how to tackle Bernardo.

A week later and, save for in the ditches, the snow had all but disappeared in the March sunshine as Tina trudged to the Fara estate. The path was wet and although it was hard going in her rubber boots, at least Tina's feet were dry. How wonderful it would have been to ride this morning upon dear Baffi. She pushed that sad thought away.

Having been cooped up inside for so long, it was good to feel fresh air on her face. The sun was surprisingly bright, the sky clear of clouds and she took care to cover her cheeks, having learned that the crooked lines of her scars showed up more if she burned. She passed a wild cherry tree, its buds waiting to burst with blossom.

At the field where Baffi and the other horses had grazed, she paused to catch her breath. How often had she thought about her handsome bay, hoping death had been swift? She shook her head and continued up the steep slope and then she heard the sound of hooves and her heart missed a beat. Were her thoughts conjuring up spirits? No, it was real and she stood back as a rider holding the reins of two bays approached. Bernardo. He pulled up when he saw her standing on the bank.

'*Whoah!*' he commanded, bringing the animals to a halt. 'Signorina, *mi scusi*, I didn't expect to see anybody—' He broke off. 'Ernestina?'

'Yes, Bernardo. It's me.' Perversely, she moved the scarf lower so her scars showed. She needed him to see how she'd been reduced – what had happened to her on the mountain. Because he'd been there. She knew he had because she remembered hearing his name called by one of his men. His face expressed horror at her disfigurement. She had hit the mark.

He stayed up on his horse. 'I'm bringing the horses down to graze. They're restless in the stables. Need exercise—'

She understood he was filling the space where shock had crept in with unnecessary talk and she interrupted him. What was the point of being subtle?

'Bernardo. I need to ask why you warned me to stay in the castle that day of the raid.'

He adjusted his grip on the reins as one of the horses behind him pushed forwards. 'Easy answer,' he said. 'We'd received orders via Kesselring, who'd commanded a thousand plus troops to carry out brutal reprisals in the area. How could I not warn you? You were...' He corrected himself. 'We *are* friends, are we not?'

She moved to help the restless horse. It was instinctive and he let her take the reins as she talked soothingly to the excitable animal and led him to the gate. Bernardo followed and dismounted to push it open. Together they removed the tack and watched as the horses galloped off, snorting, tossing their manes and whinnying with joy as they chased around the field in freedom.

'I'm sorry about what happened to you, Ernestina.'

'How did you know where the *partigiani* were?'

He sighed. 'Because they'd been tracked. I know these mountains as well as anybody. I've lived here all my life. I'm not the only one who knew where they were hiding. But I didn't inform anybody they were there. I merely followed orders to join in with the raid.'

'You didn't have to join in the slaughter.'

'I didn't fire a single shot.'

'You didn't prevent the shots being fired.'

'Tina, the war is over. You don't understand what it was like to be a soldier, so don't meddle.'

'Meddle?' She pushed herself forwards to confront him. 'Your own townspeople were murdered that day because of what happened on that mountain. Not only soldiers but innocent children, the elderly, women nursing babies. Don't tell me I don't understand.'

'I tried to warn you. It's your own stupid fault if you didn't listen.'

'I despise you. You're weak and as much to blame as the evil German who issued orders to you. You should do the right thing and admit that to your so-called friends. You're no friend of mine.'

Tina turned to go, her eyes blinded with the tears she didn't want him to see. She half ran, half slithered down the hillside, aware that he was calling her back. But she had nothing to say to him. How could he exonerate himself so easily by saying he didn't fire the shots? The man was loathsome.

She was tired when she pushed through the kitchen door of the castle, pleased that Allegra wasn't there. Fetching a glass of her walnut grappa, she knocked it back in one and then poured another. What the hell had she achieved by going to talk to Bernardo? Not much at all. She had shown her anger and hatred but what had she learned? Nothing that she didn't already know: that most people were like sheep, following the flock to keep safe. She still had so many questions.

CHAPTER 49

Spring 1946, Arezzo

Journeys of hope

Tina had to get away from the castle. Its ancient walls pressed in on her, echoing with memories she didn't want. Allegra had left for a short break down to the Maremma area in southern Tuscany, to stay with her sister and brother-in-law.

Tina decided she would kill two birds with one stone. The train for Rome, where she would try to see Antonio, left from Arezzo, where she'd learned Donatella now lived. A break would be good. She needed time and distance to gain perspective. Her talk with Bernardo had achieved little.

'You need a calmer head, *carina*,' Allegra had told her. 'Instead of flying off the handle, you must be stealthy, catch your prey unawares like Tigressa, who crouches patiently for hours waiting for mice to make the wrong move.'

Tina packed the bare minimum to travel light but at the last minute, she rummaged in the suitcase of Huber's belongings for the stolen Fabergé eggs. Funds were low and in Rome, it might be possible to sell them. She left a note on the kitchen table for Allegra's return, telling her she was going away for a few weeks and not to worry, adding she hoped her stay in the Maremma would be what the doctor ordered. Tina was only too aware of the decline in Allegra's health. It would be good for her to be looked after for a change.

Spring had definitely sprung. *Primavera* – the word meant first truth, rebirth and Tina felt optimistic and proactive. Yes, that was the word. As she climbed onto the country bus to Sansepolcro carrying her small valise, she felt she was doing something off her own bat. From Sansepolcro, she would catch a train to Arezzo.

Everywhere still bore evidence of bomb raids. In Arezzo, the station roof had buckled and workmen hammered away on repairs. The platform was crammed with people waiting for the next train. It was impossible to push through them.

'Who are all these people?' she asked the guard.

'They're southerners mostly, signorina, waiting for today's *treno di speranza*, the train of hope going north. Over the past weeks, I've seen thousands travel. They're leaving Italy in search of work abroad. Good luck to them I say. Our country's on its knees.'

She waited while the throng pushed its way onto the next train that steamed into the station, covering her face as children stared at her. It was not because they were ogling at her. By now she was growing used to strangers rapidly averting gazes from her puckered face, or, particularly with children, pointing with fascination at her scars. Some of them even asked what had happened to her in the straightforward, blunt way of the very young. No, she pulled her scarf up on her face and mouth because of the stench of body odour and something else she couldn't put her finger on. Could it be soot from the belching engine? Maybe it was poverty? These emigrants wore little more than rags, their possessions tied up in cardboard boxes, thick ropes wound round and round to keep the tattered containers together. Their faces were pinched, eyes scared. Some of the women wore threadbare blankets over their heads. Rather than a train of hope, it seemed to Tina a train of misery. How many victims of war were travelling in hope of a better life? Hers too was, after all, a search for something better. She too was travelling in hope.

Tina breakfasted in the beautiful Piazza Grande of Arezzo where as a child she'd watched the June *palio* with her father, clapping hands at the spectacular jousting tournament when flag throwers, drummers and skilful knights representing the four quarters of the city competed against one another.

She sat beneath the loggia to sip coffee and watch the world go by. A toddler chased a pigeon under the watchful eye of his mother and in the far corner, beneath the tower of Santa Maria della Pieve, a woman sold cheeses. It was the first time in too long that Tina had sat and done nothing and she luxuriated in that half hour. At the base of one of the towers in the piazza she spotted a sign for a *pensione*, a simple boarding house, and after paying the waiter she carried her valise over and knocked on the door. Yes, they had a room but they also wanted her to pay for her stay in advance.

'I'm not sure for how long,' she told the elderly owner in her blue and white polka-dotted overall. 'Maybe three days at the most.'

'Suits me,' she answered. 'After that I'm sprucing up my place for bookings for the *palio*. First one the city has put on since the war ended. People are eager to see it again. I can do you an evening meal but you take breakfast over there.' She pointed to the same bar Tina had come from.

Her room was basic but clean and she opened the shutters to let in the spring air. She had a perfect view of the whole piazza and she leant her elbows on the sill to observe the world, like watching a stage with actors passing to and fro. A group of young boys kicked a ball and their whoops and calls bounced and magnified from the walls of the buildings. She remembered how frightened she'd been as a little girl at the noise from the tournament players and spectators. Sant'Agnese was a quiet town but, like a tortoise that sticks its neck out from its shell, it did no harm to broaden horizons. And the added bonus was nobody knew her in this city where she'd briefly spent time as a scholar.

On the following morning, she waited for her cappuccino and cake to be brought to her table. The bar was popular and the choice of pastries mouth-watering. She couldn't remember the last time she'd been to a bar in her own town where the inhabitants made her presence so unwelcome. Across the cobbled piazza, she watched a young woman struggle to push a wheelchair, the grumbles of the elderly passenger loud and clear as he was bounced and jolted over the uneven surface.

'Slowly, slowly. I'm not a pig being taken to market. Have some care, woman.'

The young woman was flushed from exertion and she stopped to catch her breath and light a cigarette. There was something about her: her dress cinched at the waist with a fashionably wide belt, her nails sparkling red, hair combed up in two bouffant curls at the side of her head.

The waiter blocked Tina's view as he approached with her breakfast tray but when he moved away, there was no mistake.

'Donatella!' Tina exclaimed as the wheelchair was parked at the table next to hers. 'I don't believe it. I was coming to look for you today.'

Donatella looked momentarily shocked and then recovering, she flashed a smile at Tina.

'Fancy seeing you here. What are you doing here?'

'As I said: looking for you.'

'Well, you've found me now. What's up?'

Donatella turned to cover her charge's knees with a blanket and he slapped her hands away. 'Stop fussing me. It's not cold.'

'This is my husband. Cavaliere Cesare Paolucci,' Donatella proudly announced.

The old man smiled wide, displaying an empty-toothed mouth. 'Pity about your face,' he said.

'Husband?' Tina's surprise was impossible to hide.

'Yes. Husband,' Donatella said firmly, her eyes narrowed with an expression that forestalled further comment or query as to why Donatella should have ended up with a man at least sixty years her senior.

'I love it here in Arezzo,' she continued. 'So much more life than in the backwater where we grew up. Are you here to sightsee?'

'No. I'm here because I want to talk to you. When would be a good time?'

'How about right now?'

'But—'

'Don't worry about my husband. He'll hear what we say but he'll forget about it a minute later. I'm like a parrot the way I have to repeat everything over and over. Isn't that right, Cesare *carissimo*?'

'Shame about your friend's face,' the old man repeated.

'What did you want to talk about?' Donatella asked after the waiter had set down two coffees and a plate of pastries.

The situation was far from ideal but the old man was obviously suffering from dementia. Donatella had likely married him to inherit his money, Tina assessed. She took a deep breath.

'You might have heard I'm being blamed in Sant'Agnese for the massacre.'

Donatella nodded. 'Well, you can't blame them, can you? Your father was always entertaining *tedeschi* and *milizia*. And you must have known what was going to happen. People put two and two together and get their sums right.'

Tina reacted with her mouth gaping and observed Donatella as she added three large spoons of sugar to her husband's coffee and the same to her own. 'They always have sugar here but it's impossible to buy in the shops. Bloody war is supposed to be over.'

'But that's the thing,' Tina said, recovering her powers of speech. 'I *did* try to warn what was going to happen but I didn't find out from my father. It was Bernardo who told me.'

'Oh him! Can't trust that bastard. The things he promised *me*.' Donatella shook her head. 'I don't blame you, Tina, for what you did. We have to look after ourselves in this world. Take it from me.' She leant towards the old man to arrange the blanket and the old man once again shouted at her not to fuss.

Donatella lowered her voice. 'Anybody else would let the old man catch a chill and die from pneumonia. But I'm rather fond of the old thing. And his children would probably blame me for his death. They can't stand me.'

Donatella's attention was distracted by the sight of three young men dressed in mediaeval costumes who were practising a complicated flag-throwing routine in the middle of the piazza. She gave a low whistle. 'Just look at them, would you? The muscles on those thighs. Their tights tell no secrets. Incidentally, have you heard from Olivio recently?'

Tina gave up with her questions. Donatella was impossible but, rather than being devious, she was stupid. What would she have personally gained from a betrayal? Would she have done such a thing to her friends simply in exchange for benefits? And anyway, she had worshipped Olivio. Why deliver him into the hands of the enemy?

The old man enjoyed his breakfast, most of it ending up as crumbs and stains on his expensive shirt, his cuffs fastened with chunky gold monogrammed links.

Tina bid the depressing couple farewell and returned to the *pensione*. She paid for the night she wouldn't stay in Arezzo. There was no point in remaining. As she crossed the piazza, she ducked as a pigeon flew low over her head, its wings flapping like sheets in the wind. She checked the bird hadn't deposited anything on her head or shoulders. According to Allegra and her superstitions, it was supposed to remind you of your loyalties. But the pigeon had missed her and it wasn't her own loyalty she was concerned about. It was the proving of who had caused such dreadful suffering in Sant'Agnese and who was still out there.

CHAPTER 50

The Eternal City

For the first few days in Rome, Tina used a modest hotel where her father had stayed on his business trips. She was enjoying being anonymous in the sprawling city and slept well. Although she walked a little each day, she never strayed far from the city centre. There was time enough to visit Antonio in the Vatican.

Rome too was a muddle of ruins despite it having been nominated '*città aperta*' or protected city. She came across vestiges of occupation hard to ignore: fading posters in German and English ordering its citizens to not do this or that, scarred buildings and bridges over the Tiber waiting to be reconstructed, old hand-written slogans barely decipherable on bombed buildings. She caught sight of a half word: *VINCE* – all that remained of an exhortation to win. It would take time to rebuild the country, she thought, as she wandered about. She stopped near the Jewish quarter at a little bar in a piazza with a fascinating fountain of bronze turtles. Once again bitter memories of dear Luisa came flooding back. As she sat in Piazza Mattei, tears streaming down her face, a pretty young woman with hair swept up in fashionable curls, a colourful scarf draped artistically over her shoulders, stopped to console her.

'*Mi dispiace*, signorina, I'm sorry.' She said nothing else, her hand resting gently on Tina's shoulder, her presence soothing. She disappeared into the bar and returned with a tray holding two cups of coffee. 'I've asked Matilda to bring us a *maritozzo* each: a special bun we make in Rome. We deserve treats now the war is over and I think you deserve more than one.' She held out her hand. 'I'm Silvia and that's my shop over there in the corner. I can't stop long – I need to catch business from the tourists who've started to return, but come and see me whenever you want...' She paused, a question in her voice and Tina filled her in.

'I'm Tina. How kind you are.'

The buns when they came were delicious, stuffed with a generous filling of whipped cream and Tina laughed as both of them managed to end up with plenty of it round their mouths.

'It's impossible to eat a *maritozzo* without this happening,' Silvia said. 'Not something to choose on a first date but definitely on a first meeting with a new friend.'

She rose to leave, refusing to allow Tina to pay. 'I have a rule that I do something for somebody each day. There's been too much suffering in the past years. I try to lighten it in small ways.'

What a breath of fresh air, Tina thought. *How different from Donatella, Bernardo and their self-centredness.* She watched Silvia dash back to her shop where a couple of uniformed Americans were gazing through the window.

'We're looking for something to take back to the wives,' Tina heard one of them say, thinking how fortunate they were to still be alive and have family to think of, unlike the many victims of the April massacre in Sant'Agnese.

On the following morning Tina returned to breakfast in Piazza Mattei and wandered over to Silvia's shop. *Semplice-*

mente Fiori, Simply Flowers was written in petals on a recycled door panel, a handle still attached and used as part of the letter 'S'. Inside were picture frames studded with pressed flowers, silk scarves patterned with roses, daisies and sunflowers, handbags made from material patterned with plants.

'How enchanting!' Tina said, picking up a frame.

'I make everything myself. Mostly from what others consider rubbish that I find on bomb sites. I only take pieces of broken wood and scraps of unclaimed clothes patterned with flowers. My aim is to make something beautiful from the ruins. Even the flowers I picked from soil between fallen masonry. I press them here.' She pointed at a simple gadget made from an old tie press.

'I love it. You're so clever.' Tina watched as Silvia finished a seam on the patterned lining of a shopping bag.

'It's my turn to treat you today with coffee and cake, if you have time,' Tina said.

'*Certo!* Sure. I'm really hungry. Last night I forgot to eat, I had so much work to finish off.'

Seated at the same table as the previous day, the minutes spent in Silvia's company flew by. Without realising how their conversation had developed into so much detail, Tina found herself sharing the reason for her visit to Rome.

'So tomorrow, I'm going to try to see my friend in the Vatican,' she concluded. 'I need to know if he played any part in what happened.'

'My goodness, how much you've been though, my friend.' Silvia stretched her fingers to the scar on Tina's face.

Her gentle touch was spontaneous, like the touch of an angel.

'The Vatican, you say,' Silvia went on. '*Hmm!* You might find that difficult. It's such a closed world. During the war the Vatican was supposed to be independent, out of bounds. And it still is to a large degree. You'll need an appointment. My brother worked there as a Swiss Guard.'

Tina hadn't thought of making an appointment. 'But he's nothing important. An ordinary priest who works in the legal department.'

'Doesn't matter.' Silvia looked at her watch. '*Caramba!* Goodness – look at the time. I've got to go. But why don't you come to my place for supper tonight and we'll talk more? That way I'll remember to eat something. I get carried away when I'm creating new items.' She smiled, her beautiful face lighting up as she scribbled an address on the receipt. 'I live not far from Castel Sant'Angelo.'

Silvia's apartment was on the top floor of a narrow building. The name on the door read *Famiglia Baldassari*.

'*Avanti, avanti*, come in!' Silvia said, welcoming Tina, leading her straight into the kitchen area. Her hair was tied back in a scarf patterned with poppies, her face flushed. 'I'm preparing you a typical Roman dish. Deep-fried artichokes. But, phew! It's a hot business,' she said, fanning herself.

The table in the kitchen was laid for two, dishes and cutlery mismatching. A jam jar holding primroses took centre stage on an embroidered mat.

'My favourite flowers,' Silvia said, following Tina's gaze. 'A flower of promise. I picked them by the Tiber.'

'They grow where they want in my garden,' Tina said. 'My favourite place.'

'You're very lucky. That's a dream for me: to own my garden. But in the meantime' – she pointed at a wooden box planted with herbs on the kitchen windowsill – 'this will have to do.'

Silvia poured Tina a glass of Frascati and they started with the artichokes.

'This is a Jewish recipe,' Silvia said as she served up.

The fried vegetable resembled a flat brown flower and was crispy on the outside, soft in the centre. Tina listened carefully to Silvia as she explained the recipe, thinking Allegra would love to try it.

'And now for another of my favourite Roman dishes.' Silvia fetched a dish of greens.

'*Le puntarelle*,' she announced. 'Made from the heart of a chicory, cut very fine and left in cold water to curl up. My absolute favourite.'

The prepared salad had been marinating in a mouth-watering sauce of crushed anchovies, garlic and olive oil. Another recipe for Allegra, Tina thought.

They finished their simple, delicious meal with Roman pecorino cheese, walnuts and honey. Silvia poured more wine. Tina felt deliciously mellow and she relaxed back in her chair as the sky darkened. But unlike in the countryside, the city was coming to life and lights twinkled everywhere.

'Do you live here alone, Silvia?'

'I do now. Yes.'

Sensing there was more to come, Tina waited.

'I too have had my share of tragedy, Tina. You remind me of myself in so many ways. I'm an orphan. My parents were caught in crossfire in the city and I lost my brother two days before war's end.'

It was Tina's turn to offer sympathy as tears ran down Silvia's face.

'For a time, life wasn't worth living. But I've found my way again. And...' She raised her glass to Tina. 'When I meet special people, then it's worth it!'

It was strange how they were connecting, Tina thought. They hardly knew each other and yet there was this affinity between them. Silvia was the sister she'd dreamt of having.

'You're going to be all right, Tina. I sense it.' Silvia paused, her look pensive. 'You'll think I'm crazy but... I see things.'

Tina frowned. 'What do you mean?'

'Your mother. She was beautiful like you? She had your same long auburn-red hair?'

'She died when I was born. I only have one portrait of her and in that she's masked, so I don't know what her face was like.'

'You have her face,' Silvia said, her stare intense. 'The same eyes and snub nose. Beautiful!'

Tina shook her head. 'I'm not beautiful. Not now at any rate. But I've never considered myself beautiful.'

'Your mother is always near you. She loves you and wants your life to be smooth. Hers was unhappy.'

Tina had been about to swallow more wine and she stopped, her glass held in the air. 'How do you know?'

'I told you why, Tina. I sense things. Don't be alarmed. It's a... gift, some call it. My nonna was the same and people came to her to connect with the spirits of loved ones.'

Tina had never come across anybody like Silvia: one foot firmly planted in this world but the other, somewhere unearthly. She was transfixed.

'I've... never met anyone with your gift, Silvia. You... in a way you seem to know more about my mamma than I do. I... until I discovered her garden, she was very remote to me but when I work on the beds she created and handle the soil that she must have plunged her hands into, I... feel her presence.' She looked up at Silvia, knowing her new friend would not think her odd. 'I've not spoken about this to anyone before.'

The two young women smiled at each other and there was silence in the kitchen. Outside, life continued. In the distance, a guitarist strummed a popular folk tune, a bicycle bell was rung in the narrow street below, dogs barked.

'I don't do what Nonna did,' Silvia said. 'But I like to help when I see distress.' She rose. 'Coffee? I found a shop this morning that had a delivery of proper beans. I love reading mystery stories,' Silvia said as she added a splash of sambuca liqueur to their coffees. 'And your hunt for your traitor reminds me of one. I think you should consider inviting all your suspects to your romantic castle to see what happens when you confront them.'

Tina laughed. 'First off, my castle is *definitely* not romantic. It's a draughty, crumbling old building full of sadness.'

'Surely you feel the presence of your mamma inside there too? The sense you're not alone? That she's watching over you? No doors slamming? Lights switching on an off? A scent you catch from time to time?'

Tina pulled a face. 'Plenty of draughts through ill-fitting window frames.' She laughed. 'Maybe you're mistaking horror for mystery stories?'

'I'm not talking about evil happenings. I'm certain your mamma is with you there. She's here with you now, you know.' She pointed at the open window where a butterfly rested on the glass.

'Now you're making me think you've had too much Frascati,' Tina said but she felt comforted by Silvia's words and rose to gently cup the beautiful winged insect in the cradle of her hands while Silvia opened the window to release it. Tina watched until she could no longer see the wings flapping above the roofs.

Silvia smiled her approval. 'Now, to return to your hunt. You should hide your real identity from your guests so they don't think they're being investigated. I can help with all that.' She came over to Tina and tilted her face to the dim lightbulb that hung above the table. 'Your scars won't be so difficult to hide, you know. There's a clinic in the centre where film stars go. They could straighten out those puckers across your face, I'm sure. And I'm clever with cosmetics.'

She left the kitchen and returned with a basket. 'Will you

let me have a go? My darling mother was a singer in a nightclub and she let me apply her makeup before evening performances.'

Spending time with this fascinating young woman was like having the friend she should have grown up with years ago: whiling away time as young girls talking about boys they liked, painting each other's nails, planning futures. Luisa would always hold a special place in her heart but Silvia – she was different and now she'd found her, Tina didn't want to let her go.

She relaxed as her new friend gently smoothed foundation over her cheeks and round her nose and mouth area.

'Some dark green, I think, to accentuate those amazing eyes,' Silvia muttered as she selected a small brush and applied shadow to Tina's lids. 'And lipstick. Red. And you must dye this beautiful hair because it will give you away immediately. Black, I think. Wait!' She fetched a black scarf and tied it round Tina's head to conceal it. 'A black wig would give you a better idea. Maybe I can get hold of one. A short style, like Valentina Cortese.' Silvia stood back, hands on hips and smiled at her work.

'Take a look, Tina – or should I say, Valentina? Oh yes, and you should choose an alias. Ooo, this is such fun!'

She held up a mirror to Tina and an unrecognisable woman stared back. The scars were still visible but in the dim light, less obvious.

'It may be fun to you,' Tina said as she peered at herself. '*I'm* deadly serious about what I want to do. But...' She turned her head this way and that. 'It's not such a bad idea, you know.' She stood up. 'It's late. I must get back. They'll lock me out of the guest house.'

'Please come and stay here. I'm rattling around on my own and it'll make me eat. In fact, can you cook? You can be my maid. Please say you will, Tina. Don't you see? Our friendship was meant to be.'

. . .

It was confirmed that Tina needed special paperwork to gain access to the Vatican City. But already half expecting this, she had another ploy up her sleeve. She was not leaving Rome without trying.

'I urgently need to speak to my brother,' she told the Swiss Guard and started to cry. 'He has to sign forms for the operation on my face tomorrow, otherwise it can't go ahead. We've lost our parents so he's my guardian now – the only family I have.' She pulled out a handkerchief and stifled noisy sobs. 'His name is *padre* Antonio Gerico,' she said, thrusting an envelope at the guards, a bundle of banknotes protruding. 'Please help me contact him.'

The young soldier looked from right to left, pushed the envelope away and lowered his voice. 'Signorina, keep your money. I have a sister too. If you come back in one hour, you'll catch him as he comes out. Regular as clockwork every afternoon, he likes to take a stroll around Piazza San Pietro.'

Tina stayed in the piazza while she waited. One hour would pass quickly and she didn't want to miss Antonio. She felt very small in the shadows of the vast colonnades where the sun didn't reach. A man lay at the back of the walkway, an empty bottle by his side and a street sweeper worked around him. At three o'clock, she was back at the entrance, waiting for Antonio to emerge. True to the guard's statement, the priest emerged and Tina shrank back against a column to watch Antonio stride away along Borgo Angelico. The route was taking him in the direction of Castel Sant'Angelo where she was lodging with Silvia. How ironic if he did this walk each day and she hadn't crossed his path. He entered a park and she watched him approach a bench where a young woman sat with a young boy. The child jumped up and ran towards Antonio, who swept him in his arms. Was the woman a relative?

Tina sat on a bench in the lee of the castle walls and waited for her chance to talk to Antonio. After a quarter of an hour or so, Antonio kissed the top of the child's head and rose from the bench, waving before returning the way he had come. Tina trailed him again and before he stepped from the gardens, she called his name. He turned and she hurried over.

'Antonio. Can I have a word?'

He stared at Tina and it was obvious he didn't recognise her. By now, she was used to this reaction. 'It's me. Tina,' she prompted and watched his puzzled look turn to annoyance.

'You again. What are you doing in Rome?'

'I need to talk to you.'

He looked at his watch. 'I'm in a hurry.'

'I'll walk with you. I… er, didn't want to disturb you while you were with your family.'

He stopped. 'What do you mean, "family"?'

'The woman and the little boy.'

He grabbed her arm. 'Not family. A widow I am helping. I… knew her husband,' he said. 'What is it you want to talk to me about, Tina? I'm very busy.'

Conscious it might be her only chance, she spat it out. 'I must clear my name. I'm being blamed for the killings in Sant'Agnese and I want to talk to you about that day.'

'I really don't know how you expect *me* to help... How should I know what goes on in Sant'Agnese?' He increased his speed. 'I have to get back to my duties. You've had a wasted journey, coming all this way to ask me foolish questions. Please don't bother me again.' He hurried off, his cassock flapping round his ankles like the oily feathers of a raven.

Another useless encounter, she thought. Didn't he care about all those lives lost? *I am getting nowhere fast.*

CHAPTER 51

Two months later, Sant'Agnese

The return

Tina had planned her evening return across the little piazza of Sant'Agnese deliberately. She passed the bar by the theatre where a few old men sat outside playing cards. They looked up as the smartly dressed woman in black walked by, carrying a tapestry valise, a jaunty hat pulled at an angle on her head, its fine veil covering half her face. She heard one of them mutter, 'Who the Lord is that?' and the reply, 'No idea but she's likely lost and got off the *corriera* at the wrong stop.'

She stopped to ask them the way. 'Is the Castello di Montesecco far from here, signori?'

All four pointed up the hill in the direction she was bound and beneath her veil she smiled. *That will get the tongues wagging. Few tourists visit this sleepy town lost in the mountains and they will wonder who I am with my fancy clothes.*

She continued on her way and stopped at Allegra's door where she noted light shining through the kitchen shutters.

Under the street lamp, she pulled out the compact case Silvia had loaned her and checked her reflection in the little mirror before smearing on more red lipstick. 'Here we go,' she muttered to herself, taking a deep breath.

Tina knocked three times on the door, her heart hammering. How she wanted to wrap her arms around Allegra and smother her apple cheeks with kisses. She'd been away more than two months and had missed her so much. But first, she needed to gauge the old lady's reactions.

The door opened mere centimetres.

'Who's there at this time of night?' Allegra asked.

With concern, Tina heard the tremor in the old lady's voice.

Tina adjusted her voice to imitate Silvia's Roman accent. 'Signora, I am lost and need to get to the Castello di Montesecco by nightfall.'

The door fully open, Allegra stepped out, peering at the woman on her doorstep.

Tina gasped. Allegra looked awful. She'd lost more weight, her eyes enormous in her hollowed face.

'You've not far to go at all...' Allegra broke off and stepped nearer. 'Do I know you, signora?'

Tina shook her head. Part of her was shocked her pretence was working. The woman who had raised her no longer recognised her, such was her disguise. How long was this going to continue, this play-acting? The longer, the better, for her purposes, but, oh, how she wanted to embrace Allegra.

'May I come in for a while?' Tina asked, dropping her valise to the cobbled street and pulling out a fan from the crocodile-skin bag round her shoulder. 'I've been travelling all day and I've...' She swayed a little... oh, but she was enjoying herself playing this part. 'I've come over dizzy. Maybe you can offer me a glass of water, signora?'

'Of course, of course. Please come in. I could make tea?'

Tina sank into Allegra's kitchen chair and looked around

the cosy room while Allegra filled a pan with water and set it on the stove. How comforting to be back in Allegra's haven.

'The *castello* is locked up, signora. Why do you want to visit? The owner is away. She's in Rome.'

'I know, signora.' Tina continued with her game. 'I bought the *castello* from a signorina Ernestina when we met in Rome. Such an interesting young woman. But such an unfortunate turn of events.'

Allegra turned from the stove, alarm on her face. 'What? Is she ill? Where did you meet her?'

'Why at the casino, of course. Surely you know of her addiction to gambling?' No longer able to keep up this charade, Tina burst out laughing.

Hands on hips, Allegra stepped nimbly over to Tina.

'Ernestina di Montesecco. Where have you been all this time?' she said, the anger in her tone reminding Tina of many an occasion when she'd been naughty as a child. 'You're a minx, you are. You've had me half worried to death. I've a good mind to give you a thorough spanking. Bought the *castello*, have you? For how much?'

At last Tina could embrace lovely Allegra. The pair fell into each other's arms, laughing and crying.

Allegra mopped her eyes and moved the pasta drying on the table gently to one side. 'I must have known you were coming back. I've made *pici*... unless of course you've grown too grand for my simple food with your Roman ways.'

She watched as Tina removed her hat.

'My, but your scars. They're almost invisible.' Allegra drew nearer, placing her hands on Tina's shoulders and scrutinising her. 'Your hair, your beautiful hair. You've chopped it off and it's ruined.' She swept the stubby black fringe from Tina's forehead.

'I nearly fooled you, didn't I, Allegra? And if you didn't recognise me, then I have a plan that might even work. A surgeon in Rome worked on smoothing out the worst for me and I've learned how to use makeup to conceal. Oh, Allegra, where shall I begin? I have so much to tell you.'

'Well, usually, we begin at the beginning, my dear. Now, tell me everything.'

And so, her joy at seeing Allegra again tinged with sadness for the awful history that had led to the task ahead of her, Tina filled Allegra in on her plan to seek justice for the people of Sant'Agnese, explaining how Allegra could help.

CHAPTER 52

2 November 1946

La Festa dei Morti – The Feast of the Dead

Days before she sent out invitations, Tina was still unsure if she was going to arrive at a conclusion. But she had paid a visit again to the monastery at La Verna to double-check Olivio was not staying up there. In their discussion, the abbot had spoken of the massacre and shared details that had been concerning him. Tina was hopeful his information had led her to the truth.

Everybody in Sant'Agnese now knew the slim dark-haired woman with the Roman accent and fashionable short hairstyle who had begun to take coffee every Friday in the bar del Teatro was the new owner of Castello Montesecco. She kept to herself, always sitting at the same corner table, leaving after half an hour. So far, nobody had dared strike up conversation with the aloof newcomer.

As far as Olivio was concerned, Tina had drawn a blank about his whereabouts until one morning at the start of September. It was the season when sudden rainstorms brought rainbows and washed away summer dust. As the heavens opened, a man had rushed into the bar. Tina's hands began to shake as she'd picked up the newspaper from the table to hide behind.

Finally, her Friday coffee vigils had paid off. It was the first time she'd seen Olivio since that fateful day on the mountain and she was glad her face was caked in foundation, masking her red cheeks as she shot him furtive glances. As soon as the rain stopped, he left. When the waiter came to take her cup, she asked him if he knew the gentleman who had just taken coffee.

'That's young Buratta, signora. Olivio Buratta. He lives near my father's mill in Santa Sofia.'

'Oh, I must be mistaken then. He looks like someone I knew from the city.'

The waiter had laughed. 'Definitely not a city type, signora. Moody chap. Keeps to himself.'

Tina paid him a generous tip and as soon as she was back at the *castello*, she told Allegra to keep lunch for her. Changing into walking clothes, she drove out to Santa Sofia to nose about, pretending to the curious inhabitants she was looking for properties to buy. It didn't take long to find where Olivio lived and she scribbled down the address.

Weeks later, on the second day of November, Tina paced the dining room, her nerves jangling. The invitations to all five guests had been posted back in September and Tina fully hoped the invited would all be in Sant'Agnese on this important traditional feast of the dead. It was expected of everybody to come to their town cemetery to pay respects to the dead of their family. But Tina had no idea if everything would fall into place and she could only hope all eventualities were covered. Her contact at the Allied Advisory Commission, her former lodger Captain Jimmy Metcalfe of the Intelligence Corps, was waiting in the study as planned, together with two armed men, the door slightly ajar so they could listen to the person she hoped to reveal was an evil traitor who had caused the deaths of many innocent Sant'Agnese civilians. When Tina had communicated with the British officer and subsequently travelled once again to Rome to consult with him, Captain Jimmy had insisted on being present, pressing on her the danger in which she would find herself with her plan.

'We've experienced a few of these confrontations, Countess,' he'd said. 'On one occasion the guilty party pulled a gun and shot his accuser before we had a chance to intervene.'

Allegra had insisted on being present too, despite Tina reassuring her she was fine and suggesting it might be better if she stayed in the kitchen to keep an eye on the cooking.

'None of them deserve anything,' Allegra grumbled when Tina reminded her of what might unfold, warning Allegra to not give anything away. 'They abandoned you when you needed them and I'm not abandoning you now.'

'We don't know for sure if they did, Allegra.' Tina bent to kiss the papery-thin cheeks of the woman closest to her in the world. '*Pazienza*, you always say to me. Let's see.' But despite by now having a good idea of the culprit, she was jittery. Had she got it wrong?

Tina examined the reflection of the young woman with the short, dark hair in the mirror above the mantelpiece and adjusted the veil on her hat. She tweaked the roses in the vase at the centre of the table, checked the name places: Donatella opposite Bernardo, Antonio at the far end opposite herself, Olivio to her right, Sergio to her left. She picked a bright red petal from the white tablecloth and crushed it between her fingers.

Would they turn up? Would anybody recognise her? Allegra hadn't immediately when she'd knocked on her return from Rome. But she'd recognised a hand gesture and the way she moved, so since then Tina had adapted the way she walked and assumed a Romano-American accent, practising in front of Allegra until the old lady was totally satisfied with the disguise. Allegra had missed no opportunity in spreading the word in Sant'Agnese about how contessina Ernestina had left for America and sold the *castello* to a rich heiress: *un' americana* whose grandparents had emigrated from Tuscany years earlier.

Vigorous knocking at the door jolted Tina to the present. Allegra hauled herself from her armchair and shuffled to the hall. Tina positioned herself to await her guests and suddenly they were in. She breathed deeply to calm her nerves.

Donatella, of course, was the loudest, her laughter and chatter like breaking glass, rising above the murmur of the men.

'Allegra, *come stai?*' Olivio said, holding the servant's hands in his own. 'How are you and how is your new mistress?' he asked, lowering his voice and looking over at Tina, positioned against the tall French windows, the weak sun making her outline hazy.

Tina watched as Allegra ignored his question and moved to usher in the others, suffering their greetings with a pursed mouth.

Donatella looked round, gazing at the ceiling where a chandelier with three missing lightbulbs dimly lit the room.

Tina guessed she was assessing how worn and tired the furnishings were, how the castle had fallen on bad times. That was what happened when you spent your paltry inheritance pursuing justice: tickets for travel, hotels, not to mention cosmetic surgery. Unconsciously, her hand went beneath her veil to where the scars across her cheek had been repaired and just as quickly, she removed her fingers. If this was to work, nobody must recognise her.

They looked care-worn and older, Tina thought, as her gaze fell on each of her guests. Except Donatella. She was dressed expensively, her tiny waist nipped in by a wide patent-leather black belt, the full material of her black and white chequered skirt held out with stiff petticoats that threatened to knock the tray of Prosecco glasses to the faded rug. Was her husband still alive, she wondered, that she could turn up here today?

Antonio was rake thin. His glasses needed cleaning and he squinted at everybody, his long, tapered hands fiddling with his black cassock, the white band round his throat loose, his Adam's apple prominent as he swallowed.

Sergio, she'd already observed in Rimini. He was a little plumper. Life was treating him well and she was pleased. He still moved with a slight limp and he stuck to Olivio's side.

Bernardo had put on weight, his smoking jacket tight across his shoulders, his cheeks jowly and veined. She pitied the horses he rode.

Tina could hardly bear to look at Olivio. He'd lost weight too but it suited him and his hair, longer and swept back behind his ears, was streaked with fine silver threads. He was still impossibly handsome. Her gaze fell to his hands, bare of rings. She forced herself to look elsewhere. Anywhere else but him.

Tina's new accent, slightly foreign but fluently Italian was, she hoped, unidentifiable. Her voice was deeper, more measured than her usual excitable pace and she prayed nobody would recognise her. She took a deep breath and a dainty step forward.

'It is I who invited you all here today to my castle. As you might know by now, my name is Cristiana della Silva. I want to discover more about the wonderful place I have purchased. I know that you all, in one way or another, have connections with my *castello*. And I thought it a good idea to start integrating. I truly hope we shall know each other better by the end of our luncheon. So, welcome. Please find your seats and we shall begin.'

Tina took in the looks passed between them, pleased her invitations had been successful.

Donatella was the first to speak. 'It's been simply ages since I've been here. Sant'Agnese hasn't changed one little bit. Still scruffy and down at heel. Where I now live in Arezzo, there's such a bustle. You should visit, signora Cristiana. Theatres, operas, festivals, smart restaurants: everything I adore. You'd hardly believe there'd been a war.' She fiddled with her long satin gloves and the emerald bracelet snaking round her wrist.

Bernardo offered to hand round the glasses of Prosecco and Donatella held her glass up to him. 'Almost like old times, dear Bernardo,' she said.

He nodded and having distributed the flutes to each guest, he held up his own. '*Alla salute!* Good health, everybody.'

'I'm considering acquiring a couple of horses for my empty stables,' Tina announced. 'Where should I start?'

'Why, Bernardo's your man,' Donatella said. 'He tried to teach me to ride back in the day, but I was hopeless, wasn't I, *caro*?' She leant into him with a girlish giggle and he nodded.

'Indeed, you are better *off* the horse.' He turned to Tina. 'What breed were you considering, signora?'

'Signorina,' she corrected him. 'I'm not married.' Her glass contained sparkling water, as she needed a clear head to navigate the next hours and she took a sip. 'Oh, I don't know. Something sturdy to ride over the mountains.'

'I may be able to help. Your predecessor was an excellent horsewoman. I rode with her frequently despite the obstacles of war.'

At her raised eyebrows, Bernardo explained. 'During the time of Il Duce, riding for women was frowned upon but contessina Ernestina Montesecco managed when her father was away. She came to my estate more than once. She was a complicated woman.'

'How so?'

'I...' He hesitated. 'I never knew from one time to the next what was in her head.'

Donatella laughed. 'Even we women don't know what is in our heads half the time, *caro* Bernardo. Surely a man of the world like you should know that.'

Sergio took up the conversation. 'Ernestina was a good woman. I wouldn't say she was complicated. Of course, it wasn't easy for her being the daughter of conte Ferdinando. Growing up, she was isolated by her father. But she went on to help plenty of townspeople when food was short, including my own family.'

'*Nobody* had an easy time during the war,' Olivio said, breaking his silence. 'Il Duce split our country. Pitted neighbour against neighbour. What happened here will never be forgotten.'

Tina asked, 'Is this the reason why you have all abandoned Sant'Agnese?'

'I accepted a position at the Vatican,' Antonio said. 'Not for me the life of a country priest.'

'It was too hard to keep our bakery going with my father gone,' Sergio said. 'Life down by the coast is different but I'm happy. I'm accepted and earning a good living. But my mother finds it hard here without me.'

'I have not left. Our *podere* is doing well. Our estate is gaining an excellent reputation and selling to America again,' Bernardo said.

'And you are a politician,' Olivio said. 'For the other side now.'

'Life does not stay still. I was young. To every season—'

'We were all young, Bernardo. We all have brains and minds of our own to choose the right way from the outset,' Olivio countered.

Wanting to avoid a full-blown argument which might end in the luncheon party breaking up prematurely, Tina asked her guests to be seated.

'Signor Fara, as you are the expert, can I ask you to pour the wine? I found one bottle of this excellent Sangiovese hidden in the cellar and purchased another case. There is much I need to do before this old *castello* can be comfortable again.'

'Well, the conte was a drinker, wasn't he? It's what finished him off,' Donatella said.

Allegra rose at that untruth and disappeared to fetch the *antipasti*. When she reappeared, it was Olivio who hurried to his feet to take the tray and help serve from the platter of cold meats and cheeses.

'Ever the people's man,' Bernardo said as Olivio placed slices of Bresaola ham and *salame* on his plate.

'There's no other way,' he retorted.

'Then you should have stayed to fight with me in the local elections.'

'My heart wasn't in it, Bernardo. Politics in this country is a mess.'

'Are you still living like a hermit in that place by the river?'

'I do emerge from time to time. Witness today.'

'You should get out more often, Olivio. I'm sure you're missed in Sant'Agnese. Better still, pop over to Arezzo to visit me,' Donatella said, dazzling a flirtatious look at him as he served her.

And all the while, Tina observed and assessed, seeing whether her theory was wrong or right. Was her hunch about the traitor correct? So far, nobody had given away anything she didn't already know. Wine was the answer. Ply them with it so they were off guard and started to reveal their true selves.

'I'm leaving soon,' Olivio announced. 'I've had it with this country. We've lost our identity. The politicians are kowtowing to America for what they can grab at the table and in return for so-called good behaviour and the abandonment of socialism, the financial bribes roll in.'

Tina's heart skipped a beat. Here was a surprise. Was he really leaving? What was he really running from?

The others too were stunned into silence.

Sergio broke it. 'It's not the end of the world to leave, I can assure you, Olivio. Make a new start, like I have down on the coast.'

'I intend to travel further away. I've heard about *italiani* who have emigrated and are making a success. I need a change,' Olivio commented.

'Aren't you rather abandoning the ship?' Bernardo said.

Olivio shrugged. 'There's nothing here for me anymore.'

'Are you running away?' Antonio cut in.

'I'm running *towards* a new life, Antonio.'

Tina watched and listened to her guests throughout the meal as they ate the courses Allegra had prepared: tagliatelle accompanied with her special hare sauce, followed by tender meatballs of minced turkey in a rich tomato base and finally, her home-made *cantuccini* biscuits, dipped in glasses of sweet Vin Santo. There were also seasonal persimmon fruits piled in an antique bowl, the skins yellow-orange and sunny like a final burst of summer.

It was time for Tina to speak. 'I always smile at the name of this dessert wine,' she said, holding up her liqueur glass. 'Vin Santo. Holy wine. The same used at Mass after we have confessed our sins and are absolved to take Holy Communion.' She paused, observing the faces directed at her.

'I asked you all here today because my head has been full of questions about each one of you.'

There were looks shared and Tina heard Donatella murmur to Bernardo, 'How very strange this woman is.'

Olivio leant back in his chair and asked permission to smoke and Tina nodded. 'There are cigars on the sideboard.'

Olivio fetched the box, offering them to the men. Bernardo accepted but Sergio and Antonio declined.

'Any for a lady?' Donatella asked and Olivio indicated the compartment of slim, dark cigarillos.

Allegra had moved to stand behind her mistress and Tina reached behind to pat her hand. 'It's all right, Allegra. Please don't worry.'

It was Olivio who fetched Allegra a chair and moved himself further down the table.

Tina swallowed more water and looked around her guests.

'You really have no clue, do you? Of who I really am?' Now, she spoke in her own voice and watched for reactions. She wondered if anybody would try to leave but they all remained, each one looking more uncomfortable than the other. Bernardo stubbed out his cigar and folded his arms over his chest but Olivio and Donatella continued to smoke.

'Over two years ago, a grave injustice was committed. In our town of Sant'Agnese more than forty souls were lost. You all know this. Each one of you in some way or another was involved in the massacre. Some of you lost loved ones, God bless their souls, and for some, there was more involvement than was healthy.'

The guests were now watching her intently, more looks exchanged, everybody no doubt wondering what this woman would say next.

'You knew me as contessina Ernestina Montesecco. Yes! My face might not be one you immediately recognise, my hair is dyed and styled differently but my mind and broken heart are still Tina's.'

She paused, allowing for the gasps she had guessed correctly would ensue.

'Since the day of that awful massacre, I have been accused by almost everyone in this town of causing that tragedy. I have been spat on, excrement has been smeared over the doors of the *castello*, poisonous letters sent and dead crows nailed to the wood. My reputation has been torn to pieces. At the time, I was deeply hurt and there were times when I began to doubt my own sanity and think I was in some way guilty. But as the years have passed it is the innocent dead of Sant'Agnese that have preyed on my mind. The innocent who deserve truth and justice.' She paused, looking in turn at each one of her guests, some of whom averted their eyes.

'Very soon I shall reveal the traitor who ruined the lives of the people of Sant'Agnese.'

She grasped Allegra's hand tightly and turned to her. Tears ran silently down the old lady's cheeks as Tina spoke. 'Allegra saved me. I disappeared to a dark place after my father died. And I visited Rome. People thought I too had run away.' She looked pointedly at Olivio as she said this and he bit his lip and shook his head but she continued.

'It was not I who gave away the location of the *partigiani* on the mountain that night.'

She paused, listening to the deafening silence of her guests. When nobody spoke, she continued.

'Sergio, it was not you. I can say that with utter faith. You are too straightforward. Your father's life was in the balance too. You're a good man.

'Donatella,' she said, 'you are a flighty, frivolous woman. During the war you flirted with the *tedeschi* soldiers, you flirted with Bernardo and you schemed to make sure you always knew where your next meal ticket was. I cannot blame you entirely for your weakness. I do believe this is why you prefer to live in the city of Arezzo where your past is unknown. But you are selfish.'

Donatella looked down at her lap, fiddling with the emeralds on her bracelet. For once she remained silent while Tina continued.

'You should have been more discreet. When you asked on the evening of that concert if I had seen Olivio recently, what were you thinking of? Bernardo was standing next to us. Bernardo, a fully committed member of the *nazifascisti*, who picked that question up and stored it in his armoury. He guessed from that moment Olivio must be somewhere in the vicinity. You raised that suspicion in his mind, provided him with information that came in useful. You were foolish. But you are not guilty of informing on the *partigiani*. At least not directly.'

Tina took a deep breath. What she was about to embark on was the hardest thing she had ever done but she continued. She was doing this for Luisa, for the orphaned children of Sant'Agnese and all the helpless victims of the massacre of April 1944. She pushed herself on.

'Bernardo.' Tina directed her gaze full and square upon the aristocrat's face. 'You and I were both born into wealthy families. Our paths were seemingly plotted for both of us. You chose to keep to the path that I decided to stray from. We all have choices, as Olivio mentioned earlier, and you too are weak and opted for the path of least resistance. Towards the end of the war, you said you were wavering. But I do not believe a leopard changes its spots. You are like a dandelion that blows this way or that according to favourable winds. You were up on the mountain that night when I was there. I heard one of your men call you by name. But why were you up there in the first place? Who told you where we were?'

And now, Tina was coming to the hardest part of today's gathering. She willed her tears to remain unchecked and not ruin the rest of what she was about to reveal. She swallowed a mouthful of her water and turned to Olivio. 'I do not believe you are a traitor. I think I know you. But I don't understand you, Olivio. You believed I'd died and so you went away. I discovered you joined another Garibaldi division of *partigiani* and you fought hard on the plains of Rimini. You were with the *alleati* when Rimini was conquered. I saw a photograph of you in the newspaper and... I have kept it ever since on the wall of my tower room where I mapped the progress of you all.' She shook her head, banishing sentimentality. 'I was never certain you'd survived. And I shall never understand why you didn't return to Sant'Agnese, Olivio. Allegra told me you didn't even come to the funerals to honour the dead of your town. I thought you cared, but I am wrong.'

There was an uncomfortable silence whilst the guests waited for what was to come next. Antonio was the first to speak. He rose.

'Well, I have heard nothing of interest so far. You have invited us here to be judged but he who casts the first stone should think twice. Who was it who shared her *castello* with a German officer and helped entertain the *nazifascisti* in this very room?' He pointed a bony finger at Tina. 'Is this going to take much longer? I have a train to catch.'

Donatella spoke next. 'I've always been jealous of you, Ernestina Montesecco. Coming along as you did to the river with your fancy ways and your monied background, changing everything in our group. I thought Olivio and I were a couple. At least I did until you arrived on the scene. And then, you had your way with Bernardo too. No matter whom I set eyes on, you always come between us.'

'I admit I once had feelings for Ernestina,' Bernardo said. 'Until I understood she was simply using me. She wanted to ride her horse and to that end I was useful. But I soon realised she is nothing but a tease.'

Sergio and Olivio remained silent and Tina continued to talk, ignoring Bernardo's comment.

'Antonio. You have always intrigued me. We can never know what exactly goes on in another's mind, but we can surmise. Your vocation, for example. A true calling or passport from poverty? During the war you were sheltered in the monastery. You didn't have to fight. You had food in your belly, a bed at night. The monasteries were out of bounds to the enemy and so you were relatively safe. But I do not believe you are a true man of the cloth. I'm not here to judge you about this but I discovered you fathered a little boy and pay for his upkeep in Rome.' At Antonio's protest, she raised a hand. 'Don't try to deny it; I talked to his mother. She brought him each day to the gardens near where I lodged in Rome and it wasn't hard to strike up conversation. She's a lonely young woman. Leaving aside the rules of celibacy that a priest should adhere to, the fact you recognise your duty to your son, to me that is honourable, but it adds to the conundrum of you.'

She paused for breath. His loud objections and eagerness to leave the room made her more certain than ever of his guilt. Her heart was thumping, her firm tone in contradiction with the nerves she felt. Pointing a finger at the priest, she said, 'Antonio Gerico, your ambition is your failing. To attain your position in the Vatican you ingratiated yourself with the *clerici-fascisti* in Rome and kept them informed of the movements of the *partigiani* in this area and they in turn relayed it here.'

Olivio and Sergio leant forward in their seats.

'Is this true, Antonio? Tell me it's not,' Olivio blurted.

Tina rose. '*Please!* Let me continue. You can question him afterwards. I have more to add.'

She waited until the murmurs died down and took a deep breath before continuing, her stomach churning as she willed her tears not to spill.

'My dear friend, Luisa, how I miss her.' She paused to control her emotions. 'During my discussions with the abbot up at La Verna, I found out that poor Luisa's father had asked for shelter at the monastery for his family while they waited for arrangements to leave for Switzerland but you, Antonio, turned them away because you knew they were Jewish.' Tina brushed aside an annoying tear that threatened to unravel her at the last moment, as she imagined the despair of Luisa's family, their deportation and subsequent horrific demise in the death chambers, the fate of so many persecuted Jews. But then, it was as if Luisa was standing at her side, willing her to go on, her skinny frame and cropped hair belying the strength she had shown on so many occasions when they'd worked together to help the *partigiani*.

Tina continued. She was almost there. 'You, Antonio, obviously did not give this reason to the abbot. You told him Luisa's father had a reputation as a thief and philanderer, that he could not be trusted and should not be harboured at the monastery. I know now that as a direct result of your gross deception Luisa's family was sent to Fossoli concentration camp and then to Auschwitz.'

There were gasps all around as Tina revealed this horror. Antonio made to leave but Olivio and Sergio immediately leapt from their chairs to apprehend him as he struggled.

Above his noisy protestations, Tina raised her voice to continue.

'It is because of *you* the *nazifascisti* dragged Luisa from the chemist's on the night of the massacre and tortured her to death, leaving her mangled body hanging from the bridge we now call the bridge of the martyrs. It was *you* who told the *fascisti* she was Jewish. I shall never forgive you for that, although the God you purport to follow asks us to. And it was also you who gave away the location of the camp where the *partigiani* were hiding. You knew where they were bound because you had overheard them talking when they were sheltering in your monastery. You! A childhood friend whose classmates believed it safe to talk in front of. You betrayed them and your own townspeople. I never imagined a man of the cloth stooping so low.'

She turned to her guests, their expressions horrified. 'I was not immediately convinced of my suspicions, but I am certain now after talking to the abbot.'

'This is all codswallop,' the shamed priest shouted. 'You haven't one ounce of proof to substantiate your wild accusations. Who do you think you are you to pass judgement on us like this?'

Tina rang a bell at the side of her place setting and Captain Metcalfe and his two military police burst into the room, coming to the aid of Sergio and Olivio, who had rushed to Antonio's side, ordering the two ex-*partigiani* to let them take over.

'Let the official bodies pass judgement on you, Antonio Gerico,' Tina shouted. 'And may God forgive you for your treachery for I never shall. You have caused too much heartbreak.'

She sank back in her chair as Antonio's shouts continued loud as he was dragged away in handcuffs by the officials. Bernardo left the room after stating, 'You are wrong to involve me in this, Ernestina. And I shall prove through my lawyers I was simply carrying out my duty.'

She shook her head, her body suddenly limp.

'Now leave. All of you. I'm tired.'

She had nothing left in her. Like a hollowed rag doll, she slumped forwards, her arms supporting her against the table. She was aware of the remaining guests slipping from the dining room and Allegra rubbing her back.

'There, there, *carina mia*,' Allegra's gentle voice soothed. 'It's over now. It's over.'

CHAPTER 53

Sweet sorrow

Not even her garden could raise her deflated spirits. Through the November mist, roses drooped their heads, soggy putrid-brown petals of Albertine, unpruned branches of the climbing rose long and straggly, fallen leaves dry and withered like her feelings. The air was still and moisture glistened on her mother's old shawl around her shoulders. It was not the kind of garment that Cristiana della Silva would have worn but she was Tina Montesecco again and she craved comfort after the ordeal of confronting the people she'd considered friends.

Allegra had retired to her house straight after clearing up and the *castello* was sombre as a morgue. Tina had wanted to chat a while and go over the reunion. But the exhaustion on Allegra's face had made her send her to bed. Her hacking cough was definitely worse. Tomorrow, Tina would insist on making an appointment to consult a specialist in Riccione. Allegra put it down to damp weather but Tina worried it was more than a common cold.

She had finally exposed the traitor. Word must have already

travelled round Sant'Agnese about Antonio. The women at the fountain would be whispering to one another and carrying the news to their homes, shouting that justice had at last been served as they shared the news with women sitting mending at their windows or sweeping their thresholds. Husbands would overhear and exchange the scandal about the *castello* later in the *osteria*, exaggerating details as they knocked back tumblers of rough red wine. And Tina knew the next time she stepped across the piazza on her way to shop, there would still be furtive whispers as citizens of Sant'Agnese looked the other way. What did they think about her casting Antonio as the villain? A priest? A citizen of Sant'Agnese who had studied in the school, destined to a great future? Would anybody approach to say sorry? Perhaps they still wanted to cling on to falsehoods because salacious gossip, *pettegolezzi*, was more interesting than truth. What difference had any of her investigations made?

Sergio was the only one who had embraced her with warmth after Antonio was arrested. Tina had handed him an envelope containing money to bring his mother to Rimini and make his new home comfortable for her.

'Your mother will find purpose through caring for you down at the coast,' she'd told him. 'With a new life, her mind will be less consumed with the loss of your father and sister. She'll be useful in the restaurant rolling out home-made pasta and baking cakes.'

Bernardo was long gone while she was talking to Sergio and Donatella's exit was noisy as she flounced through the door. And Olivio... he had left without a word.

Her world was more barren than before. Had any of it been worth it?

A sound came from the greenhouse and she turned from where she sat shivering in the garden.

Olivio emerged and stopped before her, cap in hand, his fingers fidgeting with the peak as he stood.

She patted the seat beside her. 'I'm glad you returned, Olivio. Sit with me for a while.'

He lit up a cigarette after offering her one, which she declined.

'Where did you go all this time, Olivio?'

'I... was lost. For the first time in my life, I didn't know what to do. When I found you dead, under the body of Claudio, it was the end of rational thought. I wanted to die too. I couldn't see any point to life. The deaths, the agony of loved ones... I believed it was all my fault.'

His fingers continued to turn the cap round and round as he leant forwards, shoulders hunched. He reminded Tina of a cowed, beaten dog.

'It wasn't your fault, Olivio. How could it be?'

A shrug of his shoulders. 'I should have looked after you myself in those woods, but I couldn't think straight. And that continued for a long while afterwards. I... retreated somewhere I couldn't return from. I remembered a cave deep in the forest far from any tracks. I stayed there at first... like a coward. All fight and purpose drained from me.'

He turned to look at her and his eyes were pools of melancholy. 'Everything I had fought for was suddenly pointless.'

'You're not a coward. Bullets and bombs are not the only things to wound. The mind can only take so much. And you did *so* much: fought hard for your ideals and, in the end, you helped rid our country of *nazifascismo*.'

'Yes, the *tedeschi* are gone but we still have plenty of *fascisti*. They will crawl again from the woodwork and worm their way into politics. Investigations of war crimes are taking place but it's harder than expected and...' Another pause before Olivio continued. 'I read what the papers say about the relationship between *americani* and nazi criminals. How the German police commander here during the war, General Wolff – the evil *bastardo* – how he had secret talks with the *americani* to secure an early surrender and in return demanded immunity from prosecution. Nothing changes. Don't you see? And Kesselring, the instigator of so many deaths. His own death sentence has been conveniently commuted. Our new prime minister, De Gasperi, he's fiercely anti-communist, like the *americani*. He wants to limit the scope of war crimes trials and move on, forget what our nation went through. What *was* the point of it all, Tina?'

'But you can't blame yourself for any of that, Olivio. And what happened on the mountain that night was because of Antonio's betrayal, not because of you. I proved that tonight, didn't I? You need time to recover, Olivio. You've been ill.' She added in a smaller voice, 'I think you may still be ill.'

'I'm sorry the people of Sant'Agnese blamed you for the killings. I heard the rumours. What you did today was a good thing. I didn't for one moment ever believe it was your fault, Tina.'

'I would have appreciated you telling me that before,' she said. 'But now I understand you were sick.'

He looked up, staring into her eyes for a long moment. 'I did come a couple of times to town, to buy provisions and... I wanted to see you. And each time I stood under the tower room where you sleep. But...'

'But what, Olivio?'

'I... wanted to see you but I knew you wouldn't want to see me.'

She shook her head. 'You are wrong to think that. We were friends, weren't we? Good friends. I hope we still are.' She threw up her hands in frustration and stood up.

'Enough of this beating ourselves up. Come inside. I want to hear you sing again.' She pulled him to his feet and she thought she detected the faintest glimmer of hope in his eyes and maybe a twitch of his mouth into a reluctant smile.

'The *castello* is funereal,' she said. 'Let's liven it up.'

She strode through the secret passageway to the kitchen where ferns had begun to cluster thickly from the roof and brush against their heads.

In the study, she threw another log on the fire and stirred it to life with a poker. 'It's always cold in this place. I swear there must be ghosts that come behind me to blow out the flames. Come, Olivio. Stand beside me. The piano needs tuning but let's see what we can do.'

'I fear I'm out of tune too. It's ages since I sang a note.'

She played the opening bars of *Nessun Dorma* her fingers tentative at first for all of a sudden she was nervous. She wanted it to be right for Olivio, wanted to capture the old magic they'd created in the past and pull him from his sadness.

Slowly but surely Olivio found his voice, gaining confidence with each line, until his voice soared, the notes clearer and resonating with each line.

She stopped playing before he reached the final phrase, the words '*all'alba vincerò*', 'I shall win at dawn', bringing up goose-bumps. Her fingers rested on the keys as she listened to his pure voice, the acoustics of the room perfect for his tenor's pitch. Tears came to her eyes and she willed them not to spill. The moment was special, one to store in the heart and when he sang the last note, she turned to him on the piano stool, gazing up at him, her hands clasped. He was no longer hunched and dejected. He stood there proud, head raised, and she saw tears glisten in his eyes too.

'A glass of wine, I think,' she said finally, 'and we shall have an interval like in the theatre and after that please stay to sing more.'

Down in the kitchen she pulled a bottle of Montepulciano from the pantry shelf, bought recently from the *alimentari*. Olivio turned the corkscrew while Tina fetched two simple glass tumblers, knowing instinctively his preference for drinking from those rather than a fine crystal chalice. They sat opposite each other at the old table.

'You're not the only one to beat himself up, Olivio,' she said after they clinked glasses. 'I should have stood up to my father a long time ago and then I could have been of more use to the cause.'

'I admire what you did. It can't have been easy.' He stared at her and she tore her eyes away, trying to deny the desire she felt, welling up so strong she was sure he could sense it.

'Whoever mended your face did a fine job,' he continued, pouring more wine. 'You look different. At first I didn't recognise you. But you're still Tina, with that spirit I so admire.'

For a fleeting moment she thought he was going to touch her as he reached his hand towards her face and then he grinned.

'Those few remaining freckles are a giveaway, though.' He thumped his chest with his free hand. 'It's what's inside that counts, isn't it? That hasn't changed in you. In fact, I do believe your spirit is stronger than the day I pulled you from the river.'

'Going to Rome was good for me. Nobody knew me there. I wasn't contessina Ernestina. I was an ordinary young woman who had been badly scarred. I made my own decisions and I didn't have to justify my upbringing. I met a wonderful young woman called Silvia who had been through so much more than I and she helped me a lot. Coming back here, though, it feels like nothing has changed. Maybe I'll go away again.'

'I know what you mean. I'm leaving Italy,' he said abruptly. 'I'm leaving for New Zealand. There are plenty of jobs there.'

He must have heard the intake of her breath for he said, 'Why don't you come with me? Make a *new* start. What is there left for you here?'

'Just like that?' she stuttered. 'Leave this place? What would I do?'

She regretted her nervous laugh at his suggestion when she saw his immediate embarrassment.

He drained the rest of his wine and stood up. 'It was foolish of me to suggest. You've met someone else. I—'

'No, Olivio. There's nobody but what you asked is a huge surprise to me... a *wonderful* surprise.' She was blustering, covering her upset that he was leaving for the other side of the world. Yet another blow. And yet, she was charmed he had asked her.

'I should never have asked,' Olivio said, retrieving his cap from the table.

'I can't leave Allegra, Olivio. She's ill. Sergio's mother is leaving Sant'Agnese too, and there's nobody else to look after her except me. And I want to do that for her. But, will you write to me? I... want to know how everything goes. It's... such a long way. The other side of the world.'

She couldn't bear to say goodbye to this man whom she wanted to know better and better – the man she now realised was the one for her.

But what did she know about that side of life? She'd never loved a man. Like many young women, she'd dreamt about meeting a special person and falling in love. Olivio had been there all the time and she'd never understood. Had any chance of romance ended before it had begun?

When he held out his hand to say goodbye, she ignored it and flung herself into an embrace instead, her head nestling under his chin. It felt right.

She was so close to him she could feel the beating of his heart and she wanted to stay there forever but he stepped back, disentangling himself from her arms.

'*Addio*, Tina.'

'Promise me you'll write.'

He gave her a long look which she couldn't fathom and then he was gone. She listened to his footsteps as he made his way up the kitchen stairs. The bang of the huge door as it slammed behind him reverberated deep within her.

So final. She couldn't bear it.

Tina sank down in her chair, the lump in her throat refusing to budge so she picked up her glass, finishing the rest of the wine which offered small comfort. She was cold to her core. The ashes in the stove glowed red, reminding her she must bank the fire for the night. Sighing, she fetched sticks and logs and then made her way through the damp *castello* to her cold, lonely bed.

CHAPTER 54

Early 1947

The letter

Winter dragged on, its long, miserable days penetrating Tina's being. As time passed the castle grew increasingly damp and she spent most of her days in Allegra's house, nursing her fading health. With nobody to light the fires, furniture in the *castello* grew patches of mould, cobwebs hung in corners and despite Tina urging Tigressa and her kittens to stay in the castle, mice took over. The only room near to cosy was the kitchen. Tina had learned by now to keep the stove burning. She vacated her tower room after pulling down the maps, photos and notes that had consumed her whilst planning her hunt and moved a truckle bed into the kitchen.

'You don't have to stay with me all day, Tina *cara*,' Allegra said, her words slow as she struggled to catch her breath. 'And you need to add more celery to the broth next time you make it.'

Tina encouraged Allegra to take one more spoonful, smiling

at the old lady's advice. Allegra waved the spoon away. 'I have no more appetite.'

It was true she was no cook. Tina had come to it late and would never match Allegra's natural talent.

She was deteriorating fast. *Dottor* Brilli had warned her but Tina didn't want to accept that soon Allegra would no longer be with her. Allegra had been mother, friend, counsellor and confidante in most matters. She couldn't bear the idea of saying goodbye to the woman she loved so much.

As she tucked her up and made sure the stove downstairs was fed with logs, melancholy scratched at her heart. If it were not for Allegra, she'd have nothing to live for, her weeks and months dreary with routine. There'd been no news from Olivio and the people of Sant'Agnese continued to avoid her. Tina's life was empty. To add to her mood, a persistent drizzle soaked her as she made her way up to the *castello*. Tomorrow, she would lock up and stay down with Allegra. It made no sense to return nightly to the dank, dismal place and soon Allegra would need nursing all the time.

Tina let herself in through the back door. To her relief, embers still glowed in the kitchen stove and as soon as she added twigs, a cheering flame lit up the space. For a while, she sat in the chair where Allegra used to rest after her day's work. When Allegra left this world, Tina's days would be as empty as a bucket full of holes. Whenever she ventured into town, it was obvious she was not accepted. What was the expression: *né pesce né carne*, neither fish nor fowl? She was not one of them, living as she did above the town with aristocratic blood in her veins. In truth, how could she know what it was like to eke a living from day to day? With the conte dead, the factory was closed and several families had given up scraping a living from the arid land, packed up and emigrated. Some had departed for the north of Italy to seek work in the big factories, some abroad as far away as America. Even though she'd proved her innocence and word had trickled round town, Tina sensed rejection in people's stares, in the silence as she walked to the *alimentari* to buy provisions, in the frightened looks the children gave her and the way women pulled up their shawls to cover their faces as she passed. What was she going to do with her life?

Sighing, she banked up the stove with fresh logs, noting how low the pile was. How wonderful it would be to have someone help her with chopping wood and replenishing supplies as in former times. She had learned to do all these tasks but after her father's death, the lawyers had informed her there was little money left and, in any case, even if she'd had the wherewithal to take on new servants, she doubted anybody would be prepared to work at Castello Montesecco.

On the following morning, after another restless night, she passed through the hallway and something white on the floor by the great doors caught her attention. An envelope. Another poison pen letter, she thought, although there hadn't been any for a while. She bent to pick it up and her heart skipped a beat. It was postmarked Picton, New Zealand and on the back was the sender's name: Mr Olivio Buratta. So, he was a Mister now, was he? No longer an Italian signore.

Clutching the envelope, she hurried to the warmth of the kitchen. She poured a cup of yesterday's coffee, wet and warm. She hadn't thought Olivio would ever write. She'd asked him to, she'd hoped for it, but she'd picked up on his non-committal nod when they'd parted.

This letter, then, was a gift. Even though she hardly dared read the contents, he had actually contacted her. The envelope remained in front of her on the table as she prolonged the moment and sipped lukewarm coffee. What news would it hold? Perhaps he was writing to tell her he was returning to Sant'Agnese; that there was nothing for him in New Zealand; that he missed his fatherland after all. Maybe he had met a woman: he was engaged. Maybe he needed help, money, a reference.

She couldn't wait any longer and she slit open the envelope with a knife, being careful not to rip the address.

A photograph fell out as she unfolded the thin papers, one side covered with his scratchy scrawl, the rest taken up with sketches of a house, plants and a strange-looking bird. She peered at the black and white photograph, showing a healthy, happy Olivio. He was at the oars of a boat on what looked like a lake, mountains soaring in the background. His shirtsleeves were rolled up and he wore a kerchief round his neck. He looked younger and more carefree than when she'd last seen him.

Picton, January 1947

Dear Tina,

I bet you never expected to receive news from me but I think about you most days and wonder how you're getting on. How is Allegra?

Well, I love it over here on the other side of the world. Yes, it's miles from la bella Italia, *but Italia was no longer right for me and New Zealand has offered me a new life. I've moved around a fair bit in a short space of time. I started off in Auckland (on North Island) – there are two main islands here. In fact, somebody pointed out that if you look at the map, NZ resembles an upside-down Italia. Quite apt, I think when I think how my own life has turned out.*

Anyway, in the city I was directed to Club Italiano where I met fellow Italians who'd been here a while, searching for 'la bella fortuna'. They filled me in on job opportunities and suggested I make my way over to Nelson where there's another Italian community who are mostly market gardeners. But the place to earn good money is here in Picton on the whale ships. The business is run by the Perano family who came from Genova way back. Don't think I can stomach slaughtering these amazing mammals for long but another possibility has cropped up and it set me thinking. And on this first day of a new year, I thought why not write to you about it.

Someone heard me singing while I worked, and suggested I trot along to the social club in town and entertain people there. So, I tried it out and it was good. I get to keep tips but it's only part-time and not enough to live on forever. I remember the music we made. How I'd love to have you by my side accompanying me on the piano.

I share a small hut with Brunello. I have no idea what his real name is but he likes his red wine (there are plenty of vineyards in Marlborough, and that's how he got his name). You see, Tina, out here there are Italians who prefer to forget their real identities, why they left Italia and all that. And there's an unwritten understanding we don't pry and we accept what is happening in the now and yet... it's strange this feeling of being rootless. Sometimes I feel as if I have run away.

Our hut is pretty basic: the walls made of clay – some are made from flax and rushes – especially the native Maori dwellings – and there's a veranda that runs across the front where we smoke and take refuge from the sun. It's summer here right now. Christmas Day down by the sea, swimming and cooling beer in the surf was strange. One of the men made us a bowl of cappelletti *like we have in Sant'Agnese, but somehow it doesn't fit the climate out here. We threw some goat meat on an open fire and that was better. Is there snow on the mountains in Romagna? I saw snow on Mount Cook but here it's warm.*

If you feel like replying, I'd love that. In any case, I'll write again soon. There's so much to tell you. Picton is situated in one of the many inlets on this part of the island and although it's the sea, it feels like being on the edge of a lake, with mountains all around and any amount of bays to fish and explore. The climate is great for growing vegetables. There are huge purple flowers that grow like weeds and colourful creepers and orchids. It reminds me of you and your garden.

Oh, there's so much to share with you, Tina. I could fill a book with what I've seen so far.

Write soon if you can.

Affectionately,

Olivio

Tina read the letter twice more. He was missing her. Her heart had skipped a beat when she read that. He sounded like the enthusiastic Olivio full of life she'd first met and she was pleased he'd shaken off his bitterness and melancholy. Some of his mood rubbed off on her as she hummed and prepared a small valise with clothes for her stay with Allegra. At the last minute she added her mother's gardening diary and some sheets of blank paper to jot ideas for new projects on her garden. She wanted to reply to Olivio. Allegra would enjoy hearing Olivio's news and she would sit and read her the letter. It would cheer her up.

After letting herself into Allegra's small house, she heated a pan of water on the stove for a peppermint tisane, the only drink Allegra seemed to manage now. Although it might not be eaten, she cut a small slice of *ciambella* cake she'd baked two days earlier. Made from flour, eggs, oil and sugar, it contained nothing to upset the old lady's stomach. Finally, she went outside and picked the last red rose growing in the shelter of the house and stuck it in a small drinking glass to add to Allegra's breakfast tray.

'It's only me, Allegra. *Buongiorno*, did you sleep well?' she called as she climbed the stairs.

She set the tray on the bedside table and opened the inside shutters to let in wintry sunshine. The robin that came each morning to sit on the sill to await breakfast crumbs appeared immediately and started its noisy chirrup.

Tina approached the bed to help Allegra sit up but she was still sleeping, so she left her and carried the tray back to the kitchen. It didn't take long to chop fresh vegetables for a simple *minestrina* for Allegra's lunch and to sweep the kitchen floor. Upstairs was still quiet and she tiptoed up to the room. Allegra had always told her sleep was the best medicine.

She sat down next to the bed and pulled out Olivio's letter to read again while she waited for Allegra to stir. Halfway through the descriptions of Olivio's new life, something told her Allegra was not going to wake up and, tentatively, she reached for the old lady's hand resting on the bedclothes.

It was cold as a river pebble and Tina knew when she put her face to Allegra's mouth there would be no breath. And yet Tina wanted Allegra to hear the words in Olivio's letter so she picked it up again and started from the very beginning, tears spilling down her cheeks as she read aloud. Afterwards she climbed onto the bed and lay by Allegra's side.

Tina remained next to Allegra for a while, hoping the old lady had understood how much she'd been loved, how much she'd be missed. While Tina pondered her future, the robin continued to trill and, eventually, with a flutter of feathers, flew away.

CHAPTER 55

Fiammetta

I grow weary, oh so weary. My spirit is fading and my time here dwindles but my darling is almost there. My work is almost done.

I see trails of sadness but through the trees I see sun and beauty, friendships, hope.

If my daughter can learn to understand, then she will know I am not gone forever. She will never be alone. I shall be the first ray of morning sun, the light flashing a promise through bare trees on an icy winter's day, a pollen-dusted bee feasting upside down within an unfurling rose. I shall be crystal raindrops slipping down lime-green leaves, the butterfly batting at a window until my child cups her hands to gently carry me to the open, from where I shall dance away into the sky. If she looks, she will see. If she listens, she will hear me in the breeze that plays through her hair and whispers through the grass. She should stop to hear the robin's song rising above other birds in my garden and see the promise of blue speckled eggs in the nest above the arbour.

My work is almost done. Almost but not entirely.

CHAPTER 56

Visitors

The piano needed tuning, making the Chopin nocturne sound even more mournful, but she ploughed on. She'd lit a fire in the library to make an effort. Everything was an effort at the moment but it was no good wallowing. Allegra would have told her to snap out of it, given her a job in the kitchen, encouraged her to work on the garden.

She broke off playing mid-phrase and rooted in the piano stool for something more suitable. Vivaldi's 'Winter' from *The Four Seasons*. Tina played the opening bars but it was no good. It matched the harsh view of skeletal trees against the cold grey sky. She closed the lid and trailed downstairs.

A shutter banged somewhere and a blast of cold air stirred the curtains in the hallway causing the material to billow like long skirts. She thought she heard a whisper and turned sharply but, oh how ridiculous, now she was imagining things in this wretched place. A warming tisane was called for and a hunk of bread and cheese, if the mice had left it alone. She couldn't remember the last time she'd prepared a proper meal.

Tomorrow she'd make a hearty stew. It would last for days and Allegra would have approved.

Another shutter banged and banged. She really should go and investigate before it fell off. There were half a dozen waiting to be repaired but she'd failed to find anybody in town to help with odd jobs. *Knock, knock, knock.* It must be a shutter outside the sitting room window. While the water for her drink simmered on the stove, she ran back upstairs and then stopped in the hall. The knocking was coming from the door. Who was visiting at this time of evening? In fact, who was visiting at all? Nobody came to her door these days, except the *postino* with bills.

'*C'è nessuno?* Anybody there?' a woman's muffled voice called from the other side of the door.

On unbolting it, a figure in a red cape, hood pulled over the head jumped towards her and enveloped her in a hug.

'*Auguri!* Greetings, my lovely friend. I'm late with my festive wishes but I haven't heard from you and I wanted to check up, so here I am. But, *Dio mio*, it's perishing out there. *Gesù Maria!*'

'Silvia!' Tina gasped. 'I… what… but this is wonderful. I had no idea you were coming!'

'Of course you didn't. It's my surprise. I've closed my shop for five whole days, so here I am! What a journey from Rome, though. You really do live in the back of beyond.' She peeled off her gloves and the long scarf wrapped around her neck. 'And in a real castle. But *brrr*! It's so bloody freezing.'

'Come down to the kitchen. It's the warmest place. I was about to prepare a hot drink.'

Ashamed at the lack of food in the pantry, Tina ventured down on the following afternoon to Sant'Agnese with Silvia. In her company, the looks and whispers from townsfolk didn't seem to matter. Silvia found everything quaint, old-fashioned and her cheerful manner rubbed off on the shopkeepers. They returned with a decent cut of beef, a round of fresh pecorino cheese, a bag of precious oranges and vegetables, Silvia remarking that shopping was far more fun here than Rome.

That evening, they laid Allegra's kitchen table with the best dinner service and lit a dozen candles to create a magical festive scene, Silvia declaring it was never too late to have a party and as both of them had ignored Christmas and the New Year, now was the time to do so. They draped strands of ivy from Tina's garden along kitchen shelves, round beams and on the table and Silvia laid two extra places, taking care to fold linen serviettes into intricate swan shapes.

'One place for Allegra, I guess,' Tina remarked. 'And the fourth?'

'For your mamma,' Silvia replied. 'She's everywhere in your *castello*, you know. I think she'll be pleased we've invited her.'

Tina swallowed. It was a strange gesture. But it was beautiful too.

They shared a full bottle of Frascati Silvia had brought from Rome and talked and talked about their childhoods, dreams, their futures.

'One of my dreams has been realised already,' Silvia said as she cracked walnuts to eat with the pecorino. 'I love my little shop but I should like to have a family. The trouble is finding a father!'

'If I have a family, I want them to enjoy childhoods filled with the fun I never had,' Tina said wistfully.

'What *are* you going to do with yourself stuck up here?' Silvia asked later when they sipped at a bottle of Allegra's basil liqueur retrieved from the back of the pantry. 'I'd suggest turning the castle into a grand hotel, but...'

'I have no money for repairs and, anyway, who would want to come here?'

'Rich *americani*. They love castles. Where there's a will, there's a way, *amica mia*.'

Tina shrugged her shoulders. 'I really do not know, Silvia. But I need to decide soon. I can't continue like this.'

'Well, if you grow lonely, come and visit me in Rome and I shall return in the summer to pick flowers from your mountains to adorn my creations.'

After Silvia had left with promises to come again soon, the thick walls of the *castello* closed in further on Tina and she was lost again. She lay awake questioning everything. Silvia had asked what she was going to do with her life and that question loomed heavy over everything. For a while during the war Tina had found purpose. But what now? She didn't want to spend the rest of her life rattling around in this cavernous building worrying about its upkeep. She could try to sell it but what then? And by selling it would she be cutting off her roots? What did that even mean? She was a contessina but what good had her aristocratic ancestry brought her so far? Did it matter?

Where there's a will, there's a way, Silvia had said, but the trouble was dredging up that will. Olivio, Sergio and even Donatella had made their moves. Why couldn't she? She'd read Olivio's letter so many times, the flimsy notepaper was beginning to tear at the folds. He sounded so much happier on the other side of the world. If she had the money, then perhaps she could travel to see everything he wanted to show her. She certainly missed him, but basically, they hardly knew each other. Maybe she could sell more items from the castle, the knick-knacks and ornaments were merely gewgaws to her, and raise some money for the fare. But shouldn't she be putting money towards restoring the *castello*? And what if she travelled all the way there and it was a huge mistake? What then? Was she simply running away and hoping Olivio would be the answer to everything? What did that make her? A helpless female without gumption. Oh, she felt so weak and indecisive. Round and round went her fears and frets until she wanted to scream for them to end.

The garden was her solace. Tina spent hours planning what she would work on when the warmer weather arrived. She imagined herself turning into an eccentric old lady in the future, spending her days working on flower beds, pruning and trimming, designing new features while the castle fell apart around her. In one of her children's story books, the plants in an old garden came alive at night and she imagined herself as the gnarly trunk of an olive tree dancing in the moonlight, her limbs twisted, her long silvery-green hair growing like creepers, turning slowly crazy.

Tina escaped in her dreams: dreams where life was perfect, but mornings when she woke a disappointment. One night she woke too early. She'd taken to not drawing the drapes at her window because starlight was a comfort but the stars were covered tonight and a strange ethereal mist clouded the panes. Maybe it was snowing again. It sometimes did in April in the mountains. She turned over, willing sleep to keep her in her dream. But light was showing beneath her bedroom door and she cursed. She'd forgotten to turn down the oil lamp in the corridor before retiring and not wanting to waste more fuel she padded from her bed and opened the door.

Whoosh! The draught ignited a flicker of orange flame whirling like a woman with flowing auburn hair along the floorboards. Tina shielded her face and screamed, returning to her room to pull a cover from the bed to stamp out the dancing flames. But it was impossible. Sparks had already ignited the woollen tapestries hanging on the wall and to her horror, the bannisters were now ablaze.

Wrapping the cover tightly around her, and, at the last minute, grabbing her mother's journal from the bedside table, she rushed through the hoops of fire, slipping and sliding down the stairs to the hallway. The fire had not taken hold down here yet but from upstairs a loud crack and the sound of breaking glass as a chandelier plummeted to the marble tiles made her rush for the main doors.

The *pompieri* when they came were too late, the tinny siren on their single truck ringing hollow as the firemen played hoses on angry flames, orange, pink and yellow in the fire as they devoured old timbers and doors. There was nothing anyone could do against this wild furnace, even if she wanted.

In the smoke-filled light of morning, Tina wandered round dozens of small fires that smouldered and nibbled at what was left of the past. Antique tables, chairs, cracked porcelain, paintings and books lay in the hot ashes and Tina picked her way through the devastation. The painting of her mother was mostly intact and she pulled it free to take down to Allegra's place. This and the journal were the only possessions she had of her mamma. A handful of Sant'Agnese families whom she had helped throughout the war turned up to see if they could help and she was grateful. She had very little left and these friendly gestures were a deep source of comfort and hope.

In the weeks that followed, she sheltered in Allegra's house, where she replaced the religious painting above her bed with her mother's scorched portrait. Most days, she found a plate of pasta or soup left on the doorstep. Not all of the citizens shunned her now and she was grateful for their small kindnesses.

On one spring morning, Tina wandered down to the *alimentari* and the greetings of '*Buongiorno*, contessina' as she passed people in the piazza replaced the old hostile stares.

'*Come va?*' 'How is it going?' they asked. It was as if, through the adversity of the *castello* burning down, she had joined the ranks of the unfortunate: she was one of them. Or was it that word had finally hit home and she was not the traitor that gossip-mongering had led them to believe? At any rate, the change was pleasing. She felt less isolated and the heavy burden of restoring the family *castello* was now out of her hands. She entered the parish church to light a candle for Allegra and knelt for a while beneath the mediaeval painting of the Madonna and child.

It's hard, Allegra, she mouthed, *and I do miss you so much but I know you're telling me to get on with life. I'm going to see if I can help in the school and offer music lessons to the children of Sant'Agnese. And soon I'll catch the train to Rome and visit Silvia. Yes, you're right. There's much to look forward to. See you again next week.* She added an *Amen* as she left.

She preferred to visit Allegra in church. It was more comforting in there than the cemetery with its stark white stones and photos of the dead next to the inscriptions. The cemetery was so final.

On a whim, she decided she would try the tunnel to her greenhouse. The *castello* kitchen had been reduced to a mass of fallen rocks, too dangerous to navigate, and the side path to the original entrance she'd used at the beginning had completely collapsed. She wanted to see the damage to her garden.

She left her groceries in Allegra's kitchen and picked up the torch Allegra had used to go back and forth to the *castello* and returned downtown. Checking there was nobody around, she pushed her way through the curtains of thick *vitalba* fronds covering the secret tunnel. A robin flew in, startling her, accompanying her as she stepped over fallen stones. She fully expected the passageway to be blocked as a result of the destructive fire but her spirits lifted as she ascended the narrow tunnel without difficulty. Perhaps the door at the end would be blocked though and the greenhouse burned down, but she had to try.

The low door was ajar. Sunlight and a current of fresh air beckoned her forwards for the last metres, her back aching from hunching down in the low tunnel. She pictured the soldiers who might have used this passageway in the past, encumbered with weapons and armour, bent on destruction or escape. She remembered how she'd crept out at night to leave baskets of food for those in need in Sant'Agnese and how Olivio had used it to come and go during the war. How many secrets this place held. How much history nobody would know except the walls of this ancient tunnel.

To her absolute joy, she was greeted as she crawled into the greenhouse by the robin hopping about on the workbench keeping up a chattering song as she advanced further. Its little head was cocked to one side, as if to say, *What took you so long?*

Everything around her was as it had been the last time she'd worked in here: her trowel and secateurs hung from their hooks, a row of pots waited to be planted up for the summer, sacks were piled neatly at one end of the worktop. And outside... Oh, outside was nothing short of a miracle.

The fire had somehow not reached the garden, the surrounding high walls protecting her special place. Yes, there was the odd weed here and there sprouting between her perennials displaying the first shoots of summer growth but everything else was how it had been. The climbing roses nodded opening buds in the warm breeze and she caught the scent of her favourite blush-pink rose, Félicité-Perpétue. Tina trailed up and down paths, nipping off last season's sedum heads, brushing her fingers along stems of lavender that would soon attract bees and butterflies. She sat on her bench and gazed round in wonder.

How had her special place escaped the enraged fire that had obliterated the *castello* and not even scorched a single plant or tree in this forever garden? She double-checked the tops of the olive and lime trees, leaning with her head tipped back to scrutinise the perfect canopy above.

Two weeks later, her hair screwed up beneath a battered sun hat, Tina was intent on trimming straggly yew in the maze. Her gardening companion flew back and forth, packing a nest with wisps of dried grass and every now and then Tina spoke softly to the robin, encouraging her in her work.

The sound of footsteps surprised her and she jumped up. '*Chi c'è?* Who's there?'

Rounding the hedge, she almost bumped into him. His hair was shorter, his face had filled out and he was bronzed but it was definitely him. Here in her garden. Was she dreaming?

'Olivio,' she gasped.

His smile was tentative, his hands clenched at his sides. 'Sergio wrote me about Allegra passing, so I wanted to come to you. I'm so sorry, Tina. But' – he pointed to where he'd come from – 'the *castello*. The fire. I only learned about it today when I arrived. Were you hurt?'

She couldn't stop herself. It was the most natural thing in the world to run to him, embrace him and for her lips to find his. It was where she belonged. She had missed him too much.

'You came back,' she whispered when they came up for air.

'I couldn't stay over there without you, Tina. Yes, I'm back.'

EPILOGUE

There was once a young woman who married a young man from her hometown in a very simple ceremony in the church of Sant'Agnese, attended by a few close friends and a straggle of townspeople. As in all tales, they make an unlikely pair: she a contessina and he from ordinary working stock, but they love each other. Despite the cultural differences people like to consider problematical, love conquers all: it supports and nurtures and what this couple have is strong, tolerant and full of trust. Their love is fulfilling, a force that brought them together in an emotion that changed how they both now see the world.

Over time Olivio built a new house for his bride from the scattered stones of his wife's ancestral castle and now the laughter of three children – twin boys and a baby girl, all with hair the colour of fire – echoes amongst the ruins that form part of the garden surrounding their special home.

Their father is in his second term as mayor and has designated his town a place of peace. Each year the massacre of Sant'Agnese is commemorated, when the lives of more than forty innocent men, women and children are remembered. Visitors travel from afar – from France, Switzerland and even

America to where some citizens emigrated at war's end – to attend a special Mass and to lay flowers at the statue erected at the end of the martyrs' bridge. Afterwards there is dancing in the main piazza and food prepared by the women is shared at long trestle tables set outside the church and everybody vows to never forget.

Each year, the children from the music school perform the words from the special symphony of remembrance composed by their teacher, contessina Tina di Montesecco, who accompanies them on the grand piano Olivio Buratta bought on the occasion of their fifth wedding anniversary.

The forever garden at the back of the ruined *castello* is open to the public on half a dozen days each year and is listed in *The Guide to Italian Gardens of North Central Italy*. Visitors from abroad stay in the renowned hotel in town which provides employment for those townspeople who do not work in the famous, newly refurbished Montesecco leather factory that exports its products all over the world.

Rumour has it there are hauntings on certain nights of the year, when the harvest moon hangs heavy, casting dull golden light over the terracotta roofs of Sant'Agnese. If you look carefully, a woman with fly-away hair the colour of fiery autumn leaves can be seen running over the rooftops to leap over the ruined castle battlements. But the only witnesses so far have been men who drink late in the *osteria* in the piazza.

These days, for the most part, there is peace and harmony in the small town of Sant'Agnese but the old folk are never far from their warnings of how war and discord can strike at any time.

A LETTER FROM ANGELA

Dear reader,

A huge thank you (*mille grazie* as the Italians say) for choosing to read *The Lost Garden*. If you enjoyed it, and want to keep up to date with all my latest releases, simply sign up at the following link. Your email address will never be shared and you can unsubscribe at any time.

www.bookouture.com/angela-petch

Each year when we drive to our home in Italy, before we enter Tuscany, on the border with Emilia-Romagna we pass beneath an incredible castle perched on a rocky crag. It's like something belonging to a children's book illustration and fascinating in all seasons. In autumn, the mist swirls round its base, cutting it off from the town of Sant'Agata Feltria huddled below. In the winter when it snows, it's absolutely spellbinding in the sunshine. I've often thought it would make an excellent location for a children's illustrated storybook.

I can't draw and I've never attempted to write for children, but I can paint with my imagination. I have always known I wanted to include this ancient castle in a book and as my stories so far have been set in World War Two, I set out to research as much as I could. I already knew about a dreadful massacre nearby of thirty innocent civilians, including women, old people and very young children, the youngest months old.

On the night of 7 to 8 April 1944, the tiny hamlet of Fragheto suffered a dreadful reprisal as a result of ever-increasing activity in the area by partisans of the Garibaldi Romagna and Vth Garibaldi Pesaro brigades. Six hundred German soldiers and one hundred and fifty Italian militia had been gathered in an effort to stamp out the *partigiani*, whom they had underestimated. A group of *partigiani* had sought shelter in the tiny hamlet of Fragheto and were warned by two young women sympathisers that a troop of German soldiers were digging in not far away, preparing to hunt them down. These partisans were subsequently able to inflict casualties on the Germans. One partisan was injured and left behind in the village. When he was discovered, murder ensued at the hands of the Italian militia and German troops. I included more detail about this event in my very first book, *The Tuscan Secret*. But as to the actual town of Sant'Agata Feltria, its prominent castle and the role it may have played during the war, I came up with nothing, not even from the tourist office.

So, my imagination started to brew stories. I visited the castle only to discover there were no texts relating to the war. Instead, the castle has been transformed into a display of classic tales with rooms devoted to, for example, the story of Cenerentola (Cinderella), with a mannequin dressed in rags, seated by the fire. The castle has been turned into a kind of mini-Disneyland display, with scant information about its history. Other rooms display scenes from *Peter Pan*, *The Little Prince* and other famous stories. '*Tutto è fiaba*', a huge notice at the start of the display told me: everything is a fairy tale. It felt like my imagination was being prodded to get to work. And get to work it did. I wanted something more serious for my book. What if a young aristocrat from the town became embroiled with the partisans, with a father heavily involved in the fascist party? With its commanding position in the valley leading to the coastal plain, it surely would have been used as a defensive post by the occupying German army? I knew from my husband's family history that communities were divided politically during this period. Italy was suffering a civil war. So what might have gone on in the little town where everybody knew each other? There was a lot to consider.

I walked around the town taking photos, stopping to listen to the swifts screeching in and out of the battlements. I took coffee at the little bar in the piazza. I watched the world go by and eavesdropped, placing characters in my story, hunting down where they might live and shop. Whilst scribbling in my notebook, as I leant against the wall outside the castle, a ginger cat brushed against my legs and then jumped up before disappearing over the edge of the wall. I was so worried: the drop was sheer, but the cat had landed on a ledge and looked up at me (with amusement, it seemed to me) and started to groom itself, back leg in the air. What if that ledge led to a secret part of the castle: a garden maybe? I was off and ideas began to crowd in. *Grazie*, Tigressa!

The Lost Garden is totally fictitious but I think the castle needs a war story, built as it is upon the rock of the wolves. Sant'Agnese is the fictitious name I chose for Sant'Agata and although the story is threaded with fantasy, there are many true facts woven in, as I always like to do.

I lost my mother when she was far too young but I think of her every day and I feel her presence often. I feel her in a benevolent way as if she is still caring for me, loving me like she did when I was growing up. Fiammetta is not my mother and readers might be sceptical about her appearance in *The Lost Garden* but there is a lot we do not know about the afterlife. Make of her what you will.

If you enjoyed *The Lost Garden*, it would be wonderful if you could write a review. It only need be a couple of lines but I'd love to hear what you think, and it makes such a difference helping new readers to discover one of my books for the first time.

I enjoy hearing from my readers – you can get in touch through social media, or my website.

Thanks,

Angela Petch

www.angelapetchsblogsite.wordpress.com

facebook.com/AngelaJaneClarePetch
instagram.com/angela_maurice

ALLEGRA'S RECIPES

GNOCCHI DI PANE E UOVA FRITTE – FRIED GNOCCHI MADE FROM BREAD AND EGG

To serve four, remove the crusts and tear up 200 grams of stale Romagna bread slices into a basin of water containing 150 mls of warm milk and leave for half an hour. Squeeze out most of the milk and mix in one beaten egg. Add 80 grams of plain flour and 20 grams of grated Parmesan, a pinch of nutmeg and salt to season and mix well to form a kind of dough. Knead well, then cut into gnocchi shapes. Add to a pan with enough oil to fry. (If liked, you can cut up 50 grams of pancetta into cubes and fry these first.) Serve with 50 grams of fresh cream and chopped parsley and a further sprinkling of grated Parmesan cheese.

TORTELLI DI PATATE

Boil 1 kilo of potatoes, skins on and washed first and pass them through a ricer, adding one egg and a small ripe tomato so the mixture turns pink, plus 4 grated garlic cloves, 70 grams of grated Parmesan cheese, a pinch of salt. Mix well and leave to cool in a bowl, covered with a clean cloth.

Make some home-made pasta with 500 grams of plain flour and 3 large eggs by piling the flour on your kitchen table, making a well in the middle and breaking the eggs into this hole, plus a pinch of salt. Mix the eggs in gradually until you form a dough. Leave to rest, covered, for half an hour.

Roll out the dough with your mattarello *(long pasta rolling pin) until you have a thin sheet of dough that you should be able to see your fingers through. Place dots of the potato filling mix onto half the pasta sheet and cover with the remaining half to make squares of tortelli, sandwiching the potato mix in the middle of each parcel and cutting the squares with a knife. Drop into boiling salted water for five minutes and then strain. Eat with a meat or tomato sauce or sage leaves in melted butter with plenty of Parmesan cheese grated on top. Instead of boiling them up, the pasta shapes can also be cooked directly on a hot plate and eaten piping hot in the winter.*

———

PARTRIDGE STUFFED WITH JUNIPER BERRIES – GALLINA NUMIDICA (FARAONA) FARCITA AL GINEPRO

Marinade the cleaned partridge overnight in a mixture of water, wine, sage, a handful of juniper berries collected from the meadows, and crushed garlic cloves. Prepare a mix of crushed juniper berries and bread dipped in wine with which to stuff the partridge. Put in a medium hot oven and halfway through roasting, flavour with crushed anchovies, capers and fresh sage leaves.

———

ALLEGRA'S FRESH TAGLIATELLE

Allow 1 medium egg and 100 grams of plain or semola flour per generous portion.

Make a well in a mound of flour on your clean table.

Sprinkle a pinch of salt round the edges and then slowly amalgamate the beaten egg into the flour. It will seem dry but do not be tempted to add water – or beer, Madre mia, as I have heard some do. Whatever next? Knead it until all the flour is combined, then wrap in a clean cloth and leave for half an hour.

Roll it out using your long rolling pin, until you can read your lover's letters through the pasta – that is what my wonderful mother always told me but, sadly, I have never received a love letter in my life. Cut into 10-centimetre strips and when you are certain the pasta is dry but not so dry it will crack, fold it over and over and then use a sharp knife to cut your tagliatelle strips.

———

PAPPARDELLE CON SUGO DI LEPRE (HARE SAUCE)

For one medium-sized wild hare, skinned and cut up into pieces that fit easily within your closed hand, you will need: 500 grams of pappardelle, which are a thicker version of the finer tagliatelle. Make your pasta as instructed in an earlier recipe.

You will also need: 500 ml of red wine, 4 dessertspoons of good olive oil, one onion, 2 garlic cloves, grated, 1 carrot, 1 stick of celery, 2 bay leaves, 2 sage leaves, 750 ml of bottled tomato passata, grated pecorino and salt and pepper to season.

Marinade the hare pieces in the wine, vegetables and herbs and leave overnight or for at least two hours. Remove the meat and put to one side. In a thick, deep frying pan or terracotta pot that can cook on the top of your stove, add the marinaded vegetables, cut into small pieces and brown them in oil. Add the hare and brown these pieces too, then add the wine you used as marinade and the bottled passata and cook on a very low flame until the wine evaporates. Cook on for a total of 90 minutes, adding a ladle of water every now and again to stop the meat drying out.

When cooked and tender, tear the meat from the bones and

add the pappardelle pasta to the sauce and grate pecorino cheese on top. (If you like, you can also add chopped pancetta to the hare at the initial browning stage.)

ALLEGRA'S EASY RECIPE FOR PRESERVING ZUCCHINI FOR THE WINTER MONTHS

1 kg courgettes, 500 mls of water, 250 mls of white vinegar, 2 dessertspoons of coarse salt, 2 cloves of garlic, pepper grains (black, white, green or pink), fresh mint, a pinch of fine salt, sufficient olive oil as required. Carefully wash the courgettes and cut into strips. Place in a bowl and sprinkle over 2 dessertspoons of coarse salt so they can release their excess liquid. Leave for two hours.

1. *Rinse and pat the courgettes dry with a clean cloth.*
2. *Boil the water with the vinegar and add a pinch of fine salt. Cook the zucchini in the liquid for five minutes and then remove and allow to cool down.*
3. *Sterilise two clean jam jars by gently simmering in boiling water for ten minutes and then arrange the courgettes in them, compacting them and adding chopped garlic, pepper and sprigs of mint, finally adding olive oil to cover completely. Screw lid tightly and store them in a cool dry pantry, away from heat for at least one month before eating.*

ACKNOWLEDGEMENTS

A book does not write itself. I adore setting off on the 'what-if' stage and I love it when it is all over too and I feel I have worked as hard as I can. The middle part is when I am grateful for other eyes to untangle my ambitious imagination. Authors cannot easily give birth to their books without editorial midwives and objective perspectives.

Bestselling author Lisa Jewell has allowed me to use a quote I found at the back of one of her stunning books and I agree wholeheartedly with these words:

'People might think that writers are possessive of their work, think that no one but them can possibly know how it should be. But a sensible writer knows that's not true. Sometimes the writer is the least able to see the solution and sometimes the editors are the geniuses.'

Thank you, Ellen Gleeson, for your wise and diplomatic counsel in helping me see the solutions. It's a cliché but I couldn't have done this one without you: a brilliant editor from a brilliant Bookouture team.

I'd like to also thank a lovely friend who writes as Rosanna Ley and leads very special writing retreats at Finca El Cerrillo in Spain. My structural edits arrived on my first day there this year and sent me into a Spanish spin but she was able to calm me and offer wisdom and the benefit of her experience. Thanks to the group at the *finca* too, fellow writers whose feedback I pondered.

There are many others to whom I'm grateful and I fear I

might leave somebody out. I hope not. All these thanks sound like an extract from one of those awful award ceremony speeches but my thanks are heartfelt.

My Italian friends – *Noi di Rofelle e dintorni* – are amazing and go to great lengths to ferret out information on all things Italian that occasionally flummox me. *Grazie a voi* – 'It's wonderful', as Paolo Conte sings. And the other trio of The Tuscan Scribbly-Wibblies – you are wonderful too. I love our brainstorming, wine-filled writing sessions. Sue, thanks for lending me Baffi and for your horsewomanship (is that even a word? I think it should be). And Jane Cable, my perspicacious friend and honourable writing buddy, I am so lucky we have our writerly chats. Thanks also to Cariad from Facebook, Jessie Cahalin and oh so many people. Professor Augusto Tocci from Badia Tedalda and Piero and Manuela from the Rofelle restaurant l'ErbHosteria all inspired me with delicious, local country recipes. *Grazie a tutti!*

But most of all, thanks to my soulmate, Maurice. You know how grateful I am for everything in this amazing bi-Italian adventure we are blessed to be living.

PUBLISHING TEAM

Turning a manuscript into a book requires the efforts of many people. The publishing team at Bookouture would like to acknowledge everyone who contributed to this publication.

Audio
Alba Proko
Sinead O'Connor
Melissa Tran

Commercial
Lauren Morrissette
Hannah Richmond
Imogen Allport

Cover design
Alexandra Allden

Data and analysis
Mark Alder
Mohamed Bussuri

Editorial
Ellen Gleeson
Nadia Michael

Copyeditor
Jane Eastgate

Proofreader
Becca Allen

Marketing
Alex Crow
Melanie Price
Occy Carr
Cíara Rosney
Martyna Młynarska

Operations and distribution
Marina Valles
Stephanie Straub
Joe Morris

Production
Hannah Snetsinger
Mandy Kullar
Nadia Michael
Charlotte Hegley

Publicity
Kim Nash
Noelle Holten
Jess Readett
Sarah Hardy

Rights and contracts
Peta Nightingale
Richard King
Saidah Graham

RAISING READERS
Books Build Bright Futures

Dear Reader,

We'd love your attention for one more page to tell you about the crisis in children's reading, and what we can all do.

Studies have shown that reading for fun is the **single biggest predictor of a child's future life chances** – more than family circumstance, parents' educational background or income. It improves academic results, mental health, wealth, communication skills, ambition and happiness.

The number of children reading for fun is in rapid decline. Young people have a lot of competition for their time, and a worryingly high number do not have a single book at home.

Hachette works extensively with schools, libraries and literacy charities, but here are some ways we can all raise more readers:

- Reading to children for just 10 minutes a day makes a difference
- Don't give up if children aren't regular readers – there will be books for them!

- Visit bookshops and libraries to get recommendations
- Encourage them to listen to audiobooks
- Support school libraries
- Give books as gifts

There's a lot more information about how to encourage children to read on our websites: **www.RaisingReaders.co.uk** and **www.JoinRaisingReaders.com**.

Thank you for reading.

Printed in Dunstable, United Kingdom